Death
by
Candlelight

BOOKS BY EMMA DAVIES

EMMA DAVIES

Death
by
Candlelight

bookouture

Published by Bookouture in 2022

An imprint of Storyfire Ltd.
Carmelite House
50 Victoria Embankment
London EC4Y 0DZ

www.bookouture.com

ISBN: 978-1-80314-063-6
eBook ISBN: 978-1-80314-062-9

Previously published as *Death in Disguise*

1

Francesca Eve had never met Sara Smith before but she'd heard lots of good things about her. She only knew her as a friend of a friend of a friend, but that was how it worked when your children were at secondary school; everybody knew everybody, *vaguely*.

What she hadn't been told, apart from the fact that Sara's house was beautiful, was quite how useless the postcode would be when it came to finding the address among the multitude of leafy lanes and blind corners that Fran was currently navigating. She was only ten minutes from where she lived in Shrewsbury but now she was late, and she hated being late.

At least, being self-employed, it was her schedule she was chasing and no one else's. It was one of the best things about working for herself. That and the fact she was a caterer, which meant she could think about food pretty much the whole day. Food was her most favourite thing in the world. Except possibly for her husband, Jack. And maybe her daughter, Martha, although she was skating on very thin ice right now; yesterday's 'accident' had brought the total number of pairs of ruined school shoes to three so far this year, and it was only April.

Fran drew her car to a halt and peered at the lane ahead of her. The road had been steadily climbing for a while and a spread of Shropshire's finest countryside fell away on her right. To her left, hedgerows were just beginning to green again after an unusually harsh winter. It was a view she would never tire of.

The house had to be around here somewhere. She'd passed the postbox she'd been told to look out for, and the corrugated-roofed hut which lay abandoned in a field. Moving off again, Fran tried not to think of the minutes that were ticking by. She'd never catered for a murder-mystery party before today, but Sara Smith was celebrating a big birthday, much bigger than Fran's recent milestone, and something special was required. Fran had celebrated her fortieth with a trip to Pizza Hut and one too many glasses of wine; she had a feeling her fiftieth would involve slippers and a comfy chair. She sometimes felt she was ready for them now. She could cater for pizzazz, but it had no place in her own life. Not that she was complaining – life was good, just a little... ordinary at times. And being forty wasn't all bad. She wasn't blonde, so couldn't claim her small eccentricities on her hair colour, but she had soon learned that the phrase *it's my age* came in very handy at times. Perhaps she could use it to explain her inability to find her client's house...

FRAN PUT down the last of her boxes and gave a satisfied nod. She was half an hour behind but that was nothing, she could easily make it up, and this kitchen was a dream; it would be a pleasure to cook here.

'You'll have a coffee first though, won't you?' asked Sara from behind her. 'Before you get started.'

Fran turned just in time to see her client grimace. 'Although I need to stop drinking them, I've had far too many already today and...' She broke off. 'I'm gabbling. Sorry, I do that when I've had too much coffee.'

Or are nervous, thought Fran, summing up the situation with practised ease. It was time to take charge. She glanced around the room.

'Sara, why don't you sit down and I'll make *you* a cup of tea. You have my services for the duration, don't forget. You might as well make use of them. And, trust me, you have nothing to worry about. The party is going to be fabulous, I can tell. I've never seen a place more suited to a murder mystery; the setting is perfect.' The Gables was a classic Georgian stone-built country house: flagged floors, huge fireplaces and thick rugs, which were just begging to have a body sprawled across one of them.

Sara wrinkled her nose, looking around her kitchen. It was easily twice the size of Fran's. 'I don't know why I'm getting so worked up about this one,' she replied, tucking a longish strand of golden-blonde hair behind one ear. 'I have parties all the time, but...' She pulled a face. 'Maybe it's my age.'

Fran smiled; looking like she did, Sara had nothing to worry about. She was an attractive woman, one who nature had created and nurture had carefully maintained. Impeccably made-up so that the rosy bloom of her skin still shone through, laughter lines and fine wrinkles animating the delicate features of her face.

'If I didn't know any better, I wouldn't have guessed it was your fiftieth,' Fran replied. 'I've just turned forty and, well...' She shrugged her shoulders, holding her hands out to the sides as if to demonstrate quite how much her body was letting her down. 'So you've nothing to worry about on that score. Fifty is the new thirty anyway.' She considered Sara's anxious face for a second. 'But I don't think that's what's bothering you. What's bothering you is giving over your kitchen for a day to a woman about whom you know virtually nothing. You don't know whether you should be in here or not, or offer to help. And if you don't, whether I'm going to think you rude.

'Then there's everything in your kitchen, which is wonderful by the way, including all those dishes you never use because they belonged to your mother-in-law. Aside from that, this is the heart of your home, and you have everything just as you like it. So you're wondering whether tomorrow, when all this is over, I'll have rearranged your cupboards or chipped your favourite mug, and things will be ever so slightly different. It's tantamount to having someone riffle through your underwear drawer.'

She smiled at Sara's astonished face.

'So, I'm going to make you a cup of tea and then you can tell me what's off limits and which china and so on you'd like to use. Then you can absolutely leave the rest to me. I will cook you and your guests a wonderful meal, serve it, and clear away afterwards. I will take care of everything as if it were my own, and I have a photographic memory, so tomorrow, you'll find everything back in its rightful place as if I was never here. And the kitchen is still your kitchen, so if you wish to be in here, that's fine, and if you don't, that's fine too. I'm quite happy to ask questions if I need to and, as my aim today is to provide you with the very best of everything I can, I will also say if you are in my way or if there's something which might prevent that from happening, tactfully of course.' Fran smiled.

'Oh my God, *thank you*,' breathed Sara, practically melting into her chair with relief. 'Natalie said you were good, but I didn't know how good.'

Fran dipped her head. She hadn't a clue who Natalie was but that didn't matter.

'You're very welcome. Now, tell me how you take your tea, and then I'll tell you about the party I catered for where the host's brother thought it his sole mission in life to grope the cook at every available opportunity, despite the fact that he was married with two children.'

'He didn't!'

'Oh he did... But I soon sorted him out.' Fran tipped her head on one side, catching Sara's bright-blue eye.

Five minutes later they were chatting as if they'd known each other for twenty years.

Sixteen minutes later, Fran picked up the pencil from beside the pad she'd used for jotting notes. 'I think that's it for now,' she said. 'Except for the guests. Just give me a quick run-down on who's who. It's much easier to blend seamlessly into the background if I know who people are and can put a name to the face. So who's Lois? She's the only vegetarian, yes?'

Sara nodded. 'You'll spot her a mile away. She has bright-red hair down to about here,' she replied, pointing at her bum. 'And it's still natural, which is the most annoying thing ever.' Sara ran a hand through her tresses as if to reinforce her point.

Fran stared at her. You'd never know she wasn't a natural blonde.

'And then with the drinks... you mentioned that you wanted non-alcoholic wine for one of your guests.'

'Yes, Diane. She doesn't drink.'

Fran made a note on the pad, she didn't need to know the details.

'She's about your height,' added Sara.

Short, wrote Fran.

'And wears glasses.'

'Okay, got that. She's the only one, is she?'

Sara's eyes narrowed. 'Becky wears glasses, but only for reading, so not all the time. I don't think you'd mix them up. Besides, Becky is more my height. And she's blonde too, whereas Diane is very dark.'

Fran nodded. 'So Becky...?'

'Yes, she's blonde, dead straight hair, and has a broad York-shire accent. She'll be wearing huge rings, too, she always does.'

Another note made. 'So that's Lois, Diane, Becky... who else?'

Sara's expression changed slightly and Fran thought she saw the beginnings of a wry smile. 'Can't forget Camilla,' she said. 'Although you'll probably hear her before you see her.'

Fran's pencil stilled. 'Camilla?'

'Yes. She'll be the one in killer heels and tight trousers.' She laughed. 'A bit of a character is Camilla, but she's so adorable we all love her to bits.'

Fran swallowed. That was unfortunate. With any luck she could stay out of Camilla's way. Besides, it was true what people said: no one ever notices the caterer.

'Then there's me, and that's it, just the five of us,' added Sara. 'It's going to be great fun, I think. I've never been to one of these murder-mystery parties before.'

'No, me neither,' admitted Fran. 'But it does sound good.' She glanced back down at the notepad. 'Right then, if there's nothing else you think I need to know, I'd best make a start or there'll be a dead body and no pudding over which to contem-plate whodunnit.'

2

So far so good, thought Fran, picking up a tray laden with another round of drinks – champagne this time. Aside from food, her husband and daughter, people watching was next highest on the list of Fran's favourite things, and the party was shaping up to be a good place for it.

Fran wouldn't have considered herself inherently nosy, but people were just so fascinating, particularly when you threw them together into a group and then stood back and watched the personalities at play. Big family parties were the absolute best. You could tell immediately where allegiances lay, who didn't get on with who quite so well, who downright loathed whom, which ones were in love, and which ones were supposed to be in love, but weren't. Some family members were like the sun, drawing everyone around them into their orbit, while others were small ice planets, tucked in the outermost reaches of the galaxy where no one ever went; some were tiny, while others were huge gaseous planets, full of something or other but with absolutely no substance. Sara's group of friends were no different.

It was Sara's party, so one might have expected her to be the centre of the universe on this occasion, but if she were the sun, bright and warming, then Lois was the moon, beguiling, mysterious and the owner of a quite substantial force field. Perhaps it was her red hair which, as Sara had described, hung low against her back, or the soft shimmery fabric of the dress she had chosen to wear, but there was something compelling about her that the others simply didn't have.

Diane was the quietest and not just because her lack of height made her less noticeable. She moved unobtrusively, standing back from the others by just a pace or two, but it was enough to separate her slightly. She listened avidly to the conversations around her but said very little, even though she appeared to be on good terms with everyone.

Camilla was her polar opposite: loud, brash and yes, fun, Fran supposed, if you liked that kind of thing. And that left Becky. She was much younger than the others, down to earth and, if Fran wasn't very much mistaken, the one who bound the group together. Becky was everyone's favourite.

The guests had been gathered for about half an hour, but all had brought gifts for their hostess, so it wasn't until these had been opened, and kisses and exclamations exchanged, that Fran was able to serve drinks. A champagne toast for Sara's birthday.

She approached Diane first, angling her tray so that the non-alcoholic drink faced her. After that, she could let the others take whichever drink was closest, keeping her eyes low and her voice soft. Camilla didn't even seem to notice her; no one ever notices the caterer.

With a loud cheer, a toast was made and drinks sipped. The evening had begun. And the game was afoot.

Fran was quite intrigued by the mechanics of the game, which Sara had explained earlier over their tea. She watched now as the guests opened the first of the envelopes which would direct the action.

Prior to the party each of them had been sent details of the character they were to play, a role they had to maintain for the duration of the game. Alongside these were a few details about the other characters they would encounter during the evening, a hint to a darker side of their nature perhaps, or even something which might prove to be a motive for murder. Opening the first envelope gave each player further information, and so for this first part of the game their mission was simply to work out which information was true and which might be false. Characters were not allowed to lie when asked a direct question and, as the game progressed, further envelopes would be given out until, during dinner, another would reveal to its recipient if they were the victim, murderer, or simply a suspect.

It could have been rather dull for the victim, who would otherwise have had to spend the latter part of the game pretending to be a dead body, but at this point they would assume the role of a new character, that of a visiting police officer called in to help investigate the crime. If the shrieks of laughter were anything to go by, the guests were clearly excited by the prospect of the evening ahead.

With a smile, Fran retreated to the kitchen, where several full plates of canapés awaited her attention. She turned around, eyes scouring the work surfaces; she could have sworn... When Fran had left the kitchen to serve drinks, she had left the canapés ready to go. Now two of the platters were half empty.

Not surprisingly, none of the places in which she looked held the missing party nibbles. Fran was methodical and precise in her work. If she thought she had prepared the trays ready for service, then that was exactly what she'd done, not left half of the food in the fridge, or worse, burning to a crisp in the oven. She frowned. The bloody nerve of it; someone had pinched them. The party might be about to produce a dramatic murder, but no one had told her that theft was also part of the evening's entertainment.

Sara couldn't have been the culprit. Out of anyone here this evening she would have understood that the canapés were for her and her guests and consequently left well alone. Or, she would have at least asked if she'd wanted anything, surely? Besides, Sara had been in the dining room the whole time Fran had been away from the kitchen... She tutted loudly. Plan B it was then.

Experience had taught Fran to always plan for the unexpected, to have a contingency should things go wrong. Like the time an oven packed in halfway through the cooking of her main course, or the family party where the eighty-year-old guest of honour was pronounced allergic to fish at the very last minute. She shuddered to think what might have happened if she hadn't found out, or worse, been able to produce another entrée at the drop of a hat. A few missing canapés wasn't about to scupper this party, and Fran simply took out a few of the 'spares' that she always produced.

Back in the dining room the conversation was flowing as the guests got stuck into their interrogation of each other. Fran quickly delivered the selection of appetisers, handing them around before placing the trays down on the central table so that guests could help themselves to more. She bit back a smile. Her money was on Lois being the killer; she had femme fatale written all over her.

The next half hour passed in a blur for Fran as she put the finishing touches to her starter and prepped the remaining vegetables that she would serve with the main course. She had no idea exactly when the murder would take place, but she hoped they waited until the salmon en croûte was on the table; she'd be mortified if her pastry went soggy as a result.

FRAN WAS in the middle of clearing away the plates, when Sara's voice came from the far end of the table.

'Is everything all right, Becky?'

The young woman had her eyes closed, a hand to her forehead and her mouth parted as if focused on her breathing. At Sara's words, her eyes flickered open. 'Yes, I... Sorry, I just feel a bit odd; hot and—' Her mouth opened, chest heaving as if she were about to vomit.

Sara moved backwards rapidly just as a violent cough erupted from Becky's mouth.

Becky's eyes widened, fixing on Sara's with a look approaching horror.

Conversation stilled around the table as all attention narrowed to where Becky was sitting.

Lois half rose, lifting the water jug that stood in the centre of the table and refilling Becky's glass. She pushed it forward. 'Here, have a drink.'

But Becky couldn't reply. Her mouth opened but no words came out, just a horrible gurgle that trailed away to nothing. As they watched, horrified, Becky clutched her throat dramatically, waving at her glass of water with a gesture that was becoming increasingly feeble as the seconds ticked by. Her eyes grew wider and wider and Fran stared transfixed, a faint flicker of unease tickling the back of her neck. Surely this was all part of the game... wasn't it? She peered at the plates in her hand, at the scraps of salmon that clung to them, suddenly panicked. The fish had come from her usual supplier and she'd checked them over herself. She was certain the fillets were free from bones...

Becky's head dropped to the table with a heavy thunk that was so theatrical, Diane actually laughed. It broke the slightly nervous silence and Fran sighed with relief, grinning at Sara, who had her hand over her heart, clearly not sure whether she should be phoning for an ambulance. Fran moved around the table, scooping up the remaining plates as unobtrusively as she could. A spontaneous round of applause broke out for Becky's acting skills as Camilla's voice rang out loud and clear.

'My, oh my,' she drawled, in an affected, deep-south American accent. 'I do believe she's dead... Murdered!'

Becky lay unmoving, her eyes wide open and unseeing as giggles broke out around the table. Fran had to wonder whether the woman had a background in amateur dramatics. She shuffled her load of plates so she could hold them a little firmer and picked up an odd glass in her spare hand before moving away to the door.

'Becky?' It was Lois who spoke, sitting on Becky's left, her hand resting lightly on her shoulder. 'You can wake up now.'

Fran turned back from her position near the door, alert to the raised note in Lois's voice, concern tinged with a slight frisson of fear. But the head on the table remained still, the huge ring on Becky's hand beside it glittering in the overhead light. Fran could feel her heart pounding; something was very wrong here.

The beats of silence ticked out in the room, each one seemingly thicker than the last. A chair was pushed away from the table, leg scraping against the flagstoned floor. Someone coughed, a small nervous sound.

Suddenly Becky's head shot up as if it were on a spring, causing Lois to shriek and Camilla to gasp out loud.

Becky's face was split by the widest grin. 'Ha!' she snorted. 'Gotcha!' She wiped her eyes. 'God, you should see your faces.' And then, 'Sorry, I couldn't resist.'

Fran smiled, heart still hammering, and continued on her way back to the kitchen. If Becky hadn't been on the stage before now, she certainly should be.

By the time Fran served coffee, she was beginning to breathe a little easier. Her job was almost done and the guests were evidently enjoying themselves. They had moved on from the scare of Becky's 'death' and were now in the thick of trying to work out whodunnit. Importantly, she had also managed to evade Camilla almost completely. Either Camilla wasn't the observant type or, out of context, she simply hadn't realised who Fran was. But, just as Fran laid the tray of coffee on the table in the living room, she heard her name being called across the hallway. Camilla, having possibly just been to the little girls' room, was on her way back into the dining room, with one intention on her mind. She clearly wished to pick up where she had left off in her pursuit of Fran the last time they had talked at school.

Worse, there was nowhere Fran could escape to, the route back to the kitchen would mean crossing Camilla's path. She was bracing herself, ready for interrogation, when Diane came out of the dining room and stopped to talk to Camilla. Seizing the opportunity of distraction, Fran shot out of the room and darted through the first door she came to. Even an understairs cupboard potentially full of spiders was better than meeting her nemesis.

About a month ago someone, and Fran still didn't know who, had given her name to Camilla, who was chair of the school PTA, a role tailor-made for her. To help with the school's delivery of their career advice and guidance for GCSE students, Camilla had been tasked with finding speakers to share experiences of their chosen path in life. As someone who was self-employed and, to quote Camilla, *such a positive and entrepreneurial role model*, Fran was deemed the perfect person to help, and subsequently found herself top of Camilla's 'hit list'. Thus far Fran had managed to avoid being signed up, but she had a horrible feeling it was only a matter of time. She couldn't think of anything worse than speaking in front of a hundred or so students; her daughter would never speak to her again.

Fran sighed. This was ridiculous. She should face up to Camilla and tell her no, firmly and politely. Except that she didn't think Camilla was someone who took no for an answer. What was almost as bad, if not worse, was that Camilla had given Fran the impression she'd be heartbroken to be turned down, and that she was banking on Fran becoming her new best friend. All of which left Fran feeling guilty and uncomfortable.

Inside the cupboard, Fran pressed her ear against the door, hoping to hear when the coast was clear. Camilla might wonder where she'd gone, but she'd never guess to look in the cupboard, would she?

It was as she was standing, perfectly still, straining to hear what was going on, that Fran slowly became aware of something else, a sound that was not of her own making. Instead, it seemed to be coming from behind her...

She whirled around just as a silvery-blue light lit up the enclosed space, revealing a spectral head which seemed to float in mid-air.

'Jesus!'

The face grinned at her. 'Hi,' it said.

Once Fran's heart had settled back in her chest, she realised the light was coming from a laptop computer, balanced on the knees of a young man who was sitting on a box. He was seemingly a very good-looking young man – though, admittedly, the lack of light made it a little hard to tell – with a small, elfin face, well-defined cheekbones, and large, almond-shaped eyes. A beanie hat was pulled down low on his head, dark curls protruding from beneath it.

'What the hell are you doing in here?' she asked, forgetting for a moment that this wasn't her house.

'I could ask you the same thing.'

Fran's mouth dropped open. 'Well, I... I'm...' – she screwed up her face – 'hiding from someone,' she said. 'God, this is embarrassing.'

'Why is it? I'm hiding from everyone.'

Fran stared at the young man. 'But...' She sighed. She still didn't know what to say.

'Who are you hiding from?' he asked. 'I bet it's Camilla, she's the worst of my mum's friends. Although there's Ronnie, who calls me her favourite barmpot as if I'm four years old. I quite like Becky though, at least she doesn't talk to me like I'm a child, but if I'm not much mistaken, I think she's dead, so...' His grin widened. 'I was right, wasn't I? It is Camilla.'

Fran didn't say a word. She didn't have to, his quiet amusement told her she'd been rumbled.

'I thought it was only me who hid from people,' he added. 'I didn't realise adults did it too.'

'I don't make a habit of it,' replied Fran, her embarrassment threatening to turn to irritation. 'I just...' She spied another box beside the young man and sat down gently, feeling it give slightly under her weight. 'Anyway, what do you mean, you didn't realise adults did it too? How old are you? You're hardly a child.'

There was a shrug. 'Touché,' he said, holding out a hand over the lid of his laptop. 'I'm Adam,' he said. 'Adam Smith, aged twenty-three and son of Sara. Pleased to meet you.'

Fran took the proffered hand and shook it. 'I'm Francesca Eve, Fran, aged forty, the caterer. And very possibly having a mid-life crisis. I'm pleased to meet you too.' She smiled at the ridiculousness of the situation. 'Do you come here often?' she asked.

'I do, actually. Mum's on a mission to get me to be more sociable – apparently, I hide away in my room far too much. So as long as she doesn't catch me in here, I can pretend I've been out and about doing something. And I quite like working in here. It's very peaceful. I like the dark and you can hear all kinds of stuff without anyone realising. Like the time, one Christmas, when I heard Uncle David whispering sweet nothings on the phone to someone called Louise, when his wife's name is Lesley.'

Fran stared at him, wondering if she was being teased, but he was perfectly serious. 'Right... And have you heard much of interest tonight?'

'Not much, just the usual chit-chat and gossip. I use it for research too.'

'Research?'

'Yep.' Adam swung his laptop around so that she could see what he was working on. 'I'm a software designer, games mostly. And I struggle a bit with the characters sometimes, particularly the female ones. I don't know many, you see. So I use what I learn from watching and listening to people. You'd be amazed how much you can pick up.'

'I don't doubt it,' said Fran, desperately trying to recall what she might have said in the vicinity of the cupboard.

'Camilla makes a cracking alien, as it happens. She preys on people and bites their heads off, really enjoys it too.'

Adam was absolutely serious, Fran realised.

'Don't tell her though, will you?' he said.

Fran was trying very hard not to laugh. Adam might be a little socially awkward, but he had remarkable insight.

'No, I won't tell her,' she replied. She was about to make another comment when something else caught her attention.

'Did you steal my food?'

'No.'

Fran looked pointedly at the plate on the floor. 'So those aren't my canapés then?'

'I have no idea,' replied Adam. 'I found them in the kitchen.'

Fran studied the expression on his face, which was quite without guile. 'You found them in the kitchen, clearly laid out on a tray as if they were about to be served. But it didn't occur to you that they weren't just for the taking?'

There was a thoughtful silence.

'I might have taken them, yes...' he admitted eventually. 'They're very good. All apart from this one.' Adam picked up a thin rectangle of pastry. 'Whatever's on there is revolting.'

Fran lifted her head a little. 'They're anchovies,' she said.

'And what's that when it's at home?'

'A small fish.'

Adam dropped the pastry as if it were on fire. 'No wonder,' he mused. 'Anyway, apart from those, the rest are very good.'

'I'm so pleased you approve.'

He smiled. 'You're very welcome. Are there any more? I'm really still quite hungry.'

Fran smothered a smile. 'Not those, but if you want something you'll have to come to the kitchen and I'll see what I can find. I'm not bringing food back to the cupboard. Your mother will think I've lost my mind.'

'Plus, she might also discover my hiding place and I don't want that to happen.'

'No, quite, well, I had better get going anyway. It's been a pleasure meeting you, Adam.'

'You too, Miss Eve.'

It took Fran several hours to clear up and pack away all her things, as well as washing and returning everything of Sara's to its rightful place, exactly as promised. She was tired but pleased. The guests had all had a wonderful time, and were full of praise, for both the inventiveness of the party, and the food Fran had provided. It was always heartening when an event went particularly well, but Sara's offer of meeting up for a thank-you cup of coffee the following day was also a lovely surprise. Clearly Fran's impression that she and Sara had got on well was reciprocated. She had even managed to evade Camilla's clutches the rest of the evening as well.

It was almost midnight by the time she crawled into bed beside her husband.

'Night, Jack,' she whispered, tucking herself into the crook of his arm.

'Did you have a good evening?' he mumbled, still half asleep.

'I did actually, it was...' She was about to say the best fun she'd had in ages and the thought brought her up short. *When had her life become so humdrum?*

'Was tonight the murder mystery?'

Fran yawned, snuggling closer and turning the thought away. Now was not the time. 'Yes, it was good fun, actually. They all seemed to really like the food and no one died, which is always a bonus.'

Thirty seconds later she was fast asleep.

3

THREE WEEKS LATER

Adam hadn't intended to arrive at Fran's house quite so early in the morning, but he hadn't slept at all well and doing something seemed preferable to doing nothing, particularly as the police weren't involved yet. Because when they were, Adam had a feeling his mum could very quickly run out of time. He hadn't intended to sit in his car for quite this long either, but he'd only met Fran once and that had been nearly three weeks ago. He had no idea what to say, or how to say it, and summoning courage was a slow process.

But the fact of the matter was that Adam had absolutely no one else he could speak to. He couldn't say anything to his mum, obviously, he barely saw his dad these days, and he didn't have the kind of friends who might help with anything like this. Fran was his only hope.

And Fran had seemed different from most of his mum's friends. Adam wasn't very good with people, and even worse at figuring them out, but there had been something about her that he had warmed to. Perhaps it had just been the ridiculousness of the situation – two grown adults skulking in an understairs cupboard – but this in itself spoke to him; the fact that she was even there in the first place. Plus, there had been something open about her face; full of freckles and friendly, looking at him not with an expression full of mockery or scorn the way most of his mum's friends did, but instead with understanding and empathy. Course, it had been dark in the cupboard, but that was the impression she had given him. And now he really needed to find out if his instinct had been right.

He knew Fran was at home. He'd been watching the house since he'd arrived and had seen her kiss her husband goodbye on the doorstep and then, not long after, wave to a girl in school uniform who must be her daughter. He took a deep breath and climbed from the car. Pausing for a moment to let a van pass, Adam walked across the road to the house where Fran lived. It wasn't as big as his, but the red brick was homely and the bay windows on either side of the door made it look like the pictures of houses he drew as a child. He knocked quickly on the door before he had any more second thoughts.

There was music playing somewhere deep in the house and for a moment it paused, as if whoever was playing it had stopped to listen for something else. He took advantage of the opportunity and knocked again, even louder this time.

As soon as Fran opened the door, he realised that he hadn't expected her to be quite as short as she was. She hadn't seemed that way in the cupboard, but then he had been sitting down... And it had been quite a confined space... He rearranged his features into a smile.

'Hello, I'm sorry to bother you, I—'

'Oh, hi,' said Fran breezily, as if she wasn't in the slightest bit puzzled to see him. She stared at the object in her hand. 'Here, taste that,' she said, holding out a plastic spatula on which a brown viscous mixture sat.

He pulled his head back, looking at it warily.

'There're no anchovies in it,' she said, smiling. 'It's caramel. Go on, try it. I can't decide whether it needs more whisky. Trouble is, I think I've eaten too much of it. Or drunk too much of it...'

She watched him, clearly amused by his indecision. 'You can take the spoon if you want,' she added, correctly identifying the true reason for his wariness. 'And my mouth has been nowhere near it, just so you know. I know all about Typhoid Mary.'

He frowned at her. 'Who?'

'Typhoid Mary...' She raised her eyebrows. 'Don't they teach that at school these days... or in your day?'

He shook his head a little nervously. 'I don't think so. I did mainly science subjects and I—'

She tutted. 'Well, just in case it ever proves useful for you *to* know: Typhoid Mary, or Mary Mallon to give her her proper name, was an Irish-born woman who emigrated to the States and lived in New York at the turn of the last century. She worked as a cook for several well-to-do families and ended up killing half of them. She was a carrier for typhoid disease but, because she didn't show any symptoms of the disease herself, she carried on cooking and carried on infecting people.' Fran paused, waggling the spatula in inviting fashion. '*She* was obviously a spoon licker whereas *I* am not.' She grinned at him. 'Come in.'

Before Adam even had a chance to reply she turned on her heel and disappeared along a dim hallway. He had no choice but to step inside, closing the door carefully before following her. He emerged into a room full of light, which made him blink. Her kitchen ran the full width of the house and looked so reassuringly messy that relief welled up inside of him. This was somewhere he could *be*...

Fran pushed away a bowl from the edge of an island unit

which almost spanned the centre of the room, waving her hand at the resultant space she had created. 'Sit, sit,' she said, motioning to one of several stools which had been pushed underneath.

Adam did as he was told. He was about to make some comment about the niceness of her kitchen when the spatula was thrust back in his direction.

'Come on, I want your opinion. I've been faffing with this all morning and I need to get it finished.'

'What's it for?' asked Adam, eyeing an array of dishes and bowls which were piled along a counter to his left.

'Tiramisu,' Fran replied. 'Well, sort of, my take on a tiramisu anyway. The sauce is to go on top, but I really can't decide whether I like it or not.'

Adam took hold of the spatula, scooping a finger through the caramel. Holding it to his mouth, he touched it tentatively with his tongue before rapidly licking off the rest. 'That's amazing,' he said, tackling the sticky spatula with gusto.

Fran beamed at him. 'Excellent. That's what I was hoping you'd say.'

Taking a pan from atop a large cooker she poured its contents over a dish that was waiting on the side. Then she removed two bowls from a cupboard above her head, dished out two portions, sunk a spoon into each and carried them back to where Adam was sitting.

'There you go,' she said.

Adam stared at the enormous pile of creamy pudding in front of him.

'Don't you like tiramisu?' she asked.

'I have no idea,' he replied. Although true, he was actually more concerned with the fact that it was only ten past nine in the morning. 'Are you allowed to eat pudding this early?'

Fran plonked herself down on a stool opposite him and plunged a spoon into the mess inside her bowl. He watched while she ate a huge mouthful, eyes closed in what he could only describe as ecstasy.

'God, that's good,' she said. 'If I do say so myself.'

Adam had to agree with her. It was incredibly good. 'Did you make that just to eat yourself?' he asked.

'Mmm.' She nodded, through another mouthful. 'I have to road test things, otherwise how would I tell if they're shite or not? But Jack and Martha will eat the rest. I'm five foot three, Adam, if I ate this much pudding all the time I'd be as wide as I am high. You, on the other hand, probably have hollow legs.'

His spoon paused in mid-air. 'Hollow legs?'

She nodded. 'Yes. Didn't your parents ever say that to you? Or your grandparents? As in, you can eat however much you like because your legs are hollow so it takes a lot to fill you up.' She frowned at him. 'Never mind, it's not important.' She flapped a hand. 'Anyway, what can I do for you?'

Adam rested his spoon back in the bowl. 'I've come about Becky,' he said, face falling. 'You know, the woman from Mum's party, the one that... died.'

'Oh yes. Does she want something catered for?' Fran smiled up at him before taking another mouthful of pudding.

'No...' Adam pressed his lips together. 'She's dead.'

Fran's head shot up. 'Dead? As in dead, dead?'

'Yes, not living.'

'Oh. Shit.' Fran slumped back on her stool. 'That's awful. She was... what, my age? No, younger than that.' Her hand went to her mouth. 'How did she die? *When* did she die?'

Adam wriggled backwards on the stool so he could push his hand inside his jeans' pocket. He pulled out a piece of paper and slid it towards her. 'I don't know. A week or so ago, maybe.' He hesitated. 'I'm not sure. I only found out 'cause Mum mentioned that she's going to the funeral tomorrow. But look, I've written down what I remember.'

Fran picked up the piece of paper, lips moving fractionally

as she read. 'Sorry, Adam. You've lost me. "I don't know what the hell Becky's playing at, but she needs to be careful. This could very easily get out of hand and something nasty happen." I'm not sure what that means exactly. And what do you mean, it's what you remember?'

'From the party. It's what I heard them saying.'

Fran peered at the note. 'Heard who saying, Adam? You're not making any sense.'

Adam sighed. 'Okay.' He tried to slow down all the thoughts in his head and get them in the right order again before he spoke. 'At the party, where everyone was playing the murder mystery thing...' He looked up to check that Fran was following him. 'I'd been in the cupboard for quite a while before you came in, and I didn't think much of it at the time, but I heard two women saying *that*.' He pointed to the piece of paper. 'And now Becky's dead, and under mysterious circumstances too. I think someone killed her.'

Fran looked up from reading the words again, obviously shocked. 'Adam, you can't just go around saying something like that. The party was nearly three weeks ago, and whatever those people may or may not have said doesn't really mean anything.'

'But don't you think it's odd?'

'Well, I admit it doesn't sound particularly nice. But it's hardly proof of anything, is it?' Fran fell silent for a moment, her brow furrowed. 'To me, it sounds as if Becky was doing something she shouldn't and her friends were concerned for her, that's all. It may have been something they didn't approve of, but I can't see how it's significant.'

'Maybe not. But it was a *murder*-mystery party...'

'Adam, it was a *game*... Becky didn't really die and no one killed her. They all had a great time and went home happy at the end of the night. If she's dead now it will be because of some tragic accident or... I don't know, cancer, or something else that she'd already been suffering from. What did your mum say?'

Adam pressed his lips together. He should have known that Fran would want all the details. And he'd been economical enough with the truth already. 'That one minute Becky was right as rain and then the next...' He motioned his head flopping to one side. 'So it wasn't cancer or an accident.'

Fran considered him carefully. 'Even so, people die suddenly all the time. It isn't nice, but Becky might have had a heart condition no one was aware of, had a brain haemorrhage, anything...'

'She didn't.'

Fran tipped her head to one side. 'And?'

Adam stared at her, growing more uncomfortable by the minute.

Fran dipped her spoon back in her pudding, collecting a dollop of caramel sauce and sucking at it thoughtfully. 'Only it sounds to me as if you do know how she died, after all. If you're certain it wasn't cancer, or an accident, or a heart condition, or a brain haemorrhage... What was it then, Adam, if it wasn't any of those things?' Her eyebrows rose in an almost straight line.

He swallowed. 'There was a post-mortem.'

'I would imagine there was. That's routine when the cause of death isn't obvious. That doesn't mean anything either.' She narrowed her eyes. 'Unless you know what the post-mortem said.'

Adam dropped his head. 'I think she was poisoned,' he said quietly.

Fran frowned. 'You *think* she was poisoned? Or you know she was?'

'Just that I heard... Well, she, Becky that is, thought she had a stomach bug to start with. Only she didn't. She couldn't have, because it got worse. Much worse.'

Several beats of silence ticked past. Seconds when Adam could feel Fran's eyes boring into the top of his head.

'Right...' she said slowly. 'And you think it was my food, do you? Is that it? You're here because you think—'

'No!' Adam's head shot up. 'No, nothing like that, but...' Damn, now Fran had gone and got the wrong idea.

'Then if this has nothing to do with me, what does it have to do with? Sorry, Adam, but you've come here this morning, saying you think someone killed Becky, but that you're not sure when she died, or how she died exactly, but that you *heard* she had a stomach bug. None of which makes any sense at all. I think you'd better tell me exactly what you heard because, by all means correct me if I'm wrong, but I don't think you're being entirely honest with me.'

Adam grimaced. He might have known. Mothers were the worst. They had this knack for sniffing out when people were being less than truthful, his was just as bad. Or maybe it was simply that he wasn't a very good liar.

'Okay,' he said. 'I listened in on my mum's phone call. I didn't intend to, just... I was passing and it sounded interesting.' He flashed Fran a sheepish look. 'I heard her say poison and it caught my attention.'

He was expecting admonishment but, instead, Fran simply smiled. 'Go on,' she said. 'Start at the beginning.'

He nodded. 'Okay. Well, I missed the start of the conversation, but I guess Mum was talking about the funeral arrangements with one of her friends because she mentioned that again later on. I heard her say that there'd been a post-mortem, sometime last week, and this is why the funeral has been held up. Some sort of poison was what she said after that, in reply to a question, I suppose. But I didn't know she was talking about Becky until almost the end of the conversation, when she said she couldn't believe Becky had gone. That's when she said about Becky thinking she had a stomach bug.'

Fran nodded. 'What else?'

'That was about it really. They talked about what they were going to wear to the funeral, but it was just boring stuff after that.'

'I see.' Fran was silent for a moment. 'And from that little snippet of conversation you decided that Becky had been killed, did you?'

'No. I didn't think about that until much later. But I was upset when I heard she'd died. I quite liked Becky... She used to be my teacher for a while and... Anyway, she was okay, she understood me better than a lot of my mum's friends. Stood up for me sometimes too.'

Fran dipped her head. 'I'm sorry, this is horrible news. I wasn't thinking. So you spoke to your mum, did you?'

Adam nodded. 'And she told me what happened. Not all of it, but she said that Becky had been fine until a week or so after the party. Then she got sick, like food poisoning or something, and that's when she thought she had a bug. She seemed to get better after that, and no one thought anything of it. Next thing Mum knew, Becky was in hospital, and it was serious. I mean, really bad. And then she died about a week later. Whatever it was, they couldn't save her.'

Fran's look was full of sorrow. 'That's horrible. The poor woman.'

'Mum was really upset. I didn't want to ask her much more.'

'No, of course not. I only met Becky the night of the party but she seemed nice.'

'She was...' replied Adam. 'Only now I'm not so sure.'

That caught Fran's attention. Her brow furrowed.

'Because afterwards, when I thought about what Mum had said, that's when I remembered what I'd heard at the party. And now it's all I can think about. That Becky was involved in something which led to her death. I saw her too, that night. And she didn't look right.'

'When? The night of the party?'

Adam nodded. 'It was after she'd died. Not actually died, obviously, the fake one. I'd gone to the kitchen for some of those pastry things – the ones you said I could have,' he added quickly, 'and Becky was in there. She jumped a mile when she saw me, and made out she'd gone to get a drink of water. But I don't think she had.'

'What makes you say that?'

'Because if you're thirsty, you drink, and Becky got a glass and filled it from the tap, but then it was as if she forgot I was there and she just stood, staring into space, with this weird expression on her face.' He thought for a moment. 'I don't know why, but it wasn't like her. Becky normally smiles, but she wasn't smiling that night.'

Fran wrinkled her nose and spun around the piece of paper Adam had given her. She read the words again.

'See,' said Adam, pointing to the note. He didn't need to read it again; he knew the words off by heart. 'They said that they didn't know what Becky was playing at, but that she needed to be careful, otherwise things could get out of hand and something nasty could happen. Well, it has, hasn't it? Becky's dead, struck down with something less than a week after the party.'

Fran bit her lip. 'I'm sure it's just coincidence. Don't forget that everyone was playing a part during the game that night,' she added. 'They'd all been given a character to play and had to stay in that character all evening. No one knew who the murderer was, or the victim for that matter, both those things were revealed as the game went along, together with a lot of other "clues". I think what you heard was simply two of your mum's friends trying to work out from each other whodunnit, and that was the whole point.'

Adam rolled his eyes. Did she not think he'd already thought of all that?

'But that isn't what you'd say, is it? If you were acting in character and talking about another character in the game, you'd use that name. You'd say *what is so and so playing at*, wouldn't you? Not, what is Becky playing at?'

'Could have been a slip of the tongue.'

'Then how do you explain Becky's death?'

Adam should never have come. Fran was beginning to sound exasperated, and if she didn't believe him, he doubted anyone else would. Until the police decided something funny was going on and then his mum would be in the frame for murder.

'Yes, but they were just talking, they were...' Fran's mouth worked, trying to form words which would contradict what Adam had been saying, to find some plausible reason why he was wrong. She stared at Adam. 'Shit,' she said.

'See? It *is* connected with the game.' He took a deep breath. 'And there's something else as well. I could well be a witness to murder.'

Fran's eyes widened.

'Because it was my mum who murdered Becky that night. She poisoned her.'

'In the *game*, Adam, not in real life.' Her hand shot to her mouth. 'Is that why you're here? Did one of the voices you overheard at the party belong to your mum?'

'No, but—'

'Shit... Sara? You surely don't think your mum actually killed Becky, do you?' Her eyes were wide and staring.

Adam shook his head, several times. 'No! But... Just because it wasn't, doesn't mean that Mum's innocent. Someone killed Becky, and if the police link her death back to the party then my mum, all of them, could be suspects. Even you and me, we were there too...' He left his sentence dangling in the air. 'That's what the police will think, anyway.'

Fran stared at the spoon still in her hand and then gently

laid it back in her bowl. 'I don't know what to say,' she said, her face full of concern as she searched his. 'But I can see you're really worried about this.' She gave a small smile. 'For what it's worth, I can't believe your mum was involved. We met up after the party for a coffee and she's not a killer, Adam, I really like her, she can't be a murderer. Actually, I can't believe anyone could do that... Murder, Adam? Really? It's like something from the TV, not sleepy suburbia.' She ran a hand through her hair, tucking it back behind her ears. Her freckles seemed larger than they had before. 'I'm sure everything will be okay.'

'But what if it's not?' whispered Adam, his throat trying to close.

'Okay... Think. Is there anything about Becky's death which would actually link it to the party?'

'I don't think so, but there might be, how would we know?' replied Adam. 'What I heard could be the only evidence there is so far.'

Fran nodded, her eyes narrowing. 'True, but for all you know I could be the murderer, I might even have poisoned that tiramisu. I haven't,' she added quickly, stretching out a hand to forestall him flinging away the spatula, 'but why have you come to see *me*? Why do you think I can help? I'm a caterer, Adam, not a detective.'

He hung his head a little, embarrassed now. 'Because I really don't have anyone else I can talk to about it,' he admitted. 'I don't understand people and I'm not very good with them. They make me nervous.'

'They make me nervous sometimes too, and if you recall the circumstances under which we met you'll know this to be true, so...' She gave him a penetrating look and Adam could almost hear the penny drop. 'Aah... you think I'm a kindred spirit?'

She didn't confirm or deny that fact, Adam realised after a moment. Perhaps he'd got it all wrong. Perhaps Fran *would* help him after all.

And then she smiled. 'I'm not agreeing to anything, you understand, but what is it you want me to do?' she asked.

'I wondered if you could speak to my mum. Find out what you can about how Becky died. That might give us some more information about what happened and we could take it from there. Maybe you could even go to the funeral.'

'Well, I could, I suppose. But won't Sara think it's odd? I didn't know Becky personally, she was simply a guest at the party as far as I was concerned.'

'Mum would think it even more weird if I asked her. I usually don't want anything to do with her friends. If I start asking questions she'd rumble me in a minute.'

Fran nodded. 'Okay, I guess I could speak to her. She was going to phone me to arrange another get together, but I haven't heard from her – I guess this explains why.' She narrowed her eyes at him, clearly thinking. 'Now, finish your pudding.'

Adam needed no second invitation and loaded up his spoon, much relieved. He knew Fran would be able to help him, and the fact that she made food like this could prove useful. He was a very limited cook.

'Adam, one other question. How did you find my address?'

He looked up, spoon an inch away from his mouth. Damn, he was hoping she wouldn't ask that.

'Only my address isn't listed on my business cards, or on my website. Just my phone number and email.' She took a deep breath, as if warming to her theme. 'In fact, I'm not even sure Sara knows exactly where I live.'

Adam cleared his throat. 'Oh, I just looked it up,' he said casually.

'Looked it up where?' Fran was leaning towards him across the table.

'From a website I know.'

She stared at him, allowing the seconds of silence to build up awkwardly.

'It's a database. For council tax, only it's not very, er...
secure.'

There was a rather long pause.

'Adam, isn't that illegal?

He pressed his lips together and swallowed. 'Only a little
bit.'

4

An hour had passed since Adam had left and Fran was no closer
to phoning Sara; she was still trying to take in what Adam had
told her. That Sara, or one of the other party guests, could be
guilty of murder. It didn't seem possible. Fran had only met
Sara a couple of times, but they'd got on like a house on fire, and
Becky had seemed lovely too; they all had. Just a group of
friends enjoying an evening together. Surely it was nothing
more than that.

Fran sighed and carried the now-covered bowl of tiramisu
over to the fridge. But if it was just an innocent party, then how
did you explain Becky's death? It didn't have to be related to the
party, of course. There could be any number of other explanations for it, rational explanations. It was still tragic, but anything
else was... The thought died in her head. *How many people
were poisoned on purpose?* she wondered. The thought made
her feel both hot and shivery because the answer, she suspected,
was not many. And what Adam had overheard painted things in
a very bad light.

Which brought her straight back to what Adam had asked
of her – talking to Sara to establish the circumstances of Becky's

death. It seemed a bit morbid to say the least, even though she
would like to offer her condolences. And that was without the
consideration that Becky had been murdered and Sara could
well be a suspect – if Fran wasn't careful she could end up
looking like a real idiot. Or worse, that she was accusing her of
murder. Only...

The possibility that Sara could have been the one responsible raised the hairs on the back of her neck. *Imagine how
Adam must feel.* He didn't strike her as the type to jump to
conclusions; more the type who'd had to screw up his courage to
talk to her in the first place. It was a measure of not only how
seriously he was taking his fears, but also the degree of trust and
faith he was placing in Fran by doing so. She huffed, puffing out
air between her teeth in frustration. Then she picked up her
phone and dialled.

WHICH WAS HOW, after a very pleasant phone call and an
unexpected invitation, the day of the funeral had rapidly
arrived and Fran found herself standing nervously outside the
church of St Barnabas, a place she hadn't visited since her
wedding over fifteen years ago.

St Barnabas's Church of the Blessed Virgin, to give it its full
title, was a tiny church which had suited her and Jack and their
small families and close but small circle of friends. Today,
though, the huge number of people who had turned out to pay
their last respects to Becky Pearson threatened to overwhelm it.
Fran's assessment of Becky as the most popular among the
group of friends at the party evidently held sway in the rest of
her life as well. The churchyard was full of people, as was the
surrounding area, and, although it made Fran feel somewhat of
a fraud for attending, it also meant that she wouldn't be so easily
observed.

Fran checked her watch. She had deliberately come early,

thinking it would give her ample opportunity to scout about for a bit before Sara arrived. Clearly, other people had had the same idea, although in their case it was perhaps because they knew the church would not hold everyone who wished to attend. She stepped backwards into the shade of a tree as she spied Lois's flaming-red hair and watched as she approached. She was accompanied by another woman who Fran had never seen before but, as she looked in the direction they were heading, she spotted Diane waiting for them. Of the other friends, however, there was no sign as yet, not even of Sara.

Fran moved so that she was standing behind a large crowd, sidling closer when she heard Becky's name mentioned.

'How's Nick doing?' someone asked.

'In bits,' came a reply. 'I heard from Stella that he's blaming himself, but then I guess you would, wouldn't you?'

'From what I've heard it wouldn't have made a scrap of difference if Becky had gone to the hospital sooner or not.'

'I heard they told her. That she knew they weren't going to be able to save her. Can you imagine how that must feel?'

'Don't,' said someone else. 'It's too horrible.'

And at that the conversation dwindled.

Fran was about to move on when she felt a light touch on her arm and almost jumped out of her skin. It was Sara, looking amazing in a fitted black suit.

'Hi, Fran,' she murmured. 'Thanks for coming.'

Fran nodded in reply. 'I know you said it was okay, but I still wasn't sure if I should come today. I didn't even know Becky, but then again it feels right somehow, for someone so young... It's just so shocking, isn't it?'

'Makes you think about life, that's for sure,' replied Sara, looking around her.

Fran followed her line of vision to where Lois, Diane and the other woman were standing.

'I saw Becky two days before she died,' Sara volunteered. 'She'd been feeling better but then... It's all so hard to take in.'

'Was it sudden then?' asked Fran, wondering how many questions she could get away with. 'Something unexpected?'

Sara swallowed. 'Not exactly, but at the start, yes, totally out of the blue. Becky just thought she'd picked up a sickness bug from school. She was a teacher,' she added for clarity. 'Always catching colds off the kids. Only I don't think it was a bug...' She turned her head away for a moment. 'Becky even joked about how she hadn't been able to leave the bathroom. I wish I'd taken what she said more seriously, but you don't, do you, something like that? You just think nature needs to take its course. No one imagined for a minute that leaving nature to take its course was the very worst thing anyone could do. And then, just as she was beginning to feel better, she collapsed, and by the time Nick found her and got her to hospital, it was too late. Major organ failure and nothing they could do.'

Fran could feel her nose beginning to prickle, the first sign of tears. 'I heard someone mention Nick before,' she said. 'Is that Becky's husband?'

Sara nodded. 'Poor sod. I have no idea how he's going to cope without Becky, they were soul mates, had been ever since they met. And all this hanging about between her death and now. Well over a week, almost two. I know people have to do their jobs but first the post-mortem and now an inquiry as well... Nick couldn't even organise the funeral. Too much.' She looked over to where her friends were standing. 'Excuse me a minute, Fran.'

Fran nodded and watched Sara walk away. This was too awful for words. She really shouldn't be here. She was threading her way through the crowds of people, aiming to simply slip away, when the hearse pulled into the kerb in front of the church and, behind it, two black cars. She stepped back onto the grass again. There was no way she could leave now, she'd have to pass through the gate at the entrance to the churchyard, right in front of the coffin. It would be so obvious.

Almost immediately the voices around her hushed as if by some unseen signal, and the graveyard grew still. Beside her, another mourner dressed in black stood, eyes rimmed with red, waiting silently for the family. Fran couldn't move even if she wanted to. Before she knew it, she was swept along with everyone else, filing into the dim church to honour the life of a young woman taken far too soon. And because Fran was as soft-hearted as they came, she cried along with everyone else too.

It was as she was listening to the vicar at the close of the service that Fran caught herself looking at everyone around her, studying their faces, watching their actions. From where she was standing, tucked up against a pillar down one side of the church, she had a clear line of sight to the front row of pews where Becky's husband and immediate family and close friends were sitting. What on earth did she think she was going to see? Someone looking vengeful, triumphantly gloating over Becky's death by their hand? Of course she wasn't, it was ridiculous. Someone very much loved and respected had died, and that death had made its mark on the lives of those around her. But that was all. There was nothing sinister about any of it, there couldn't be. It was a simple mix-up, no more. Fran hung her head in shame for thinking otherwise.

As the service ended, all she could think about was escaping back home and hoping that the family would forgive her for thinking such awful things about their loved one. Not that Fran had done anything wrong as such, but her presence at the church felt like a horrible intrusion into their grief. She couldn't blame her actions on Adam, either. He was young and impressionable, had probably watched far too many crime dramas on TV and was perhaps prone to bouts of exaggeration. Plus, he cared about his mum; nothing wrong with that and he was only doing what he thought best.

She shuffled forward, letting others go ahead of her, waiting until last so that she could file out behind them. No one would be looking back and she could just slip away while folks regrouped. And that would have been fine had Sara not been waiting by the lychgate, a balled-up tissue in her hand.

She smiled wanly as Fran approached. 'God, that was awful,' she said.

Fran could only nod.

'The burial is for immediate family only, but the rest of us are going over to the Swan in a minute. Lois and Diane have just gone to get something from Lois's car, but you're welcome to come with us.'

Fran hesitated, but then shook her head firmly. 'No, I shouldn't really. I didn't know Becky and it seems a bit, I don't know, mawkish.'

Sara gave her a sympathetic look. 'I know what you mean. It's bad enough that Becky died without everyone speculating about what happened. It doesn't seem right, does it? Just leave the poor girl alone. I'm not sure I want to go to the pub myself and sit there listening to gossip from people who should know better. In fact, I probably wouldn't go if I didn't know the family as well as I do. You've got to then, haven't you? To show your support.'

Fran was about to agree and take her leave when she realised what Sara had said. 'Why are people gossiping?' she asked. 'What are they saying?'

Sara glanced over to a group of people standing on the other side of the road. 'Oh, stupid things. That Nick had something to do with Becky's death. Or that Becky had done something silly. It's just ignorance, but it makes me so mad. On today of all days.'

Fran nodded, hoping that Sara would continue.

'Nick is gutted, anyone can see that. There's no way he could have had anything to do with it, and Becky was deliriously happy, they both were – after all this time trying for a baby, they'd finally agreed to put it behind them and start fostering. They were over the moon. So saying Nick poisoned her or that Becky did it deliberately is ridiculous. No, it's worse than that, it's goddamn hateful.'

Fran's eyes widened. '*Poisoned?* Sorry, I don't understand.'

Sara pressed the soggy tissue into the corner of her eye, sniffing. 'That's what it was, apparently. Diane told me, and Veronica told her, and she was closer than all of us to Becky, she would know. Some kind of mushroom it was, I forget the name of it now, death something or other. But Ronnie looked it up. It's fatal, shuts down your organs and there's no cure.'

Fran could feel her cheeks growing hotter and hotter.

'I don't know how it got into Becky's system and I don't know why. I don't want to know. It was a tragic accident and that's all. Anything else is just plain...' Her mouth dropped open as she fished for the right word. 'Impossible.'

THE VERY FIRST thing Fran did when she got home was to peel off her clothes and throw them in the laundry basket. The stiff trousers and blouse were things she only ever wore out of necessity, and the soft leggings and linen smocks she usually favoured would bring her some of the comfort she so desperately craved.

The other thing that would help, lived in the fridge. Moments after dressing, Fran took off the lid of the Tupperware container which held the remains of the tiramisu and began to eat it with a spoon, straight out of the tub as she leaned up against the sink.

It was a good ten minutes before she felt sufficiently revived to sit down. At the same island unit where she had sat with Adam only three days before as he had expounded his wild theories. Now... Now, she needed information. She pulled her laptop towards her and opened an internet tab, clicking into the search bar. *Death mushroom,* she typed.

She found it almost straight away. There were several entries for mushrooms which wouldn't do you a whole lot of good. Fly Agaric was one – the red toadstool with white spots on it so favoured by gnomes to sit on – that would give you a nasty stomach ache, but there were only two which were lethal. One was *Amanita bisporigera* or the destroying angel, as it was commonly known, and the second was *Amanita phalloides.* The death cap.

Fran checked article after article, but they all said the same. Just a few mouthfuls of the death cap mushroom would kill you, its toxin was so deadly. A toxin that could not even be removed by cooking the mushrooms. Baking them, boiling them, freezing them or drying them made no difference, they remained just as virulent. Poor Becky never stood a chance.

From ingestion, the first symptoms would have appeared between six to twenty-four hours later. Stomach cramps, nausea, diarrhoea – all the symptoms of food poisoning and also the stomach 'bug' that Becky thought she had picked up. If she had stayed hydrated to manage her symptoms, it was very possible that Becky would have begun to feel a little better, but all the while the toxins were stealthily and inexorably destroying her liver, kidneys and intestines in a vicious circle of death. The only things which might have saved her were knowledge of what was killing her, and time. Becky had neither.

Fran sat back, looking at the words blurring on the screen in front of her. She felt sick. Heavens only knew what Becky had been through. And just at the point where she had been taken to hospital, where she would have felt reassured that help was on its way, it was already too late. Her organs were shutting down, her body was failing and there was nothing that anyone could have done to save her.

Fran refocused on the article she had been reading, anger

setting her jaw into a hard line. The facts were unassailable. But you didn't get something like the death cap mushroom into your system by accident. Neither did you buy them off the shelves at Tesco.

Adam was right. As ludicrous, far-fetched and sinister as it sounded, Becky Pearson had been murdered.

5

'So what are you going to say?' asked Adam.

'I have absolutely no idea,' replied Fran, pulling up behind a row of stationary traffic. 'But I'm trusting the God of Improvisation to come up with something.' She checked the road ahead and then gave Adam a sideways glance. 'What I will not say, however, is that you found Nick's address in the same way you found mine. If he asks, I'll say that Sara gave it to me.' She pulled a face. 'Nick is quite likely to show me the door otherwise, or call the police, and either of those two things is going to get us precisely nowhere.'

'Yes, boss,' said Adam, tipping an imaginary cap although his beanie was still stuck firmly to his head.

Fran ignored him. 'You know, I probably should speak to your mum about this first, instead of barging in on Nick. So should you for that matter.'

Adam shook his head, alarm widening his eyes. 'Uh-uh... She wouldn't believe me, and that would be an end to it. Until the police came knocking, of course, by which time it would be too late.'

There was a certain ring of truth to Adam's words, but that

didn't make what Fran was about to do sit any more easily. 'I can't begin to imagine what he's been going through, and I'm just about to make his day a whole lot worse.'

'But we agreed,' argued Adam. 'If the police come to the same conclusion that we have, then they're going to make Nick's day far worse than we ever could. We're trying to help, remember.'

Adam was right, but Fran's conscience still prickled.

'Plus,' added Adam, 'if the police *do* become involved, then everyone is going to clam up very quickly. No one will want to say anything.'

Fran sighed. That was true as well. And it was just one conversation, how could that hurt?

The line of traffic moved off and Fran followed, turning right when she got to the bottom of the road. Nick's house was a little further along, one in a row of Victorian villas. She slowed, scanning the street for a parking space.

'Are you sure you don't want to come in with me?' she asked Adam, still hoping for a little moral support, whoever the provider.

'Fran, I'm nerdy, awkward and odd things come out of my mouth when I'm least expecting it. I'll only upset Nick and he'll either phone my mum or throw me out. He certainly won't take anything I have to say seriously.'

She studied him. 'Fair enough,' she replied, before climbing out of the car. She dipped her head back down again. 'I'm not sure how long I'll be, though. You could be waiting a while.'

Adam waved her away. 'You'll be fine,' he said, summing up how she was feeling far too accurately.

She started walking in the direction of Nick's house, cheeks flushing pink with embarrassment. Nerdy, awkward and *perceptive*...

The properties in this row all sat a little way back from the pavement, with small front gardens bordered by wrought-iron

railings, some thick with numerous coats of smart black paint
and others sorely in need of some. Nick and Becky's was well
cared for, their garden filled with bold architectural plants and
neat paving. Fran's hand was already on the gate when the front
door opened and a woman stepped backwards onto the path in
front of her.

'I'll call you,' she said. 'Or you call me, any time, Nick, and
you know I mean that.' She darted forward and impulsively
hugged the man standing in the doorway, before releasing him
just as swiftly and turning away. Her smile fell as she spotted
Fran, morphing into an unashamed stare as Fran stepped backwards to allow her through the gate. The woman passed
without so much of an acknowledgement.

The front door was still being held open and Fran mustered
her biggest smile as she turned to face Becky's husband. She
had an impression of height, a slim build underneath jeans and
tee shirt, but her attention was claimed almost immediately by
the look of raw grief in his eyes which even his glasses couldn't
hide.

'Hi... Um, I'm a friend of Becky's, or rather...'

But Nick had already stepped backwards to admit her, a
polite, but resigned smile on his face. He looked unbelievably
tired, stubble adding shadow to an otherwise pallid face. Fran
almost turned tail and ran.

'I'm sorry to intrude on you like this. I know it must be such
a difficult time, but I wondered if I might chat to you about
something. Something which...' She stopped. 'Oh.'

Fran had stopped speaking partly because she was aware
she was gabbling, but also because Nick had led her down a
short hallway to a kitchen that ran along the back of the
house, much like her own, and there was food piled everywhere. By the look, some of it had been there for a day or two
already.

Nick gave her a weary smile. 'I don't know what to do with

it all,' he said. 'Everyone is being so kind, friends, neighbours...
but the very last thing I want to do right now is eat.'

Fran stared around her in dismay. She was a fine one for
putting the kettle on in times of difficulty and she was also a
firm believer that a chocolate biscuit could fix most things, but
this was ridiculous.

'For goodness' sake, what do they think, that you're a five-
year-old?' Fran asked, bewildered.

Nick picked up a casserole dish covered with a tin-foil lid.
'Beef and ale stew, I believe,' he said, looking at her with
pleading eyes. 'You know, you're the first person to acknowledge
that I might be anywhere near capable of looking after myself. I
have a broken heart, not a sudden inability to cook for myself.
This has been going on for a week or so now. Everyone arrives
with more bloody food.'

Fran gave him a sympathetic smile. 'People mean well,' she
said, concern wrinkling her forehead. 'They want to help, but
often they don't know how, so they assume, instead of asking.
Would you like me to sort this lot out? I'm a chef, so one thing I
do know about is food.'

'Would you?' he said. 'The fridge is full as well, I just can't
face it but it seems wrong to throw it all away.' His face was
angled, the light catching the lens of his glasses. They were
covered in smudges.

'Then let me; I won't have any qualms about doing so. Especially as eating some of this food would be a really bad idea, not
unless you'd like a side order of food poisoning as well...' She
closed her eyes, suffused with embarrassment. When she
opened them again, Nick was studying her.

'And that's something else no one tells you about – that
when someone dies there's suddenly a whole list of taboo words
or subjects. Please, I'd rather you just say what you want, then
we all know where we are.' He gave an exasperated sigh. He
was a man rapidly approaching the end of his tether.

And now Fran was about to make it all ten times worse.

'Okay,' she smiled. 'Perhaps mentioning food poisoning seems horribly tactless of me, but what I've said is true. Please don't eat anything that hasn't been refrigerated, especially if it has meat in it. Let me sort this lot, and then maybe I can tell you why I'm here.'

He nodded gratefully. 'I don't even know your name,' he said, sinking onto a stool at the breakfast bar. 'But thank you.'

'No problem,' she replied. 'I'm Francesca – Fran – and I'm also a dab hand with washing up, as it happens. Some of those pots look like they'll need a good soak, but hot water and plenty of washing-up liquid will sort them out.' She eyed the door on the other side of the room. 'That's the back door, is it? Is that where your dustbin is?'

Nick nodded. 'And bin bags are—'

'Under the sink? No problem, I'll get them.' She flashed him a brief smile. 'Nick, tackling this lot might take me a few minutes, so if there's anything else you'd rather be doing, please do. I'm used to being in other people's kitchens.' She rummaged in her handbag. 'And just in case you'd like to see proof that I really am a caterer, this is my card. That's how I knew Becky, actually.'

Nick gave a sad smile. 'I should have had you to do the funeral tea, the pub food was rubbish.' He stared at her, pulling off his glasses and rubbing a hand over his face. She could hear the scratch of stubble on his chin. 'Do you know what I'd really like to do? Have a long shower. I haven't had a moment to myself since Becky died.'

'Good idea,' said Fran. 'You can have a damn good cry at the same time and no one will be any the wiser. I did that all the time when my mum died. Just let the water wash it all away.'

She watched as he walked off. He could only be mid-thirties, she reckoned, but he moved like a man twice his age.

By the time Nick reappeared half an hour later, the side was clear of dishes and a pile of empty and now spotless containers stood on the table.

'You'll have to let folks come and claim these,' said Fran. 'One or two of the dishes have the owners' names stuck on them. Someone called Helen seems to have been very industrious.'

'My mother-in-law,' supplied Nick. 'I think it's helped her to keep busy.'

Fran nodded, taking in the changes to Nick's appearance. He did look like he'd had a good cry, but the tension along his jawline had eased and a fresh shave had brought some colour to his previously pasty skin. Thick black hair, combed back off his face and slightly to one side, was still wet, slick like sealskin. His brown eyes were dark and troubled. Was it the face of a killer? Fran didn't think so.

Nick mustered a smile, looking around the kitchen. 'It's quite some transformation,' he said. 'I'm sorry, I should never have let it get like that, but—'

'You had other things to think about,' replied Fran. 'Don't worry, it's what I do. If it's helped at all then I'm glad. Now, anything I knew was safe to freeze, I have done. One or two people helpfully added notes to that effect, including today's casserole, so you don't have to worry about those now. They can stay frozen until you want them – *if* you want them. I've emptied the fridge of anything that is past its best too. There was a collection of what might have been vegetables at one point, but were now mostly slime so I've given the salad drawer a good clean out too.' She grimaced. 'Leafy green stuff, it's the absolute worst for that.'

'Becky used to make those hideous smoothie things after she'd been running,' replied Nick. 'Kale and the like. She must have bought them weeks ago now though, sorry.'

'It's no problem. In any case, I don't think you'll starve. The cupboards are also groaning with food.'

'Helen did some shopping for me too,' he said. 'Something else she seems to think I'm incapable of.' He frowned, as if annoyed by his ingratitude. 'Sorry, this is all so incredibly hard. I want to scream at people sometimes, even when I know they're only trying to help.' He looked at her expectantly, no doubt wondering while he'd been in the shower just how sensible it had been to let a stranger loose in his kitchen.

Fran swallowed, catching sight of a memo board over his shoulder. A photo had been pinned to one corner, a smiling, carefree Becky, tucked under Nick's arm, both of them wearing colourful bobble hats. Happy days.

It was time for her to come clean.

'I think I should explain why I'm here,' she began. 'Because you may well want to shout at me too.'

Nick remained silent although his look changed to one of caution.

'I *did* know Becky, but we weren't friends. I only met her a few weeks ago when I catered for a party that Sara threw.'

'So then why are you here?' he asked, suspicion lending his voice an edge.

'Because of something Sara told me,' she replied. 'And something I overheard at the party. Two things on their own which don't amount to much, but put them together and it's a very different story.'

Nick's eyes were fixed on hers. 'The party? What's that got to do with anything? Apart from the fact that it totally freaked Becky out.'

'Did it?'

It was an innocent enough question, but Fran could immediately see anger flicking across Nick's face.

He thrust his hands in his jeans' pockets, hunching his shoulders. 'Well, think about it. Becky had to pretend to die at some bloody party, poisoned by something she'd eaten, and by her own account she hammed it up, gargling, choking, head thudding onto the table... Can you imagine how she felt when she thought she had *actual* food poisoning? By the time we reached the hospital she was in so much pain and convinced she was going to die. She *knew*, before anyone had even looked at her. She said the party was like a bad omen, like a prophecy.'

Fran's fingers clenched inside her fist. She *could* imagine how Becky must have felt, and she was certain Nick had. She swallowed. 'The thing is, Nick, what if it was...?' Her words hung in the air, seconds stretching out, tightening the tension until it felt as if it might snap.

Fran was about to say something else to lessen the impact of her words, when Nick vented a huge sigh that crumpled him like a deflating balloon.

'You know how she died?'

Fran nodded gently. 'Sara mentioned it at the funeral.'

'I did everything I could to save her! Everything. But it wasn't enough.'

Fran's heart went out to him. There it was, laid bare, the thing that would always haunt Nick about Becky's death – the fact that he should have been able to save her, but couldn't. *If only...* How many times had that been said? Hindsight *isn't* a wonderful thing. It's one of the hardest things to ignore.

'I know,' she said quietly. 'But I'm sure you also know that once the mushrooms were in Becky's bloodstream there was nothing anyone could do. The only thing that could have saved her was to turn back time.'

'I still can't understand it,' said Nick. 'Becky used to go mushrooming with her dad when she was a kid, but they haven't done that for years. She knows how important it is to make sure you're absolutely certain about what you're eating. So why would she pick those mushrooms? Where would she have got them from? It makes no sense at all.'

He stared at Fran, searching her face for an answer, but then she saw his expression harden.

'Oh, I get it, that's why you're here, isn't it? Well, don't worry, I've heard what people are saying. Our so-called friends. Not all of them... But enough.' He clenched his jaw. 'I didn't kill my wife. And she didn't take her own life. There, is that what you wanted to hear? Straight from the horse's mouth. Have I convinced you, or are you going to go back and report on what you've just heard? The poor grieving husband who's hiding a dark secret. You lot disgust me, that you could ever think—'

Fran held up a hand. 'Nick! That's not why I'm here. Not at all, quite the reverse, actually.' Her voice had taken on the tone she reserved for her daughter, and she deliberately softened it. 'I came here to help you *because* I'd heard the rumours.'

His eyes bored into hers. 'Becky and I were about to embark on the biggest adventure of our lives together – parenthood – and so there's no way she would take her own life, just as there's no way I would have killed her. We had everything going for us, for God's sake. We loved one another, we—' He broke off, choked.

'Nick, I'm not saying I think you had anything to do with it, or that Becky would have taken her own life. But the fact remains that she was poisoned.' She took a deep breath. 'And if you didn't give the mushrooms to her, and she didn't take them herself, how else did they get into her system? I'm sorry, Nick, but I don't think it was an accident.'

Nick's expression had relaxed a little but now his eyes shot open. 'You think someone killed her?' A pulse was beating in the side of his neck. 'You actually do, don't you? For God's sake, you make it sound like one of those far-fetched soap operas. Don't be so bloody ridiculous.'

'Ridiculous it may be, but I heard someone at the party making what could be construed as a threat against Becky. I wouldn't have thought any more of it if I hadn't learned how Becky died. It's too much of a coincidence to ignore. I know you don't want to admit to the possibility of what I've just said, and I understand that perfectly. But I don't believe you're stupid either. Deep down you know what I'm saying makes absolute sense.'

Fran could see the tussle on Nick's face. The desire to be left alone to mourn his wife. The desire to make everything nasty go away and for things to be as they were before. But she could also see that he wanted answers. If someone *had* ruined his life, then he wanted to know who.

He made his way to the breakfast bar, holding onto its edge as a child might, and sat down on the stool he had used earlier, turning so that he faced Fran. 'I think you'd better tell me what you heard,' he said softly.

6

It didn't take long. There wasn't much to say, after all. But it didn't matter that there weren't many words, it was what they imparted that was important.

Nick received the news calmly, albeit white-faced with shock as he listened to Fran with a sombre expression on his face. It was the face of a man who knew that his world had changed irrevocably. How much worse could anything be?

'I can't believe I'm saying this, but what do we do?' he asked, after a moment's silence.

'That's really why I'm here,' said Fran, taking up the conversation again. 'At the moment no one else knows what I heard, but I don't think it will be very long before other people start asking very probing questions and, apart from Becky's death casting suspicion on you, given what I've told you, it could also cast suspicion on anyone else at the party. Particularly Sara as she was the one who "murdered" Becky in the game. And I really don't want that to happen.'

Nick nodded, and swallowed, the first flickers of unease starting to show. 'So how do you think I can help? Do you know whose voices you heard?'

Fran shook her head. She hated deceiving him but she really wasn't sure what else she could do. 'No. Only that I'm pretty sure it wasn't Sara. I don't know the other women well enough to be able to judge and I didn't think anything of it at the time, it was just a random snatch of conversation like countless others. It was only when I heard Becky had died that it came back to me.'

'And if you heard them now, would you be able to tell?'

Fran thought for a minute, making sure that her story was plausible. 'No, I don't think so. Not with any degree of certainty. I was in Sara's kitchen when I heard them. The door was closed and they were out in the hallway so the sound was a little muffled.'

'Yet you're certain about the words you heard?'

'I'm sorry, but yes, I am.' Fran had been watching Nick carefully while she spoke and caught a flicker of something on his face. 'What is it?' she asked. 'Something's just occurred to you.'

He sat forward a little, obviously interrogating his memories. 'When Becky got home the night of the party, I asked if she'd had a good time, but it was late and she was tired so she didn't say much. The next day when I asked her again, though, she was a little dismissive. Simply said she'd really enjoyed it and left it at that. Which was odd for Becky 'cause she usually rabbited on about what she'd got up to with her friends. To the point where I had to stop her sometimes, too much information.' He paused, a sad smile on his face. 'She was a very social person. Life was always fun with Becky around.'

Acknowledging his grief, Fran waited a moment before asking her next question. She was thinking about Adam's comment – how Becky had appeared troubled when he had met her in the kitchen. 'So you think maybe she had something on her mind?'

'Perhaps... It's true that she'd go quiet when she was worried about something. And she did mention that pretending to die had been unnerving. Weird, she said. On the one hand really fun, but on the other, a little... surreal. I'm not sure if that's the right word, but that was how she made it sound. And it obviously stuck in her head because why else would she have made the comment later on about the party being a bad omen?'

'Why indeed? But she didn't mention anything in particular about the game that evening? Or anything about her friends?'

Nick shook his head. 'Not that I can think of, sorry.'

'How well did you get on with them?'

'Okay, I suppose. As well as any husband gets on with his wife's friends. I didn't know them all that well, although I know that Becky was very close to them. Lois, she met at the school where she worked... I'm not really sure about the others.' He frowned, no doubt chastising himself that he didn't know this group of women better.

'So you don't know why any of them would want to kill Becky?'

Nick's shoulders sloped even further downwards. 'That's what the police are going to want to know, aren't they? *Who hated your wife enough to kill her, Mr Pearson?*' His face began to crumple. 'But that's just it, who would want to kill Becky? She was... perfect.'

'Well, that didn't really get us anywhere, did it?' said Fran a few minutes later as, back in the car with Adam, she navigated the junction at the bottom of Nick's road. 'Other than the fact that Nick is obviously heartbroken about his wife's death and clearly didn't kill her so—'

'Why *clearly* didn't kill her?' asked Adam from the passenger seat.

Fran pursed her lips. 'Because of how shocked he was at the thought that someone had. He was so pale at one point I thought he was going to faint. Besides, there were a gazillion photos around the place. They were obviously very much in love and they'd just decided to start fostering children; that's a really long-term commitment and something you'd only contemplate if you were in a really solid relationship.'

'Yeah, but he would say that, wouldn't he?'

Fran frowned, concentrating on the road. 'Sorry, I'm not sure what you mean.'

'If Nick did kill his wife he's hardly going to go around telling everyone he hated her, is he? He probably doesn't have a concrete alibi for her death, because at the moment no one really knows what happened on the day she was taken ill so the only thing he can do is suggest a reason why he couldn't possibly be guilty. But husbands are *supposed* to be in love with their wives, so saying that he adored her isn't a good enough reason for him not to have killed her... but fostering might be. Fostering not only implies commitment, it implies that other people were involved in that decision. But do we really know if that's the case? Had they actually gone as far as contacting authorities to apply to be foster parents?'

Fran slid him a look. 'Are you always this suspicious of people?'

'Maybe my experience of life thus far has been different from yours,' he said, which didn't really answer the question. 'Mostly I've found people to be weird,' he added, shrugging.

'Perhaps some of them are, but not all of them. Mostly *I've* found folks to be kind and generous, honest and—'

'Is that why you were hiding in a cupboard at the party?' The corners of his mouth were twitching in amusement.

'Oh, ha ha!' she replied, equally not answering the question. 'You're right about the sequence of events though; that is something we need to find out. We need to piece together Becky's movements on the day she was taken ill. You know what they always say on TV detective shows: that the last person to see someone alive...'

Fran turned to look at him when there was no reply.

'The last person to see someone alive is the person that killed them,' she said.

Adam considered this for a moment. 'But that doesn't work in this case.'

Fran wrinkled her nose. 'No, I guess not. But I still think we need to establish when, and indeed where, Becky ate the mushrooms.'

'Agreed.'

'As for the possibility that Nick *did* have something to do with her death, I'm prepared to keep an open mind. And it was your mum who told me about Becky's fostering plans.'

'Yes, but who told *her*?'

Fran smiled. 'Okay, okay, I'll be sure to ask.' She paused for a moment, wondering how best to say what she needed to. 'You know, I really think you need to come with me when I talk to your mum. Tell her that it was you who overheard the threat against Becky. I know you might have to admit to where you were when you heard it, but—'

'No.' The reply was immediate.

'Adam, I've just lied to Nick. I told him *I'd* overheard two women talking at the party. So what do I say if the police come knocking? Do I have to lie to them as well?'

'I'm hoping it won't come to that.'

'So do I. But the possibility remains. This could get me in a whole heap of trouble. We can't keep this evidence from them if they ask and it isn't going to look good if they find out I've been lying.'

Adam shook his head repeatedly. 'I know that. Which is why we need to find out as much as we can before the police do start asking questions. But I can't talk to Mum, Fran, I absolutely can't.' Fran noticed his head drop. 'She could be a suspect,' he said quietly.

'So could I,' replied Fran, raising her eyebrows. 'You don't really think she could be guilty, do you?'

'No, of course not! That's why I want to find out what happened, *before* someone accuses her.'

Fran shot him a glance. 'But you're also mindful of the fact that once we start looking into this, we might uncover things we might not want to...'

Adam didn't reply. He didn't need to.

'Okay,' said Fran gently. 'Let's agree that Sara had nothing to do with Becky's death, because I'm sure that's the case. *If* we find out differently then... well, we'll deal with that if the situation arises. Besides, I'm just about to go in your house and explain to your mum that I think Becky was murdered and I don't think I can do that believing she might have had anything to do with it.' That much was true, but Fran was only too aware of how wrong she might be. She gave Adam a sideways look. 'But I am going to have to tell her why I've come up with such a wild idea, which will mean me lying, yet again.'

'I know, I'm sorry.' Adam slid his beanie from his head and ran a hand through his hair. 'But I don't know what else we can do. There's also the fact that if Mum knows I'm involved in this at all, she'll forbid me from delving any deeper. Please, Fran, I'm positive this is the way to go. You talk to her and while you do I'll be in my room, making no noise and pretending I don't exist.'

'Adam, you're hardly Harry Potter.'

'No, but I do still live at home, and I have no desire to make my life any more difficult. And before you argue, have you told your husband what you're doing?'

'What do you mean?'

'Have you told your husband that you're investigating a murder?'

'Adam, we're just asking a few questions, we're not—' She

stopped. *Were they? Was that what they were really doing? And if it was, why did the thought set off a little tingle of excitement?*

'No, I thought not.'

Fran could feel him smiling across at her but there was no way she was going to look at him. Damn it, he was right too. Of course she wouldn't tell Jack what she was up to. He'd hate the idea. He'd tell her to leave it to the police, to not get involved. He'd tell her that it could be dangerous and that she didn't know what she was letting herself in for. Ergo, if she didn't tell him, they wouldn't be able to have that conversation. She narrowed her eyes. She would have to keep an eye on Adam, he was far too clever for his own good.

'I think the word you're looking for is "touché",' he said, the corners of his mouth twitching upwards.

'Oh, shut up,' said Fran, pretending to be cross as she turned up Sara's drive.

Once out of the car, Fran waited while Adam went around the back of the house to let himself in before she knocked on the front door. Sara answered almost straight away, and all but pulled Fran inside.

'Oh, thank God you're here,' she said. 'I've just had the police on the phone asking me how well I knew Nick Pearson, Becky's husband. I had no idea what to say, so I fudged things a little and said I didn't really know him. It's true, I don't, but... Fran, I have a horrible feeling they were going to ask me about Becky too, about her relationship with Nick. It was bad enough that people were talking that kind of nonsense at the funeral, but now...' Her eyes were wide and staring. 'How could anyone think that Nick killed Becky?'

'Sara, the police are just doing their job. I know it sounds awful, but Becky did eat mushrooms which poisoned her, and if it wasn't an accident then someone gave them to her deliberately. The police will only be trying to work out which it was in this case.' She felt the weight of all that had already been said that morning. 'I don't suppose we could put the kettle on, could we?'

Sara nodded. 'Yes, of course. You said on the phone that you wanted to talk to me about something. Was that it? Have the police spoken to you too?'

'No, nothing like that but... Let's get that drink and I'll explain.' Fran would be much happier if Sara were sitting down when she told her what she had come to say. Sara was very obviously out of her comfort zone. She already looked anxious, the poise and confidence that were so evident at her party all but gone.

It took a few minutes before they were both seated, Fran gratefully clasping a mug. Sara possessed a rather grand coffee machine and wouldn't countenance Fran's suggestion that instant would do. Sara didn't say as much, but her raised eyebrows spoke for her. Taking a fortifying swallow, Fran began.

'There's no easy way to say this, Sara, but I wanted to see you for exactly the same reason that I went to see Nick this morning. Because, as you now know, the police *are* looking into Becky's death, and whether or not they think there is anything suspicious about it, I'm afraid I do. I overheard something at your party which makes me think that Becky's death was no accident, especially now that I know how she died.'

Sara stared at her, face contorted with emotion. 'You think someone killed Becky,' she exclaimed. 'You actually do!' She shook her head. 'I'm sorry, I can't believe it. People gossiping is one thing, but this...' Her mug lowered to the table, borne on a shaking hand. 'What did you hear? You must have got it wrong.'

Fran pressed her lips together. 'I don't think I did, Sara,' she said gently. 'I know this is a shock, but I heard two people make a threat against Becky and—'

'But what did they say? Why would they do that?'

'I don't know.' Fran was very conscious that Sara's voice had risen. 'But in a way, it almost doesn't matter. What matters is that, if I'm right, and the police *do* begin to suspect foul play, then the first thing they'll do is put together a list of suspects. I think it's a pretty well-known fact that most murder victims know their killer, and that being the case the list of suspects is going to include Becky's husband, other members of her family and her friends, one of whom is you.'

Sara's mug stopped halfway to her mouth, her eyes wide. 'Me?'

Fran nodded. 'And if the police were to learn what I over-heard then that could narrow the list of suspects considerably, perhaps even to just a handful of people.'

'You mean someone who was at the party?'

'Yes, that's exactly what I mean.'

'But what did you hear?'

'That they didn't know what the hell Becky was playing at, but that she'd better be careful before things got out of hand and something nasty happened. I'd say being poisoned is pretty nasty, wouldn't you?' Fran studied Sara's face. 'Does that mean anything to you?'

Two white spots had appeared in Sara's otherwise florid cheeks.

'You think *I* said those things?'

Fran's eyebrows raised.

'Well, I didn't!'

Fran had been very interested to see how Sara responded, but now she softened her expression a little. 'Actually, no, I don't think you were one of the people I heard.' She thought quickly how to elaborate while making no reference to the fact that she had ever been in the understairs cupboard. 'I was in the kitchen at the table and the voices came from out in the hallway, but they were too muffled for me to identify. It doesn't take a genius to work out who it must have been though – either Diane, Lois or Camilla.'

Sara shook her head. 'But maybe you got it wrong. Maybe you misheard or misunderstood. Things taken out of context are often not what they seem.'

'Perhaps, and yet Becky's still dead.' She paused to let her words sink in. 'So let's assume for a moment that what I heard was a threat. Don't you think it's odd that two women who were supposedly Becky's friends would say those things? Can you think of anything that Becky could have been doing? Something that someone might want to kill her over? Having an affair maybe?' added Fran, thinking on the spot.

But Sara's reply was instant.

'God no,' she said. 'Not Becky. She and Nick had been together since uni and they were... well, you can just tell, can't you? They were very close.'

'And about to start the process to become foster parents, you said. Did Becky tell you that herself?'

'I think so. Now you say it, I'm not a hundred per cent certain, but it was common knowledge among her friends. Everyone knew about their difficulties in conceiving, it wasn't a surprise as such.'

Fran nodded. 'Okay,' she said, but it was interesting that Sara couldn't confirm how she'd come by that information.

'I can't believe it,' protested Sara. 'That anyone could have killed Becky, least of all one of her friends. Or that she was guilty of anything either. What, like *blackmail*? Honestly, Fran, if you don't mind my saying, that's a great motive for a murder-mystery game, but in real life?' She made a dismissive noise. 'Come on, don't you think that's a little far-fetched?'

'Blackmail?' Fran blinked. 'Why would you say that?'

Sara looked puzzled. 'Well, that's the reason why Becky, or rather Clarity Makepiece, was killed. In the game we played. She'd been blackmailing everyone.'

Fran felt her stomach drop away in shock. 'Was she now? Well, that is interesting.'

Could that be the motive for Becky's death? Not just in the murder-mystery game but in real life too... She thought for a moment, trying to make sense of the threads that were swirling in her brain. *Oh, for goodness' sake, Fran, listen to yourself. Don't be so ridiculous.* Becky was loved among her friends. And you only had to see how many people attended the funeral to know how well liked and respected she was. Why would she do something as devious and manipulative as blackmail?

'Sara, where did you get the game from?'

A wary look crossed Sara's face. 'It was bought online, why?'

'I just wondered who chose the blackmail motive, that's all.'

Sara still looked confused. 'No one did. That's not the way it works.'

'Oh,' replied Fran, disappointed. 'How does it work then?'

'You can buy a specific game. There were lots of off-the-shelf kits, but those seemed more suitable for larger groups so, because there wouldn't be many of us, we decided on a bespoke game. We simply entered a few details on the website and then they sent a game which was tailored to our needs. We didn't know exactly what it was going to be until it arrived, though.'

'Can you show me?' asked Fran.

'Yeah, sure.' Sara slipped off her seat and crossed to the other side of the kitchen, where her mobile phone was charging. 'I'll have to check the email Becky sent me. I can't remember what the company was called.'

Fran waited as patiently as she could, her heart beating much faster than the seconds that were ticking by. She stared expectantly as Sara returned to the table.

'Here it is. The company's called Red Herring Games.' She made a slight moue. 'Not exactly original, but if you look at the menu there are different games with different themes.' She passed the phone to Fran. 'And you can either pick one you like, or you can go there' – she pointed to a custom tab on the website menu – 'and put in your details.'

Fran did as she was shown, looking at the page as it loaded. She quickly read through the information. It was just as Sara had said, an explanation of the service they offered if a standard game wasn't suitable. Fran looked at the details the company requested and her heart fell. They simply wanted to know the number of guests, how many were male and female, a broad age range and the theme of the game required, nothing more specific than that. Choices ranged from historical murder mysteries to Christmas-inspired themes, pirates, even the Wild West.

'We picked Hollywood,' added Sara, seeing where she was looking.

Fran nodded, scrolling to the bottom of the page. 'Just a thought,' she said. 'Thanks anyway.'

'What were you looking for?'

'I was thinking about the blackmail motive, that's all.' She handed back the phone. 'But you mentioned that Becky had emailed you. In connection with the game?'

Sara nodded. 'Yes, she organised it.'

Fran sat a little further forward in her seat. 'Did she? Why would she do that if it was your party?'

There was a pause but then Sara's face unscrewed itself. 'Oh, I see what you mean.... I didn't buy the game, it was my birthday present; the girls all clubbed together, and Becky offered to organise it. We got together a while back and someone asked what we were going to do for my birthday. I can't remember who suggested a murder-mystery game, but we all thought that would be a great idea.'

'So could that person have been Becky?'

'Possibly... No, actually, I think it was Ronnie. Her family had played one previously.'

'But it was Becky who suggested which company to use?'

Sara scratched the end of her nose. 'It might have been. I'm sorry, I can't remember. But it was me who picked the Hollywood theme. We couldn't decide, so in the end they made me choose, seeing as it was my birthday. I just thought it would be fun.' She dropped her head, tucking her hair behind her ears.

Fran could see how awful she was feeling. She gave her a sympathetic smile. 'And you did have fun,' she said. 'Everyone had a wonderful time.' She didn't know what else to say.

Sara sank back heavily onto her chair. 'Do you really think that we might all be suspects?' she asked.

'Yes, I'm afraid I do,' replied Fran. 'Like I said before, if the police decide Becky's death was suspicious then they're going to look to her family and friends first. They're going to ask if anyone might have wanted to kill her. And why. And if they find out that Becky "died" at a murder-mystery party recently, well, it doesn't take a genius to work out what their next line of questioning is going to be.'

Judging by the look on her face, Sara was beginning to understand just how serious all this could be and Fran's first instinct was to reassure her. She liked Sara – surely she couldn't be the guilty party?

'But, apart from Nick, and now you, no one else knows what I overheard, and I think we should keep it that way. It's the only thing which suggests the party was anything other than a bunch of friends having a fun evening. And as long as the police don't know there's a possible connection between the party and Becky's death, the better it will be.'

Sara's eyes grew wide. 'You're saying you think I'm going to be the main suspect, aren't you?'

Fran nodded. 'One of them, yes. Along with Nick. They always look to the husband first, so he's the most obvious suspect, but you—' Fran could hardly bring herself to say it. 'You were the one who actually poisoned Becky, even if it was only a game.'

'Is that really what the police are going to think?' Sara whispered, her cheeks burning in a sudden flush. 'But that's crazy. We all loved Becky.'

'Someone didn't,' said Fran.

'No...' replied Sara, the skin around her eyes puckering. 'But *you* don't think it was me, do you?'

Fran smiled, thinking about Adam's face when she spoke to him earlier. How worried he was. 'No, I don't think it was you. I wouldn't be here if I did.'

'Oh, thank God.' Sara looked hugely relieved but then almost immediately Fran saw anxiety spring back into her eyes. 'But the police might not think that.'

'No, they might not. Which is why we need to be one step ahead if we're going to catch a killer.'

7

Sara stared at the cup of coffee in her hand as if scarcely able to believe that normality had suddenly become so tenuous. 'So what do we do now?' she asked, the fingers wrapped around her drink, white at the knuckle.

Fran drained her mug and held it out. 'Have another one of these?' she suggested, hoping to lessen some of the tension. 'And if you have any cake, or biscuits, I suggest you crack them open too. The sweeter the better.' She paused a moment. 'Sara?'

Adam's mum was staring into the distance, eyes unfocused. It took several seconds for her to realise that Fran had spoken.

'I'm sorry... I just can't believe that anyone would want to kill Becky. It sounds like a plot straight out of a soap opera, not something that could happen around here.'

'Don't you believe it. The things which drive people to murder are the same the world over. It makes no difference where or how you live; rich, poor, inner city or countryside. When emotions run high, anything can happen and, believe me, I've catered for enough family get togethers to know that even the closest people can hate one another. Despise each other. Feel jealousy, white-hot anger and simmering resentment too.

God, that's the worst. Of course, there's a lot of love, fun and laughter as well, but you take my point. It can happen anywhere, Sara, and often does.'

'But we've all known Becky for a while now, some of us a very long time. Don't you think we would have noticed if anyone felt that strongly?'

'Possibly. Possibly not. People are often very good at hiding how they feel. Even from their closest friends and family.'

Sara looked down at her coffee and nodded sadly. 'Yes, I guess they do.' Her voice sounded far away. She drank what remained and held out her hand to take Fran's mug. 'I've got some custard creams somewhere, will they do?'

'Perfect,' replied Fran, making a mental note to bring some biscuits with her next time she came. 'So how did you and Becky meet?'

'At the school,' replied Sara, her back to Fran as she fiddled with the coffee machine. 'Becky was Adam's form tutor for his last year, his drama teacher too. We had a few... issues, shall we say, and Becky did her best to help out. Not that it made any difference. Adam was, is, very bright and he was bored rigid at school.' She turned back to face Fran. 'I don't think they knew what to do with him, actually, but Adam didn't exactly help matters, he... never mind, it's all water under the bridge now. But Becky and I got to know one another quite well. She was a huge help to me personally. We met up a couple of times and hit it off straight away. That's how I met Lois too.'

Fran nodded, trying very hard to hide the smile that wanted to be let out. She wondered what Adam would make of his mum's description of him. 'So how would you describe Becky?'

'Warm, optimistic, generous and loyal. She cared about the people and things in her life.' Sara's reply was immediate. 'And would go out of her way to help anyone. Out of us all, I think she was the one who kept us together, made sure that we all stayed in touch, that kind of thing.' A slight pause. 'Not that we wouldn't but, you know how it is, we're all busy, all tied up in our own lives, and sometimes it's easy to let things slide.' She turned back to the coffee maker. 'In a way, that's why this is so awful. I don't think I realised how bad things had been for Becky before, perhaps even how unhappy she'd been, how much wanting a child had coloured her whole life. I knew she did everything she could to get pregnant – ate the right things, took supplements – and she was the only one of us who took keeping fit seriously. I play a few games of tennis, but it's more of a social thing. She and Nick had talked about IVF in the past too, except the cost made it impossible. Looking back, though, I can see how much happier Becky had been of late now that they'd made the decision to foster. She was more accepting, resolved. She'd lost the slightly desperate air she sometimes wore, like she was running out of time—' Sara stopped suddenly, turning back around. 'Oh God, and now she has, hasn't she?' She raised her hands to her face, trying to hold in her emotion.

'So, for argument's sake, you don't think she could have been capable of something like blackmail?'

Sara shook her head firmly. 'Absolutely not. No, I just can't see it.'

'Not even if it might have paved the way for IVF treatment?'

Sara thought again. 'No.' She bit her lip. 'Is that what you think was going on?'

'I really don't know, Sara. I'm just trying to explore all the possibilities. And her friends are the people that knew her best, aside from her husband, of course.'

'I accept your point about not always showing people what you're feeling, even those closest to you. But I don't think Becky was like that. What you saw was what you got.' Sara stared at her. 'This is horrible... making assumptions about people. Speculating who might have—'

'I know it is, Sara. And I know I'm pushing you to think about things you don't want to, but unless we do...' There was no need to finish the sentence. 'And the police won't have any qualms about asking these questions. What I overheard at your party is the only thing we have to go on at the moment. We need to find out what Becky was doing which had everyone so upset. It's a motive for murder and whether that's blackmail or anything else, we need to pursue it. And the only people we can ask are your friends, however unpleasant that may be.'

'I know.' Sara's shoulders hunched. 'But I still don't like it.' She turned resolutely back to finish making the coffee and Fran let her be. It was a lot for anyone to take in.

A few minutes later Sara brought over a tray with two mugs on it and a plate of biscuits. 'Sorry,' she said. 'I'm just finding all this very difficult.'

'It *is* difficult,' replied Fran, smiling warmly. 'I think it would be odd if you didn't feel like you do.'

'Okay,' said Sara, taking two biscuits and visibly straightening her shoulders. 'What do you need to know?'

'Let's start with your other friends from the party. You've told me your impressions of Becky. What about the others?'

'Okay... so, Lois then. Well, she's—' Sara broke off. 'This is really difficult, I've never had to describe anyone in this way before. Lois would say she lives a small life, but I think in truth we're all very envious of her. She's never happier than when surrounded by her family, a real homemaker, whereas the rest of us have struggled with various aspects of that. Some more than others.' Sara pulled a face. 'Lois and Martin have been married forever; they were childhood sweethearts, but you couldn't meet a nicer couple, so in tune with one another. They have two beautiful daughters who never seem to cause them a moment's trouble, and Lois's house... well, she just has this incredible eye for what works and what doesn't. There's nothing I could add to it and I work in interior design. It might not be as big as some

houses but it always looks so beautiful, but the homely kind of
beautiful that takes a lot of work to achieve so that it doesn't
look it. Does that make sense?'

Fran nodded. 'I have a friend like that too. She's very
creative and seemingly throws things together. If I do that, they
just look a mess.'

'Yes, that. Absolutely.'

'Do you know how long Lois has worked at the school?'

'I don't know for definite but she was there before Becky
started. So at least five years or so. I get the feeling it's been a
long while.'

'And she's been friends with Becky all that time?'

'I think so. Longer than the rest of us anyway.'

Fran filed away these new facts about Lois in her brain,
where they sat with the assumptions she had already made.
They didn't exactly meet in the middle, but perhaps Fran's
initial impression of her had been wrong. It wouldn't be the first
time.

'And so what about Diane? What can you tell me about
her?'

There was a longish pause which Sara tried to hide by
taking a slurp of her coffee. It was long enough for Fran to lean a
little closer, however, senses on alert.

'I've known Diane longer than anyone, but... it sounds
weird, but in many ways, I'd say she's the friend I know the least
about. We actually met through work. I did a stint in accounts
before I decided to train in interior design and ended up
working for the same company as Diane. She's still there,
although I always got the feeling that her husband didn't
approve of her going to work at all. He's something big in the
city, and I think thought Diane should be a stay-at-home house-
wife. It's odd, because I don't think she ever said as much, but
she's certainly never tried for promotion or anything like that.
She's still doing the same job she was when I met her. I guess

over the years I simply accepted that Diane's home life was something she was very guarded about, and so we based our friendship around other things. They don't have any children and recently moved to a beautiful house in the very poshest part of town, but I've never been there.'

'She seemed quiet during the party,' put in Fran. 'Is she very shy?'

'I wouldn't say shy as such, more... nervous? No, that's not quite the right word. Reticent maybe? She *is* quiet, but has the most wicked sense of humour once you get to know her. Trouble is, folks often don't get to appreciate it because she'll mutter under her breath almost as if she's not confident of saying it. But she has me in hysterics sometimes. Loyal too, and very supportive of anyone with a problem, even though her own life isn't without a share of its own.'

Fran took another bite of her biscuit. 'You asked me to serve her non-alcoholic drinks at the party. Is that what you mean?'

Sara wrinkled her nose, frowning. 'No, Diane's teetotal, but not because she's had a drink problem in the past, well, not that I know of anyway. You see, that's just it, there's so much about Diane I *don't* know – especially things from her past. And I know what you're thinking,' she added, as if reading Fran's mind, 'we've all talked about whether we ought to find out more regarding Diane's past but, apart from the odd comment, she never seems down about it. She also has an incredibly sunny disposition. Real happy-go-lucky.' Sara drank a mouthful of coffee. 'She's a bit of a conundrum is our Diane.'

Curiouser and curiouser, thought Fran.

'Which just leaves Camilla,' she said. 'Although I admit I know her myself, through the PTA at school.'

Sara laughed. 'Then I probably don't need to tell you any more. Camilla – larger than life, loud, pushy, ostentatious, flam- boyant, wickedly funny, with a heart of gold and the best fun to be around.'

'She terrifies me,' admitted Fran, wondering if she should divulge the fact that she'd spent a good half hour in Sara's understairs cupboard because of her. She decided against it.

'Me too,' replied Sara. 'But I still love her. And she's as direct as they come, which you probably also know. There's nothing hidden about Camilla at all, she certainly wears her heart on her sleeve for all the world to see.'

Fran had to agree, which meant she had almost decided what her and Adam's next course of action should be. There were two people, to her mind, where the information Sara had given her simply didn't stack up. And the first of these was Diane. The sooner they delved a little deeper into her life, the better.

'Thanks, Sara, that's really helpful.' Fran took a bite of her biscuit, lips scrabbling to catch some breakaway crumbs. 'And is there anything you can remember about the party itself? Anything which might have seemed unusual, anyone acting oddly, or out of character?'

'I don't think so,' replied Sara, thinking. 'Although we were all playing a role, don't forget, so half the time everyone was acting weird – saying and doing odd things. We were meant to, those were the clues, you see, so that everyone could work out who the murderer was and why they'd done it. That's the theory anyway. I don't think I was very good at it, too busy worrying that everyone was having a good time... I wasn't worried about the food at all, don't think that, but I don't think I was paying as much attention as I should have been when I was questioning people. Actually, Becky seemed to be the one who had found out the most.'

'Sorry, I'm not following you.' Fran tucked her wiry curls back behind her ears. 'If Becky organised the game, didn't she know what was going to happen? I assumed that's why she played the victim.'

'No, we wanted her to play as well, you see. She got her

instructions along with everyone else so no one would know how the game worked out.'

'So Becky didn't even choose the parts that people played?' Fran groaned.

'No. Like I said, the company organised everything. All I knew about the game was what was sent to me; basically, just the character I was to play and what the game was about. Becky was also sent a set of envelopes to be given out during the game. You saw us opening those, together with the running order of when to open them, but I didn't even see those, Becky got the lot.'

'And when you opened these envelopes during the game, it told you what to do next?'

'Yes, that's right. They were addressed to each character, so, for example, halfway through the evening I found out I was the murderer and so on. It was dead easy. Because we'd told them we wanted to play the game around a dinner party, the action was divided into courses. We opened the first set of envelopes after the starter, then there was a gap where we all tried to act on what we'd learned. Then we had dinner and opened the next set after that. And so on.'

Fran nodded. 'Yes, I see. I don't suppose you kept any of the instructions, did you?'

Sara's face fell. 'I threw them all out, I'm sorry. I think some people may have kept theirs as a bit of a souvenir, but there was no point otherwise.'

'No...' Fran sighed and shoved a biscuit in her mouth, crunching it as she mulled over what she'd learned.

'I've just had a thought,' she said, after a moment's more chewing. 'You mentioned before that the character Becky played in the game was blackmailing everyone, so that would have been the motive for her character's murder?'

'Yes, that's right. It turned out that Becky, or rather Clarity, was threatening to reveal everyone's secrets – we all had them, so we were all suspects. We were supposed to work out what everyone was hiding and that would lead us to the killer.'

'But you don't know what those secrets were?'

Sara grimaced. 'No. Like I said, I wasn't very good at it.'

'So what about you, Sara? Your character must have had a secret, so what was it?'

Sara stared at her. 'You know, I hadn't really thought about it before, but that's the one thing that's odd about all this...'

8

Fran watched while Sara blew across the top of her coffee, trying to cool the liquid beneath the frothy top. If Fran was being uncharitable, she'd say Sara was stalling for time, but then she looked up, smiling.

'Sorry, this is a little... I didn't think I'd have to be sharing this.'

Fran raised her eyebrows.

'I'm not making sense, am I?' Sara laid a finger on some crumbs which had found their way onto the table and whisked them away. 'I guess if the police do get involved and learn what you overheard at the party, it's all going to come out anyway.' She laced her fingers around the mug without drinking. 'In the game, I played a character called Fortuna Dempsey, an actress with a bit of a wild past, now sadly widowed and fallen on very hard times.' She paused, smirking. 'At least that part bears no similarity to reality. But Fortuna also had a son, the apple of his mother's eye, not least of all because he had amassed a huge fortune doing dodgy real estate deals in Hollywood. Trouble was that Fortuna's son was also suffering from a terminal illness and, with no wife or offspring in the picture, as his doting mother, Fortuna was set to inherit. All well and good – tragic – but Fortuna was stoic in her grief. Unfortunately, Clarity Makepiece, Becky's character, had somehow discovered that Fortuna's dead husband hadn't actually been her son's biological father. And should that news get out, there was every possibility that Fortuna's dreams of a comfortable retirement were not going to come true after all. Not once her son's real father came crawling out of the woodwork.'

'So Clarity had to be done away with,' finished Fran. 'That's a brilliant story. Quite an invention. You said it was odd though?'

Sara looked at her, with something approaching fear on her face. 'Yes...' She swallowed a mouthful of coffee, pausing for a moment and taking a breath before continuing. 'I had a one-night stand when I was twenty-seven, with a guy I met in a pub. He was a university lecturer, a physics professor. I'm not proud of it, and in truth, it only happened because my boyfriend, Ben, and I had had a stupid argument about getting married of all things. He wanted to and I didn't, or not then anyway; I wanted to wait a while. I subsequently saw the light, went back to Ben and... well, I'm sure you can guess the rest.'

Fran's eyes widened. 'You discovered you were pregnant?'

Sara nodded, catching at the side of her lip. 'And I told myself that the baby was Ben's, that it had to be. Ben and I got married, sooner than I'd wanted, but that was all.' She held Fran's look for a moment, before glancing away. 'After that, well, I guess we simply got on with life. We were busy, and time just went by.'

'What happened? Did you ever find out the truth?'

'Not until things started going wrong between Ben and I. Given that I doubted Adam could have inherited his brains from either me or Ben, I always had my suspicions, but, thing is,

I didn't really want to know. Maybe that sounds stupid, but Ben was Adam's father in every sense of the word; we were a family. It was only when cracks appeared in our relationship that it became an issue.' Sara stared at her hands. 'I mentioned before that we had a few problems with Adam at school. Well, Ben and I had been having a bit of a tough time. One reason being that Ben blamed me for the way Adam behaved, saying it was my fault, that I spoiled him. He never really understood that Adam was gifted. Instead, he saw his intelligence as a problem, as the reason why Adam didn't fit in. We had a massive argument one day and, whether he had suspicions about Adam's true parentage, I don't know, but he declared that Adam was no son of his.' She broke off, looking at Fran sadly. 'It was just an unthinking remark, flung out in anger, but it festered. Ben took a paternity test and we divorced shortly after that.'

'And Adam doesn't know?'

Sara shook her head. 'I know I should tell him. But...' She sighed, holding Fran's look. 'It was such a difficult time for all of us. Throwing that into the mix, well, I just couldn't see how it would have been helpful. Now, I don't know. I haven't thought about this in a long time.'

Fran nodded, her smile offering empathy.

'It sounds daft,' continued Sara, 'but when I received the information about the character I was to play at the party, I didn't even think about the similarity between this aspect of my life and the one that had been given to Fortuna Dempsey. When Ben and I embarked on our life together, I so desperately wanted it to work, and I convinced myself that Ben was Adam's father. And now, even though I know differently, I still think of Ben as Adam's dad and I haven't thought about any of this since. Adam's my son and I consider Ben his father, that's all there is to it.'

'Except that, bizarrely, a part of your history seems to have found its way into the plot for a murder-mystery game. Coincidence?'

Sara swallowed. 'It has to be. What other explanation is there?'

Fran wrinkled her nose. Something wasn't right about all this. On the night of the party, Fortuna Dempsey had murdered Clarity Makepiece to keep her secret from being revealed, a secret which bore an uncanny resemblance to Sara's own. Despite the silly names and the hammy staging of the game they had all played, could there somehow be a connection between the game and Becky's death? It was a wild theory, but what else did they have to go on?

'But what if it wasn't a coincidence?' she asked Sara. 'What if Becky *was* blackmailing people, just like her character in the game. I said we needed to find out what Becky had done which had everyone so upset, that we needed to find a motive for her murder. What if that's it?' She smiled sadly. 'I'm sorry, Sara, but I have to ask: was Becky blackmailing you?'

'No!' retorted Sara. 'No, nothing like that.'

Fran stared at the anguished expression on Sara's face. She looked weary with it.

'Becky knew about Adam's dad. She's the one person who did.' Sara's shoulders drooped as she slumped back in her chair. 'Becky and I became very close when everything kicked off at the school. Then with Ben and the divorce... Hers was the shoulder I cried on. Why on earth would she have tried to blackmail me? Becky wouldn't do such a thing.'

'Is everything okay?'

Adam smiled and nodded. 'Yes, fine,' he replied. 'I was thinking, that's all. So what do you think we should do now?'

They were sitting in Fran's car, halfway down his driveway,

tucked behind a high hedge that shielded them from view of the house. Fran had messaged Adam as she was about to leave, just as she had promised, and he had described the spot where they should rendezvous, away from his mum's all-seeing eyes. He'd used it quite a few times in the past when taking delivery of things he really shouldn't have been.

'I'll be a bit pushed for time for the rest of the day,' replied Fran. 'I've got a christening tea to get ready for, and an engagement party at the weekend, but I definitely think our next step should be to find out as much as we can about the women at the party. And Diane definitely warrants further investigation. In fact, in my opinion, she should be top of the list. But there's also something about Lois that strikes me as curious.'

'I can take a drive by Diane's house today if that helps?' said Adam. 'See if I can spot anything unusual. What time did Mum say Diane ought to get home from work?'

'About three thirty. Here's the address.' Fran held out a piece of paper onto which she had scribbled the details.

Adam nodded, snapping a quick shot of it on his phone. 'Do you have the address of where she works as well?'

'No, but...' Fran turned the paper over. 'That's the name of the company. I'm sure you can find the rest of the details.' She grinned at him cheekily.

He smiled back. 'No problem. I'll see what I can find out and I'll let you know, okay?'

He waited until the car was gone from view before walking back up the drive, keeping the cover of the hedge between him and the house. His mum had an uncanny way of knowing when he was up to something.

Checking his watch, he smiled to himself. Provided his mum wasn't in the kitchen he had plenty of time to slip in the back door and make himself some lunch, or what he liked to call a 'Scooby snack' on account of its size.

. . .

Just over an hour later, Adam slowed his car and, squinting at the houses up ahead, pulled into the kerb and parked. From here he had a perfect view of the house opposite, Claremont Villa, where Diane and her husband lived. And Fran had been right, it was very big and very posh. In fact, ridiculous when you considered there were only two people living there. But that was just one of the many things wrong with the world in Adam's opinion. Diane's husband was obviously the sort that liked to flash his entitled life around. Adam opened a bag of Hula Hoops and settled down to wait.

Adam had never actually spied on anyone before. People watching, however, was another matter. He did that all the time, trying to understand what motivated his fellow citizens, working out why they behaved the way they did. It was mostly so that he could make his games as realistic as possible, particularly the dialogue, but it was also so that he could try to make sense of a world where he rarely felt he belonged. Today's exercise, however, would take his observations to a whole new level.

In the space of only a few short minutes, he spotted someone out jogging, someone walking their dog, two delivery drivers and a man in a very sharp suit having an argument with someone on his phone. Small snippets of lives, but enough for Adam to easily conjure a story from them. So far Diane's house had been quiet, but it was probably only a matter of time, and Adam didn't mind waiting. He could chalk all this up as 'research'.

He'd already made quite a few notes on his phone when a navy-blue van caught his attention, slowing as it approached Claremont Villa, and then pulling up onto the driveway. Adam didn't catch the wording on the side, he was too far away, but the graphic of a paintbrush underneath it gave him all the clue he needed: Diane had the decorators in.

She wasn't due home for another ten minutes or so yet, and

Adam wondered whether that gave him enough time for a little chat – he imagined that tradesmen overheard all sorts of things that could well prove useful. Almost without realising, his fingers found the handle on the car door and opened it. Which was precisely the point at which he panicked.

What on earth was he thinking? Despite having his cover story all worked out, now that he was actually at Diane's house the thought of talking to a random stranger was deeply unnerving. For goodness' sake it had taken him several days to pluck up enough courage to visit Fran that first time. And he'd only done that to help his mum. He swallowed. And breathed deeply. This was something he needed to do, he reminded himself, because, as it stood, he and Fran might be the only ones who could get his mum out of trouble. Besides, Adam would most likely never see this man again. What would it matter if he made a prat of himself? *Just remember, Adam, despite what you think, people are not looking at you all the time.* That was what he'd been told anyway. He took another deep breath and climbed from the car.

Well, that was *odd*... Adam had been keeping one eye on the van, fully expecting the driver to remain inside it while he waited for Diane to arrive home, but now the man was out of the cab and heading for the front door. Adam walked quickly across the road before he could change his mind.

By the time he got to the house, pausing momentarily behind a tree to hide himself from view, the man had opened up the front door and let himself in. Diane was clearly on very good terms with her decorator if she'd given him a key, and he wondered what her husband would have to say about that.

Adam was all set – thanks to Amazon's wonderful array of products which never ceased to amaze him, plus a bit of technical jiggery-pokery. He pulled his newly fashioned warrant card from his pocket and DC Adam Smith rang the doorbell.

And waited.

And then waited a little bit more.

He hadn't banked on there being no answer. He was about to ring the bell again when the door was pulled open by an apologetic-looking man holding a sandwich. He also had bare feet. Diane's decorator obviously knew how to make himself at home.

The man raised the sandwich, several bites already taken from it, Adam noticed. 'Sorry, mate, I've just got home, forgot me bait tin today, didn't I? I've had no lunch and I'm bloody starving.'

Adam smiled, he wasn't sure what else to do. There was so much wrong with that sentence.

Belatedly, he flashed his warrant card. With hindsight, he probably should have used a fake name, but he was working on the assumption that it wouldn't be remembered anyway. Plus, these things were easily altered.

'Detective Constable Adam Smith,' he gabbled, clearing his throat. 'I was hoping to have a word with Mrs Cook.' Adam was finding it very difficult not to look at the man's feet.

In the time it had taken Adam to speak, the man had taken another two bites of his sandwich and Adam had to wait while he hurriedly chewed his food, following it with an enormous swallow.

'The wife's still at work, mate, sorry.'

Did this man call everyone 'mate', Adam wondered. *Even police officers? Fake police officers admittedly, but he wasn't to know that.* His train of thought suddenly slammed to a halt. *Did he just say 'the wife'? But that would mean...*

'Ah... I was told she usually arrived home around this time?'

Mr Cook shook his head. 'Not for hours, mate, sorry. It wouldn't do if the boss went home earlier than everyone else, like. And she's a *very* busy lady.' For the first time a glimmer of interest showed in his eyes. 'Is this about that friend of hers? The one that died?'

Adam nodded. 'But I'm not at liberty to discuss the case, I'm afraid. I just have a few routine questions for Mrs Cook. But if she isn't due home, I'll visit her office, it's no problem.' Adam's desire to run away was getting stronger by the minute.

'I wouldn't if I were you,' Mr Cook remarked. 'She'll be in a meeting, or on the phone, and she doesn't see anyone without an appointment, not even me. Or take personal phone calls for that matter. The company is very strict about these things and she might be the CEO, but she still has to follow the rules, same as everyone else.' The rest of the sandwich was stuffed in his mouth as he gave Adam a sympathetic look. 'You can come in and have a cup of tea if you want? While you wait, like.'

Adam shook his head. 'Thank you, but I'd better not.'

Diane's husband shrugged. 'Up to you. I'm going to have a shower, but I trust you to wait without pinching anything, you being a copper an' all.' He grinned, showing teeth not quite free from the food he'd been eating.

It was tempting. Adam would very much like to look inside, but he wasn't sure how long he could keep up his current persona. Plus, he didn't want anyone to be able to identify him. The quicker he got going, the better.

'That's very kind, but best not. Not sure the super would like it much.' Adam squirmed, beginning to blush at the horrendous words coming out of his mouth. He had a horrible habit of mirroring people's speech and accents when he was talking to them and he was doing it now. Mr Cook might be a Liverpudlian, but Adam certainly wasn't. 'It's a lovely house though.'

'Isn't it?' came the proud reply. 'Best in street. I always knew my Diane was a winner.'

'Right, well, I'd best be on my way then. Thanks for your help.'

'You're welcome. Not that I really helped, like. I'm not sure

I can say anything that might either; I don't really know Diane's friends.' He leaned a little closer in conspiratorial fashion. 'Not really my type of people,' he whispered, raising his hand and pointing to the driveway. 'I'll come out with you,' he added. 'I need to put the van away in any case.'

Adam took a few steps backwards, letting Mr Cook walk past him, leaving the front door wide open. Adam couldn't see a great deal, but what he did see was very inviting; light and space and the deepest pile on a carpet he'd ever seen. He didn't blame Diane's husband for taking his boots off; he reckoned he'd do the same. It must feel lovely to scrunch your toes in that.

Keys in hand, Diane's husband pressed a button on the wall beside the garage, partially hidden by some large, artily shaped bush, and Adam watched as the big triple doors rolled silently upwards. Rather impressive, but he guessed that was the point.

Adam raised a hand. 'Thanks again,' he said, turning to leave.

'Any time, mate, no worries.'

Adam was almost at the bottom of the driveway by the time the garage doors had raised to their maximum, but he just had time for a look before the van was driven forward. The inside of the garage was almost as impressive as the house, just without the carpet. It was also depressingly tidier than Adam's room at home.

An array of hooks was fixed to one wall, each hung with some particular tool or other, keeping everything in its place. There was also a workbench and some gardening equipment, but very little else. Save for the three spaces where the family vehicles would go – two empty, one for Mr Cook's van and the other for whatever Diane was driving, and the third filled by a dark blue and very sleek sports car. The only thing which looked at all out of place was an estate agent's For Sale board, propped against a wall.

Adam got straight into his car and drove off, turning the

corner at the end of the road and almost immediately pulling back into the kerb and killing the engine. He needed to think. Because what he had just witnessed was very strange and made no sense at all. The very opposite, in fact, of what he had expected to find. Pulling out his phone from his jacket, he quickly searched for the name of the estate agent he had seen on the board, tapping his fingers impatiently on the steering wheel as he waited for the page to load.

Making a few selections from the drop-down menu presented to him, Adam began to search for their highest-priced properties, including those already sold. He was hoping the agency would continue to display such properties as an indication of their selling prowess and, after four pages, his hunch scored a hit. A little over four months ago, Claremont Villa had sold for the princely sum of £875,000. Adam almost dropped his phone.

Breath coming faster and faster, Adam sat back in his seat, winding his window down for some fresh air. *Think, Adam, think.* He needed to speak to Fran, that much was clear, but he also had the address of the firm where Diane worked. She was supposed to have left for the day by now, he could easily go over there and check a few things. But the way his heart was pounding, he wasn't sure he'd be able to pull off his cover a second time around. He'd got away with it once, he should quit while he was ahead. One thing was certain though – at some point he would need to get to the bottom of this particular mystery.

It was as he was sitting there, trying to sort out the muddle of questions in his head, that Adam became aware of something else which confounded his expectations. His mum had seemed pretty certain that Diane finished work at three and yet her husband wasn't expecting her home for a while yet. So what was she doing in the hours in-between? He thought for a moment. If he were in her shoes and needed to kill some time, what would he do?

Restarting the car engine, he checked his mirrors and pulled away from the kerb, slowly navigating the residential street. If Mr Cook were a painter and decorator, then he could quite feasibly arrive home from any direction, depending on where he had been working that day. Diane couldn't simply park her car nearby, she would run the risk of being spotted, so, if she didn't want her husband to see her, where would she go? And the answer came to Adam straight away.

It was a horrible assumption to make, and it irritated him that he had even considered it, but somehow he didn't think Mr Cook was an avid reader. And even if he were, then with the kind of money the couple clearly had, the local library didn't seem the most obvious location to source their books from. But it *was* the place where Adam had spent a significant amount of his time a few years ago, so he knew that the library had a large car park, and importantly, one that was situated *behind* the building, tucked out of sight from prying eyes. No one would know Diane was there.

He arrived in ten minutes, and a quick sweep around the rows of parked cars told him all he needed to know. Diane hadn't even looked up as he'd driven past her, head bent to her book. For some strange reason he had an almost overwhelming desire to know what she had been reading, but that wasn't the biggest question he needed an answer to. There was the small matter of a husband who was supposedly something big in the city, a guy who, if Diane's friends were to be believed, was domineering and possibly even a little controlling, but also undoubtedly someone who earned a great deal of money. He was also the nicest, friendliest, painter and decorator Adam had ever met. Then again, there was also Diane, an unambitious woman who had stayed in the same relatively lowly admin job for years, and yet according to her husband was an incredibly successful go-getter, the CEO of the company no less. The kind of woman who worked long hours and was so important that no one could get to speak to her or see her while at work, not even her husband.

But the biggest question that Adam sought the answer to was that, given the reality of the situation, rather than the fairy-tale version they'd been led to believe, how on earth did a couple like that afford a house which cost £875,000?

Just who was fooling whom?

9

Saying you were going to catch a killer and actually doing it were two entirely different things, as Fran was finding out. And that afternoon she'd been up to her eyeballs in forty-eight identical, decorated-to-within-an-inch-of-their-lives cupcakes for the christening tea tomorrow, with no time for anything else. Plus, she'd mislaid her phone and was suffering from that annoying sense of disconnect with her life which, given that a hunk of metal was the root cause, irritated her immensely.

It was further exacerbated by the fact that, as she was collecting an envelope for her invoice from the study, she caught sight of the calendar pinned to the wall. How had she not remembered it was parents' evening tonight? It was another reminder that her head was far from where it should be – focused on her work and her family. Instead, it was full of strange imaginings and wild scenarios involving convoluted murder plots and desperate killers – distracting and not especially helpful. It also didn't help that a voice in her head kept reminding her that this was precisely why they had a police force. She was doing her level best to ignore it.

But the fact was she had no idea how she and Adam were

going to tackle things going forward. Adam might well take a drive past Diane's house that afternoon, but what did she expect him to find? It was hardly going to be a huge banner affixed to the side of the house saying *Yes, I did it* in large red letters.

Likewise, if they spoke to any of the victim's friends, what would they ask them? *Did you kill Becky Pearson?* To which the answer would be *No, of course not.* And Fran and Adam would have to thank them for their time and be on their way. No, what they needed was something to question them about. Or cold, hard evidence as Adam had so eloquently put it, putting the wind up Fran in the process. And she had no idea how to go about getting any.

So it was somewhat of a surprise when, several hours later, Fran all but bumped into Lois during parents' evening.

It was the red hair which made her easy to spot. Aside from this there wasn't much to separate Lois from her colleagues at the school. She wasn't especially tall, nor particularly short, neither slender nor well rounded, but no one else had a fiery sheen of hair hanging almost to their waist. It was taking all Fran's willpower not to stare at her. Firstly, in envious acknowledgement that Fran would love to be a ginger, with Pre-Raphaelite curls and pale skin à la *Ophelia* by Millais, and secondly, to see whether there was anything about Lois which would give Fran a sound reason for suspecting she had murdered her best friend.

Pulling her gaze away, Fran turned her attention back to the task in hand and shifted uncomfortably in the regulation plastic chair which the school had provided for parents to sit on. Parents' evening was torturous enough without being made to feel like you were sitting outside the Head's office, waiting for some sort of punishment to be meted out, but it had always been this way. And every year, Fran thought there must be a more efficient way of doing things.

Fortunately, Martha was an uncomplicated child and tried hard in all her subjects. Even so, she was still slumped in a chair beside Fran, squirming with a mixture of embarrassment and boredom. She hated these evenings just as much as Fran did.

Fran had never spotted Lois at a parents' evening before, but then she'd never spotted Becky either. Not that there was anything unusual in that; it was a big school and the brain had an uncanny way of ignoring anything which it deemed irrelevant. And according to Sara, Lois worked in administration and so there was probably even less reason for Fran to have come across her. Tonight, therefore, it would seem that a certain amount of serendipity was at play.

Fran glanced across as the chairs in front of Martha's English teacher were vacated, only to be almost immediately filled by two sets of parents simultaneously, one pair finally giving way in a grudging admittance of defeat. Looking around the rest of the hall, Fran spied a vacancy in front of Martha's history teacher and gave her daughter a nudge. They were out of sequence with their appointments anyway; English should have been fifteen minutes ago and history wasn't due for another ten. Would it really matter if they took advantage of an empty slot? Martha gave her an exasperated look, but got to her feet anyway, following Fran over to where Mr Holmes was sitting, trying his best not to look like a wallflower who no one wanted to talk to.

Mr Holmes was also evidently of the opinion that the booking system had its limitations and he smiled gratefully as he indicated that Fran and Martha should take a seat. He riffled through his notes, trying to jog his memory about yet another child. With Martha duly located on his list, he began to rattle off her most recent test scores and predicted grades.

'So, all in all, I'm very pleased with Martha's progress,' he continued. 'We're moving on to a new topic next week, but if Martha maintains the same level of commitment that she's shown with the last two modules, I would predict a similar set of scores, come the summer. Which, of course, all bodes extremely well for her mock GCSEs.' He looked up and smiled at them both. 'Is there anything else you particularly wanted to know about Martha's grades?'

Fran would have replied but, unfortunately, her attention was captured by the sight of Lois delivering a cup of coffee to a teacher two tables along from where they were sitting. Her hair swung forward as she bent down and, just for a second, Fran could have sworn...

'Mu-um?'

Martha's voice jolted her back to the current conversation and she tried desperately to recall what Mr Holmes had been saying.

'No, I think that's all fine,' she replied. 'Great, thanks.' She smiled and nodded, trying her best to look focused and sincere.

'Good. Well, other than that, there's nothing much else for me to say. Martha is a pleasure to have in the class and I have no... Mrs Eve, is everything all right?'

'What...?' Distracted, Fran turned her head back, seeing Martha's frown of disapproval and Mr Holmes's one of irritation. 'Yes...' she stammered. 'Yes, absolutely, all fine. Wonderful, in fact. I was just...' She smiled again. 'Never mind. And thank you, that's all brilliant news, isn't it, Martha?'

Her daughter gave her an odd look and got up, moving away to leave Fran holding out her hand for Mr Holmes to shake. He did so, with a look of total bewilderment on his face. Flushing beetroot, Fran scuttled back to the waiting area.

'God, you didn't have to shake his hand, Mum,' hissed Martha. 'No one does that. *You* don't usually do that.'

'No, sorry, I just thought I saw... I was distracted, that's all.'

Suitably chastened, Fran muttered another apology and

vowed to redeem herself. But it was so tempting to have another look... She kept her eyes focused straight ahead and her ears attuned to her daughter, but even so, she still spied Lois from the corner of her eye, disappearing out of the hall. And that would have been fine, had the teacher she had just plied with coffee not followed her, less than half a minute later.

Fran took a deep breath and smiled at Martha. 'It doesn't look like your English teacher is going to come free, does it? I might just pop to the loo while we're waiting. Won't be a minute.'

She received the inevitable eye roll, but got to her feet anyway, heading for the door that would take her back out into the main school corridor. It took nearly all her willpower not to break into a run.

The corridor was busy with milling parents looking at displays of artwork on the walls and Fran had no idea which way the teacher had gone. She looked first in one direction, then the other, craning her neck to see past a succession of tall fathers who were completely blocking her view. She sighed with frustration. She could hardly go wandering the building looking for the teacher and was about to return to the main hall when she spotted him in conversation with another set of parents further down the hallway. She pretended to look at the collection of paintings on the walls, edging her way closer, while simultaneously watching his every move. After a moment or two she was rewarded when he excused himself from the parents and moved away. With a glance behind her, Fran took off in hot pursuit.

Or, rather, what turned out to be lukewarm pursuit when the teacher disappeared through a blue-painted door after only a handful of steps. Fran sidled past, ostensibly looking at more displays, while at the same time preparing to be looking for the loos should anyone ask what she was doing.

The blue door bore a sign telling her that *Resources* were to be found within and Fran might not have thought more of it, had she not heard a key very clearly turning in the lock as she passed.

Curious...

Who goes to replenish their stock of glue sticks and then locks themselves inside the room while they retrieve them?

And then she heard a giggle. A very feminine giggle.

Really? The old assignation in the stationery cupboard cliché? Fran hated to admit it, given that adultery seemed to be afoot, but she was disappointed. With her flaming-red hair, Lois could have thought of something a little more original than a furtive fumble among the spare biros. Femme fatale it was not.

But then Fran suddenly sobered, because if it *was* Lois in the cupboard with a man who was definitely not her husband, and if they were engaged in something rather more illicit than stocktaking, then Lois was not the person everyone thought her to be. The question was, did Becky know? And if she did, was that a motive for murder?

Damn, if only she had her phone. There was a memo-taking app on it that would have been ideal to record what she was hearing. Far less obvious than pressing her head against the door to listen. But she really needed proof and—

'Mum?'

Fran spun around in shock.

'What are you doing?' Martha's face loomed in front of her.

'Nothing, I just—'

'The loos are *that* way,' said Martha, pointing in the opposite direction.

'Are they? Oh yes. I thought this didn't look right.' She indicated the corridor ahead of her. 'Shall we go back in?' She started to walk back the way she'd come, only to be stopped again.

'I'll wait for you, Mum, I don't like sitting in there on my own.'

Fran gave her a puzzled look.

'The loo?'

'Oh yes, not to worry, I can wait,' replied Fran, firmly attempting to regain some semblance of control. 'I've been out here long enough as it is, and I bet we've missed our English slot now. Come on, there are only a couple more teachers to see and then we can get home.' She eyed her daughter's anxious face. 'We could even stop and get some pizza if you want.' She smiled. *Was that a bit too much?* Martha was very well aware of Fran's opinion on takeaway food.

Fortunately, however, Martha was simply looking forward to the evening's trial being over and didn't notice how unusual a statement this was. They trooped back into the hall and resumed their previous seats. It was a full sixteen minutes before Lois reappeared, lipstick reapplied and hair brushed.

And that might have been the end of it, had Fran not actually needed the loo once they had finally finished for the evening. Too long a wait had been interspersed by far too many cups of the canteen's revolting coffee. Unfortunately, it seemed that the same was true of quite a few other mums. *Women of a certain age*, thought Fran glumly, as she joined the queue for the ladies.

By the time they finally managed to get going, the car park was virtually empty and, as Fran pulled up behind another car waiting to turn onto the road beyond the school gates, Lois's red hair proved to be her downfall yet again. It made her and the bright-red Mini she was driving stick out like a beacon among the series of silver and white cars which were ahead of them.

On impulse, Fran flicked her indicator switch and turned in the opposite direction to the one which would take them home. Because Lois wasn't heading home either; Fran already knew via Sara where Lois lived, and it certainly wasn't the way she was going, not unless she was taking a very circuitous route. Fran had never followed anyone before, and for all she knew,

Lois was simply heading to the supermarket, or to run some other errand before returning home, but somehow Fran didn't think so.

With her head bent, glued to her phone, it took Martha quite a few minutes to realise that they weren't on the right road either. She looked up, turning round to stare out of the side window of the car.

'Why are we going this way?' she asked.

'Sorry, darling,' replied Fran, glancing in her direction. 'We won't be long. It suddenly occurred to me that I have no clue where I'm supposed to be going with the food for tomorrow's christening tea party. It's around here somewhere, so I thought I'd just check it out while we're here.'

'Isn't that what the satnav is for?'

Fran glared at the car's glowing instrument panel, a map of the area they were driving through in full view. Fran wasn't very good at lying.

'Yes, but I just wanted to see where the house was. My client said the access was a bit tricky, so forewarned is forearmed.'

Martha nodded and turned her attention back to her phone.

A set of traffic lights was coming up, and had been on green for some while now. Lois might get through, but surely not the two of them together, and Fran offered up a silent prayer to the God of all Things as she accelerated towards the light.

Red. She might have known. Amber, and she might have risked it, but not red, and she pulled on her handbrake, tutting loudly. *Come on, come on...* Up ahead, Lois had already turned right, and by the time Fran got there, and then had to wait for the inevitable traffic to pass before she could also turn, Lois could be anywhere. Fran sighed. Well, if she was, there was nothing she could do about it.

She lurched forward off the lights, giving Martha a quick glance but, fortunately, she was still glued to her phone, thumbs working at lightning speed to type out a message. No doubt expressing joy that the torture which was parents' evening was over for another year. Fran flicked on her indicator, slowed, checked there was nothing coming, checked again, and turned, praying for a flash of bright-red Mini.

To her surprise, Lois's car was still up ahead, caught behind a cyclist trying to navigate a row of parked cars. Fran slowed and made a pretence of looking left and right as if she were checking out an address, just in case Martha needed reassurance that her mother wasn't going mad.

Fed up with being tailgated, the cyclist very sensibly tucked himself in-between two parked cars and Lois sailed past. Fran sped up accordingly, nodding a cheery thank you to the man on the bike as she passed. He might very well have saved the day.

A left turn and then a right. They were deep into the Abbeygate estate now and finally, Lois slowed, before pulling onto one of a row of identical driveways in front of a row of identical houses. Fran drove on, just in case she was spotted, and pulled in to the kerb a couple of houses down. She hadn't wanted to stare too obviously as she passed the house where Lois was climbing from her car, but then she hadn't needed to. She'd already clocked Mr Maths Teacher standing on the threshold of what was presumably his house. Because it certainly didn't belong to Lois; she lived on the same side of town as Fran. And she'd also lay money on the fact that Mr Maths Teacher was not Lois's husband either.

Fran pursed her lips, narrowing her eyes at the view in her rear mirror. *Well, well, well, Lois Shepherd, not so much the homemaker now, are you? More like home-breaker…*

Fran was right, she knew she was. She'd seen the way Lois had held her fingers against the teacher's as she'd delivered the mug of coffee. It wasn't an accidental brushing, there had been something altogether more suggestive about it. The touch had lasted a second or two, no more, but it had reminded her how she'd acted with Jack when they first met and couldn't keep their hands off one another. She blushed at the memory.

'Are we lost?' Martha was looking around her, as if startled to find herself somewhere unfamiliar.

'No, no, this is it,' replied Fran. She made a show of peering through the windscreen. 'The house over there, I think.'

Martha gave her a disparaging stare. 'Well then, I don't know what that woman you're baking for was talking about,' she said. 'There's clearly no problem accessing that place, is there?'

Fran cleared her throat. 'No... there certainly doesn't seem to be. Well then, let's go and get that pizza, shall we?'

10

At ten to midnight Fran eventually found her phone, where it had slithered under the passenger seat of the car. She was tired, and a little grumpy at having been unable to find it, the impact of what would have happened to her business and her life if she hadn't reverberating in her head. But all that disappeared when she saw the string of missed calls and messages from Adam.

Inside the house her husband and daughter lay sleeping, which was exactly what she should have been doing but, instead, she was sitting furtively in her car, in her pyjamas and dressing gown, peering at her phone screen, which lit up like a beacon against the backdrop of pervasive darkness.

Adam, are you awake? she texted, worried that something was wrong.

His messages hadn't given any detail, simply asked her over and over to call him as soon as she could. And now she was terrified that the police had caught up with Sara. Perhaps even now, as Fran huddled in her car, Sara was huddled in a police cell under arrest for murder.

Yes... Where have you been?

Fran almost dropped her phone as the screen flashed into life again.

Sorry, I lost my phone. What's wrong? Is Sara okay?

Mum's fine... But I know who killed Becky! 🕯️ *It was Diane! I don't know how she did it yet, but she's got the biggest secret!*

Fran frowned at the screen.

Diane? No, I think it was Lois – she's having an affair. It had to be her!

What??

Fran typed some more, fingers fumbling in her haste.

Lois is having an affair – if Becky found out that has to be why she was silenced.

But the same must be true for Diane. It has to be. You're not going to believe this...

Fran jumped as a light came on inside her house. Her bedroom light.

Adam, I have to go. I'm sitting in the car and my husband has just woken up.

A pause.

Why are you sitting in the car?

Because that's where I'd lost my phone. She kept one eye on the house, certain that Jack would be walking down the stairs by now. *But that doesn't matter. I have to go, but I need to speak to you.*

Yes!

Tomorrow. I'll ring you.

The hall light came on and Fran frantically pressed the button on the side of her phone to get it to turn off. *Shit...*

She scrambled out of her seat, slamming the hem of her dressing gown in the car door in her haste.

'Fran...?'

'Hi. Jack. God, you made me jump!'

Her husband stood shivering on the damp driveway, his bare legs dimly illuminated by the light coming through the hallway.

'What on earth are you doing?' he asked, seemingly uncaring that his boxer shorts were on display to the whole street. *Don't be silly, Fran, everyone else is fast asleep. No one is looking at your husband's underwear.*

'Nothing, I just... I couldn't find my phone earlier and it was bugging me. Sorry, I couldn't sleep.' She tugged her dressing gown free from the car door. 'I had to come and get it or I'd be lying awake the whole night.'

He sighed, rubbing a hand across his face. 'It's really late.'

'I know,' she whispered. 'I'm sorry, but I've got it now.' She held up her phone as proof, forgetting that the screen would automatically wake as she did so. She quickly lowered it again in case Jack could see Adam's messages. 'I've got a job tomorrow. You know how it always makes me nervous.' That much at least was true. 'I was convinced my customer had cancelled, or told me she wanted yellow icing, not blue.'

Jack stared at her, bleary-eyed. 'What?'

She shook her head. 'Never mind. Come on, let's get back to bed.' She took Jack's arm, chiding herself under her breath. She really must be more careful, before her whole family thought she was losing it, or worse.

Minutes later, she lay snuggled against Jack's side, listening to the even tones of his deep, regular breathing, which started up again almost as soon as his head touched the pillow. She was warm, comfortable, and her limbs at least were relaxed. The same, sadly, could not be said about her mind. Fran knew that she was going to spend the entire night wondering what secrets Diane had been keeping. It was evidently true what they said: it was always the quiet ones you had to watch. And she'd been so sure it was Lois...

THE MORNING DAWNED with the raucous blaring of the alarm clock which set Fran's heart hammering in her chest. She groaned. It seemed as if she'd only just fallen asleep. She rolled over and breathed deeply, hoping her heart would calm down sufficiently for her to get out of bed without falling over. Jack was already up and, despite how Fran was feeling, it was high time she got her day started as well.

Fran had deliberately left her phone downstairs before going to bed but, even before she picked it up, she knew there would be more messages from Adam. She had a feeling he rarely slept. Besides, he was young, he certainly didn't need his beauty sleep the way Fran did. She poured herself a cup of tea from the pot that Jack had already made and willed herself back to life.

Two-and-a-half hours later, Fran could finally think about what she needed to do. Husband off to work – check. Martha off to school – check. Cat fed – check. Dishwasher emptied – check. Breakfast, more tea, clothes on, hair brushed, check check check check. And it was still only 9 a.m. Number one on her to-do list was to deliver forty-eight christening cupcakes to her customer, to an address five minutes away which she was already familiar with and was not at all difficult to access. Number two was to finally call Adam and find out what on earth had been going on.

She was nearly home, however, when her phone rang and she connected the call via the hands-free option on the car's dash. She didn't even need to look at the caller display to know it was Adam.

'Where are you?' he asked without preamble.

'Well, good morning to you too,' she said. 'Yes, I did sleep well, thank you. Even though I didn't, obviously.'

There was a long pause and she thought she'd lost the call.

'Oh... Good morning, Francesca. It's a lovely day, isn't it? And how are you this morning? Did you have a peaceful and refreshing sleep?'

'Adam, I was just teasing.' She smiled at his awkward speech. 'And please don't ever call me Francesca again, otherwise I might be forced to do something you really wouldn't like.'

Another pause. 'That was a joke too... right?'

'Yes, Adam, it was a joke. Listen, I'm nearly done with my work today, where are you, at home?'

'No, I'm—'

The call dipped out as Fran turned into her road. 'Sorry, Adam, say again, I lost that bit.' She drew level with her house. 'Oh—'

She turned into her drive and waved at Adam, who was sitting on her front doorstep. He raised a hand, grinning.

'Morning,' she said, once she'd extricated herself from the car, juggling her bag, phone and coat.

'I thought I'd pop over,' he said.

'So I see,' she replied, waiting for him to move off the step so she could open the door. 'Come in.'

She smiled all the way down her hallway. There was something about Adam which was incredibly endearing.

'So this thing with Diane all sounds very exciting,' she said, entering the kitchen and dumping her things on the table. 'Let me put the kettle on and you can tell me what you've found out.'

When he didn't answer, she turned around to see him looking around the kitchen, eyes raking the work surfaces.

'I don't suppose you have any more of that pudding thing we had the other day, do you?'

It took a moment for Fran to remember what he was talking about. It seemed an age since they had first met. 'Oh, the tiramisu, do you mean? No, sorry, that's long gone. But... Hang on a sec.'

She crossed to the pantry and took down the spare cupcakes she had made for the christening. She placed the tub on the table. 'Help yourself,' she said.

Adam sat, pulling the cakes towards him and cranked off the lid. He sniffed cautiously. 'What are these?'

'Cupcakes,' she replied. 'St Clements.'

He blinked.

'Some are orange flavoured, some are lemon,' she supplied.

He nodded and took out one, peeling back the wrapper and sinking his teeth into it, the frosting reaching almost to his nose. Fran smiled and began to fill the kettle.

It took three cakes and a half cup of coffee before Adam's hollow legs were sufficiently filled for him to begin explaining what he had discovered about Diane, and she listened, eyes growing wider and wider.

'But that's... That's... I don't know what that is, but I'm struggling to understand how Diane could even pull that off. How do you live a life so complicated? I struggle to keep tabs on mine. So let me get this straight... Diane works as an office manager – we know that's true because that's how your mum met her – and everyone who knows Diane believes that her husband has a mega-important job and earns pots of money. And yet, in actual fact, her husband is a painter and decorator and can't possibly earn the kind of money she says he does. Possibly worse than that though, *he* thinks Diane's the CEO of the company she works for and is the one who earns a fortune, working all hours, when, actually, she sits in the car park at the library, reading, until the time she can legitimately return home.'

'That's about the size of it, yes.'

Fran blew air out from between her teeth. 'That's some lie,' she said. 'I'd have a nervous breakdown. Imagine the number of fibs Diane must tell every day, just to keep the plates spinning. The whole charade could collapse at any moment.' She frowned. 'And, this is going to sound horrible, but I thought Diane was a bit... ordinary.' She grimaced. 'Sorry.'

Adam looked at her, clearly puzzled. 'Why is being ordinary a bad thing? I'd quite like to be ordinary... But I think Diane might actually be incredibly cold and calculating, ruthless even. Some people are like that. Serial killers are.'

'Blimey, Adam. I don't think we're quite at that level. I agree, though, that she must be able to absolutely compartmentalise her life, almost as if she's living two lives, two personae...' She shuddered. Put like that, it wasn't too much of a leap to imagine Diane as some kind of master criminal. 'But the real question is, why? Why would she go to the trouble of maintaining all those lies? Her life's a façade, which means she's using it to hide something and it must be something pretty big to go to the lengths she has.

'Let's not allow ourselves to get carried away,' she added. 'But put like that, whatever it is could well give us a perfect motive for murder. Diane's been fighting really hard to keep her secrets, so she must feel she has a lot to lose should they come out.'

'Plus, there's the house,' said Adam, reaching for another cupcake.

'The house?'

'The £875,000 house. That an office manager and a decorator could never afford between them.'

Fran stared at him, claiming a cake herself. 'My God, you're right. So where did the money come from?'

Adam smiled. 'That, is the sixty-four-thousand-dollar question... or rather the eight-hundred-and-seventy—' He bit into his cake so he wouldn't have to finish the sentence.

Fran rolled her eyes anyway. 'I'm serious though – where *did* it come from? An inheritance, maybe? But if that were the case, surely she would have said? It would have been much easier than inventing the pack of lies she has. It's part of the deception, it has to be.'

'They only bought the house a few months ago though,' said Adam. 'And Diane's double life has been going on a lot longer than that. Do we know where she lived before?'

'No, but I can ask Sara. I get the feeling it would have been somewhere quite grand. Diane has always suggested they live a very comfortable life, as far as I know.'

Adam pointed to her mouth. 'You have a bit of cream on your face,' he said, with no trace of embarrassment. 'You know what I think?'

Fran scrubbed at her lips, blushing slightly. 'What?'

'That we should follow the money. That's how it works in films. Follow the money, they say, and you'll catch the killer.'

Fran thought for a minute. 'Damn,' she said eventually.

Adam raised his eyebrows.

'I was so sure it was Lois,' she said. 'But all she's been doing is having an affair. Somehow I don't feel it's in the same league as Diane's shenanigans.'

'No, but that's still good... bad, I mean. Because now we have two suspects.'

'Do we *need* two suspects? Isn't that just going to confuse things?'

'Not necessarily. It's the truth we're after, don't forget. How did you discover what Lois has been up to anyway?'

Fran explained what had happened at the parents' evening.

'But how did you know to follow her?' asked Adam, looking confused.

'I didn't really. It was just a hunch. I didn't actually see Lois after she left the hall, so I don't know that it was her in the stationery cupboard with the maths teacher, but there's definitely something going on between them.'

'Because of the hand?' Adam stared at his fingers.

'Yes, you know...' Fran blushed again. She could hardly show Adam what she meant, but it was such a hard thing to explain. 'Lois brushed her hand up against the teacher's as he took the mug of coffee from her. But it wasn't accidental, it was... suggestive.'

'Suggestive?'

'Yes. And also, she *leaned*—'

'Now I have no idea what you're talking about.' Adam looked genuinely baffled.

'Okay.' Fran adopted the tone of voice she used with Martha whenever she was imparting information. 'So, when Lois brought the maths teacher his coffee, she leaned forward, invading his personal space, but she did so deliberately. It's what people do when they're, um, familiar with one another. And then, the hand thing... Most colleagues are really careful not to touch one another, even accidentally, in case it gives the wrong message, but she made sure their fingers touched. It was a tiny gesture, hidden quite well, and you'd have to have been watching carefully to notice, but it was there, you're just going to have to take my word for it.'

'Oh, I do. I'm just amazed that you could deduce so much from a simple brushing of the fingers. That's a bit scary.' He looked at his hand again, rather nervously, as if he were worried he might lose control of it.

Fran smiled. 'Maybe it's a woman thing,' she said, clearing her throat. 'Anyway, I hadn't intended to follow Lois, but I was already suspicious, and when I happened to leave at the same time she did and saw that she turned out of the gate in the opposite direction to the one in which she lives, it seemed like too good an opportunity to miss.'

'And you definitely saw Lois and this teacher together?'

Fran nodded. 'He was at the door of his house waiting for her.'

'Lois might have been visiting him on school business,' Adam suggested. 'Maybe she had some paperwork for him?' Adam took in the expression on Fran's face and then shook his head. 'No, okay, they were definitely together. So, where does that leave us?'

'With two people definitely acting dishonestly, admittedly one more suspect than the other. I think you're right though, I think we do need to follow the money in Diane's case. Maybe we can speak to the estate agent who handled the sale of Diane's new house, see whether he can tell us where the money came from to buy it – another property, a mortgage perhaps, even cash. I also think we need to check out where she works; there might be some clue there as to what's been going on.'

Fran picked up a cupcake wrapper and began to fold it into ever smaller triangles, trying to organise her thoughts. 'Plus, we need to figure out how Becky was killed. A motive isn't enough, we need opportunity too. We need to know what Diane and Lois were both doing on the day Becky first became ill. Where they might have got the mushrooms from and how they could have given them to Becky without her knowing.'

'And I don't think we should forget about Camilla either,' said Adam. 'She was the other friend at the party, remember, and two of those guests are known to have been hiding secrets.

The same could be true for Camilla. We need to either rule her in or rule her out.'

Fran toyed with the ball of wax paper in her hand. Adam was right, but she really hoped that he wouldn't take his line of reasoning any further and ask about his mum. She really didn't want him to know about Sara's secret just yet, not until she was clear how it fitted into this whole affair.

'Camilla was who you were hiding from in the cupboard, wasn't she?' Adam added.

Fran groaned. 'Don't remind me.' She sighed. 'You're right, though, we do need to talk to her, and I should probably be the one to do it. It's just finding the opportunity that's going to be tricky.'

'You could try following her?' suggested Adam. 'That seems to have worked well so far.'

Fran smiled. 'Maybe I will.' She was about to say something else when her mobile rang, Sara's name flashing up on the display. She looked at Adam, alerting him to who was calling.

'Hi Sara, is everything okay?'

'Fran, I'm sorry to trouble you, but I didn't know who else to call. I know you said this was going to happen, but I still can't quite get my head around the seriousness of it. It's like something which happens to other people, not folks you know.'

'Sara, what's happened?'

There was a long pause.

'I've just had a phone call from Nick, in an absolute panic. The police have been to see him and... Fran, he thinks they're going to charge him with murder.'

11

Fran got out of her car and walked slowly up the path to Camilla's house. Given the choice, she would very much like to be back in Sara's understairs cupboard, but this was something she had to do. When Sara's news had arrived a little while earlier, an anxious hush had fallen over Fran's kitchen. She and Adam had stared at one another, feeling almost overwhelmed by the responsibility which seemed to be sitting squarely on their shoulders. They not only knew things which would be very useful to the police and their investigation but, right now, that information was possibly the only thing standing between Nick and potential arrest.

The trouble was that if they relayed what they knew to the police then it would only be a matter of time before Sara became implicated too. And her best defence lay in Fran and Adam proving her innocence before the police could decide otherwise. It had all become very serious indeed.

Which was why Adam was currently on his way to see a certain firm of estate agents, and she was about to talk to Camilla. It was time for some very honest discussion. After all, Camilla could either talk to Fran, or talk to the police, and Fran

knew which one she would prefer. She just had to hope that
Camilla felt the same.

The house was exactly as Fran expected. Sitting behind an
immaculately manicured front garden, Holmwood was
bordered by a low wall, encircling a gravel forecourt where not
a single weed had been allowed to grow. The front door was
flanked by two large urns, each containing a huge pyramid-
shaped box shrub, and Fran knocked nervously, feeling uncomfortably dwarfed by the topiary.

Anticipating a gushing welcome, Fran held back on her
greeting, preparing herself to ward off the inevitable scream of
delight which Camilla usually gave when she had a victim in
her clutches. Having Adam's description of Camilla as a head-
biting alien forefront in her mind wasn't helping Fran's nerves,
so, as the door opened, she was somewhat surprised to see
Camilla's eyes widen. Almost as if she were horrified to see
Fran, and not the other way around.

'Hi...' Fran faltered. 'Sorry to come unannounced, but... I
wondered if I might have a chat with you. It's about Becky.'

Fran waited for the invitation to cross the threshold, but
none came.

'It's rather important,' she added.

Camilla gave a tight smile and reluctantly pulled the door
wider. 'My husband will be home very soon,' she said.

Fran nodded. 'Okay...' She stepped inside, shoving her car
keys in her pocket. 'I shouldn't be long.' She'd entered an
opulent hallway, hung with a huge mirror so that the space
danced with light. Fran's mouth dropped open. It was filled
with plants, one of which, a monstera bigger than Fran had ever
seen, stood almost seven feet tall under the turn of the staircase
as it rose gracefully to the next floor.

Fran didn't really know Camilla at all well, and what she
did know had mostly come from their encounters at the school.
On every such occasion, Camilla had been immaculately made

up, with her hair freshly curled and wearing bright colours. Today was no exception. Even on a Thursday morning, in the privacy of her home, Camilla looked as if she'd spent the whole morning getting ready. For what, Fran had no idea. Didn't Camilla ever relax?

'Have you spoken to Sara at all?' Fran asked, still looking around her.

Camilla had barely moved, staring at Fran with a curious expression on her face. 'A little,' she said after a pause so long Fran wondered if she was going to reply at all.

Fran waited, but this was clearly all Camilla was going to impart. Which didn't seem like her at all. It wasn't particularly helpful either. It left Fran struggling for a way to begin the conversation when she'd banked on Camilla doing most of the talking for her.

'Is there somewhere we could sit down?' asked Fran. 'Only this might be better discussed somewhere other than the hallway.'

Grudgingly, she was taken into a huge open-plan kitchen with a conservatory at one end. Wooden beams criss-crossed a vaulted ceiling, merely adding to the already impressive space where one whole wall was made of glass. It was hard to tell where the house finished and the garden began, but Fran wasn't here to talk about Camilla's interior decor. And by the look of her, Camilla didn't want to talk about anything at all, let alone the exact shade of blush pink which adorned her walls. Fran was beginning to feel distinctly uncomfortable.

Camilla halted in the centre of the room. 'I don't know what this has got to do with you anyway,' she said. 'Becky's death, I mean.'

'No... I'm sorry, I know she was a good friend of yours, but—'

'Not really. In fact, compared to the others, I barely knew her.'

'Really? I thought you'd been friends for ages.'

'A few years... But not as long as some of the others.' She made a dismissive gesture, which Fran found oddly cold and callous.

She tried warming things up with a smile. 'I'm a little worried about Sara, to tell the truth. Only, it seems as if Becky's death might not have been an accident. The police have already questioned Nick. I'm just trying to help.'

'Well, I didn't have anything to do with it.'

Fran softened her expression, realising the reason for Camilla's defensive stance. 'I think you may have misunderstood,' she said gently. 'Nobody is suggesting that for a minute, but you were her friend, you'd been with her at a party not long before she was poisoned, and that makes you a suspect in the eyes of the police. They're already speaking to Nick and, at some point, they're almost certainly going to be talking to you. Someone *killed* Becky, Camilla.' She paused for a moment to let that sink in. 'And, unbelievable as it sounds, it appears that Becky might not have been as nice as everyone thought she was. Or why would someone have wanted to kill her? We don't have all the facts yet, far from it, but I wondered if you knew anything about that. Maybe even—'

'Well, I don't. And I'm not sure I appreciate you insinuating that I do, under the pretext of "helping" or not. Who made you chief investigator anyway?'

Fran met Camilla's gaze with one equally frank. This was getting her nowhere. 'No one,' she said, wondering why Camilla was still so reluctant to answer any of her questions. Surely she should want to help catch the killer of a friend? 'But I'm someone who could be affected by a police investigation, the same as you. And as Sara was the "murderer" in the game you all played on the night of the party, she certainly will be. I'm worried, that's all, for all of our sakes, and I was hoping you might be able to help.'

'Well, I can't. I think you might have made a mistake.'

Camilla towered over her, and suddenly Fran could see very clearly that she had. She shouldn't have come here, not by herself. She did her best to smile.

'Yes, you're right. I'm sorry. I should have called first, barging in on you like this. I'll go now... forget I was ever here.'

Fran was about to make smartly for the door when Camilla shook her head and smiled.

'Oh...' She waggled her fingers. 'No, don't go. I've just had a thought. I came across something recently but didn't think anything of it at the time, you've just reminded me. It did strike me as odd though, maybe that's why I hung onto it.'

'Hung onto what?' Fran couldn't help herself.

'I can show you. It's in the garden.'

'The garden?'

'Yes. I didn't want anyone to see it, so I hid it.'

'What is it?'

But Camilla didn't answer, simply walked over to what Fran could now see was a huge sliding glass door, opened it, and stepped outside onto the patio where she turned, holding the door. Fran had no choice but to follow her. The door slid closed like silk.

'It's in the shed. I had to put it somewhere, you see, otherwise my husband would have found it.'

Fran nodded. 'Okay. It all sounds very mysterious. What is it?'

Camilla looked around her, at the manicured hedges and lawn, the huge urns which flagged the patio, full of sculpted shrubbery. 'I'd best not say,' she said. 'Not out here anyway. You can't be too careful, can you?'

Fran smiled, nervous now. And she suddenly wished Adam were with her. Then she could ask him if she wasn't the only one thinking that Camilla was acting very strangely.

The rear of the garden was more shaded. An area of

decking stood to one side, beneath two trees which would give welcome relief from the high heat of summer. Nestled in the other corner was a shed, tucked into the hedge, unobtrusive despite its size, and partially screened by a large Buddleia bush. It was here that Camilla seemed to be heading.

Fran patted down her pockets as she walked. Damn. She'd left her phone in the car.

'This is such a beautiful garden,' she said. 'It must take hours to keep it looking this good.'

Camilla glanced backwards over her shoulder. 'It does, and I have the backache to prove it. But it keeps me out of mischief.'

'Oh.' Fran stopped, staring at Camilla's back, kicking herself for the astonished response that slipped unguarded from her mouth. 'Sorry,' she added quickly. 'For some reason I thought you must have a gardener.'

'Yes, everyone thinks that,' she replied. 'They think a lot of things.'

Fran clenched her jaw, berating herself for being so stupid. She needed to have Camilla on side, not antagonise her with every word which left her mouth. 'Have you thought about doing it professionally?' she asked, looking around her and only now seeing the extent of the careful planting. 'I'm sure people would bite your arm off.'

Camilla gave her another odd look, as if she were wrestling with something. But then she turned back and walked the last few steps to the shed. She took a key from her pocket and, unlocking the door, pulled it wide so that Fran could see inside. Not that there was very much to see.

'It's over there by the far wall,' said Camilla, pointing to the dim corner.

Fran leaned forward. 'What am I looking for?' She couldn't really see anything of note. Some sacks of what looked like compost, a bucket...

'The box. It's only small, but I'd be interested to hear what you make of it.'

Fran took a step forward and was about to ask another question when Camilla's outstretched hands shoved her hard between her shoulder blades and she was sent sprawling onto the floor. All at once the light from outside was extinguished as the door slammed shut and she heard the frantic turning of the key in the lock.

'Camilla!' Fran scrambled to her feet, wincing as her ankle took her full weight. 'For God's sake, Camilla! What are you *doing*?'

'I don't know...' came the reply, muffled by the door, but something else too. Something which had lent a tremor to her voice. *Was she crying?*

'Camilla!'

But this time there was no reply. And it was only too apparent what Camilla had done: she had locked Fran in the shed.

Fran grappled at the door, feeling for the handle. Her eyes weren't yet accustomed to the dark after the brightness of the day outside, and there were no windows in the shed. It was pitch-black. And musty. A warm, dusty smell that was all pervasive. That was...

Fran took a huge intake of breath, steadying herself against the side of the shed. *Breathe, Fran, just breathe. You're okay...* But the air seemed to stick in her throat, thick and cloying. She suddenly felt incredibly hot.

She sank to her knees then sat with her back against the rough wooden planks, gulping air into her lungs as the shock of what had just happened hit her. Her head swam, and she forced herself to slow her breathing. She was taking in too much oxygen, that's what was making her feel dizzy; it wasn't the lack of it at all. *Get a grip, Fran, you are not going to be locked in here forever, you're going to be fine*. A little uncomfortable, but fine.

Slowly, her head began to clear, and the overwhelming

panic lessened its grip until she was able to think a little more logically. She got to her feet and felt her way towards the door, tugging at the handle, even though she knew the door was locked. It was a shed, how strong could it be? But, as she crashed all her weight against it, the answer was clear: too strong for her. She kicked the door savagely. Anyone else would have a tin-pot, flimsy little shed that they'd bought years ago and was on its last legs. But no, Camilla had to have one built to the same standard as Fran's house.

Okay then, so maybe if the door wouldn't give, something else might. Fran felt her way along each side of the shed, kicking experimentally, using her heel instead this time, but all that achieved was a foot which hurt in more than one place. A surge of anger welled up inside her.

'Camilla Swinton, you crazy cow! Let me out of here!' She rattled the door handle, tugging at it with all her might, screaming and kicking until, exhausted, and panting like a horse, she dropped back onto the floor, where her thoughts disintegrated into a jumbled mush of self-pity.

Ten minutes later she had corralled them into something more sensible, because the very real possibility now existed that Camilla had murdered Becky. What other reason did she have for locking Fran in her shed? And if she had murdered Becky, where did that leave Fran? Becky's murder was calculated – poisonous mushrooms weren't something you happened across by chance. Neither were they something you would decide to give someone on the spur of the moment – they were researched and carefully obtained. The administering of them was planned; even Becky had had no idea how she could have eaten them.

Fran's thoughts jangled unpleasantly. Camilla was a gardener; in all likelihood she would know a thing or two about poisonous plants; deadly nightshade, foxgloves... did that knowledge extend to mushrooms as well? And now Fran had gone and surprised her. She had panicked Camilla, leaving her with no choice but to lock Fran in the shed until she'd had time to think. And, now that she had, she was busy plotting what she would do to Fran and how she would do it. Because the very last thing any murderer needed was a loose end.

Fran swallowed and tried to calm the fear spiking through her into something less disabling, at least to allow her to think rationally. She needed her wits about her; turning into a blob of jelly wasn't going to help one little bit. No one knew Fran was here. Camilla's house was on a quiet lane, where the houses were all set back from the road, screened behind fences and hedges. Money needed protecting from prying eyes. So no one had seen Fran arrive, and shouting for help wasn't going to achieve anything either; the garden was lengthy and the shed too far away from the front for anyone to hear her. Only Adam knew she was coming here and if, when it became obvious that she was missing, Adam enquired if Camilla had seen her, all Camilla had to do was say no. Because by then Fran would be in the freezer, or been cut into small pieces and fed to the neighbourhood dogs... *For goodness' sake, Fran, pull yourself together*.

Apart from reining in her imagination, there was one other thing Fran very clearly needed to do, and that was escape from the shed. She got back to her feet and began to systematically explore her prison. Without the benefit of light it was hard to work out exactly what she was sharing the shed with, but there was surprisingly little to be found. A quantity of ceramic pots, a metal shelving rack holding bottles and tins of varying sizes, and the sacks of compost she had seen before.

On impulse, she picked up one of the ceramic pots and, holding it above her head, and angling her face away, she threw it to the floor. There was a satisfying crack and the sound of pot shards tinkling, one against the other. She bent down, cautiously running her hand over the debris until she found what she was looking for. A nice triangular section with a sharp point. She dug it experimentally into the side of the shed, but it was immediately apparent that her hand would be damaged far more quickly than the woodwork. Reluctantly, she gave up any idea of being able to either dig or cut her way out. That was it, she was out of options. Now all she could do was wait. Wait, and then act as soon as she got her chance. Now, at least, she had a weapon.

A sudden scratching noise came from the door and she sank back in fear. *What was that?* She had bellowed at Camilla to come and release her from the shed, but now, when faced with the possibility, it was the very last thing she wanted. An image of Camilla dragging her down the garden by her hair swam into her head, followed immediately by one of her being dragged down into a cold, cobwebby cellar and—

'Fran...? Are you in there?' A whisper, no more.

Another noise came from the doorway. And she could hear something being jiggled in the lock.

On soft feet, she crept over and stood silently beside the door, turning the shard of pottery in her palm. If it *was* Camilla coming back for her, then she would be ready. Fran might only be short, but she could do quite a lot of damage if she put her mind to it. Plus, she had surprise on her side. Camilla probably thought she would be weeping in a corner, not poised and ready to strike...

'Fran...?' The voice came again. 'Fran, for God's sake, answer me. I don't want you to be dead.'

She stared at the door. 'Adam...?' *What on earth was he doing here?* She banged on the wood, dropping her makeshift knife. 'Adam, is that you?'

'Yes, it's me. Thank God, you're okay. Now quit rattling the door, I'm trying to get you out.'

She stood back, listening to metallic noises interspersed with the odd sigh and a tut of consternation. But then the noises stopped and the door was wrenched open.

Fran's arm shot up to shield her eyes as light flooded in and she stumbled through the door, blinking furiously.

Adam pulled her into a tight hug, just for a second, and then let go of her as if she were on fire. 'You're okay,' he said.

Fran nodded, overwhelmed with happiness at seeing him. 'Bloody sore foot but, yes, I'm okay.' She stopped. 'Where's Camilla? Adam, we've got to stop her, she's—'

'Back in the house,' Adam replied, with no trace of anxiety. 'I think she said she'd make some coffee.'

'Coffee?' Fran stared at him. 'Why would she be making coffee?'

Adam shrugged. 'I guess she thought you might like some. Although actually I think she needed one herself. Maybe something even stronger; she was a bit worked up.'

'*She* was a bit worked up? What about me? I'm the one she left for dead. Well, not exactly dead., but...' She frowned. None of this was making any sense. 'And now she's back in the kitchen, calmly making a drink and—'

'She's not exactly calm, she... You'll see for yourself in a minute.'

Fran stared at his hand, eyes narrowing at what she saw. 'How did you get the door open?'

Adam opened his palm. 'They're my lock picks.'

'Your what?'

'Lock picks.'

'Yes, I heard you the first time, but—'

'Then why did you ask me to repeat myself?'

She tutted. 'Never mind. Where on earth did you get lock picks from? And possibly more importantly, where did you learn to use them?'

'Amazon, of course,' he replied, smiling, looking very chuffed with himself. 'It really is quite remarkable what they sell.' He drew himself up. 'As for how I learned to use them, I'm self-taught. They come with instructions. The only lock I haven't mastered at home yet is the desk drawer in my mum's study, but I'll get there, it's only a matter of time.'

Fran held his look, eyebrows skyward.

'Sorry, is that not okay?'

She didn't know where to begin. 'Well, normally no, it wouldn't be right at all.' She saw his face fall. 'But, under the circumstances, and given that you did rescue me, I think I can overlook it. I'm just a little confused as to why, if Camilla is in the kitchen, you couldn't just ask her for the key.'

'Because she threw it away,' he said, as if that explained everything. 'She dropped it down the drain outside the back door. She panicked, she said.'

'*She* panicked...' Fran muttered something very rude under her breath. 'Why in heaven's name would she panic? Not when she's the one who killed Becky, she—'

Adam took hold of her arm. 'No, Fran, she didn't. Maybe you'd better come inside. It's a bit awkward, actually.'

She looked up at his face, searching for information. She hadn't a clue what was going on, but let herself be led back up the garden.

'Anyway, how did you know I was here? I mean, thank God you did, I really wasn't sure what was going to happen to me, but your sense of timing is impeccable.'

Adam's gaze shifted just slightly to the left. It was something her daughter often did when confronted with something she didn't want to talk about.

'*Adam...*' she said, warning sending her voice dangerously low.

He picked at his lip. 'Um... Can we just focus on the bit where I rescued you?'

'No, we bloody can't. How did you know I was here, Adam?' Her hands were firmly on her hips. 'Did you follow me? For God's sake, you were supposed to be talking to the estate agent.'

'I was and then... No, I wasn't following you.' His face contorted with anguish. 'But when I heard you were in trouble, what was I supposed to do? You were screaming quite a lot.'

Fran narrowed her eyes. 'Sorry, when you *heard* I was in trouble? And how, pray, could you hear I was in trouble?'

Adam dropped his head. 'There's a bug on your car keys.'

Fran fished them out of her pocket and held them up in the palm of her hand. 'Somehow I don't think we're talking about creepy crawlies, are we?' she said. 'Show me.'

Adam gingerly took the bunch and pulled out her keyring, a small bear hugging a heart which Martha had given her years ago. Teasing open its arms, he pointed to a small grey disc which was stuck to the shiny red fabric.

'I wasn't even sure if it would work. But it's incredibly good...' He trailed off, no doubt realising that probably wasn't the best thing for him to say.

Fran shook her head. 'I don't believe this,' she muttered. 'You've been listening to everything I've said?'

Adam could barely meet her eyes, giving the slightest of nods instead.

'Since when?'

'Yesterday. I was trying it out really, I didn't mean...' His words fizzled out at the look on Fran's face.

'And did that come from Amazon too?'

'No, actually, it was a place that sells—'

Fran took two steps forward, poking her finger into Adam's chest, an action which had him backing away in surprise.

'Adam Smith. I am very grateful to you for coming to my rescue and for opening the shed to get me out. I'm even prepared to overlook the fact that you picked the lock to do it. But don't you ever' – she jabbed her finger towards him again – '*ever*, put a bug on me again. Do I make myself clear?'

He nodded miserably. 'Yes, Fran.'

And despite herself, Fran had to bite back a smile.

12

'Take it off.' Fran pointed to her keys. 'Take off the bug and then put it away. Better yet, throw it away. Or give it here and I'll—'

Adam had pulled off the offending listening device and was holding it protectively to his chest. 'They cost a lot of money. I'll put it in my pocket and I promise I won't use it on you again.'

'Adam, you shouldn't be using it at all. You could get into a lot of trouble.'

'Not as much as a murderer would,' he replied, giving her an indignant look.

She sighed. 'Okay. Keep it, just in case we might need it again, not that I'm encouraging you, not at all.' She looked up towards the house. 'Right, let's go and get that coffee. I can't wait to hear what Camilla has to say for herself. I'm beginning to think she's a bit unhinged.'

To her surprise, Adam gave her an admonishing look. 'Don't,' he said. 'Don't judge her until... Well, you'll see.'

Fran frowned, but walked purposefully back up the garden.

Camilla was waiting for her, anxiously pacing the kitchen floor, and looking the exact opposite of her normal flamboyant and confident self. She looked at Adam as he came through the door and then took two halting steps towards Fran. She was almost in tears.

'Fran, I'm so sorry. I didn't know what to do, you see, I panicked. I really thought you knew everything. I thought you were going to accuse me of killing Becky, that you wouldn't believe me... I'm really sorry,' she repeated.

Adam gave Fran a look as if to say *I told you so*, which she ignored. She also ignored Camilla's treaty. 'I was told you were making coffee,' she said. 'And I would like one, please, as I've just had the most tremendous shock. Some madwoman locked me in a shed and I've hurt my ankle, bruised all my toes, not to mention my heel, and I have a ruddy great splinter in the palm of my hand.'

Camilla nodded quickly, with a look that made Fran squirm with guilt.

'Okay. I'm sorry, I shouldn't have said that, but I'm bloody angry. For God's sake, Camilla, what on earth were you thinking? Saying you panicked isn't good enough. Throwing and then locking someone into a shed isn't something normal people do. You had better have a very good reason for the way you behaved, because at the moment I'm really struggling to take you seriously. And for all I know you really did kill Becky.'

'I didn't, Fran, I didn't. Please, you have to believe me. I know what it looks like, but I would never hurt her, no matter what she was doing.'

Fran's attention came into sharp focus. 'And what *was* she doing?'

Camilla's face had fallen. In fact, she looked close to tears again. 'Blackmailing me,' she whispered. 'Becky, of all people. I still can't believe it. And she had it wrong, Fran, that's the worst of it, and I never got the chance to tell her. I've been so scared.'

Fran flicked a glance at Adam and held up her hand. 'She was blackmailing you? Do you know what you're saying? Shit, that's a motive for murder, Camilla.'

'I know,' she said, her voice on the edge of breaking up. 'I know it is. Please, you've got to help me. I didn't kill Becky, I swear I didn't, but I don't know what to do.'

Fran studied Camilla's face, her own expression softening by degrees. 'For some stupid reason I do believe you, but you'd better start talking, because none of this is making any sense at all.'

'I will. I'll tell you everything.' And with one last pleading look, Camilla scuttled over to the kitchen counter.

She returned carrying a tray freshly laid as if the Queen were coming to tea. There were even linen napkins. Fran was mid eye roll when she caught Adam's expression and turned it into a smile instead.

'This looks lovely, Camilla, thank you.'

'It's too much, isn't it? I know it is. I just… I'm sorry. I had to do something while I was waiting for Adam to get you out of the shed.' She set down the tray on a table and lifted the coffee pot. 'Now, how do you take it, Fran? Milk and sugar? Or there's cream if you prefer.'

'Just black, please.'

'And a slice of cake? A scone? Iced fancy?'

'Camilla… This is really kind, but I don't think we can gloss over what's happened with a slice of lemon drizzle.'

Camilla bent to the task in hand. 'No, I know. But… I don't know what to say. Or how to be. You must hate me.'

Fran accepted her cup of coffee. 'If I did then light refreshments wouldn't make me change my mind, but I don't hate you, no. I'm angry at being locked in the shed. Even a little bit scared still, but mostly I just want to know what's gone on between you and Becky. You're clearly not yourself.'

'What? Bolshy, loud, over the top?' Camilla gave a laugh that sounded almost bitter, bitter and something else. Sadness? She fiddled with her cup, turning the handle first one way and then the other. 'I've been so scared,' she said. 'When I got the first note from Becky, I didn't know what to think. I've worked it out since, of course, but—'

'Hang on a minute,' interrupted Fran. 'What note?'

Camilla blinked. 'The one that Becky sent with the invitation.' She searched Fran's face for any sign of recognition. 'I thought you knew about those,' she added. 'I thought everyone got one.'

Fran looked at Adam. 'I have no idea,' she said. 'But it's quite possible they did. Do you still have it?'

'The note?'

'The invitation and the note.'

Camilla nodded mutely and crossed to a dresser on the far wall. Pulling open a drawer, she lifted up some papers before drawing something forward and sliding it out. 'I shouldn't have hung onto it really, it only made me feel worse. And I would have thrown it away, but when Becky died, I didn't know what to think. I was terrified everyone would think I'd killed her.'

Fran held out her hand for the piece of paper. 'But why would they think that?' She read the few lines on the sheet.

This is such good fun, isn't it? Make sure you get into character for the party, won't you? I picked it just for you. Everybody has a secret...

She looked up, hairs prickling the back of her neck. 'Go on.'

'The note was clipped to the front of the invitation and I didn't pay it much attention when I first read it, it sounded just like the kind of friendly note that Becky might send. But when I saw what she'd sent with it, well, that's when I realised what her words really meant. They were a warning.' Camilla slid the invitation towards Fran. 'The note might not say anything by itself, but put it together with the information she sent about the game and it's pretty obvious what she was getting at.'

She paused a moment to let Fran begin reading. 'I was

supposed to play a character called Melody – a society heiress –
who just happened to be a thief. Coincidences are one thing,
but that's too close to home for comfort. It seemed as if Becky
were making fun of me, even having a dig at me, and it unsettled
me a bit. It didn't seem like the kind of thing she would do, I
thought she was my friend.'

'Wait a minute,' said Fran, shaking her head. 'Why would
what Becky had written unsettle you? How is it too close to
home?'

Camilla put down her cup and grimaced. 'Because I *do* steal
things.' She held up her hand. 'But it's not what you think.' She
touched a finger to each corner of her mouth as if to wipe it. 'It's
better if I show you. It's complicated.'

Fran instantly glanced at Adam, who was leaning up
against the edge of the breakfast bar, and he nodded, pushing
himself upright.

Fran waited while Camilla opened one of the kitchen
cupboards and then, stretching on tiptoes, took down a pot from
the top shelf. She tipped something into her hand and then
replaced the pot, turning back around with a hesitant smile.

'We need to go upstairs,' she said. 'To my office.' She took
two steps forward and stopped again. 'I swear I'm not about to
lock you in anywhere.'

The thing in Camilla's hand turned out to be a key, which
Fran discovered once they'd been led up the oak turned
stairway to the impressive galleried landing above. It was
painted bright white and hung with a series of enormous prints;
beautiful, vibrant things, which Fran could tell would have cost
a fortune. The carpet up here was just as deep as downstairs,
and none of them made a sound as they walked past a series of
doors, turning at the end of the hallway and, once the last door
was unlocked, into a large, airy room, decorated in a pale duck-
egg blue.

'This is where I work,' said Camilla. 'I keep it locked

because...' She sighed. 'I guess it's daft really, when you consider what else we have in the house, but the things in here, they're not mine.' She stepped further into the room and pointed to a large work area. 'On the desk,' she said.

Piled on one side of it were an assortment of boxes, several items of clothing, books, perfumes and even some jewellery. With the exception perhaps of the books, everything else was evidently expensive, the kind of things you would only find in exclusive stores. Fran looked at Camilla, perplexed.

'I take things,' she said. 'Steal them.' She gave a rueful smile. 'Except it really isn't what you're thinking because I'm paid to do it. When I've taken something, I bring it back here, write up a report of my findings, and then return the goods, together with my report, to whichever store hired me.'

Fran stared in astonishment. 'You're a mystery shopper,' she exclaimed.

'Not quite. A mystery *shoplifter*. I have a company which I set up several years ago, and which is now managed day to day by my brother-in-law. We work with high-end stores, helping them to improve their security arrangements.'

Things were rapidly falling into place for Fran.

'So this is what you thought the note from Becky was referring to – she was pointing out the parallel between the secret she thought she'd found out about you, and the one your character was to play in the game.'

Camilla nodded. 'I'm certain of it. Except that she'd jumped to entirely the wrong conclusion, of course. For obvious reasons I have to be very circumspect about what I do. It isn't something I discuss with anyone, friends or otherwise. And especially not the PTA.' Her smile was wry. 'Besides, it helps when everyone thinks you're rich as Croesus. No one expects me to work for a living, let alone do something like this.'

Fran stared at Adam. 'That makes sense,' she said. 'If Becky had seen you take something, she *would* think you'd stolen it.'

'Strictly speaking, I was,' replied Camilla. 'So you can hardly blame her.' She drew in a deep breath. 'Although I did think Becky might have spoken to me about it if that was the case. I thought our friendship was better than that. That's what I can't understand.' She dropped her head a little. 'But I've been wrong about people before.'

There was a sadness in her eyes that may have been grief at the loss of a friend but Fran wasn't so sure.

'Even so, I still thought it was a simple misunderstanding that Becky and I could easily clear up, with no harm done.'

'So when you went to the party that night you were intending to speak to Becky about it?' asked Fran. 'Or perhaps hoping that Becky would speak to you?'

'Yes. It was awful. I didn't know what to think, it seemed such an odd thing for Becky to do.'

'And did you speak about it to anyone else at the party?' asked Fran. 'Or tell them about Becky's note and that you suspected she was up to something?' She leaned forward, eager for Camilla's answer. Could Camilla's have been one of the voices Adam overheard?

'No, I didn't want anyone else to know about it. I wanted to get Becky on her own so I could explain, but I never got the chance.'

Fran felt her heart sink, but what Camilla said made perfect sense. So they were back to the drawing board again. Although, if Camilla wasn't one of the two people Adam overheard and it obviously wasn't Sara then, by a process of elimination, it must have been Diane and Lois. Interesting...

Fran's head was in a spin. She certainly hadn't anticipated the direction her day had taken, and there was an awful lot to take in.

'Who else knows about this?' asked Adam, pointing to the array of things on Camilla's desk.

'No one. When anyone asks, I just say I work for my

brother-in-law. If I'm pushed, I might add that he has a security business, but most people aren't interested beyond that. Or they're not even sure what that is, so they don't ask. It's not that I'm ashamed of what I do, not at all. But, as you can imagine, I don't want it to become public knowledge. If my face gets "out there" it's going to make business very difficult, which is why Becky's note freaked me out so much.' She looked around her. 'This house, the lifestyle, I owe it all to the business. I've worked so hard to build it up and I could lose everything. Everything.'

'So if no one else knows,' added Fran, deep in thought, 'then I can only imagine that Becky's note and the character role she sent for you to play would seem spooky.' She was thinking back to her conversation with Sara the day before. A conversation where Sara had described a very similar coincidence between her life and that of a character she'd been given to play.

'It's like it described my life. It has to be more than a coincidence.'

'But you said you were being blackmailed,' put in Adam. 'The note Becky sent with the invitation might have seemed odd or out of character, a little malicious even, but it hardly constitutes a blackmail threat.'

Camilla looked at him, her lip trembling.

'No, that's why I was sure it was something and nothing. But I never got the chance to speak to Becky, to explain. It isn't a conversation you can have by text, even over the phone. I wanted to talk to her properly, face to face, but I was away on business the first few days after the party and when I got back...' She swallowed. 'That's when I found the second note.'

Fran stared at Adam. 'I think you'd better show us,' she said to Camilla, a grim tone to her voice.

Camilla relocked her office and led them back downstairs to the kitchen. 'I'll just go and fetch it.'

Fran watched as Camilla left the room and, while they were

waiting, poured them all another coffee, cutting them each a slice of cake for good measure.

'I tucked it into my handbag,' said Camilla, returning with it over her arm. She plonked it on the table and opened a zippered compartment inside, fishing out a piece of pink paper, which she held out to Fran. 'Here.'

Fran eyed it as if it were an unexploded bomb. 'I'm not sure we should be touching that,' she said, wondering how wise they'd been to handle the other note. A band of pressure was building around her head, one which seemed to be getting tighter and tighter.

Camilla blanched and laid the paper on the table, spinning it so that it faced them. The words were stark, and their message crystal clear.

Time to pay up or I let everyone know what you get up to in Harvey Nics.

Five grand ought to do it. For now. By Monday, please.
10-04-29 61266740

Lots of love, Becky xx

'I received it the day before Becky was taken ill,' said Camilla. 'When it arrived, I went into a flat spin. I didn't know what to do, and then the next day Becky got sick and I obviously couldn't speak to her then, so I did nothing. The police are going to think I killed her, aren't they?' Her eyes filled with tears.

Fran didn't know what to say. What Camilla had said was almost certainly true.

'You don't think I killed her, do you?' added Camilla. 'Please tell me you don't. I'd never hurt Becky, despite what she was doing. She really was the nicest person, out of us all.'

'No, I don't think you killed her, and barging in here probably wasn't my wisest move,' admitted Fran, eyeing her cake. She took a bite and then paused. 'Not unless that was all a pack of lies and you've poisoned the lemon drizzle.'

Beside her, Adam almost choked and Fran reached over to pat his hand. 'That was a joke, Adam.' She looked back at Camilla. 'It was, wasn't it?'

Camilla picked up a fork and toyed with her own slice. 'Yes, don't worry.'

'Seriously though,' said Fran. 'I really hope you can prove what you've just told us about your business. Because I won't lie, Camilla, without it, things will look really bad.'

Camilla's frightened eyes met hers.

'It's the only thing which turns the blackmail demand from something very real into a harmless, empty threat.'

Adam frowned. 'Run that by me again,' he said.

'Think about it,' replied Fran, punctuating her sentence with her fork. 'If Camilla was a thief then arguably that makes a very good case for blackmail – if her "secret" came out, she could go to prison. Except that, as we've just discovered, Camilla's secret is completely innocuous. What would be the point in blackmailing her? And no blackmail, no motive for murder.'

Adam's eyes widened. 'God, you're right. You *can* prove it, I hope?'

He turned to Camilla, who gave a wan smile.

'I can. In fact, I still do work for the man who first employed me. A long time ago now, I was seventeen at the time.' She looked out to the garden, eyes glazed, as if she were peering into her past and not really seeing the plants at all.

'It's a pretty niche career,' commented Fran, watching her carefully. 'How do you get involved with that kind of work?'

Camilla refocused her attention and inhaled a deep breath. 'It's a long story,' she said. 'The one other occasion in my life when a so-called friend has played games with me.' She dug her fork into her cake. 'It's quite pathetic, really. I'm the daughter of

a very wealthy family, the type of money that goes back genera-
tions, and I grew up with people who thought anything and
everything was theirs for the taking. Determined not to be like
them, I became the original rebellious teenager. Went to art
school. Did things I shouldn't just to prove a point. I also made
friends with someone who I thought liked me for who I was, or
at least who I was trying to be, and one hot summer when we'd
just had our exam results, she dared me to pinch something to
prove I'd turned my back on my capitalist upbringing.' She gave
a tight smile. 'You can probably guess what happened after
that.'

'You got caught?' said Fran.

'No, I didn't. But when I showed my friend what I'd taken,
what I'd done to prove our friendship, she laughed in my face.
Said she'd only done it to let the poor little rich girl see how it
felt to be treated like a criminal. She'd wanted me to get caught.'

'Bloody hell,' said Adam. 'What did you do?'

'Marched back into the store and told them what I'd done
and why.' Her smile was wistful this time. 'I think it was the
most terrifying thing I've done in my entire life but, instead of
being arrested, the manager wanted to know how I'd managed
to pinch something so expensive without anybody seeing. It
impressed him that I'd had the nerve to own up to what I'd
done, so we got talking and he offered me a job, of sorts. It kind
of grew from there.'

Fran shook her head. 'That's an incredible story.'

'I was very lucky. Right place at the right time maybe. But,
yes, with his help I started my own company a few years later.
And, like I said, I still work for him now from time to time. His
security is obviously a lot better than it was.' The beginnings of
a smile crept over her face, but then it fell again. 'That's what
hurt when I realised what Becky was trying to do, that someone
else was laughing in the face of our friendship. I still can't
understand it though – what could have motivated Becky to do

something like this? Something must have been very wrong in her life. And now we'll never know. That's what really hurts. If we'd known, we might have been able to help her.'

Fran laid a hand on Camilla's arm. 'I don't think anybody knew. You mustn't blame yourself.'

'Do you think she might have been blackmailing other people?' asked Camilla.

Fran nodded gently. 'I think it's quite possible, yes. Camilla, would you mind if Adam took a photo of the blackmail demand? Only I want to check out the details in it with Nick.'

Camilla shook her head, dropping her gaze. She shuddered, clearly thinking about a friend who wasn't who she thought she was. 'It was still a horrible way to die. No one deserves that. And she knew, didn't she? That's what Nick said. Becky knew she was going to die.'

Fran swallowed. 'Can you think of anything else? Anything you saw or heard at the party that might help us?'

'No, honestly. I've thought about it. Over and over, but I didn't come up with anything,' she added quietly.

Fran suddenly remembered something. 'You wouldn't know anything about mushrooms, would you? I wondered, seeing as you're such a good gardener. Only we have no idea where the mushrooms that poisoned Becky might have come from. Where they grow, if there's any round here, that kind of thing.'

But Camilla shook her head. 'I'm sorry, no. Plants, yes, there's a whole long list of those which are poisonous, but fungi is a rather different field of knowledge.'

Fran smiled. 'Okay, it was worth a shot. If you think of anything else which might help, will you let us know? Even if it's something that doesn't seem to make sense.'

She nodded. 'I will.'

Fran took another bite of cake. 'You could do something else too, if you wouldn't mind, and that's not mention a word to Sara about Adam being here with me today. She doesn't know he's involved, you see. We're trying to get a head start on all this before the police. As soon as they begin asking questions about the party, as the "murderer" in the game, it's not going to be long before they arrive at Sara's door.'

Camilla smiled. 'Don't worry, your secret's safe with me.'

13

It seemed a very long time since Fran had arrived at Camilla's house, so much had happened, and now, as she walked back out to her car with Adam, she felt almost overwhelmingly tired. The prospect of several hours baking ahead of her wasn't a happy one.

'Are you thinking what I'm thinking?' she said.

Adam gave her a surprised look. 'Do you want to run away too?' he asked.

'What?' Fran took a deep breath. Adam's verbal gymnastics were hard to keep up with at times. 'Why do you want to run away?' she asked.

Adam paused, wrinkling his nose as he tried to think of the right response. 'I don't really, just that... I'm normally in my room all day. This is the most I've been out in weeks and... I think I'm still having a hard time getting my head around the fact that Becky was murdered. That someone could do that deliberately. And that someone really isn't a very nice person.'

'Except that, by the sound of it, Becky wasn't the angel everyone thought she was. She was a blackmailer, Adam.'

'If what Camilla said is true.'

She narrowed her eyes at him. 'Why? Don't you believe her?'

He smiled. 'No, I do believe her. I was just playing devil's advocate. Her story is obviously true and although I can understand why Camilla doesn't want what she does for a living to become common knowledge, it's hardly the end of the world if a few people do find out. It certainly wouldn't get her thrown into prison, which was obviously what Becky was banking on as leverage for blackmail.'

'Unless there's another reason why Camilla doesn't want people to know about what she does.' Fran thought for a moment. 'But I can't see it. Camilla was obviously still utterly unable to accept what Becky had done, but even though she knew it to be fact, you could see how much she cared about her.'

Adam nodded. 'So do we cross her off our list of suspects?'

Fran wrinkled her nose. 'It's odd, isn't it, because before I came here today I had no idea that we were going to find out what we have. Camilla has gone from innocent to the best suspect we have, and then back to innocent again, all in the space of a morning. I can't keep up with this.' She shook her head. 'But I think for now, we should discount her. Camilla might have had opportunity, but a straightforward chat with Becky would have cleared the whole thing up, so she has no motive that I can see.'

'Agreed.'

Fran looked at him over the roof of the car. 'I need to thank you,' she said. 'And apologise too. I shouldn't have yelled at you when I found out about the bug, not when you'd come to my rescue.' She paused. 'And it's made me realise how stupid I've been about this. I went waltzing into Camilla's house today, ready to if not quite ask, then certainly imply, that she killed Becky and then wait calmly for her to tell me what she was hiding. I'm lucky that being locked in a shed was all that happened. Imagine what the outcome might have been if Camilla actually *was* the murderer?'

'I'm not sure being locked in the shed was all that lucky,' Adam replied. 'Not really. You could have been in there for hours. But you're right, and it's my fault too. I didn't think about the consequences either. This is beginning to get very complicated; it's making my head hurt.'

'I'm beginning to feel that way too. First, Lois, then Diane, now Camilla. It makes the story of my life look like a piece of cake.'

Adam grinned. 'Ha, I like that, very funny.'

Fran stared at him. 'Oh,' she said, once the penny dropped, 'an unintentional pun. But, really, I've never met a bunch of people who have so many things to hide, even if Camilla's "secret" isn't anything to be ashamed of. It does make you wonder. And think. We have to be a lot more careful than we have been.'

Adam nodded. 'And I think we should stick together too. No going following up clues on our own.'

Fran touched a hand to her mouth. 'I guess that is what we're doing, isn't it, following up clues? Blimey, never thought I'd hear myself saying that.' She squinted across at him. 'It's kind of fun too though. Is that wrong?'

Adam grinned and gestured towards the car door. They could chat in there safely.

Fran flashed her key remote obligingly. 'So before you came to rescue me, did you find out anything about Diane from the estate agent?'

'It's interesting.' Adam pulled open the door and slid into the passenger seat, waiting until Fran was behind the wheel. 'Because the same agent also handled the purchase of their previous house too. They have a "fine and country" tag so I guess that means they only deal in places worth a lot of money. Diane and her husband bought their previous house about three years ago and, even allowing for a pretty hefty increase in house prices, this latest one cost significantly more. They have a very small mortgage, which they transferred against this property, but the difference was made up in cash.'

'So to outward appearances they have a mortgage which a lot of couples on their kind of income might have?'

Adam nodded.

'So where did all the extra cash come from then, if it wasn't just from the sale of their old house?'

'Where indeed. The agent didn't enquire, but doesn't recall there being any mention of a windfall of any kind, or an inheritance. Most people talk about that kind of thing, apparently.'

'I'm amazed he was so loose-lipped, but that could prove to be very useful information. So how do we follow the money now? What would the police do in this kind of situation?'

'Demand access to Diane's bank accounts, probably. See what was coming in and going out, and how regularly, that kind of thing.'

'Right, well, we can't do any of that, obviously – and before you say it, given what's already occurred, I've no doubt you could hack into Diane's bank account. They're all online these days, aren't they? But under no circumstances are you to do that, and I want a promise this time.'

Adam grinned. 'I'm flattered you think I'm capable,' he said. 'But banks have encryption that's rather more sophisticated than I can deal with, so it's out of the question anyway. Unless Diane has a habit of leaving her bank statements lying around, either at her house or at work...'

Fran looked up sharply. 'No. Absolutely not. We are not breaking —'

'I'm not suggesting we break in, but it's occurred to me that if Camilla received a note from Becky with her invitation, then it's possible the others did too. We might not be able to see where Diane's money comes from, but there's another way of checking if she's paid anything out. Let's ask Nick if he can check Becky's account, see if any money has come in from Diane. We have proof of at least one blackmail demand now, it's a necessary question. And surely he'd do anything to help prove that Becky wasn't guilty.'

'True,' said Fran. 'I'll ask him.' She frowned. There was something else niggling her about all this, as if she'd missed something important which had been said. The kind of thing which irritated you all day and then came to you at three in the morning.

'And...?' Adam raised his eyebrows.

'And what?'

'Well, if Becky sent out at least one note, what's to say that she didn't manipulate other things as well?'

'I'm not sure I'm following you.'

'So far we know that Becky ordered the game and paid for it on behalf of Mum's friends. Then later, when requested, she sent the company everyone's addresses so that they could send out the invitation and the details of the character they were each to play. But the note from Becky that Camilla received with hers wasn't handwritten, it was typed. So Becky must have contacted the company and asked them to do that. What if that's not all she asked them to do?'

Fran made a rolling motion with her hand. 'Go on.'

'That coincidence between Camilla's secret and the one which her character, Melody, was hiding – it wasn't a coincidence at all. It was a warning shot across the bows, alerting Camilla to the fact that Becky knew her secret. You saw what she'd written on Camilla's note – *I picked this one just for you.* What if she didn't just pick it? What if she wrote it from scratch?'

'My God, you're right! The note seemed quite innocuous, really, when actually what it was could have been was very, *very* clever indeed.'

'And if Becky did that for Camilla, what's to say she didn't do that for everyone else at the party? We know that Lois and Diane are hiding secrets too.'

Fran stared at him. 'This whole murder-mystery game was invented by Becky. Or purloined by her at the very least. She's used it as the stage on which to play out her own drama. It's the key to the whole thing!' Her heart was pounding. Finally, they were getting somewhere.

She looked at Adam's face, flushed with exhilaration, while unease began to snake around her shoulders. Oh, this was horrible. They were just beginning to work things out but now she needed to end this conversation, and quickly. Adam was far too smart. Any minute now he was going to mention the possibility that his mum might have a secret too, and she really didn't want him to do that. Not before she'd had a chance to speak to Sara first. She swallowed, checking her watch.

'Damn. Adam, I'm sorry, we're just beginning to work things out and I have to go. I've got an engagement party tomorrow to cater for.' It wasn't a lie, but she was using it as an excuse to leave.

His face fell. 'Oh, okay. Well, I guess I could go home and have a think about what else we need to do.' He readied a hand on the car door. 'Or' – his face brightened – 'I could help you. I'm no cook, obviously, but I bet there's stuff I could do. Fetch and carry, mop your fevered brow. Make the coffee?' He smiled. 'Besides, I thought we were a team now?'

'Adam, that's a really kind thought, thank you. And it isn't that I don't want you to come and help, but...' She glanced at her watch again. 'Martha will be home from school soon and I'm not sure you'd want to—'

'No, no, you're right and I've probably got work I should be getting on with too,' he said, smiling. 'All this running around trying to catch a murderer eats into your day rather, doesn't it?'

Damn, now he was trying to make *her* feel better.

'Come round first thing in the morning,' she said. 'We can have a catch-up then.'

'Okay.' This time he did open the door. 'See you then.'

She watched as he climbed from her car and walked back to his. Maybe it would be okay. Maybe Sara would find some time to talk to him this evening and Fran wouldn't have to explain to Adam that yes, his mum did have a secret as it happened. She sighed. Blimey, life was complicated sometimes.

She started her engine and pulled away, giving Adam a cheery wave as she passed.

It wasn't until Fran was almost home that the thing which had been niggling her for a while now suddenly made itself very clear. And she was hit so hard by its implications that she almost drove straight through a red light. She jammed on her brakes, heart beating fast. 'Shit, shit, *shit...*'

NOT SURPRISINGLY, Fran had a very sleepless night – worrying about Adam, who was no doubt worrying too. How on earth must he be feeling? But now that the morning was here, she was even more anxious; she had no idea what she was going to say to him.

At least he's punctual, she thought as she went to open the front door. Hanging around waiting for him to arrive would have been the worst kind of torture. She tried to surreptitiously assess what she saw as he stepped into her hallway. Was he more tired than usual? Or more preoccupied? He could be forgiven for either. Indeed, the bags under her eyes now seemed to be packing for a fortnight rather than a week.

'First things first,' she said. 'Have you eaten?' It seemed the most obvious thing to say. And the thing most guaranteed to ease them past any awkwardness as Adam stepped over the threshold of her kitchen.

His smile was still there at least. 'I have,' he replied. 'Unusually for me, I've been up since seven.' He tapped his head. 'I think I must have a few of Poirot's little grey cells in here, because they seem to be constantly busy. But my early start meant that I found time for some toast. Peanut butter as well. I'd forgotten how incredible that is.'

Fran pulled a face. 'I'll take your word for it,' she said. 'So, I don't need to feed you then? Before we get to down to business.'

There was a pause where Adam clearly gave her question very careful consideration. 'Hmm. Probably not. Although, I'm not absolutely sure why, but I was thinking about ice cream on the way over here. I don't suppose you have any, do you?'

'Have you secreted video cameras around my home as well as bugs?' Fran quipped, instantly regretting it.

He gave her a puzzled look.

'I have several batches in the freezer,' she said in response. 'In fact...' She went to the pantry and returned with a small Tupperware tub containing one of her latest creations. 'You could taste test this for me, if you like?' She collected a spoon as well and placed both on the table. 'I'm not even going to tell you what it is, I'd like to see whether you can tell.'

'Okay,' replied Adam, happily taking a seat.

Fran waited until he was settled, pretending to clean her work surfaces, which were already spotless. Because if she didn't say something now, she doubted she ever would.

'Something's been niggling me,' she said. 'And I've been trying to remember what it was.'

'Urgh, that's so annoying, isn't it?' said Adam, through a mouthful of ice cream. 'And did you?'

'I did, actually. I was sure someone had said something. Something which alluded to another thing entirely, a really quite important thing. And if I could remember who it was that said it, I might be able to recall *what* was said.'

Adam looked up, spoon poised.

'And it turns out that the someone who said it was you.'

'Oh. That's handy then, seeing as I'm here. What did I say?'
Fran took a deep breath.

'When I asked you *when* you'd bugged my car keys, you mentioned that you'd done it yesterday. And seeing as another day has dawned since then, the yesterday in question would have been Wednesday.'

She checked to make sure he was following. 'And a lot of things happened on Wednesday. We spoke to Nick, obviously, but we also spoke to your mum, at least I did. You went to wait upstairs, making no noise, just like Harry Potter...'

She looked at him again, at the downward turn of his face, the slope of his shoulders.

'And your mum mentioned something odd about the character she'd been given to play during the party. One that coincidentally mirrored a little secret she had of her own, just like Camilla's did. Not so little, as it turns out. You heard everything, didn't you? About your dad.'

There was the smallest of nods. And an even smaller glimpse of a smile. 'My mum used to tell me that eavesdroppers never heard anything good,' he murmured.

'I tell my daughter the same,' replied Fran. 'Although, as we know, that isn't always the case. I might well still be in Camilla's shed if it wasn't for you.'

He smiled at her words but she could see that it was scant compensation for what he'd recently learned.

'Although perhaps it isn't all bad,' he mused. 'I think maybe it's given me a few answers too.' He stared at the tub of ice cream and spooned in another mouthful. And then another. Eventually, he rested the spoon against the side of the container, although he continued to play with it. 'I've spent years thinking my dad left because of me. The fact that he isn't my biological father makes that decision a little easier to understand. I was right, albeit for the wrong reasons. And I suppose at some point in the future, I might even see it as a blessing.' He gave a sad smile. 'I'm scared my mum might be guilty of murder. I should be grateful that in comparison, this pales into insignificance.'

Fran gave him a sympathetic look. 'It's hardly insignificant, Adam.' She paused. 'Would you like to talk about it?'

'Probably,' he admitted. 'Although I wasn't really paying attention when you and she first started speaking. What prompted the confession?'

'We were talking about the premise of the game – how Becky's character was blackmailing everyone because she was about to expose their secrets. So I asked if she knew what those were. She didn't, said she was rubbish at working out the clues on the night, so the next logical question was for me to ask her what her character's secret was. It was your mum who mentioned the coincidence, though. After that, I guess she had to tell me why.' She studied his face. 'But, remember, she made no mention of actual blackmail, Adam, or that she'd received any kind of note with her invitation. Given that she pointed out the very thing that this whole affair seems to rest on, I don't think she can be guilty. It certainly didn't seem that way to me. Besides, she wasn't one of the people you overheard, was she?'

'No, but that doesn't mean she isn't guilty,' he replied. 'Just that no one heard her make any threats.'

'Adam, I know you must feel angry with Sara for keeping things from you, but you must also know that she plans on speaking to you about it.'

Adam toyed with his ice cream, breaking it into curls with his spoon. 'Apple and cinnamon?' he said. 'Although I think there may be a touch of honey in there too.'

Fran smiled, her heart going out to him. 'Have you always been this clever?'

'I guess that's been part of the problem,' he replied. 'Although that's where finding out that my dad isn't my dad makes a lot of sense. He isn't stupid, neither is Mum, but where my brains came from has always been somewhat of a mystery.'

'Your mum said that the problems didn't really start until secondary school.'

Adam nodded. 'I aced my tests in primary, but then so did a lot of other kids. It wasn't until the testing became more rigorous at secondary school, and the subjects more challenging, that I began to realise I was reading and understanding far beyond what my classmates were. And that wouldn't necessarily have been a problem, except that my enthusiasm and thirst for knowledge were met with bored indifference by the school.' He took another mouthful of ice cream.

'Go on,' encouraged Fran.

'I was bitten by the bug,' he continued. 'I craved new things. And someone to talk to about them. I met a retired university lecturer one Saturday at the local library, and that helped for a while. It made me realise that I wasn't weird, or a teacher's pet, or any of the other names I got called, but, instead, just like countless other people. What I hadn't done yet was find them, that was all. Lesley set me projects to explore, homework, if you like. I couldn't believe there was someone who not only understood the things I was saying, but challenged them too, made me think harder and further.'

Fran realised she was smiling as Adam spoke. She could picture him and his retired professor, the teacher and protégé. 'What happened?' she asked.

'He moved away,' replied Adam. 'His wife died and he went to live with his son and daughter-in-law. And so that was the end of that. I was back to being the nerdy geek, utterly bored by school, and becoming more and more angry as the months went by. Angry that no one would listen to me, worse belittled me, and furious that none of my teachers could be bothered with me. I was too much like hard work.'

'Wasn't there anyone who saw your potential?' Fran asked.

Adam gave a bitter laugh. 'Only Becky. She was my drama teacher,' he replied. 'She channelled my angst and teenage hormones into as many parts in her plays as she could. I'm not sure it helped particularly, but at least she encouraged my endeavours. She also fostered a life-long love of theatre and storytelling.' He shrugged. 'She's probably the reason why I do what I do.'

'Writing computer games?'

He nodded. 'A game is essentially the same as a film, or a book, just in another format. The world it takes place in has to be envisaged, the characters have to be drawn and the plot has to be robust enough so that whoever is playing can manipulate parts of it without ever losing the central premise. The people who play them don't want something which is unrealistic or has loopholes or plot narratives that don't hang together. It might be set on some distant planet where the main protagonists are lizards, but it still has to make sense, the facts still have to be right, and the weirder and more nerdy the science, the better. Same with the more conventional stories. Puzzlers like puzzles, and they can spot one that doesn't work a mile away. That's what I get a kick from, devising something that takes some figuring out, leading players through my clues, allowing them to act out their fantasies as well as directing the action. Essentially, it's all a stage, the only difference is that the stage is virtual.'

A staged game, just like the one Becky seems to have created.

Fran considered his words for a moment. 'I think I owe you an apology,' she said. 'Because I, like countless others, no doubt, have always thought computer games were a bit... well, a poor relation when compared to a book perhaps, or a film. Thank you for enlightening me.'

Adam dipped his head in acknowledgement, but he was grinning now. 'You're welcome.'

'Your mum mentioned a few... issues. At school. Things you got in trouble for.'

'That was a polite way of saying it. I got expelled, although I think we're supposed to say excluded now.'

'What did you do?' She couldn't help herself, she was intrigued now. From what she knew of him, Adam wasn't an obvious troublemaker.

'More a case of what I *didn't* do. I decided that if the school couldn't, or wouldn't, teach me the things I wanted to know, then I would teach myself. The official viewpoint is that I became a non-attender, in their eyes no doubt drifting through my days, high on whatever, a loser... whereas, in actual fact, I spent my days at the library or online, learning about whatever interested me. But that didn't fit with the profile of someone playing hooky, so no one believed me. And that made me angry – that I was in the wrong for doing something which the school had a responsibility for. They were so certain that their perfect systems were the answer, so I decided to show them they weren't.'

A trace of a smile flickered around his mouth.

'Go on...'

'To start with, I created a series of spoof social media accounts where I had teachers posting about things that... well, let's just say things you wouldn't expect them to. And it wasn't long before a good proportion of the school was obsessed with them. I got caught, of course – some Year 10 girl who fancied her form tutor ratted on me – but it was while I was languishing at home after my first exclusion that I devised an even more wicked plan.' He spooned up several mouthfuls of ice cream, eyes gleaming with mischief. 'And the best part was that I could do it all from home.'

Fran screwed up her face. 'I hardly dare ask.'

'I hacked the school network and altered a few grades... changed a few security settings, and made all the internal exam papers available via an encrypted folder, the password to which just happened to find its way into the hands of every GCSE student...'

Fran had to cover her mouth quickly in order to contain her

laughter. 'I shouldn't be laughing, but I confess I rather like your style. Robin Hood would be doing that kind of thing if he were alive today.'

'Hmm... my parents didn't think so.'

'No, I guess not. What happened?'

'Permanent exclusion... and, not the greatest period in my life.'

'I can imagine. That's when your dad left?'

Adam nodded. 'He went ballistic when he found out what I'd done. Mum was angry, but at least she tried to understand why I'd done it. Dad's view was that punishment, not understanding, was the answer and, wait for it, he banned me from going to university.'

'But that might have made things worse. And, in any case, you'd have been eighteen by then, you could still have done your exams and gone anyway.'

'I could, but he would have made it difficult, financially for one. The trouble was he simply didn't understand me at all, or want to. He saw my intelligence as a threat, not a gift. Mum didn't realise the extent of it, or not at first anyway, but at least she tried to understand how I was feeling.'

Fran gave him a sympathetic look. 'And it was during one spectacular row that your dad declared that you were no son of his...'

Adam hung his head.

'Adam, it wasn't your fault. You heard what your mum said – that their relationship had been troubled for a while. The stress of what happened might have shone a light on it, but it wasn't the root cause. Personally, I think your dad leaving was a pot coming slowly to the boil. Do you think you'll go and look for him now; your real dad, I mean?'

'I haven't really thought about it yet, not properly anyway. I need to speak to Mum about it, but—'

'How do you go about that when you'll have to admit to listening to our conversation?'

'Exactly.' He pulled a face. 'Although the point as to who has the moral high ground in this particular situation is very much up for discussion. It makes a lot of sense, though, the fact that my real dad was an academic. And a physicist, no less. God, the conversations we could have had, the things I could have learned. That's what I'm finding hard, what hurts, the fact that I've been denied him all these years. That my childhood could have been so different.'

'True. But even if he knew about you in the first place, he might not have wanted anything to do with you. Plus, it was a one-night stand. Maybe he wasn't such a great person, after all.'

'The grass is always greener...'

'We do have a tendency to think that way, don't we?' She paused for a moment, watching Adam push his spoon around what was now a pool of ice cream. 'So what happened next? How did you get from where you were to where you are now?'

He gave her a puzzled look.

'I don't mean sitting in my kitchen eating ice cream. You're how old, again? Twenty-one, twenty-two? What happened after you left school?'

'I'm twenty-three, but essentially, I continued my education on my own. You're right, I could have gone to university, but I couldn't see the point. What would I have studied? I already knew a lot of degree-level stuff... and I'm not just saying that to sound arrogant, it was a real dilemma. And in the end, more study, formal study anyway, seemed a waste of my time. By then, I'd found a bunch of people just like me online, through forums and chat rooms. We sit a little outside the circle of everyone else, but that's okay, we all know where we stand. I've made loads of friends that way, real friends, and through them I started exploring gaming, and I soon realised that it was a really good match for my skill set. And the rest, as they say... Mum still thinks I should get out more, but she kind of gets it.'

'And now here you are, sitting in my kitchen, eating ice cream and halfway to solving a murder.'

Adam pulled a face. 'I'm not sure I'd say we're halfway...'

'Maybe not.' Fran smiled. 'I was trying to cheer you up. But don't knock what we've found out. We have a motive and that's a huge step forward. Every person at your mum's party had a secret, and it seems certain that Becky must have been blackmailing them too, just like the characters in the game. And now we have motive, we need to crack on with establishing opportunity and means. Quite conceivably, everyone wanted to kill Becky, but who had the opportunity to do it?'

Adam nodded. 'I think we need to keep digging a little deeper into Diane's secret. We still don't know what that's all about. Maybe we should find out some more about this company Diane works for. I think we're both agreed that she isn't the CEO, but what does she do exactly? Is that where her money's come from?' He pushed his bowl away a little distance. 'Oh, and there's this...'

Adam lifted his phone and navigated to whatever it was he wanted Fran to see. He held it out to her. 'While I was waiting to see the estate agent yesterday, I got thinking about the company where Becky bought the game from, so I paid a visit to their website, hoping that something might leap out at me. It didn't, but look, they're advertising for a developer to help expand the range of products they offer as digital downloads.'

Fran held Adam's look.

He continued. 'I'm wondering if I should apply. We know Becky must have manipulated everything that got sent out to Mum and her friends. If I got an interview, I might at least get the opportunity to have a snoop around the office, maybe even have a chat to a few people. It wouldn't hurt.'

'That's a brilliant idea.' Fran smiled. 'You know, if it's any consolation at all, I think you're doing all right, Adam Smith. And given that your talents also extend to identifying mystery ice-cream flavours, I'd say you're very all right.'

He smiled, suddenly, a brief bright twinkle in his eyes. 'Thanks, Fran, really. I feel... better. Full up, but better.'

Fran held out her hand for the Tupperware tub. 'Then I'm glad,' she said, raising her eyes to the clock on the wall. 'Oh my God, is that the time? Adam, never mind secrets and life histories, now I really need your help. *Again.*'

14

The next few hours passed by in a blur of gastronomic industry. The engagement party Fran was catering for was later that day and, thankfully, the finger buffet the couple had chosen to serve their guests consisted of classic items that Adam was more than capable of helping with. So, together, they chopped, mixed, marinaded, rolled, filled, assembled, baked and wrapped. And, at the end of that time, Fran's long kitchen table was covered with an assortment of temptations. Mini fishcakes with their sweet chilli sauce sat next to baby chicken Caesar wraps. Assorted sandwiches nestled against bruschetta, mini quiches, and sausage rolls, while tiny scones huddled alongside fresh fruit tartlets, cupcakes and sinfully wicked miniature chocolate tortes.

Fran straightened her aching back and grinned at Adam, who still had his finger in the mixing bowl that once held chocolate, but which they had long since finished with. He had been more than conscientious, listening to her instructions carefully and carrying them out to the letter. Importantly, he hadn't tried to eat anything either and, given that she had warned him against the perils of spoon licking the very first time she met him, he hadn't put a foot, or finger wrong. Even so, there was a point midway when she thought they would never get finished, and then, miraculously, it had all come together.

Adam gave a low whistle. 'This lot looks amazing... and you do this every day?'

'Not every day. Some days it's just baking, or cooking for a dinner party. Bigger events are rarer, and I usually make sure I have plenty of time to do everything I need to. Not like today... and believe it or not, this is only a smallish job.' She took in the slight drop in his expression. 'And I couldn't have done it without you, so don't you go thinking that my lack of time had anything to do with you being here today.'

Adam was still staring at the mountain of food on the table.

'Would you like something to eat before we go and deliver this lot? I can rustle up some beans on toast or something?' Fran smiled, hoping to jog him out of his reverie.

His eyes flicked up to hers. 'I was just thinking... about how you would poison someone. All this food and you think it would be easy, wouldn't you? But how would you ensure that you poisoned the person you intended, without everyone else getting sick too?'

'How indeed? Particularly given that most poisons have a very strong taste... not so easy to hide at all.' She looked back at the table. 'And a party, or some other gathering, would make it virtually impossible, I would have thought. If it was intentional, that is. Unintentionally poisoning people is much easier. Although, seeing as we're just about to deliver this lot to my customers, perhaps we could change the subject.'

Adam caught her eye. 'Oh yes, sorry. I wasn't suggesting that... What do those mushrooms taste like then?' he asked. 'Would Becky have been able to tell?'

Fran shook her head. 'They taste lovely, apparently.

According to the very few people who've taken them and lived to tell the tale, they're slightly sweet, with a faint honey flavour. Why, what are you thinking?'

'I'm not sure yet. And do they have to be eaten raw?'

'No, that's one of the most insidious things about them. Nothing you do to them makes them any less deadly. Cooking, freezing, even drying them makes no difference to their potency.'

'And would Becky have had to eat them on the day she first reported symptoms?'

Fran considered his question for a moment, matching it against what she knew. 'Not necessarily. Stomach pains would have come first, or sickness, just like any other case of food poisoning, but it can happen between six and twenty-four hours after ingestion. So it's possible that Becky could have eaten something in the night, or at a push, the previous evening. Are you thinking what I'm thinking?'

Adam nodded. 'That, at the moment, our two most likely suspects are Lois and Diane. And yet we have no idea what they were doing during that window of time the night before Becky was taken ill.'

Fran checked her watch. 'Come on, let's get this lot delivered and then we can decide what to do next.'

Adam's stomach gave an audible growl. 'Will that include the beans on toast?' he asked.

IT WAS late afternoon by the time they got back, and Fran's daughter was obviously home from school. It looked as if the kitchen had been raided; cupboard doors open, a pot of marmite on the side with the lid off, squash on the table and the bread board abandoned by the sink, a sticky knife clinging to it. A mug and a glass holding the dregs of what looked like milkshake completed the look. Fran sighed and rolled her eyes at Adam.

'As you can see, I am well used to catering for hungry people. If Martha has friends over, it's like a swarm of locusts in here some days.' She automatically closed the cupboard door and began to collect the dirty things together for washing. 'So, still beans on toast, is it?'

Adam cleared his throat, looking rather nervously about him. 'I can have something at home,' he said. 'Honestly, I should get going.'

Fran raised her eyebrows. 'Martha will be long gone, don't worry. Once she's eaten, she beats a retreat to her room until it's time to eat again.' She smiled. 'And, despite her usual ravenous disposition, she won't eat *you*.'

She was about to fetch a tin of beans from the pantry when the back door slammed and the sound of giggling could be heard. Seconds later, two teenage girls in school uniform stopped dead in the doorway, faces frozen in horror. They looked from Fran to Adam, back to Fran again and were on the point of doing an about turn when Fran stopped them.

'Hi, Martha, hi, Louise. More rehearsals, is it?'

'Hi, Mrs Eve,' said the slightly taller of the two girls, blushing furiously. 'We've just been in the garden.' Her arm lifted in a graceful gesture that Fran knew was an illustration of the dance they'd been practising, but just as suddenly, she withdrew it and clamped it to her side.

'Good,' said Fran brightly. 'How's it going?' She looked at her daughter, who was desperately trying to edge backwards out of the room.

''S'okay... I suppose. But we're going to do our homework now. Can Lou stay for tea?'

Fran smiled. 'Sure. Just spaghetti bolognese, is that okay?'

Both girls nodded and would have quickly escaped, had she not deliberately turned to Adam to beckon him forward. He shot her a glance that might have felled a lesser mortal.

'Adam, this is my daughter, Martha, and her friend Louise,

who are both talented ballerinas and very soon to star in their dance school's spring show. And, girls, this is Adam who—' She had no idea how to introduce him. 'Who is the son of a lady I catered a party for a little while ago. He's on work experience with me for a few weeks.' She turned her head away slightly so she couldn't see Adam's face.

Murmured responses were made by all parties and seconds later there were just the two of them again.

'I know,' she whispered loudly, tutting at his expression. 'I couldn't think of what else to say.'

'But *work experience*? You made me sound like a fifteen-year-old. Couldn't you have come up with something better than that?'

'Evidently not,' replied Fran, grinning at his discomfort.

Adam groaned.

'Would you like to stay for tea as well?' She couldn't help herself.

'No, I bloody would not,' he huffed. 'And they were just as embarrassed.'

'Probably,' agreed Fran airily. 'But you wait until you're a parent. Embarrassing your children is one of the few pleasures you get.' She took in the startled look on his face. 'That was a joke, by the way. Right, listen, am I making you beans on toast or what are we doing?'

She could see the tussle on Adam's face. The desire to scuttle back to his place of safety, contrasted with the needs of his stomach, which had already growled several times.

'I'd better be going,' he said, looking pointedly at his watch. 'You've got things to do and... Anyway, thanks for the ice cream this morning and the... chat.' He grinned. 'And the work experience, actually. I enjoyed it.'

'Well, you were a very good pupil,' she said, smiling warmly. 'You can come help any time.' She walked him to the door. 'I might come and have a chat with your mum later if she's around. I think we need to find out what everyone was doing on the day before Becky was taken ill, and I'm hoping Sara might be able to help me. I'll call you in the morning, shall I?'

AFTER DINNER THAT EVENING, Fran found herself back in Sara's capacious kitchen, sipping a glass of wine. Or at least Sara was. Fran was driving and so had opted for some sparkling apple juice instead. She'd thought long and hard whether to tell Sara what they'd discovered about Becky – that not only were they sure she'd been blackmailing people, but that she'd used the murder-mystery game to give her 'victims' the first warning. But the truth of it was that they still needed to find the means and opportunity for whoever had killed Becky and for that, Fran really needed Sara's help; she knew these women better than anyone.

'I can't believe it,' said Sara, staring into her glass. 'They're my friends, we've known each other for years. But from what you say, they've all been hiding a secret, and not just some little white lie, but a whopping big one. So, in all likelihood, if Becky was blackmailing Camilla, she was blackmailing the others too.' She looked at Fran from under her lashes. 'So why not me? You must be wondering?'

Fran held her look. 'Becky had known about Adam's dad for a while, and could have feasibly broken your confidence at any time over the last five years or so. To wait until now before threatening to spill the beans doesn't make much sense. It would have made more sense had you still been with Ben – he could have been the thing you stood to lose, but now? There's Adam, of course, but apart from a wish not to have your private business discussed I can't see why you would need to take action to prevent it from becoming common knowledge. I could be wrong, of course.'

Sara dipped her head, a wry smile on her face.

'Perhaps I gave Becky the idea?' she suggested. 'Perhaps when she learned that one of the others had something to hide she thought about me and realised the power that knowledge can give you over another person.'

Fran sighed. 'And you're certain that no one else knew about Ben and Adam?'

'No. Why would they?' She thought for a moment. 'I guess we're all very good about keeping things close to our chest, aren't we?'

'It would certainly seem that way,' replied Fran. 'Human nature, I suppose. Life's complicated – relationships are complicated – and often we hide the truth simply because we're scared of the changes that truth might bring. It's often done with the best of intentions, but then the truth has to be hidden with a lie, just a small one to start with, and you tell yourself one won't matter, but before too long the lies have grown bigger and bigger and there's seemingly no way out.'

'Please don't tell me what anyone else has done,' said Sara. 'I don't want to know. It's bad enough that you've found out these things, but what's worse is that it probably means one of my friends is a—' She broke off, unable to say the word, and took a huge gulp of wine.

Fran lifted her glass thoughtfully. 'Have you spoken to Nick again?'

'Only briefly,' replied Sara. 'The poor man is beside himself. The police have asked him lots of questions, but as yet they haven't taken anything further. But I guess that's only because—'

'As far as they're aware, there's no motive for murder.' Fran nodded. 'And we need to keep it that way for as long as we can. Have they asked anything about the party yet?'

Sara shook her head. 'No, he didn't mention anything, so I don't think so. Nick just said they wanted to know what he was doing in the hours before Becky was first taken ill.'

Fran pricked up her ears. 'I don't suppose he told you, did he?'

Sara gave a surreptitious smile. 'I asked him, actually. Said that I struggle to remember what I've been doing a *week* ago, never mind nearly a month, which is the truth. It must be next to impossible to provide an alibi, despite how easily it seems to happen on the television.'

Fran nodded. 'Yeah, I've often wondered that. So what did Nick say?'

'That he'd had to check his diary to find out where he was. It made me realise how much time had elapsed between Becky first becoming ill and when she died. It was almost two weeks, Fran. Horrible.' She gave a shudder. 'And I can only remember that first day she became ill because it was Adam's birthday, the ninth of April, a Friday. We'd been out for a pizza and I messaged Becky some time that night – which is when she replied, saying she felt dreadful and thought she had food poisoning. But Nick had been at work all day, same as usual, so there was nothing out of the ordinary.'

'And Becky became ill in the evening?'

'Yes, sometime after tea. But she and Nick had eaten the same thing, which is why he thought it odd. If it was food poisoning, wouldn't he have become ill as well? I think that was why Becky changed her mind, convincing herself she'd caught a bug from school.'

'And she'd been to work as usual?'

'The day before, yes. She doesn't work Fridays.'

'Doesn't she?' Fran thought for a moment. 'That's interesting. It can take up to twenty-four hours for symptoms to show after eating the mushrooms, so it's very unlikely that her evening meal was the culprit anyway.'

'I wondered why the police were asking Nick about the day before.'

'Hmm...' Fran's eyes narrowed. 'It's more likely that Becky

was poisoned much earlier in the day on Friday, or even the
night before.'

Sara's hand flew to her neck, a movement she tried to hide
by tucking her hair behind her ears.

'You've thought of something,' stated Fran.

Anxiety filled Sara's eyes. 'This is awful, speculating about
everyone...'

'But?'

There was a slight pause. 'I got the jitters after I'd spoken to
Nick. I realised that the police were quite likely going to ask us
all to provide alibis. And, like I said, it isn't so easy to remember
what you were doing weeks ago. So when Lois rang to see how
Nick was, I said the same thing to her, that I was struggling to
pinpoint what I'd been doing. I didn't make it sound like I was
fishing for information, more that I was sharing my anxiety. Lois
agreed with me, but she also happily told me where she'd been.'
Sara put down her wine glass and leaned forward. 'She was
babysitting for her sister on the Thursday night but, Fran, Lois
met Becky for a coffee on Friday lunchtime. She almost
dismissed it though – I think, like me, she assumed that when
Becky got sick it was because of something she ate much later in
the day.' She held Fran's look. 'I hope I haven't made her
anxious.'

Or wary, thought Fran, biting back an expletive. But it
wasn't Sara's fault, she was only trying to help. It was herself
she was angry with; she should have followed up these things
sooner.

'I don't suppose you also checked with Diane, did you?'

Sara nodded, looking relieved at being able to redeem
herself. 'I did, actually. But Diane was at work on Friday and
out the night before with her husband. Some posh work do;
they're always entertaining, it's a requirement of his job.'

Oh no it isn't...

'Okay, well, that rules that out,' she replied, playing along. 'And what about Nick? What was Nick doing on the Thursday night?'

'Nothing. Just at home, watching TV. Although he did say that Becky went out to a wine bar with one of her friends, but he can't remember who. She didn't get back until late.' Sara smiled as if thinking of memories. 'Becky was a very social person, she often met up with girlfriends.'

Fran felt a growing sense of horror. That trip out may well have been the one when she was poisoned.

Almost immediately Sara's face fell. 'Oh God. Do you think that was when... when it happened?'

'It sounds quite likely,' agreed Fran quietly. 'Is there any way we could check who Becky met that evening? Would she have a diary or something?'

'I think Nick has probably checked. But I know it wasn't Camilla, because I spoke to her too and she goes to a yoga class on Thursday evening. I know which one, so that would be easy enough to confirm.'

Fran nodded. 'Can you let me have the details and I'll follow it up.' Sara was right, they ought to get that detail confirmed. Camilla's story certainly didn't point to her being the culprit, but Fran couldn't rule her out. Just as she couldn't rule out Sara either.

'Other than that, Becky could have had dinner with any one of a number of people – maybe Ronnie, they've been friends for years. That's true of a lot of people, though.' Sara bit her lip, lifting her glass and savouring another mouthful of wine.

'And it wasn't you either?' Fran pulled a face. 'Sorry, Sara, but I have to ask.' Fran already knew the answer, of course. If Sara had had an alibi for that night, Adam would have certainly mentioned it by now; it would have been one of the first things to cross his mind.

Sara shook her head. 'No, it wasn't me, and I was here the night before Becky was taken ill, ostensibly on my own. Adam was here but we, well, he was in his room and I'm not sure I would have seen him during the evening. We don't always. I could ask Adam now if you like? See if he remembers anything. He'll just be up in his room.'

Fran smiled. 'I'll check with him another time,' she said. 'I'm more interested in finding out who Becky had dinner with first. What about the Friday though? Can you remember what you were doing then?'

'I was working during the day, except that I mainly work from home so could have easily popped out. I didn't, but... apart from at two, when I had a meeting with a client. I could show you my diary... although I guess that doesn't prove anything, but you could always check with them.'

Fran smiled. 'Sara, don't worry, that's plenty to be going on with. Listen, I'd better get back or the family will think I've gone AWOL, but thanks for the drink and the catch-up. I'll let you know if I find anything, and if you hear any more from Nick, just ring or message me.' She stood up and carried her glass over to the sink.

She was about to collect her handbag and car keys ready to leave when another thought came to her. 'It's just occurred to me that if we can't find out which friend Becky met up with, we might be able to check with whichever venue they went to. I don't suppose you know where she would have gone?'

'There are a few places we go to – The Armoury by the river, or Number Four mostly. Bistro Jacques sometimes too, and Côte.' She smiled. 'Everyone likes French food, although Becky always complained because she is – was – very careful about her weight and their food isn't exactly low in calories. She might have gone to Libertines as well, it's a cocktail bar.'

'Yes, I know it. Okay... Thanks, Sara.'

She let Sara walk her to the door, already thinking of what their next step was going to be. Because one thing was certain: the night before Becky became ill, Diane was not out at some posh do with her husband, and Fran intended to find out where she'd really been.

15

It was Fran's favourite time of day, and week – early morning on a Saturday, when it was just her, a mug of tea and silence. The rest of the house wasn't up yet, and she was alone with her thoughts, drinking in the peace, feeling restful and relaxed. It was when she did a lot of her best thinking, making plans for the week ahead, or pondering whatever problems might need solving. And this morning it was especially welcome; her head felt as if it had been through the spin cycle, and she wondered when life had become so complicated.

Just over a week ago, her days had consisted of the usual juggling act between running a business and being a wife and mother, but they had also been comfortable, safe and, although far from dull, there had been an ordinariness to them which had grown out of years of familiarity. Now though, everything felt as if it had been torn up into tiny pieces, held on the palm of a hand and lifted to the wind, leaving her frantically scrambling to collect the scattered pieces. Not only were there more thoughts in her head than she could seemingly hold, they were disturbing ones too.

Murder wasn't something which happened in ordinary, everyday life, it was the stuff of films, and books, where reality was suspended and— Her thoughts came to an abrupt halt. Because this *was* reality, you only had to listen to the news or read the newspapers to know that murders happened all the time. Lives *were* taken, and families *were* destroyed... and there was no doubt in her mind that this was what had happened to Becky. But the deeper she and Adam delved, the more they were exposed to the very much darker side of human nature. Hatred, betrayal, jealousy... none of these things had ever played a part in Fran's life before, but now, as she picked her way through motives and opportunities, and discovered secrets and hidden desires, she could feel the black shadow of them clinging to her.

She gave an involuntary shiver and drank deeply from her mug, looking around her cheerful and sunlit kitchen. However *she* was feeling about events, for some people it was infinitely worse. She narrowed her eyes, feeling resolve pushing away doubt. Becky Pearson had died in agony, knowing that there was no way through her pain, no happy ending. It was the worst possible death, and if Fran could play a part, even a tiny one, in catching the person responsible, then she would give it all she had. Becky may have been a blackmailer – the easy-going friend who everyone supposedly loved, may not have been a very nice person at all – but she still didn't deserve to die the way she had.

Fran drained the last of her tea and, hearing Jack's footsteps on the stairs, got up to re-boil the kettle. It was time to think about the day ahead.

Jack appeared, bleary-eyed, hair sticking up on end, and wearing his customary nightwear – a tee shirt and boxers. Saturday mornings usually meant a very lazy start, for everyone else at least, Fran was usually working. But, *unusually*, she had no jobs on this weekend and the day stretched ahead of her. She flicked the switch on the kettle and slid inside Jack's arms as he crossed the room.

'Morning,' she murmured, grateful for his solid warmth.

This was her second-best time of the day, on a weekend at least. The chance to catch up with her husband, released from the routines that weekdays dictated and snatched moments of time which was all they seemed to have.

He pulled her closer and pressed his lips against her hair. 'I wondered if you might be trading me in for a younger model,' he said.

She pulled back, giving him a puzzled look.

'The young man who was here yesterday,' he clarified. 'The one who made such an impression on Martha and her friend. Fairly swooning, they were.'

She smiled. 'When was that?'

'At tea. You missed them talking about him, I think, it was when you went to answer the phone.'

'Oh... *Adam.*' She lay her head back on Jack's chest for a moment. 'He's the son of a woman I catered a party for a few weeks ago.' She looked up, pulling a face. 'He wants to train as a chef,' she added. 'Or rather, he thinks he does. He isn't sure. She asked me if I could have him for a couple of weeks, on a work experience type thing, to see if he likes it. It's kind of a favour as she has the potential to be a very good customer, but I have a feeling I might live to regret saying yes.' She thought for a moment. 'Although he was pretty good yesterday, worked hard and listens at least.'

'And very good-looking by all accounts...'

'Is he?' Fran poked Jack's chest. 'He's twenty-three... and makes me feel incredibly old.' She smiled at the very obvious differences between her and Adam. 'But I'll see how it goes. At least it makes a change to have someone to talk to when I'm working.' She kissed the end of Jack's nose, pulling away, partly to make the tea and partly to hide her expression. She hated lying to him. She didn't think she had ever done so, not in the entire time they had been married. 'Are you cycling today?'

Jack stretched his arms in the air, groaning, as if his muscles were stiff. 'When I wake up, yeah. Is that okay?'

'Of course. I've got the shopping to do this morning anyway, and Martha will amuse herself. Once she's got up, that is.' Fran took down another mug from the cupboard. 'Actually, I... Never mind.' It had been on the tip of her tongue to tell Jack what her other plans for the morning were, besides the shopping. Should she tell him? The lie about Adam and who he was had tripped so easily from her tongue – the thought was disquieting. Lying was a slippery slope, she was more aware of that now than ever, but could she really tell Jack what was going on? She wouldn't even know where to start.

She turned to see his quizzical look. 'I thought I might try a different supermarket this morning, that's all.' She grinned, rolling her eyes. 'Which is probably a thought I should keep to myself. I just get a bit bored of the same old stuff, thought I might mix things up a bit, you know, buy some different-shaped pasta, cheese in a different coloured wrapper, the possibilities are endless.'

Jack's eyes twinkled in reply. 'I'm so happy for you,' he replied, heading for the biscuit tin.

IT WASN'T A COMPLETE LIE. She *was* trying out a different supermarket, in a different part of the town, but not because she had a yearning for as yet undiscovered grocery brands, but because she needed to speak to Lois, and Sara had just happened to mention where Lois shopped every Saturday morning.

Fran pulled into the car park, eyes scanning the rows for a bright-red Mini. It was still early, so there was every possibility that Lois hadn't yet arrived, which was exactly what Fran was hoping. Satisfied that there was no sign of her, Fran pulled into a free space near the entrance and, switching off her ignition, settled back to wait.

It took forty minutes, and two false alarms, but eventually the correct red Mini drove past and Fran got out of her car, heading for the supermarket entrance. It wouldn't do to arrive exactly at the same time as Lois.

They met in the chilled food aisle, Fran 'accidentally' reaching for some milk at exactly the same time as Lois. She turned, smiled, apologised and then, eyes wide, said, 'Oh... hi...' Followed by a frown. 'I know you, don't I?' she added, peering into Lois's startled face.

'I work at the school, so maybe.' Lois put the milk into her trolley, giving Fran a polite but uninterested smile.

'No, it's not that, it's...' Fran waggled her fingers and then took in a sharp breath. She flashed a look behind her. 'I know what it is. You're a friend of Becky's, aren't you? I catered for the party Sara gave, the murder-mystery party.' She delivered the last words in a stage whisper. 'God, it's awful, isn't it? Poor Nick is so worried, and I can't say I blame him.'

Lois frowned. 'Yes, I remember, but I'm not sure... I didn't know you knew Becky too.'

'Oh, I didn't, not really. I'm a friend of Nick's, actually. But...' She leaned in a little closer. 'You wouldn't have ten minutes, would you, when you've finished your shopping?'

A wary expression crossed Lois's face. 'I'm not sure, I—'

'Only you might be able to help me with something. Well, help Nick. He's going out of his mind with worry, and when I think about what happened to Becky...' She put a hand to her cheek. 'Please, I really am worried about him. He's said some things about Becky which... I can't say here. I could meet you in the coffee shop?' Fran checked her watch. 'At eleven? Will you have finished your shopping by then?' She smiled brightly. 'Oh, you're a star, thank you so much,' she finished, giving Lois no chance to reply.

She turned away, heading purposefully for the yoghurt without so much as a backward glance. She had no idea what Lois would do, but she was desperately hoping that curiosity would get the better of her. After all, if she did have a hand in Becky's death then it could be in her interests to find out what Nick might have had to say about his wife. She'd be desperate for news of any investigation into the death, or indeed if anyone else was under suspicion. And if she wasn't guilty of anything, barring adultery, of course, then she would be keen to help out a friend, wouldn't she?

Fran hurried from aisle to aisle, collecting what she needed and now cursing the unfamiliar layout of the store, but by eleven, she was almost done. She joined the queue at one of the checkouts, noticing that Lois was a little ahead of her, further down. She kept her eyes turned away and prayed the line would move quickly.

Once she'd paid, to her relief, she found Lois waiting for her at the end of the row of checkouts and together they walked to the coffee shop tucked in one corner of the supermarket. It was heaving with people, which was exactly how Fran wanted it; much less chance of them being overheard. She had wondered whether she should try to provoke Lois, mentioning the murder mystery and intimating that it was Nick who thought this might have had something to do with his wife's death. She was very curious to see what Lois's reaction would be. But, even though they were in a very public place, given what had happened when Fran had confronted Camilla, she decided against it. She wouldn't always be in a public place, after all...

By the time they had bought their drinks, there were only a couple of vacant seats left, wedged in a corner, but Fran didn't mind. The tight space meant she had to wait a few moments for Lois to manoeuvre herself into position before taking her own seat, moments where Fran could observe Lois completely unnoticed. Aside from seeming a little wary, however, which was only as Fran expected, Lois didn't appear particularly anxious at the prospect of talking about Becky's death.

Fran readied a smile, a warm, sympathetic and concerned smile that let Lois know just how much Fran was on her side.

'It's horrible, isn't it, all this?' she began. 'I didn't know Becky all that well, as I said I'm a friend of Nick's, but...' She shook her head a little.

'I just can't believe she's gone,' replied Lois, her voice tinged with the hint of longing that only the recently bereaved have. 'I've known Becky a long time, since she started at the school. We hit it off straight away and have been friends ever since. That's not hard if you know Becky though.'

Fran sucked in a deep breath. 'Nick's beside himself as you'd imagine. Blaming himself when I'm not sure what else he could have done. And now the police are involved... I know they have a job to do but, honestly, how ridiculous. Have you heard what they've been saying?'

Lois shook her head. 'Not directly, but Sara's mentioned a few things. I can guess, though. It doesn't take a genius to work out that he'll be top of the suspect list. I'm not sure which is worse, thinking someone killed Becky or that she killed herself, which, if you knew her, is the most ridiculous thing I ever heard. She was made up at the prospect of fostering kids, and she would have been bloody good at it too; she was a brilliant teacher. Why couldn't her death have been a plain accident? That's what I'd like to know. I know it might seem unlikely, but these things happen.'

Fran watched Lois's expression carefully, but there was nothing that spoke of anything beyond sadness at losing a friend. 'You're right,' she replied. 'Which is exactly what I've said. If we knew what Becky was doing on the day she became ill, or even on the day before, then it would probably be obvious what happened. Nick was at work, so he has no idea, but that's why, when I saw you, I wondered if you might be able to help fill in some of the blanks.' She smiled again. 'But I'm sorry for hijacking your morning.'

Lois blew across the froth on top of her coffee. 'It's no problem, honestly. I'm happy to help if I can. I was speaking about this to Sara, actually, just the other day. It's really difficult to remember what you were doing that length of time ago.' She straightened her head slightly and tucked her hair back behind her ears. Immediately her eyes returned to Fran's. 'I saw her at work on Thursday as usual, but the evening I can't help with, I'm afraid, I was babysitting for my sister. But I did meet Becky for a coffee Friday lunchtime, she doesn't work on a Friday – you might already know that – so it's something we often do. But, sadly, we got talking about work, *again*, and, as far as I can remember, she didn't say anything about where else she'd been, or was going. I hadn't seen much of her that week, even at school. It was exam time and the teachers were all frantically busy.'

Fran nodded, almost transfixed by Lois as she talked. It was something she'd noticed at the party, that Lois had a way of drawing you in as she spoke. She was incredibly attractive, with her striking red hair, luminous skin and bright-blue eyes, but it was this last aspect of her which was so affecting. Because Lois's eyes never left Fran's the whole time she was speaking.

'Do you know what time that would have been?' Fran asked.

'Yes, just before twelve. I go to the bank on a Friday morning, you see, on behalf of the school, so I'm already in town, that's why Becky and I meet. I go around half past eleven, take care of school business and then take an early lunch.'

'And do you always go to the same place?'

'Pretty much, unless for some reason Gingers is really busy

and then we sometimes go to Poppys. But the coffee is better at Gingers, so it's usually there.'

'So, from what time, around twelve…?' She waited for Lois to nod. 'Until…?'

'About a quarter to one. It takes me ten minutes to get back to school and I only have an hour.'

Fran drank a mouthful of her coffee, grimacing, it was scalding hot. 'I see.' She paused for a moment. 'This is really awkward, and I hate to ask, but is there any way that Becky could have eaten the mushrooms at Gingers? You obviously know the place well, so presumably you trust the food, but I'm trying to think if somehow there might have been a mix-up in the kitchen or…' She fell silent, hoping that Lois would fill in the gap.

'No, because Becky didn't have anything to eat, she rarely did.' Lois made a slight moue. 'I usually had a slab of cake, which Becky would moan about because she'd want one too, only she'd have been for a run in the morning and wouldn't want to ruin her good work. She was a bit of a health nut. I think it started when she and Nick were trying for a baby and she wanted to get herself into the best possible shape to see if that made a difference. But then it stuck and it just became the way she was.'

Fran could feel her heart sinking. If Lois was telling the truth, it dashed the possibility that Friday lunchtime had been when Becky consumed the fatal mushrooms.

'So, as far as you know, after you left the coffee shop, Becky went home and, assuming she walked into town, she would have arrived back by about one o'clock.'

Lois nodded. 'I didn't think to ask what she had planned for the afternoon, sorry.' She looked straight into Fran's eyes. 'I really wish I had.'

Fran gave her a sympathetic smile. 'That's been really helpful though, thank you. It might have only accounted for a part of the time, but it also means that there are still plenty of hours left where we *don't* yet know what Becky was doing.'

'Have you spoken to anyone else?' asked Lois. 'There's Sara, of course, and Camilla and Diane who were at the party with us; they might be able to help. I'm just trying to think who else...' She pressed her lips together. 'Veronica or Lynn? Although I'm pretty certain they would have been at work too. I can give you their numbers, if you like? I'm sure they won't mind.' She pulled her phone from her bag and Fran smiled in agreement. Lois didn't need to know she already had most of them.

Fran copied down the numbers as Lois read them out, before taking a cautious sip of coffee. She pulled a face.

'It's not very good, is it?' said Lois. 'I'm a bit of a coffee snob, I'm afraid, and...'

Fran smiled. 'Perhaps I should try out Gingers myself. I've never been there.'

'Oh, you definitely should. I can recommend the white chocolate and raspberry blondies.' She gave her watch a quick check. 'Do you really think someone might have killed Becky?' she asked, leaning forward and keeping her voice low.

Fran sighed. 'I don't know, but it seems so... stupid. I can't understand why anyone would want to hurt her.'

'That's what I can't get my head around,' agreed Lois. 'Everyone loved Becky. And she was always so happy, looked on the bright side of everything. She had her troubles, same as everyone else, but she never let them get to her. I'm sure I'd have known if something was wrong. If she was frightened or...' She lifted her hands helplessly. 'I don't know.'

'That's what Nick said. Everything had seemed fine and Becky didn't seem any different from usual...' Fran broke off as if trying to work out whether to mention something or not. 'Only one horrible thing... when Becky was in hospital, she mentioned that the whole thing with the party game was a bit spooky, pretending to die like that. She said it was a bad omen or something.'

Lois shuddered. 'Oh, don't,' she said. 'That's too horrible.' She took another mouthful of coffee, only to push it away. 'I should get going really.'

'Yes, me too.' Fran reached a tentative hand towards Lois. 'Thanks for this,' she said. 'I hope I haven't upset you.'

Lois smiled. 'It's hard for everyone,' she said. 'But next time you see Nick, please tell him how much we're all thinking of him. I don't believe that man killed his wife for one minute, but if somebody did, I hope you find them.'

FRAN SAT in her car for quite a few minutes after loading her shopping into the boot. Apart from the fact that she had learned nothing new, and was no further forward in their investigation, something else had become very apparent. Because the whole time she had been speaking to Lois, Fran never once felt that she was lying or trying to misdirect her. In fact, the complete opposite was true; Fran was now having real problems considering that Lois could have been involved at all.

There was something about Lois that was incredibly compelling, but only in a good way. That she never broke eye contact was perhaps a little unusual, but not only did this mean she gave Fran her absolute and undivided attention, it also left Lois with no space in which to hide, or to cover up her feelings. She had openly admitted to seeing Becky on the fateful day with no trace of guile, just a sadness at the last memory she had of her friend when she was happy and well. How could she have spoken like that if she had anything to hide? The fact that she had seemingly implicated herself never even occurred to her, she was simply trying to help. It would take a very clever and skilful actor to pull off that kind of bluff. Not to mention the kind of person you would need to be to do it.

And yet...

Lois was supposedly a happily married woman, the epitome of domesticity, a doting wife and mother, and yet Fran had seen clear evidence to the contrary.

So where did that leave her now?

Could Lois really be that good a liar?

16

'I think we should split up,' said Fran. 'Take three places each and see what we come up with.'

It was Monday lunchtime and she and Adam were standing in the middle of a car park in Shrewsbury planning the next stage of their investigation, namely how to determine which of the friends had met Becky for a meal the night before she was taken ill.

Fran groaned. 'I'm so confused. Before I spoke to Lois I was convinced she would be defensive about her movements or even try to hide them altogether, conjuring up some other alibi and denying that she'd been anywhere near Becky. Except she wasn't like that at all and I ended the conversation with my opinion completely reversed. I'm now convinced that Lois *didn't* kill Becky. I think she probably *is* guilty of having an affair, and that would certainly give her motive for murder if Becky were blackmailing her, but my instincts are telling me she didn't do it. I still think I'm missing something though. That I've heard or seen something important without realising how significant it is.'

Adam scratched his eyebrow. 'We seem to be eliminating suspects though. That has to be a good thing, doesn't it?'

He was looking at her with a hopeful expression on his face and she wished she could share his enthusiasm. The more she thought about this whole matter, the more something felt off.

'Agreed. Let's see what today brings. We're looking to see if anyone had a reservation for Becky on the eighth of April or remembers anyone fitting her description. Then we find out who she was with.'

Adam took a deep breath. 'Okay,' he said. 'I'll do my best. But what if no one wants to talk to me?'

'You'll be fine,' she replied, smiling. 'You're a potential customer, don't forget. Of course they'll want to talk to you.'

Her eyes darted to his head, just as he slid off his beanie with a grin.

THEY HAD TIMED their arrival to coincide with the start of lunchtime, hoping that places would be open, but not so busy that they couldn't stop to help with their enquiries. Fran had decided to start with the smallest place first, reasoning that there was more chance of Becky being remembered. Her hopes were dashed within the first five minutes, however, when she was met with a point-blank refusal to provide any information. The rebuttal wasn't all that polite either and she saw little point in pursuing her request. There were still, as yet, a reasonable number of fish left in the sea.

She quickly texted Adam and began walking to the next restaurant on her list, a wine bar that she knew was popular of an evening. At lunchtime, however, it was more of a tea-room, and this wouldn't necessarily have been a problem if the place didn't have two managers; one for the day shift and one for the evening. The staff were often different too, she was informed, albeit politely and with profuse apologies.

'But you do keep records of your reservations?' she asked, hoping that there might still be some merit in pursuing things, even if it was at a later time.

The young man on the door smiled at her. 'What day did you say it was for?' he asked.

'A Thursday, in April, about a month ago?'

But she could see from his face that her enquiry was going nowhere after all.

'She might not even have booked,' he replied. 'People don't always. On Friday nights, or at the weekend, perhaps, but we're not so busy on Thursdays. And in any case I doubt we have records back that far, I'm not sure we're allowed to keep them.'

Fran smiled. 'Okay, thanks.' She moved aside to make way for two women who were both clutching multiple bags. *Ladies what lunch*, Fran thought, perhaps uncharitably, but her mood was rapidly deteriorating.

By the time she approached The Armoury, her heart was almost in her boots and she sighed audibly as she saw how busy it was. With a prime position alongside the river, the outside tables were always popular and, on a warm day like today, there wasn't a single one free. She trudged inside, waiting a moment for her eyes to acclimatise to the change in light. Here, at least, there were unoccupied tables and she wandered through the room to one at the back in front of a large arched window. She sank into a seat and pulled out her phone to text Adam.

At The Armoury. Come and join me when you're done. There's pudding.

Fran had only ever been here once before but, as she looked around, she wondered why that was. It was the type of place she liked, admittedly playing easily into the hands of its age and heritage, but it also had a cluttered, lived-in look that made her feel relaxed. Too many places went for the slick, glossy vibe, all glass and shining metal, that might be fashionable but put her on edge for some reason. It had been some while since she might have been considered a 'bright young thing', but here she could be a middle-aged, slightly crumpled, often looks tired, but we don't mind, type of customer. There was even a huge floor-to-ceiling bookcase that hugged one whole corner of the room, making her feel instantly at home. There was plenty of space, plenty of laughter too, and a reassuring hum of conversation. She picked up the menu from the table and smiled when she saw the dessert list. That would do nicely.

She was already midway down her first cup of tea when Adam arrived, looking considerably brighter than she felt. She raised an arm and, spotting her, he hurried over.

'I've got an interview,' he said, sitting down. 'For the games company.'

Fran had forgotten he had even applied. 'Blimey, that was quick.'

He grinned. 'I know. And it's on Wednesday. At their head office.'

Fran thought back to when they'd checked out the company online. 'Isn't that in Bradford...?'

'Yep.'

'But that's—'

'A town in the eastern foothills of the Pennines, once famous for its manufacture of wool.' He grinned again. 'In fact, so much so that it was nicknamed Woolopolis. It now has a population of about 350,000 people and, more importantly, is about a two-and-a-half-hour drive away.'

'Well, that is good news. What time do you have to be there?' She was already doing the calculation in her head.

'My interview is at two,' he replied, pulling a face. 'Which is irritating because it might mean I have to hang around for ages afterwards.'

Fran frowned. 'Sorry, why will you need to do that?'

'Well, because if I can't find out what I need to while I'm there for my interview, I'll have to go back later on.'

Fran nodded and was about to ask something else when she checked herself. 'What do you mean, go back later on?'

'When they're shut. After hours.'

'As in...?' Fran hardly dared ask.

'I think the legal terminology would be breaking and entering, yes.'

She darted a look around them. 'Keep your voice down,' she whispered. 'Adam, you can't do that, that's—'

'One way of finding out exactly what Becky had been up to.'

'Yes, but it's also illegal. You can't do that.'

His face fell. 'Oh... that's a shame.'

She raised an eyebrow.

'Only I was hoping you might help me.'

Fran stared at him. 'I can't do that, I... And you shouldn't be thinking about it, either.'

'Why not? They probably won't even know I've been there.'

'Adam, that's not the point! Look...' She lowered her voice again. 'Let's talk about this later. How did you get on just now? Did you find out anything?'

'Nope.' He checked his phone. 'I've been to everywhere you said: Number Four, Côte and Spoons. No joy at any of them.'

'That's what I found too. Didn't keep details or Becky wouldn't have booked, both Libertines and Bistro Jacques said that. I even called into The Granary as well because I know it's popular. Nothing. No one even asked for a description of her, so...' She shrugged. 'They do a special deal here, look.' She tapped the menu. 'A drink and a pudding. Sounds perfect for you. We might as well, otherwise it will be a completely wasted trip.'

'What did they say here?' asked Adam, looking up from the card in front of him.

'I haven't bothered asking. This place gets busy, I can't see us having any luck.'

Even so, when they placed their order a minute or so later, Fran asked to see the manager.

'There's nothing wrong,' she reassured the waitress. 'I'm just looking for some information and wondered if they could help.'

The waitress smiled. 'Sure.' She looked around her and then headed towards a woman who was standing at a nearby table talking with its occupants. Fran watched as she spoke with the woman, dipping her head towards their table as she did so.

To Fran's surprise, instead of the look of resignation or irritation she expected to see, the woman looked up, smiled and gave a wave of greeting with her hand. Moments later, she was by their side.

'Hi, I'm Jenna,' she said. 'Can I help you with anything?'

'I'm hoping so.' Fran paused, wondering, yet again, how best to explain. 'We're trying to find out if a friend of ours was here, a few weeks ago,' she began. 'It's really important.'

The young woman held Fran's look. 'Okay,' she said. 'Let me just pop this order through to the kitchen and I'll be right back.'

Fran was quite impressed that the manager herself was working the room, taking orders, and even more so when Jenna returned to their table and pulled up a chair.

'Fire away,' she said. 'I'll do my best.'

Fran quickly explained. 'I know it's a long shot, but I wondered if you kept records of bookings or...'

Jenna was already shaking her head. 'We're not allowed,' she replied. 'Data protection, and they might not have booked, of course. Thursday isn't a busy night generally, not unless there's something on.'

Fran smiled. 'So, I'm beginning to realise,' she replied.

'Never mind, it was worth a try.' She flashed a look at Adam before smiling back at Jenna. 'Thanks anyway.'

'But someone might still know her,' continued Jenna. 'Particularly if they came here regularly. Let me ask around. What did they look like?'

'Oh... um...' Fran looked at Adam for confirmation. 'She was tall, had black hair, very pretty.' She grimaced. 'Which would probably describe half your customers. The only thing I can think that might mark her out is that she wore really big rings. Not diamonds or anything, but big costume jewellery.' She sat back slightly as their original waitress returned, bearing a tray. She placed a cafetière on the table between them.

'And she had a strong accent,' added Adam. 'From Yorkshire.'

The waitress smiled. 'Oh, Chewbacca, you mean?'

Fran looked up. 'Sorry?'

'Chewbacca,' she repeated. 'Or rather *Chew Becca*... Sorry, it's a bit of an in-joke.'

Fran flashed Adam a look. 'Yes, that could be her. Do you know her?'

'Not personally, only as a customer, but she comes in about once a month, not much during the day though, I don't think. Unless it's the summer – I think she might be a teacher.'

'Yes. Yes, she is,' replied Fran, feeling excitement. 'Oh, thank God. So she does come here?'

The waitress nodded. 'Usually with a girlfriend, sometimes with a group. Come to think of it, I haven't seen her for a few weeks.'

Fran pursed her lips. Should she be honest about why they were there? She hated telling anyone horrible news but hearing of Becky's death might compel the waitress to reveal more than she might otherwise do. There was also the risk, however, that she could deduce, quite correctly, the reason why they were asking questions, and the fewer people who knew about the circumstances of Becky's death, the better. It was a risk she had to take.

'No,' she replied, inhaling a deep breath, 'I'm afraid Becky died a couple of weeks ago.'

'Oh...' The waitress's face fell. 'God, I'm sorry.'

Jenna pulled out the fourth chair at the table. 'Sit a minute, Ellen.'

The waitress took a seat gratefully, anxiously looking around as an older couple walked past on their way to a table on the opposite side of the room. But Jenna gave a small nod; she had clocked them too.

'And the thing is,' continued Fran, 'that we need to know if she was here on a particular date and, if so, who she was with. But I'm afraid I can't tell you why, so please don't ask.' She shifted her weight in the chair, waiting anxiously while Ellen digested this information.

'Okay,' she said, nodding. 'What do you need to know?'

Fran leaned forward. 'The date in question is the eighth of April, so about a month ago. It was a Thursday night and we think that Becky had dinner with a friend.'

Ellen laid down her pad and pen, wrestling with a pocket underneath her apron. Eventually she pulled out a phone. 'Let me just see if I was here that night.'

Fran's fingers were tapping on her knee under the table and she consciously stilled them, smiling in what she hoped was an encouraging fashion.

After a moment, Ellen located the information she needed and looked up, smiling. 'Well, I was here, so that's a start. But...' She stared at a point on the wall over Fran's head. 'I'm sorry, the days all blur into one.'

'I know, it's hard to remember,' replied Fran. 'But would there have been anything on that night which might have marked it out from any other?'

Jenna was already drawing back her chair. 'Excuse me a moment,' she said.

Fran watched as she crossed the room, slipping behind the bar and retrieving a large leatherbound book. She returned to the table, placing it front of Ellen.

'Have a look while I just catch this drinks order,' she added, moving off again. She approached the elderly couple who had arrived moments before, a broad smile on her face. Once she'd made a note on her pad, she approached another waitress and it was clear from their expressions that Jenna was not only passing on the order, but alerting her to Ellen's absence from the floor. Fran had done her fair share of stints in various bars and restaurants while she was training and was impressed by Jenna's handling of the elements at play in the room. Fran suspected she had a very good memory.

She turned her attention back to Ellen, who was flipping the pages in the diary, leaning closer as she peered at the squiggles of handwriting which covered the white space. 'Yes, we had a customer with a birthday in that night.' She turned the book one-eighty degrees so that Jenna could see it as she resumed her seat. Ellen tapped the page. 'Do you know who that is?'

Jenna squinted. 'Oh... yes, Josh... you know, the guy from the bakery up in Frankwell?'

Ellen nodded rapidly. 'Yes, I know who you mean. So, there were... seven... eight of them here that night?' She looked at her boss, who nodded. 'And they sat...' She stared out across the room, clearly conjuring a picture of the room that night in her mind.

'There,' finished Jenna, pointing to the corner beneath the bookcases. 'Table sixteen.'

'Which means that Becky...' Ellen wiggled her fingers. 'Yes!' She looked at Fran and then across at Adam. 'Yes, she was definitely here. She sat behind them, in the window seats just over there.'

Jenna nodded and smiled too. 'Table nineteen.'

Fran felt the shared accomplishment flowing between the two women. 'That's incredible,' she said. 'I can't thank you enough. And now... I don't suppose you can remember who she was with, can you?'

But Ellen nodded. She already had the picture of the night in her mind's eye, the rest was easy. 'I don't know the woman's name,' she said, 'although she's been here a few times with Becky. She's small... as in short, probably about your height,' she added, looking at Fran. 'With dark hair, almost black. It's kind of this length' – she held her hand up to just under her chin – 'a little bit wavy. Oh, and she wears glasses.'

Fran's eyes shot straight to Adam's.

'Do you know who that is?' asked Ellen.

A smile was beginning to wrap itself around Fran's face. 'Yes,' she said. 'I believe we do. Thank you so much, Ellen, and you too, Jenna. That's been the biggest help.'

Jenna smiled and got to her feet, scooping up the diary as she did so. 'You're very welcome,' she said. 'And, I'm very sorry to hear about your friend.' She looked at Ellen. 'If you need any more information, you know where we are.' And then she was gone, melting back into the room and the myriad tasks that were waiting for her.

Ellen nodded. 'I'll just go and see about your puddings,' she said, picking up her pad and pen. She was about to go when Fran put out her hand.

'Just one more thing,' she said. 'This probably doesn't matter, but why did you call Becky "Chewbacca"?'

Ellen's face creased in a sheepish grin. 'It's a bit naughty, really.' She dropped her head and surreptitiously scanned the room. 'You won't tell anyone, will you? But we sometimes give nicknames to the customers. It helps us remember who they are, or sometimes what they do – like the guy who comes in and is a bit hands-on, if you know what I mean. Anyway, Becky sometimes used to come in with another lady, and one night when they were here, we had a special on, a dessert tasting menu. And one of the things we had was this big meringue pie. When I asked Becky if she'd enjoyed it, she said... sorry, this is a really bad impression of her, but she said – *I did, it were proper chew-eh* – in this amazing broad Yorkshire accent. And the name just sort of stuck. Sorry.'

17

'It was definitely Diane with Becky that night,' said Fran as they hurried back to the car park. 'It had to be. I'm so relieved, I really thought we were going to draw a complete blank, but now it looks as if we might be getting somewhere.' She paused by her car with the door open, letting the heat out for a moment before she climbed inside. 'I just hope the fact we were asking about her doesn't get back to Diane. I don't want her thinking we've got wind.' She tipped her head to one side. 'Mind you, given that the person she used to have dinner with is now dead, she might not have the same inclination to visit The Armoury as she did before.'

She looked at Adam as he slid into the seat next to her. 'You're very quiet.'

'I was just thinking... But never mind, it's probably nothing.'

Fran rolled her eyes. 'You can't say something like that and then not tell me. Come on, out with it. What have you been thinking?'

'Only that while I agree the meal that night seems the best opportunity we've seen so far to poison Becky, there could be another alternative.'

'Which is?'

'That it didn't matter who Becky ate with that night, not if someone at the restaurant poisoned her instead.'

Fran stared at him. 'But why would they do that? That just confuses things when I don't think they need confusing. What possible motive could they have?'

Adam shrugged. 'I'm not saying they *do*, just that there still remains a possibility that they *might*. They would have had the perfect opportunity.'

Fran thought back over the last forty minutes or so, shaking her head. 'But the manager and the waitress both seemed so nice, and damned good at their jobs too.'

'You can be good at your job and still be a murderer,' replied Adam quietly. 'And lots of people have dark hair and wear glasses; it could just as easily have been another of Becky's friends who was with her that night, and not Diane.'

'Adam, this isn't helping. Are you always this suspicious? The evidence is stacking up and yet you keep wanting to pick holes in it.'

He looked crestfallen at her words. 'I'm not, but people often don't behave the way I expect them to, and I'm just trying to keep an open mind.'

She explored his expression, seeing the wariness in his eyes and the reluctance to commit to a decision he wasn't one hundred per cent behind.

'Are you feeling it too?' she asked. 'That even though everything seems to be pointing to Diane, we still seem to be missing something?'

But to her surprise, Adam shrugged. 'Not particularly.'

Fran let out a loud sigh. 'Oh, just me then.'

He flashed her an apologetic smile. 'But I agree that Diane *is* still the most likely candidate,' he added quickly. 'And we already know she lied about her whereabouts the night before Becky was taken ill. She certainly didn't attend a works party with her husband. That was a lie on so many levels. Now we have pretty positive proof that she was at the restaurant with Becky. I think we should confront her with what we know.'

Fran nodded. 'That, I do agree with.' She tutted with frustration. 'Damn. I should have asked what they'd eaten. Do you think we should go back?'

'We can always ask them later, and I've just thought of a way we might be able to get absolute proof that it was Diane with Becky that night. I just need a bit of time to work on something beforehand.'

'Okay. So what's the big idea?'

Adam scratched his head, scuffing at something with his foot.

'*Adam?*'

'You're not going to like it.'

'You weren't kidding, were you?'

It was early evening and Fran was sitting in her car, staring at a lanyard in her hand, on the end of which hung an ID badge that proclaimed her to be one Samantha Fielding, employee of Baker, Woods and Shaw, Architects, the company where Diane was either the CEO or the Office Manager, depending on which version you believed. Beside her, in the passenger seat, Adam had a similar badge, only his name was Peter Reed.

'Besides, do I look like a Samantha?'

Adam looked wary. 'Why, what do Samanthas look like?'

Fran tutted. 'Not like me. Tall, with big hair and perfect teeth, large...' She held out her hands in front of her chest. 'Never mind.' She eyed the building in front of her. 'You reckon we can just waltz in there, do you?'

Adam nodded. 'Why not? We work there. The staff have left for the evening, the cleaning team have just arrived. It's not too late to arouse suspicion and we have a very plausible reason for being there.'

'Which is?'

'That we're working on a presentation and have left some files behind.'

'And what? We both forgot our keys, did we?'

'Don't have them. We're purely rank and file. We couldn't possibly be trusted with the security of the building.'

Fran rubbed her eyes. 'If my husband finds out what we're doing, I'm going to be in so much trouble.'

Adam grinned. 'What does he think you're doing?'

'Meeting a young couple to discuss a wedding package. But this is not what I do, Adam. I don't lie to my husband, and I don't go around breaking into buildings and snooping about.'

'Technically, we're not breaking in.'

She threw him a murderous look, which had Adam raising his hands in submission. 'Okay, but I still don't like it. And, yes, I'm well aware that you told me I wouldn't.'

Adam shifted awkwardly in his seat, causing odd squeaking sounds to emit from the warm plastic. He cleared his throat ever so gently and then sat with his hands folded in his lap.

Fran almost growled. 'Okay, come on then. Let's get this over with. If I'm going to get arrested, I'd much rather it be sooner than later.'

'I could go by myself,' he volunteered.

'No, you can't. Two heads are better than one, and you need someone to keep an eye open for you. Besides, your mum will kill me if anything happens to you.' To her consternation, a smile flitted across her face. 'We are doing this to get justice for Becky, aren't we?'

He nodded.

'And to prove that despite "poisoning" Becky a few weeks before, your mum had nothing to do with her death?'

Another nod.

'And because whoever did kill her did so by one of the worst possible means and needs... something really rather horrible to happen to them.' She turned to look at him. 'Those are all really important things, aren't they?'

But Adam didn't need to reply, Fran's hand was already opening the car door. 'Let's waltz,' she said.

Moments later, they were at the main door to the building, through which someone could be seen pushing a vacuum cleaner back and forth across the reception area. Fran tapped on the glass and then waved to get their attention.

'This is never going to wor-erk,' she sang softly through her fixed smile.

Ponderously slowly, the man inside walked to the door and unlocked it.

'Hi,' she said brightly. 'Sorry, can we come in? I work up on the second floor, got halfway home, and realised I've left some files behind.' She brandished her lanyard as proof.

The man pulled a headphone from one ear, peered at her ID and grunted, standing back to let her and Adam inside. By the time they had reached the staircase at the rear of the room, the vacuum was already back in operation.

Their feet made no sound as they sped down a long corridor. 'I can't believe that just happened,' whispered Fran.

'See, what did I tell you,' replied Adam, grinning as he scanned the name plates on the doors they were passing. 'Security; not his job, not his problem.'

Fran still thought what they'd done was incredibly risky, but she also felt the stirrings of illicit thrill. Not that she would ever admit to it. She focused back on the job in hand.

'Okay, so your mum told me that there's a square space at the end of the corridor, like an atrium, and Diane's office is just off that. Let's hope we don't run into anyone else.'

'And that the door isn't locked,' added Adam. 'Although that isn't necessarily a problem.'

Fran gave him a sideways glance as they entered the area Sara had described, the kind of 'breakout' space that companies seemed so fond of these days, but in reality was simply somewhere to park the photocopier and the water cooler.

Only two doors faced them and Fran headed for the nearest, quickly opening it and sticking her head inside. She backed out. 'Nope, don't think it's this one...' She tried the other, beckoning Adam inside once she'd assessed what she'd seen. 'It has to be this one,' she said. 'Plants,' she added, in response to Adam's querying look, 'and photos. While I hate to resort to stereotyping, the other office clearly belongs to a man. It's... not like this,' she finished, closing the door behind them.

Adam walked around the desk and tried the top drawer. 'Locked,' he muttered, fishing in his jacket pocket. 'Can you keep watch?' he added.

'What even are we looking for?' asked Fran, moving back to the doorway.

He shrugged. 'I think this is one of those *we'll know it when we see it* kind of situations, but there'll be a diary around somewhere, there has to be.' He tried another drawer.

'And if there is, let's just hope that Diane hasn't covered her tracks and removed anything incriminating.'

Adam sighed. 'Urgh... I hadn't thought of that, but you're right.' He straightened up. 'This is pointless. Of course she would have covered her tracks. Diane lied about her whereabouts on the night before Becky was taken ill, so she's already deduced that her meeting with Becky that night places the finger of suspicion on her. We're not going to find anything.'

Fran opened the door a crack and peeped out. 'Well, we're here now, we might as well look. Besides, there are a few other things that Diane hasn't been honest about. Maybe we can find something which sheds some light on those.'

Adam nodded, opening the little pouch he had withdrawn from his pocket. Fran didn't even need to ask what it was, and she watched as he selected a long thin tool with a series of kinks in one end.

Opening Diane's desk drawer took him about thirty seconds and she hurried to his side to see what it contained. She smiled at the predictability of what she saw. A packet of tissues, a small make-up mirror, some so-called 'healthy' snack bars, individually wrapped, which made no difference because you always ate more than one anyway, Post-it notes, pens, elastic bands, a hairbrush, stapler, sheaf of papers and, on top of it all, bang in the centre was the kind of bland office diary which stationery buyers everywhere favour for its price. Adam lifted it out and placed it on the desk.

'See what you can find,' he said. 'I'm going to have a look at this little beauty.' He tapped the top of the PC, which sat to one side of the desk. Fran made no comment; there was little point.

She opened the diary, pulling on the little ribbon which poked from the bottom of the pages. It revealed the current day, which was good – it meant that it was regularly used. She quickly flipped backwards to the date she was looking for in April. And her heart sank.

There were entries on every page, but nothing of a personal nature among them and nothing after the hour of 5 p.m. There were appointments, and notes of meetings, reminders for herself to action certain things, but nowhere could she see an entry which read *buy poisoned mushrooms* or *slip Becky the poison tonight*. She closed the book in disgust. Honestly, what was she hoping to find?

Leaving the diary on the desk, she began to riffle through the other papers in the top drawer. Copies of emails mostly, and files which Diane was obviously working on. A plastic folder held a couple of letters which Fran assumed were awaiting signature and she scanned them quickly. A stickie was attached to the second sheet of one letter with a scribbled *Fantastic!* and a smiley face. Fran smiled and turned them aside.

The other drawers held similar folders and a couple of books, while the bottom one held hanging files full of invoices, possibly those falling due for payment. Fran pulled one out at random; a mobile phone bill. Nothing unusual about that.

Beside her, Adam tutted and she glanced over at the computer screen. It had booted up, the series of clicks and whirrs it omitted as it did so settling into a steady hum. And right in the centre of the desktop was a password prompt.

'Try "password",' she suggested.

'Already have, in upper and lower case, and 1234, 4321 and all the other obvious ones I can think of.' His fingers were poised over the keyboard. 'It's not a problem, I can probably get in as the system administrator, but I'd rather not if I don't have to. It will take a while apart from anything.'

Fran crossed to the door and checked the area outside again, but all was still. She really didn't know that much about Diane, nothing that might be helpful in this situation, such as the name of a pet or her favourite film, nephew, niece, favourite holiday destination; any of the prompts which people often chose for their passwords. Adam was still trying possibilities.

'Won't the computer lock you out if you keep typing incorrect passwords?' she asked.

He smiled. 'No, it's just the bog-standard Windows login. You can set a threshold so that it defaults to lock out after a certain number of incorrect attempts, but most people never bother. Security doesn't look that tight around here, and I'm guessing that extends to their use of IT. Admin computers are often the worst... and ironically the ones with all the information.'

'Well, at least we know that Diane isn't the company CEO.'

'True, but we need to find a whole lot more than that if we want to tie her to Becky's murder. It's not just the alibi for the night Becky was taken ill, don't forget, we need evidence of motive too.'

Fran wrinkled her nose. 'Right, so, think logically. What else could her password be?' She stared around the room, eyes alighting on the more personal touches to it. But without knowing Diane herself, they were meaningless. She returned her gaze to the desk. There must be something...

And then it came to her.

She snatched up the diary again and flipped to the very back page, moving backwards one sheet at a time. Phone numbers, a couple of addresses and... yes! In among some scribbled department codes for the photocopier was a word, followed by a series of numbers.

'Try Camelot16, capital "C",' she suggested. She waited, heart thumping, while Adam typed.

'Well, f—'

'Don't say it,' she warned, as the screen flashed into life.

He stared at her. 'How did you know what it was?'

She grinned. 'Old admin trick,' she said. 'I've worked my fair share of time in offices over the years and, from what I remember, certain systems don't allow you to reuse passwords, but they still prompt you to change them every few weeks. It was always a pain in the bum to think of new words you hadn't used before and then try to remember them so we used to come up with a memorable word and then just add a sequential number on the end. You keep a running list and... bingo.' She turned the diary around so that Adam could see it. Beside the word 'Camelot', Diane had initially written the number 1, crossing each subsequent number out as she was prompted for a password change. 'I guess she's a fan of King Arthur.'

'That is the worst kind of lax security, which leaves IT officers around the globe despairing,' said Adam, grinning. 'And just the kind I love. It makes breaking into other people's PCs so terribly easy. Right, let's see what Diane's got on here.'

Fran stood back and watched as Adam grabbed the mouse and began clicking away. 'I'll check her diary first.'

'But she already has a paper diary,' remarked Fran. 'Why would she keep both?'

'She might not, but she might have more than one version of her diary.'

'Sorry, I'm not following you.'

'Her company uses Microsoft 365, which allows for anyone on the network to work collaboratively, sharing files and so on. It also hosts email and other admin systems, including diaries and task managers. And it also, as its name suggests, is available three-hundred-and-sixty-five days of the year. As the trend these days seems to be to work employees into an early grave, you can access all these systems from home too, on phones, mobile devices, all sorts. You're only ever just an email away.' He smiled at her. 'You can bet your life that Diane accesses hers from home too, and, if we're lucky, might utilise it for her personal account as well.' He clicked a couple more times. 'And there you have it.'

'Oh my God....' Fran stared at the screen in front of her as Adam deftly navigated his way around the software. He selected the previous month within the diary and there, on the eighth of April, was what they'd been searching for. One entry. Four words. *Becky. 7.30. The Armoury.*

'Got her!'

'Bloody hell,' said Fran, her head reeling. Had they really just found evidence that Diane was a murderer?

She thought quickly, trying to sift through all the questions that had previously been in her head. No, this wasn't absolute proof of Diane's guilt. What they had was evidence that placed her in a restaurant with Becky the night before she was taken ill. An occasion which, so far, seemed to be the most obvious time for Becky to have eaten the mushrooms which killed her. They also had concrete corroboration that Diane had lied about her alibi. She didn't have one. She never had.

Fran was still staring into space when she realised that

Adam's focus was still directed entirely on the computer in front of him.

'What are you looking for now?' she asked.

'We need a motive,' he replied. 'And we haven't got long. I don't want to be here any longer than we have to be.'

A rush of adrenaline made Fran feel suddenly jittery. This was serious. Not only because of what they had found, but also because of what might happen to them if they were caught. She went to stand by the door once more.

'Go on,' she whispered. 'I'm listening.'

'So we know that Diane isn't the CEO her husband thinks her to be. Neither is he the hotshot mega-earning something or other she claims *him* to be. So where did the money come from to buy their house? The most obvious ways of committing company fraud are by passing dummy invoices through accounts from fake suppliers, or by adding fictitious people to the payroll.' He stopped, looking up at her. 'What?'

'How do you even know that?'

'I googled it before coming here.'

'And Google told you how to commit embezzlement?'

'Yep.'

'Unbelievable.'

'I know. You can get answers to the most incredible things. Those examples are from a site for budding entrepreneurs, citing them as things any self-respecting businessperson should look out for in their company.'

'And you think that's what Diane has been doing?'

'I think there's a very strong possibility. She's worked here for ages, and is therefore presumably well liked, considered trustworthy. Plus, given her job, and from what I can see on her computer, she oversees both the accounting and payroll operations for the company. She has the perfect opportunity to set up all kinds of scams. And no one probably notices quiet little Diane, who's a part of the furniture and loves her job because she doesn't have much to look forward to when she goes home.'

A sudden sound outside the room made Fran jump. She waited a few seconds before cautiously opening the door a fraction and peering out. Across the other side of the breakout space she could see another cleaner wearing the same uniform as the chap downstairs. He was carrying a metal mop bucket and, as she watched, he set it down again inside another doorway and none too gently either. It was this which had made the noise they'd heard.

'We don't have long,' she whispered to Adam. 'There's a guy cleaning the toilets on the other side. But what's the reckoning he'll be doing these offices soon.'

Adam swore under his breath. 'I just need a couple more minutes.' His fingers were flying over the keyboard.

'What are you doing?' she hissed. 'Adam, we've got enough. We need to go *now*.'

'Just a minute more...' He drummed his fingers on the desk. 'Come *on*.'

Fran opened a cupboard in the corner of the room. As she'd suspected, it held various items of spare stationery and she lifted a couple of empty envelope files from the top of a stack, tucking them under her arm.

'Adam...' she warned, her eyes flying to the desk. She snatched up Diane's diary, almost dropping it in her haste, watching in panic as a piece of paper drifted out and floated under the table. She dropped to her knees. 'For God's sake...' she murmured, as she groped to retrieve it, her pulse immediately jumping when she saw what it was. Because she'd seen an identical note to this only recently. At Camilla's house. She shoved the note inside one of the folders and carefully placed the diary back inside the topmost desk drawer, just where they'd found it.

'I don't suppose you can re-lock that, can you?'

Adam shook his head, agitated now. 'No, but with any luck, Diane will just think she forgot to lock it in the first place.' His fingers gripped the mouse as he made a couple more clicks. 'Just as she won't notice this little bit of software I've installed on her computer. Almost there...' His tongue hung out the corner of his mouth. 'Especially if I hide the programme icon, and...' He clicked again. 'There, we're done.' He set the computer to shut down and clicked off the monitor. 'Go,' he said. 'Come on.'

Fran peeked back through the door. 'Coast's clear.' And without a backward glance they sauntered through the atrium and back into the corridor which led to the stairs.

'Talk to me,' Fran whispered. 'About work, anything.'

Adam looked stricken. 'And say what?'

'I don't care, anything!' She readied the files under her arm.

'So... um, do you think you'll be able to get it finished in time?' he asked as they descended the stairs into the reception area.

'I should do,' Fran replied. 'But you know what Keith from accounts is like. He'll have my guts for garters if I don't have the report on his desk by the morning.'

The cleaner smiled at them as they crossed reception. 'Get what you wanted?'

Fran raised the folders. 'Yep, thanks so much!'

And then they were out, in the warm evening air, trying not to run across the car park, hearts thumping and blood rushing and thoughts whirling around their heads.

Fran drove from the car park as nonchalantly as she could, even though the adrenaline flooding her system would have her do otherwise. She turned onto the road, drove as far as she could manage and then pulled into the kerb where she killed the ignition and sat, staring out of the windscreen.

'I can't believe we just did that,' she said, shaking her head. 'I'm a married woman, a mother, a professional caterer, I don't go around breaking into buildings and riffling through people's possessions.'

Adam pulled his beanie from the pocket in the car door and settled it back on his head. 'Apparently you do,' he said.

Fran put a hand to her lips, but it made no difference. The smile which she was trying to smother crept out anyway, and grew wider and wider, followed by an explosive giggle.

'Adam Smith, you are such a bad influence.'

A dimple showed in his cheek as he held her look. 'You're entirely welcome,' he replied.

Fran shook her head again in amusement and was about to drive away when she remembered something. 'Wait, I have to show you this,' she said, reaching around to pick up the folder that she'd thrown onto the back seat. 'It slipped out of Diane's diary as I was putting it back in the drawer.' She fished out the note and showed it to Adam. 'Where have we seen one of *these* before?'

He looked at her, puzzled. 'At Camilla's house, she...' He broke off. 'Rhetorical question?'

'Rhetorical question,' Fran confirmed, rolling her eyes. 'I only had a chance to glance at it before, but listen to this.' She read the note aloud.

> *Hi Diane, this is going to be such fun, isn't it? I hope you like the character I've chosen for you. I thought you could really get into the part, but to play her and not get caught, you need to be very clever. She's been telling lots of naughty lies, stealing money from her boss, all sorts of things, and has a feeling that she's just about to be exposed. She has a lot to lose so best acting hat on – just think how you would feel if you had a secret that was about to be found out!*

'Bloody hell!' exclaimed Adam. 'Becky was really spelling it out this time. That's far more explicit than Camilla's note was.'

'Isn't it?' Fran narrowed her eyes. 'Maybe that's because Diane's secret leaves her with way more to lose. Becky knew that. Perhaps she was feeling the water to see how much Diane was prepared to pay for her silence.'

'And instead she paid the ultimate price herself,' replied Adam. 'But this is proof. Diane had clear motive to murder Becky. We already know that she's been lying to everyone about her job, and there's the whole issue with where the money came from for their house. And I bet once I have a look at what's on her computer, I'll find evidence of how she obtained it.'

'And Diane had opportunity too,' Fran added, feeling her heart rate begin to rise again. 'But let's just get confirmation,' she said, reaching for her phone. She checked the number for The Armoury and waited for the call to connect, asking to speak with Ellen. She put the call on speaker as soon as the waitress came on the line.

'Hi, Ellen, I'm the woman who came in at lunchtime with a young man – we were asking about our friend, Becky? Chewbacca, you called her.'

'Oh, hi! Yes, I remember. How can I help?'

'You did an amazing job at remembering Becky on the night we were asking about, and I know this is a really long shot, but I don't suppose you can remember what they both had to eat?'

There was a short laugh. 'Oh, that's easy! Becky had what she always had, a Caesar salad. It's our chef's special, and she had it every time she came in. Her friend did too.'

Fran looked at Adam. 'Okay... but just to check, that's all Becky would have had? No starter, or dessert?'

'No, the dessert tasting I mentioned was a one-off event. Any other time Becky always had the salad. In fact, she rarely had a starter or dessert – careful about what she ate, I think.'

Fran could feel her optimism seeping out of her like air from a burst balloon. 'Thanks, Ellen. You've been really helpful.'

There was a burst of sound from the phone. 'I'll let you get on, I expect you're really busy.'

'Okay. Nothing else I can help you with?'

'No, that's perfect. Thank you.'

She hung up, looking glumly at Adam. 'I was so sure we had her, but where on earth do you hide mushrooms in a Caesar salad?'

18

'Damn it!'

Fran stared at the saucepan in disgust and pulled it from the heat, lifting it over to the sink and tipping the contents away. That was the third batch of caramel she had burned this morning and her lack of concentration was beginning to annoy her. She needed to focus on what she was doing, not worry about other things. Trouble was, that was easier said than done when you were trying to catch a killer and had had little to no sleep.

Turning on the tap to wash away the mess in the sink, Fran ran water into the saucepan to let it soak for a moment. Perhaps it was time to make something that wasn't quite so temperamental.

Fran had been trying to get ahead of herself, preparing some toffee apple tartlets to freeze in advance of the weekend's job. She had thought that industry was what she needed to take her mind off things, but all it was doing was making the situation worse. Her brain was simply too chock-full of information. She glanced at the clock. Perhaps a walk would do her good.

Abandoning her kitchen, she went to change her shoes and the baggy tee shirt she was wearing. The day was warm, with bright spring sunshine, but not quite yet warm enough for short sleeves; a thin jersey would be much more suitable. She stood in her bedroom, pulling on a Breton-style top over her jeans, and then fished out her trusty Converse from the wardrobe.

Catching sight of herself in the mirror, she stared at her reflection and the dark circles which had appeared under her eyes, where previously there had been none. Even Jack had remarked on how tired she had looked that morning, and he wasn't known for being a morning person. He rarely noticed anything at that time of day. She stretched her eyebrows upwards as far as they could go and opened her mouth wide, trying to inject some life into her face. It didn't work and Fran sighed. Perhaps this was the price *she* had to pay to catch a killer.

The thought brought her up short. A few dark circles were nothing compared with what Becky had been through. Or what Nick was facing. She and Adam were so close to finding the answers, she could feel it. Her chin came up a little. *Francesca Eve, don't you dare give up now*, she commanded herself. *You can sleep later*.

She was jogging down the front steps of her house when a car pulled up outside, one she recognised, and she drew to a halt as she waited for the driver to appear.

'Sara, hi!'

'Morning. Sorry, Fran, I only just got your message or I would have called first. I've been over at a client's house who lives out near the Stiperstones, and the signal there is patchy at best. Is now a good time?'

'I was just going for a walk, but sure, come in.' She was about to remount the steps when Sara checked her.

'I could come with you?' she suggested.

Fran smiled. 'A walk it is then.'

They fell into step as they walked the short distance to the end of the road. The park lay opposite, and its perfect location was one of the reasons why Fran and Jack had bought their house. Fran had spent hours pushing a pram along its winding paths and later, playing on the swings with Martha. It ran alongside the river too and, today, was quiet and peaceful.

'So you have some news?' asked Sara as they walked through the gate. 'And a request, I gather.'

Fran nodded, making sure the gate was latched behind her. 'Not as much news as I'd hoped. It's like every time we think we're there, something else crops up which makes no sense.'

'We?'

Fran felt her step falter and almost groaned out loud. 'Figure of speech,' she said. 'I've been talking to myself a lot, some days I feel as if I'm going mad.'

Sara smiled. 'Maybe *I* can help you figure this thing out. Are you any further forward?'

Fran quickly filled her in on what she had learned about Diane's evening with Becky on the day before she was taken ill, carefully glossing over Adam's involvement and the more unlawful aspects of their investigation. She'd nearly given him away once, she wasn't about to do it again.

'So, everything points to it being Diane. She clearly had motive, and opportunity, but then I find out that it would have been incredibly hard for Diane to have given Becky the mushrooms that evening. Becky would have spotted them immediately.'

'Perhaps they were dried?' suggested Sara. 'Or powdered? Would that make a difference?'

Fran thought a minute. 'Possibly... No, you're right, it might. Perhaps they could have been added to the salad dressing, but it still doesn't seem all that feasible.'

'Plus, the note from Becky seems pretty damning,' added Sara. 'I can't believe Becky could've done such a thing.' She sighed. 'But then I didn't imagine that my friends, who I've known for years, could be hiding such secrets either.'

Fran looked at Sara, her head tipped to one side. 'The thing is, I need your help with something. But if I tell you what Diane's been up to, you have to swear not to say anything.' They were right by the river's edge now. 'Shall we sit a minute?'

Sara nodded and they headed for a bench facing the water.

'I don't really have any experience in what constitutes a good motive for murder,' Fran began. 'But Diane would seem to tick all the boxes. The basic story here is that she's not who you think she is. Or rather, her husband isn't who you think. He's a painter and decorator, Sara. I don't know how much he earns, but it certainly wouldn't be enough to buy the kind of house they live in. He seemed a really nice bloke too. I don't think he's abusive, or in any way controlling of Diane, and more to the point he seems equally confused about what she does for a living. He thinks Diane is CEO of the company she works for.'

'What?' Sara's eyebrows nearly shot off the top of her head. 'But that makes no sense. Why would he think that?'

'Well, I suspect because that's what Diane told him. Just as she told you he was some hotshot in the city, she told *him* that she was the CEO. She's been spinning lies for years, never letting you meet him, suggesting things about him that your imaginations conjured into reality. She simply told him the reverse; that she had to set a good example to her employees and has adopted a no personal calls at work kind of thing. That she's incredibly busy, and because her job is so stressful, she makes it a rule never to discuss work at home. You get the picture. Easy enough to do... but to sustain? I can only imagine the strain she's been under, keeping that lot spinning.'

Sara nodded, staring out across the river at a line of ducks that were busy dabbling at the water's edge. 'Diane's so quiet, she's... I would never have thought her capable of something like that. Maybe it just goes to show, we never really know people, after all.'

'Perhaps,' said Fran quietly, well aware of what her revelations could mean for Sara's friendships. 'But the real question is why Diane would tell all those lies? And we still don't have the answer to that. Nor do we know where the money came from for their big house. Neither Diane nor her husband are earning big money, which is where it gets even more complicated. I'm pretty sure that Diane has been defrauding the company she works for. I can't think of any other explanation and, while I don't have any proof yet, it seems the most logical solution. She's been there a long time, she's well trusted. I think, if I was somehow able to check, I'd find proof to that effect.' She glanced away to hide her expression. There was every possibility that even as she spoke, Adam was busy interrogating Diane's computer for just such evidence.

Sara blew out a puff of air. 'Blimey. So Diane could have a huge amount to lose if her secrets are exposed. Fraud would carry a prison sentence, wouldn't it?'

Fran nodded. 'Which gives her a very real motive for murder if Becky was blackmailing her. I don't have proof of that yet, but it certainly seems that way. The character Diane had been given to play at the party had a secret, which bore an uncanny resemblance to reality, in just the same way yours did. Plus, Becky sent a note with the invitation alluding to the fact that she knew what Diane was up to. So far, I haven't been able to check if she actually received a demand for money, but Camilla did so logic would suggest the others would have too.'

'I missed a phone call from Camilla this morning,' said Sara. 'That's the trouble with working out in the sticks. I wonder if that's what she was calling about? She left a garbled message asking me to ring her back, said something about Becky and having made a mistake.'

'Yes, Becky was attempting to blackmail Camilla over something she thought Camilla was involved with. Turns out it was completely innocent but, to my mind, it effectively rules out Camilla as the killer. For now anyway. Diane seems a far more likely suspect.'

Sara closed her eyes. 'So what will you do?' she asked eventually.

'That's what I've been thinking about this morning,' Fran replied. 'And I think the only thing to do is to confront Diane. Tell her what we know and see what happens.'

'A bit like Poirot, you mean? Where he gathers all the suspects together and then takes them each in turn. The murderer always trips themselves up.'

'It's either that, or go to the police, and we don't have all the evidence yet. In Diane's case, we have a probable opportunity, a very probable motive, and a whole bunch of lies, but if I'm right, it's also proof that Becky was a blackmailer, don't forget. And while this might help remove the suspicion that it was Nick who killed Becky, I don't want to tarnish the memory of his wife without being absolutely certain.'

'Thank you,' said Sara. 'I like Nick, he doesn't deserve that. But you shouldn't go and see Diane alone. Would you like me to come with you?'

'That's what I wanted your help with,' she replied. 'I think Diane is far more likely to talk if you're there. Could we go this evening? Only, given the nature of Diane's lies, I think we need to confront her at home.'

Fran waited for Sara's answering nod.

'Would seven suit you? I can pick you up if you like. I'll have to tell my husband I have a work thing on, so it makes more sense to go in my car.'

Sara dipped her head in agreement, only a fraction, her eyes were full of anguish. 'God, this is horrible. I know we need to get at the truth but I don't like this one little bit.' She thought for a moment. 'I almost don't want to ask, but did you speak to Lois?'

'I did. To ask her about her lunch date with Becky on the Friday she was taken ill. Lois confirmed it. In fact, she was very open about it, and Becky only had a coffee, nothing to eat, so I think we can probably assume that wasn't when Becky ate the mushrooms. Lois didn't know what Becky's movements were for the rest of the afternoon though so there's still a lot of hours unaccounted for.' She paused. 'However now that I know Diane received a blackmail note, I do need to speak to Lois again. I'm pretty sure she'll have received one too.'

Sara switched her attention away from the river and back to Fran. 'You know something about her?' she asked.

'She's having an affair,' said Fran, bluntly. There was no point trying to soften it. 'And so the woman you think is the epitome of domesticity, and a role-model wife and mother, has been deceiving them all. And I would imagine the threat of potentially losing her husband, quite possibly her children too, would give her ample motive for murder.'

Sara tutted, angry now. 'The stupid fool. Whoever it is, she should just give him up, then there wouldn't be a problem. It didn't have to come to this.' She shook her head. 'Do you know who she's having an affair with?'

Fran nodded. 'I don't know his name, but he's a maths teacher at the school. I saw them purely by chance at parents' evening. There was definitely something going on between them, and then later on, as we were leaving, I pulled up behind Lois's car. When she turned the wrong way for home, I followed her, straight to the maths teacher's house. He was there, waiting for her.'

Fran was expecting to see an anguished expression on Sara's face, but to her amazement, her face had lit up.

'Oh my God,' said Sara, eyes wide in wonder. 'I can see exactly how you would think that, but'– she sat up straight, as if excited by what she was about to impart – 'Lois isn't having an affair with a maths teacher – he *is* her teacher!'

And now it was Fran's turn to utter an astonished, 'What?'

Sara was still smiling. 'You're right, it is a secret, but only because the school is such an incestuous place; everybody knows everybody else's business. Or they like to think they do. And cliquey; God, it's awful. I don't know how Lois stands it. Bad enough if you're a teacher, but worse if you're admin, like Lois is. Lowest of the low, I'm afraid.'

Fran shook her head. 'Sorry, I still don't understand.'

'It's no coincidence that Lois works in a school. She's always dreamed of being a teacher, but never had the qualifications necessary to do the training. Martin, that's her husband, encouraged her do it, but just as she was about to start the course, she fell pregnant with their first child. Having children was something they'd always wanted, it just happened a little earlier than planned. And so Lois took the decision, because she really is an amazing mother, to delay her training until the children were a bit older. And now that they are, she's working towards a degree through the Open University. Mr Sneddon is tutoring her, that's all. Martin knows all about it. Dave Sneddon is Lois's cousin.'

Fran groaned. So the touching hands she had taken for intimacy between the pair had been no more than comfortable familiarity shared by relatives. She had jumped to conclusions, comparing what she'd seen with memories of how she felt in the early days of her and Jack's romance, a time when they'd been unable to keep their hands off each other. It had prejudiced her view, incorrectly.

'But why is that a secret? It sounds like a fantastic thing to be doing.'

Sara made a face. 'It is, but I suspect the real reason is self-preservation. Despite outward appearances, Lois is afraid she won't make the grade. It's a very long time since she did any studying and she's lost confidence in her abilities. She gets a hard enough time from some of her colleagues in school as it is, so she doesn't want anyone to know what she's doing in case it all goes pear-shaped. Some of the teachers treat the admin staff like scum, and if they knew that Lois was trying to become one of them, they'd only laugh. It's pathetic, but there you go.'

'Hang on a minute,' said Fran, her brow furrowed. 'Surely Becky would know about that? She and Lois had known each other for years. They worked together, for goodness' sake.'

Sara nodded. 'Yes, that's right.'

'Then why would Becky try to blackmail her over it?' asked Fran.

There was a long pause.

'Maybe she wasn't?' Sara squinted across at Fran.

'Now I'm even more confused, but I still can't think of anything which could explain away Diane's lies.'

Sara smiled sadly as a robin hopped across the grass in front of them. 'You know, before Becky's death, I'd have said we were a good bunch of friends. Now, I'm not so sure. It's hard finding out that the people you thought you knew best in the world are essentially still strangers to you. Becky's death has changed everyone's lives, and not just in the obvious way.'

Fran looked at her kindly. 'Then even more reason to find out what really happened so that, while it can never truly be put behind you, at least you'll all be able to move on with your lives.' Although in Diane's case, Fran suspected that might involve a prison sentence.

'It's going to get worse though before it gets better, isn't it?'

'I'm afraid so.'

Seeing Sara's eyes beginning to glisten, Fran fished in her bag for a tissue and passed it to her. She accepted it gratefully, sniffing a little.

'I'm okay.' She gave a weak smile. 'I guess I'm realising the importance of being honest with people,' she said. 'How, what starts out as a little white lie, often done with the best of intentions, can snowball and before you know it, it's wildly out of control. Or, at the very least can be misconstrued by someone.'

'We're all good at jumping to conclusions. I think I proved that point very effectively with my suspicions surrounding Lois.'

Sara nodded. 'But it's never really crossed my mind how dishonest *I've* been about aspects of my life. I thought I took the decisions I did to protect the people I cared about, but now I can see this isn't the right way to go about things. Sooner or later it brings heartache.'

'You're talking about Adam's dad?'

'Mmm... When I first fell pregnant I wasn't sure who the father was, but I wanted my relationship with Ben to work so much that I kidded myself he had to be the one. What I should have done was be honest right from the start, even if the consequences weren't what I wanted. It would have given my relationship with Ben a solid foundation, instead of one built on shifting sands. The truth would have allowed us to weather the storms that Adam's behaviour brought, or at least given us a better chance, but instead it drove us apart. Ben is still Adam's dad in every sense of the word, except biologically. That hasn't changed, but his view of me has, irrevocably, and there's nothing I can do to change that.'

'What will you do now?' asked Fran. 'Will you tell Adam?'

To her relief, Sara nodded. 'He has a right to know. It's wrong that I've kept it from him.'

'For what it's worth, I think that's a good decision. And Adam might surprise you, maybe he'll take the news better than you think. He's very intelligent.'

'Academically, yes, but maybe not emotionally. Not so much anyway.'

Fran was torn. There was so much she wanted to say, but she knew she couldn't interfere. Or tell Sara that her son was a fast learner, with a wonderful sense of humour and a quick wit. That he was good at solving problems and that, while he might not see the world as other people do, his insights could be very useful. Perhaps it was better if Sara found out those things for herself.

'Give him the benefit of the doubt,' she said, smiling gently. 'You never know. And do it before it's too late.'

Sara stretched out her legs. 'You're right,' she replied, holding Fran's look. 'Shall we walk on for a bit?'

They strolled in silence for a while, and Fran was happy to give Sara some space. They both had much to think about.

They were coming to a fork in the paths crisscrossing the park, and Fran had a sudden desire to get on. She had caramel to make and her mind now felt much more focused. She was about to suggest they head back when she was struck by a sudden thought.

'I was just thinking about the game,' she said. 'And the notes that Becky sent everyone about the characters they were to play. But you never received one, did you?'

'No.'

'Neither did you receive any hint that she was about to blackmail you...'

Sara stared at her.

'And I thought that odd when you first told me.'

'But it isn't, is it? If you think about it. Because Becky knew about Adam's father. Like I said, she and I became friendly when Adam began to have problems at school. And then as things progressed and Ben left, well, she was the shoulder I cried on.'

Fran frowned. 'Yes, but that isn't what's odd. The fact that she already knew your secret shouldn't really make a difference, should it? She thought she knew everyone else's secret too, even if she did get it wrong. So if she wasn't going to blackmail you, why did she still send you the details of a character to play at the party whose history bore such a striking coincidence to your own?' She gritted her teeth in frustration. 'None of this is making any sense.'

19

To say that Diane was surprised to see Sara that evening was something of an understatement. Fran had never seen anyone pale so quickly and for a moment she wondered if Diane was going to faint, but then she recovered herself, staring at Fran instead, with something approaching fear.

'Hi, Diane,' she began. 'I don't know if you remember me, I catered for Sara's birthday party?'

'Yes... yes, I do remember.' She adjusted her glasses, looking up at Sara, who seemed to tower over her.

Sara smiled. 'Sorry, Diane, but do you mind if we come in for a minute? Only Fran here is a friend of Nick's and she has some bad news, I'm afraid. We wondered if we could talk to you about Becky.' She leaned in. 'I know this might not be convenient with your husband... you know.' Her voice had fallen to a whisper. 'But it's really important. Is there somewhere we could talk to you privately?'

Diane was holding the door as close to her as she could, clearly not wanting anyone to see inside her beautiful home. Her eyes darted between us. 'It isn't really convenient now,

Sara.' She flashed Fran a look that let her know Diane considered this to be her doing.

But Sara was insistent.

'I wouldn't ask if it wasn't really important. Besides, how have I never been to your house, Diane? It's gorgeous!' She smiled and stepped a little closer. Diane had no choice but to open the door and let them in.

Fran followed them both down the wide and airy hallway, a beautiful oak and glass staircase rising up out of the space beside them.

'Wow, Diane. This is incredible,' said Sara. 'I don't know who did this for you, but I'm a little miffed it wasn't me.'

But Diane didn't reply, simply carried on and led them through into the kitchen, a gleaming and glossy space even bigger than Camilla's, and Fran had been impressed by that. Diane turned and leaned up against one of the counter tops.

'My husband's watching the television,' she said. She shot an anxious look towards a set of double doors at the end of the room as if to suggest that after five minutes he would come hurtling through with a machete in his hand, demanding to know what his wife was up to. Fran could feel any sympathy she had for Diane seeping away with every moment they were in this house.

She and Sara had already discussed how they would play this, and Sara had suggested that Fran let her do the talking, initially anyway, making it seem as if Sara were there under duress, and that she didn't really believe what Fran had told her. Sara could therefore look to Diane to straighten out the whole silly misunderstanding. They both felt it was less confrontational and that perhaps Diane might even be persuaded to confide in them. If not, then Fran could chip in and lay it out straight.

Fran was more than happy with this arrangement. Not only

did it give her more thinking time, but as Adam was still franti-cally and systematically combing through everything on Diane's PC, he needed all the time he could get. Fran had wondered whether Adam might feel a little disappointed that his mum was accompanying her to Diane's house, rather than him, but a quick text had confirmed otherwise. So far, he had found nothing to incriminate Diane, but he was still firmly of the belief that he would.

I'll text you when I find something he'd messaged. Hope-fully in the nick of time. And now, as Sara smiled at Diane, composing herself for what was to come, Fran prayed that he would.

'Diane, I'm really sorry. I wouldn't be here if I didn't have to be. I know it might cause problems for you, but Fran came to see me this afternoon, she didn't know who else to turn to. You see Nick is almost certain the police are going to arrest him for murder.'

'Murder?' Diane's eyebrows drew together and her mouth parted in surprise.

'Yes, Becky's murder.' Sara feigned her own surprise. 'Oh God, I haven't seen you, have I? You don't know...' She flashed Fran a quick look. 'The police are almost certain that Becky was murdered, but more than that, she was blackmailing everyone, Diane.' She narrowed her eyes.

Diane's head jerked backwards.

'But that's ridiculous,' she said. 'Becky would never do something like that. Why on earth...?' She paused as Sara's words hit home and her mouth became a thin line. 'Oh, and you think she was blackmailing me, do you? Well, she wasn't. Becky was my friend, Sara, and I thought she was yours.'

'So did I. But I'm afraid that Fran already has proof of what's been going on. And I was as shocked as you appear to be. Still am. I've only just found this out, Diane, but it's very clear that there are quite a lot of people for whom the truth means nothing.'

Sara hardened her expression and Fran could see how difficult it was for her to confront her friend like this. 'Are you really going to let an innocent man be arrested for the murder of his wife?' she added. 'Or are you going to tell us the truth about your life, Diane?'

Diane's eyes shot towards the doorway at the far end of the room. '*My* life?' She held a hand to her mouth. 'Sara, I don't know what's going on here but' – her eyes took on a beseeching look – 'whatever you think you know, it isn't true, it's—'

'Perhaps it would be better to tell us, rather than your husband.'

'But I don't have any secrets from my husband,' she said, her voice wavering a little.

Fran could hardly contain herself. Given what they knew, it was incredible that Diane could even begin to refute the fact that she was leading a double life. And for Sara, who had known Diane for years, it must be incredibly hard to keep calm. If Fran were in her position, she'd be hissing like a snake.

'That's a beautiful coffee machine you have there, Diane. I'd love a cup, thank you.' Sara smiled, letting her eyes wander the opulent kitchen.

Diane caught the tone in Sara's voice and her look of hurt indignation turned into a glare. For a moment neither woman said a word, eyes locked, both seemingly immoveable. Fran could feel heat rising upwards from her toes. The silence was becoming unbearable.

Diane lifted her chin a little, clearly struggling to retain her poise. 'Apologies, Sara, but you've come to my house and what? You almost seem to be suggesting that I'm guilty of murder. Or, at the very least being blackmailed by someone you seem to have forgotten was ever a friend. Forgive me if I'm not reacting the way you expected me to, I'm having rather a hard time taking all this in.' She folded her arms. 'So, no, I'm afraid there won't be any coffee. I'd like you to leave now.'

'Diane, just cut the crap, will you? Murder aside for a moment, are you going to own up to the fact that Becky was blackmailing you?'

'She wasn't blackmailing me!'

'So there's nothing you want to say about any of this? Your house, for example, which I've never seen.'

'What has my house got to do with anything? Yes, I have a nice house, I told you, Gary has a very well-paid job. We have no children, we've saved our money and not frittered it away on rubbish. That doesn't make me guilty of anything.'

'Why are you doing this?' asked Sara.

'Doing what?'

'Maintaining this ridiculous stance when I know you've been lying to me for years. You've been lying to everyone. And if you persist with this charade then God help you when the police come knocking, Diane, because they will. It's only a matter of time.'

Still silence.

'Last chance, Diane. You can come clean about what's been going on, about the reason why Becky was blackmailing you, or we can tell you what we know.'

Fran held her breath.

Sara shrugged.

Diane shifted her weight against the counter top.

Still nothing.

'Okay, Fran. Tell her.'

Fran took a moment to look around the room before taking a seat at the long marble island unit which separated the kitchen area from the rest of the room. The surface was cool beneath her hands and she splayed them out, finding the sensation calming. Her legs felt like jelly.

'Maybe you should sit down,' she said.

For a moment she thought Diane was going to ignore her suggestion, but then, with an oddly defiant look, she sat down opposite. Fran waited until Sara had joined them, looking as nervous as she felt.

'I've known Nick quite a few years now, we met through work,' began Fran. It was vague enough. 'Although I didn't really know Becky, I knew *of* her, of course, and I'd met her once or twice – enough so that when I catered for Sara's party, I recognised her straight away. But I did what I always do when I'm working, which is to try to blend seamlessly into the background.' She watched Diane carefully but her face was impassive. 'And it's true what they say, that no one ever notices the caterer, so I'm quite used to hearing all sorts of things, quite often things which people would be horrified if they knew I'd heard. So when I heard two people talking at Becky's party, I didn't think anything of it at first. Not until Becky died in such an horrific way. That got me thinking.

'You see, two people at a party saying that they didn't know what Becky was playing at, and that she needed to be careful, could have been about anything. But, put it together with a violent death, and the fact that you'd all been playing a murder-mystery game where Becky just "happened" to be the victim, just happened to be poisoned, and just happened to be playing a blackmailer, *then* you begin to see a very different picture.'

'But that party was weeks before Becky died,' said Diane.

'Died, yes, but only a week before she was taken ill.' She let her words hang for a few seconds. 'And even then, I didn't really put two and two together until I talked to Nick, a man absolutely unable to fathom how his wife could have died in such a way. He blames himself, obviously. That he didn't get Becky to the hospital earlier, that he didn't spot there was anything wrong... And then it wasn't long before the police began to ask the same question. And that's when I really began to worry about what I'd overheard.' She cleared her throat.

'I knew neither of the voices I'd heard belonged to Sara, and I've since discovered that it wasn't Camilla either. So, by a process of elimination, the two people I heard speaking that night were Lois... and you. So what could Becky have been playing at that could have possibly got the pair of you so concerned?'

'I don't know, Fran, you tell me.'

Fran smiled. The urge to slap Diane was becoming stronger by the minute.

'Oh, that was easy, if you remember *where* I was when I overheard you. Namely at a murder-mystery party, where the victim was a blackmailer. So I deduced that perhaps the pair of you might have been up to something. Harbouring secrets that Becky, lovely as she seemed, couldn't help but blackmail you over.'

'But she wasn't blackmailing me. Why would Becky blackmail anyone?'

'Why indeed? I can think of one very good reason. The fact that, despite years of trying, she and Nick still hadn't been able to conceive the child they so desperately longed for. But with a bit of extra money, or more to the point, a lot of extra money, they could afford the IVF treatment that their budget simply wouldn't allow for.'

'But that's crazy. That would mean Nick would have had to be in on it too.'

Damn... she still hadn't checked with him about Becky's bank account.

'Not necessarily,' Fran pressed home. 'Lots of wives keep secrets from their husbands.'

She held Diane's look, a look that wavered, ever so slightly.

'And if those secrets were motive for murder, the other thing I had to consider was quite how the deed had been done. Do you know anything about death cap mushrooms, Diane?'

There it was again, another flicker. 'No, why, should I?'

Fran shrugged. 'I just thought you might have, that's all. Because the excruciating cramps, sickness and diarrhoea they cause can appear from anywhere between six and twenty-four hours after ingestion. And a lot can happen in twenty-four hours. Incidentally, that's why the police were interested to know everyone's movements the day before Becky became ill. It's quite possible that she met a friend for dinner, for example.'

Diane swallowed. 'I have an alibi,' she said.

'Yes, you do, don't you? You were at a party with your husband, I gather. Some posh work do.'

'Yes, that's right. Entertaining clients is part of his role. It's expected.'

Fran nodded. 'Yes, I bet it is. So, why is it then that a waitress at The Armoury in town confirmed that Becky had indeed had dinner on the night in question? With a friend whose description matches yours perfectly.'

Diane sat back in her chair. 'Okay, okay... I panicked. I knew my dinner with Becky would look suspicious, but I didn't kill her. And I can always say that I got my dates muddled up; my husband and I often do go out to entertain clients.'

'And what form do these evenings out take? Does your husband paper a wall for them, or show off a new painting technique perhaps?' Fran leaned forward. 'I know all about it, Diane. I know that your husband thinks you're CEO of the company you work for, except that when I last looked, you're the office manager – a good job, but not quite the same thing. I also know that, according to your friends, who've known you for years, your husband has some hotshot job in the city and earns a fortune. It's a very handy trade to have, that of painter and decorator, I wish my husband had a skill like that, but it doesn't really earn enough to buy a house like this, does it?'

Fran's eyes bored into Diane's and, just for a second, Fran thought she was going to argue, even now when the facts had been laid bare, but then her face suddenly crumpled and she sagged in her chair. She pulled her glasses from her face, rubbing her eyes.

'You can't tell anyone about this,' she whispered. 'Please. I've tried so hard to keep it quiet.'

20

'You murdered Becky, Diane! Why the hell should I keep quiet about it?' It was Sara who spoke, her eyes blazing.

'No... no, I didn't! Please...' Diane coughed violently, as if she had something stuck in her throat. 'I'll tell you. Okay? I'll tell you, but you have to swear not to repeat it. I like it here, Sara, and, stupidly, I love my job. And I have friends here too, good friends like you, who I'd never want to be without. I know I haven't been honest, but...' She was close to tears. 'I don't want to have to move and start all over again.'

Fran shot Sara a puzzled look. Moving house was surely the least of Diane's worries. She watched while Diane slipped from her chair and went to open the double doors at the end of the kitchen.

'Gary...' Her voice wavered as she spoke and almost immediately Fran saw a tall shadow appear in the doorway.

'Everything all right, love?'

Gary stepped into the room, his gaze flicking over to where Fran was sitting before returning to his wife's face.

Fran couldn't hear Diane's reply, but her words caused another glance in their direction, much longer this time. Gary passed a hand over his face and then, arm firmly around Diane's shoulders, he led her back towards them.

'All right?' he said, nodding acknowledgement of their presence. He took a seat as Diane pulled out from under his arm, his face strangely impassive.

Diane took something from the drawer of a sleek storage unit which sat in one corner of the room and retook her seat. Sliding the envelope wallet across the table to him, she gave a weak smile.

'This is Gary,' she said. 'And you're right, he is a painter and decorator. A damn good one too.'

Gary pulled his tee shirt a little lower over his stomach, nodding at each of them in turn. The file sat in front of him like an unexploded bomb.

'And *this* will explain why we've been able to afford the house. Show them, Gary.'

He drew out a sheet of paper and slid it across to Fran, who was closest. 'You might want to check the date,' he said.

Fran dropped her eyes to the letter, still certain that Diane was trying to pull a fast one, but as she read the words in front of her, her stomach dropped away in shock. It was the last thing she'd been expecting. She looked up.

'Nine point three million pounds,' she said, her voice rising. 'You won *nine point three million pounds*? I can't believe this.'

She slid the letter across to Sara, who was staring at her, open-mouthed.

Sara checked the date as Gary had requested. 'This was twelve years ago,' she said, shaking her head. 'I don't understand.'

Diane looked as if she wanted to cry. 'It's really very simple,' she replied quietly. 'Gary, maybe you'd like to get the box and show them?'

'Love, you don't need to do this. Them knowing is enough, like.'

But Diane shook her head. 'No, if they know, they're going to see it all.'

Gary nodded and rose from the table.

'Twelve years ago we won the lottery,' continued Diane. 'Like you said, just over nine million pounds. And, like most people, we thought all our problems were over. When, in fact, they had only just begun.' She licked her lips and Fran could imagine how dry her mouth had suddenly become. 'No one ever tells you, you see. Or maybe they do now, but they certainly didn't then. They don't prepare you for what happens. And we were so naive; this was the most wonderful thing that had ever happened to us and we wanted to share that joy. We thought people would be happy for us.'

She paused while Gary carried a large box back to the counter. He laid it down and opened the flaps, pulling out a sheaf of papers. There must have been fifty sheets in one hand alone.

'We kept these as a reminder of what we've been through,' said Diane. 'In case we ever doubt what we're doing now. Because even though it's horrible, and on our darkest days only feels like half a life, it's infinitely better than what went before.'

'Begging letters...' said Sara, looking across at Diane with sadness in her eyes.

Diane swallowed. 'Yes, that's right. Would you like to read some?'

Fran dipped her head in shame.

'No, I thought not. They aren't very nice. Oh, don't get me wrong, some are very polite, but they're still filled with terrible stories of desperate lives. Death, illness, destitution, victims of abuse, domestic violence... heartrending... And they started coming almost immediately.'

Sara sighed in heartfelt sympathy. 'I had no idea. None of us did.'

'Damn right you didn't,' said Diane, her words shaky. 'I

made sure of that. Because that wasn't even the half of it.' She lifted her chin a little and, even now, after all this time, Fran could see shiny tears filling her eyes.

Diane gave Gary a smile as he reached across to take her hand. 'We had a letter quite early on from a woman whose child was very poorly... in fact, who would die without an operation, experimental at best, and pioneered by a doctor in the States. There'd been limited success, but some success, and I guess when you're desperate... Anyway, I don't know why, I mean, there were literally hundreds of people who we could help, but there was something about this letter that got to me. And so I decided to help her. I shouldn't have, I know that now, but there's a huge amount of guilt attached to winning that much money and...' She shrugged. 'I kidded myself I would be redressing the balance if I helped her.'

'What happened?' Fran whispered.

'We gave her the money, her child had the operation, and then...' Diane stopped, staring at the wall opposite. 'Then he needed another operation. There were some complications that weren't foreseen. That was always a risk, but... you have to understand how desperate her letters were. And I'd given her my mobile number when her son had the first operation so she could let us know how things were going. Such a stupid thing to do, but I didn't think. Then we were asked for more and more money and we could see that, really, none of it was going to make any difference – her little boy was going to die. She knew it too, in her heart of hearts. And so we said enough was enough, that we had done all we could.'

'Jesus...' Sara's hand was on her mouth. 'How do you even begin to cope with something like that? She put you in an impossible position.'

'That's why we did it. We didn't want her son to die, of course we didn't, but we knew that if we carried on giving her money, there would never be an end to it. And her little boy was so poorly, he'd suffered so much. But it almost felt as if it was our decision to let him go, not hers. And that's an almost impossible thing to live with.' She looked across at Gary. 'And it hit us hard, even though we knew we were doing the right thing.' She stared at Sara as if daring her to contradict what she'd said, but Sara looked like Fran was feeling, ashamed and sickened.

'So you moved house, to get away from all the memories?' asked Sara.

'No.' It was Gary's turn to talk. 'We moved because she kept on gerrin at us. Like it was our fault her son died, and we was the ones causing her pain. We knew it was just the grief, like, but there were phone calls, nasty ones, and visits to the house. She'd hammer on the door for what felt like hours, shouting at us through the windows. It got so that we were afraid to go out, afraid to stay in an' all, in our own house. It was horrendous. Had to get the bizzies involved in the end, got one of those restraining orders. But it was them who told us to move, to start again, and this time to keep shtum about the money.' His voice was calm and relaxed, its pitch soft.

'So that's exactly what we did,' added Diane. 'We moved here and decided that we needed to behave like everyone else. We never wanted a lavish lifestyle, and neither of us wanted to give up work, we would have gone stir crazy if we'd done that. But we bought a nice house, and we gave a lot of money away to charities too. And, if anyone asked me, I would say that Gary had a very well-paid job and vice versa.'

Gary gave a small smile. 'Diane even goes to the library every day, like. After work so it looks right, her coming home when she does. We don't want no one asking questions. So we don't have any secrets from each other at all. It's everyone else we've kept the truth from.'

'I'm so sorry you felt you couldn't share any of that with us,' said Sara, real sadness in her voice.

'It wasn't that I couldn't,' replied Diane, her own regret

written large across her face. 'It was nothing any of you did, this was all down to me. But it's so hard when you start fabricating lies about your life because, before you know it, the lies have got bigger and bigger and more and more complex, and how do you even begin to have that kind of conversation. *Hey, guys, I've been lying to you for years. I'm not who you think I am.* I never thought I would be so happy and settled here and, as time went by, I realised how desperately I wanted to keep what we had, but by then it was almost too late. We were already so deeply mired in our lies that there seemed no way out of it. I was so scared. I still am. Scared that one tiny slip would be enough for our secret to get out and that we would lose everything once more. I can't go through that again.'

Silence stretched out, all four of them lost in their thoughts. Diane looked sad more than anything, although Fran imagined she must be feeling relief at some level for having finally told them the truth about her life. Gary looked a little wary, sitting among strangers, even though he knew one of them at least was a good friend. Sara looked hollow, exactly how someone would look who felt they'd let a friend down, who'd heard how much they had suffered and knew there wasn't a single thing they could do about it. But Fran was puzzled. She couldn't help but be moved by Diane's story, but there was still something else that didn't sit right, like a piece of jigsaw squashed into the wrong position. And then it came to her...

'But Becky must have found out,' she said. 'About your secret. Or at least, even if she didn't know about the lottery win, she'd figured out that Gary wasn't who you said he was.'

Her eyes widened. 'You're right, she did find out, that's why she sent me that note. Oh God... She must have seen our house, or seen Gary and realised something didn't add up. So she put two and two together and decided that I was stealing from my employer. The sad thing is that I would have given Becky and Nick the money for the IVF treatment – I wanted to, but how could I? I was scared that if I offered it, saying it was from Gary, that she would want to come and meet him, or come here and... She would have found out. It was only a matter of time, and I couldn't risk it.'

Fran obviously couldn't tell her that she had seen the note. 'I guessed she might have done something like that,' she replied instead. 'Camilla received a note too, and it was clear that Becky suggested she play her party character for a very specific reason.'

Diane nodded. 'I was terrified when I went to the party that the beans were going to be spilled during the evening. I was on edge the whole time, thinking Becky was going to say something. And you're right, I did speak to Lois about it. She got a note too, and although she thought it was a bit odd, she didn't seem to think that much of it. Not like me anyway. But then Becky was fine, her usual lovely self the whole evening. It didn't really make any sense, and I would have forgotten about it, but...' She swallowed. 'I got another note, the day before Becky got sick.'

Fran shot a look at Sara. 'A demand for money?'

Diane looked away, her nostrils flaring. She nodded gently. 'The stupid cow. It wasn't even for much money, not really, and I would have gladly given it to her if she'd asked. If she wanted it for something, or was in trouble. But now we'll never know, will we?' She dropped her head. 'I'm sick of lying.'

Fran caught Gary's eye, and gave a weak smile. 'I'm sorry to have to ask, but would you have that note?'

Diane shook her head. 'I burned it. I know I shouldn't have, but I felt sick at the sight of it. And I was going to talk to Becky, to tell her there was no need for all of that, but then I couldn't, could I? She got ill, and...' Her voice faded away as a tear dripped down her cheek.

Fran looked at Gary, his face full of concern for his wife. 'I'll put the kettle on, shall I?' she said.

. . .

THE VISIT to Diane's had relaxed a little after that. The coffee machine was pressed into action and Diane pulled out some chocolate biscuits from a cupboard. It was obvious that she and Sara were going to have much to discuss over the coming days, but Fran was pleased that they were, at least, still friends, and had hugged when they parted.

Fran felt awful that she may have come between the two women, and said as much on the drive back to Sara's house.

'I jumped to massive conclusions about Diane and, worse, made you come barging in there with me, accusations flying from our lips. I should have taken more time to be sure about my facts.'

Sara looked across from the passenger seat. 'Fran, you have no need to apologise. Everything *did* point to Diane being guilty, and she *was* guilty of lying, in pretty spectacular fashion too. And you didn't make me go with you, I offered, don't forget, because I agreed with you. Going over there was the only way to find out the truth – and it's much better now that we know why Diane has been lying, instead of discovering that what we feared was true. In fact, you've done Diane a favour. Now she's been able to open up to me and she knows I'm on her side, it must be a huge relief.'

'I hope so. It's amazing, isn't it, but sad too? Everyone dreams of winning the lottery and yet it's brought Diane and her husband such heartache.'

'And the price of their happiness has been a life built on lies,' agreed Sara. 'Maybe they never intended things to go that far, but I guess once you start down that path it becomes harder and harder to step off it.'

'Do you think it will be different for them now?'

Sara nodded. 'I think the fear of something is often bigger than it actually is. What they went through was awful, and I can fully understand them not wanting to go through it again, but hopefully now Diane can see that the friends she has are ones who understand and are more than happy to keep her secret. I don't think it will be like it was before.'

Fran concentrated on her driving for a moment. There was something else she needed to say to Sara, about Adam, and now might be a very good time to say it. But to do so would break another promise and perhaps she wasn't the person who should be coming clean... She was still toying with the idea when Sara spoke again.

'The lies have got to stop,' she said. 'Tonight was yet another reminder of what happens when you keep the truth from people, however good your intentions might be.' She pressed her lips together. 'I'm going to speak to Adam, soon. Tell him what I should have years ago. It's too late now and he's out tomorrow at a job interview, but as soon as he gets back, I'll talk to him.'

Fran smiled. 'I think that's a very good idea,' she said as she navigated the turn onto Sara's driveway. 'And if you're free tomorrow, maybe we can have a brainstorm? We still seem no nearer to figuring out who killed Becky. If we're lucky, one of us might come up with something. I can't help but feel as if I'm missing something.' A sudden thought came to her. 'Did you find out what Camilla wanted?'

Sara shook her head. 'She was out when I rang her back this afternoon, but that's not unusual.' She checked her watch. 'I might give her a quick ring now. Or if not, in the morning.'

Fran smiled as Sara turned to get out the car, but it was only to cover her awkwardness. She was beginning to feel more and more uncomfortable about keeping Adam's involvement in all this a secret, but for the time being, it would have to remain so.

'I'll ring you,' called Sara with a wave, turning for her front door.

Fran lifted a hand in reply and swung the car around, heading back down the driveway. She stopped in the lee of the hedge where she had waited for Adam previously. Gently resting her head against the steering wheel, she sighed wearily. All this cloak and dagger stuff was doing her no good at all.

She took a deep breath and, lifting her head, reached for her phone. She texted with jittery fingers.

Adam, can you come meet me? I'm in the usual place.

And then she stared out the windscreen at the night sky, wondering why her life had become so complicated.

She was so deep in thought that she almost shot in the air as Adam pulled open the passenger door.

'I don't believe it,' he said, climbing into the seat. 'I haven't found a thing on Diane's computer.'

Fran rubbed her eye. 'No, and you're not going to either.'

'She flirted mildly with a guy from the IT department, but then who hasn't in her position? Office managers need those guys onside.' Adam raised his eyebrows. 'I was so sure I would find something incriminating. Hang on a minute... How do you know I'm not going to find anything?'

She quickly explained, flinching as Adam let go a volley of expletives. He gave her a sheepish look.

'Sorry,' he said. 'I was so sure we had her!'

'I know... and now I have no idea where that leaves us.'

'Up a certain creek without a paddle,' answered Adam. 'I've just realised what her computer password was all about too.' He groaned. 'I can't believe it.'

Fran gave him a quizzical look.

'Diane's computer password – it was Camelot. And we were thinking Arthur and the knights of the round table, when really it was far more relevant than that.'

'Sorry, I still don't understand.'

'Camelot are the organisation who run the National Lottery,' explained Adam. 'When the computer asked Diane for a memorable word, whether she really thought about it or not, that was the one thing that came to mind. Perhaps it was a reminder to hold firm in her lies, to maintain the pretence and remember why.'

'Yes, maybe. But I can't believe we got it so wrong. It all seemed like it was falling into place.'

'Or maybe we didn't get it wrong,' said Adam, his eyebrows raised. 'Maybe knowing the truth about Diane doesn't change anything at all.'

Fran rubbed her eye. 'Okay, I'm tired,' she said. 'You're going to have to explain.'

'I was just thinking. I'm pretty sure that Lois didn't have anything to do with Becky's death. Becky knew about her studying to become a teacher for one thing. Camilla and Diane, however, are a different story. They both seemed to have a secret which then turned out to have an innocent explanation – something, in fact, which would make any attempt at blackmail pointless. We know that both women had wanted to speak to Becky to clear up the misunderstandings, but that was *after* they received the blackmail demand. They never got the chance to speak to Becky because she became ill. Well, what if one of them did speak to Becky—'

'And poisoned her!' finished Fran. 'Except that neither of them had the opportunity, did they? Diane's meal with Becky seems unlikely to have been when Becky ate the mushrooms and Camilla was at a yoga class that evening.'

'Which still leaves Friday as a possibility,' replied Adam. 'It's still possible there was a small window of opportunity. Plus, Camilla's not short of a penny or two, is she? And Diane certainly isn't. While she isn't guilty of the secret Becky seemed to have been accusing her of, she still has a lot to lose if word gets out about her lottery win. And perhaps she's not as generous as she makes out. Even if Diane did have a chat to Becky to explain the innocence of her situation, what's to say that Becky didn't decide to go ahead and blackmail her anyway? She could have taken her for an absolute fortune.'

Fran groaned. 'My head hurts, but you're right. So Camilla and Diane are still suspects then?'

Adam nodded. 'I reckon so. Someone must still be lying, but I don't know who.'

21

Adam's interview at Red Herring Games was scheduled for two o'clock but at just after ten, he was about to leave, saying that he wanted to arrive in plenty of time without worrying about getting stuck in traffic.

'And?' Fran enquired with a teasing note to her voice.

Adam grinned. 'And... have time for a little snoop around, obviously. What would be the point otherwise? Someone devised the characters and the plot for the murder mystery which Mum and her friends all played. Even if that person was Becky, someone at the games company must have known about it and helped, however innocently. It might be the only chance we have of getting proof of how it all worked.'

'Well, keep your wits about you,' Fran replied. 'And let me know once you get there, otherwise I'll only fret.' She handed over the paper bag she was holding. 'They're only brownies, but I thought they might come in handy.'

Adam rolled his eyes. 'You're worse than my mum.'

'I shall take that as a compliment,' she retorted, smiling. Despite his protestations, Fran could see Adam was pleased.

She walked him to his car, waiting until he had climbed

inside and settled himself before giving a wave. Satisfied he was on his way, she walked back up her driveway and, moments later, was in her own car, waiting patiently for a gap in the traffic so she could pull out.

Fran had done nothing but wrestle with her thoughts all night and was hoping that Sara might have hit on something from yesterday's discoveries to give them a breakthrough. Nothing in this whole affair was going the way she thought it would.

A car flashed past her and she frowned. *Wasn't that...?* But the name wouldn't come to her. It was probably just someone who she had catered for in the past. But whoever it was should slow down; a residential area was not the place to be travelling at speed, it was only a matter of time before someone had an accident.

Fran checked again that the road was clear before pulling out, turning towards Sara's house. The journey was only ten minutes, but she took her time, well aware of how preoccupied she still was.

She and Adam had tried to think logically, considered each of the guests at the party, one by one, found out what their motives were and what opportunities they might have had to poison Becky, but instead of being left with one very obvious suspect, as they had thought yesterday, it now seemed unlikely that any of the friends had murdered Becky. Unlikely, but not impossible. Unless...

Fran tapped her fingers on the steering wheel. *Unless...* it really wasn't any of them, but someone else instead. She didn't want to consider the possibility that Sara might be guilty, but at some point she would have to. Sara was the only person they hadn't investigated, but in many ways she was the most obvious suspect. Fran shook her head. No, she couldn't believe that. Sara had been helping them, she—

Fran slammed on her brakes as she turned up Sara's drive,

narrowly missing a police car coming the other way around the bend. The car lurched to a halt, her heart thumping as the officer pulled wide, skimming past her and raising a hand in contrition as he did so. She concentrated on breathing for a moment before slowly inching around the hedge just in case anyone else was leaving in a hurry. A collision with the police was the last thing she needed, even if it wasn't her fault. Her heart was still hammering in her chest. She had just been considering the possibility that Sara might somehow have been involved in Becky's murder and now the police were here. That couldn't be good news.

Sara met her on the driveway as she was climbing from the car. Her face was red and blotchy.

'What's going on?' Fran asked. 'I've just had a near miss with a police car.'

Sara's usually calm exterior was anything but. 'Camilla's dead! And I've had to tell them everything, Fran. There was nothing else I could do! Oh God, what's going to happen now? They're going to come back and arrest me, I know they are.'

Fran took hold of Sara's arm, her heart rate rocketing back up from the shock. How could Camilla be dead? The poor woman.

'Okay, let's just take it one thing at a time.' It was as much to calm herself as Sara. 'What happened to Camilla?'

'Her husband found her dead last night. He was late home and she was just... just sitting at the kitchen table. A heart attack, but...' The fear in Sara's eyes was plain to see. 'How can it have been natural causes, Fran? Camilla wasn't unwell. She didn't have high blood pressure, or a history of heart problems. When the police told me I—'

'Wait, the police told you?'

Sara nodded, her eyes filling with tears. 'I didn't kill her, Fran, you have to believe me. But the police aren't going to listen, are they? They're obviously connecting the two deaths.'

Fran swallowed back her own tears. 'You don't know that. Their visit doesn't necessarily mean anything, they're just following up inquiries, that's all, doing their job.' She sniffed. 'Come on, let's go inside.'

Sara nodded, but she didn't look at all convinced.

A vacuum cleaner was abandoned in the hallway and Fran stepped around it, following Sara through into the kitchen. They were almost there when Sara suddenly swung around. 'No, let's go in the garden. I can't bear to be in the house.'

She walked past Fran and back out into the hallway, heading for the dining room, where a set of patio doors led outside. Fran paused as she saw the table, remembering Becky's head resting on it during the party, tongue lolling as her friends giggled until the moment when their merriment had suddenly died. The moment when, for a few split seconds, there had been doubt. But then Becky had come back to 'life' and more laughter had rung out, albeit tinged with a hint of relief. With all that had happened since, it seemed a very long time since that night. And now two people were dead.

Sara, however, was so preoccupied by her predicament that she swept through the room without even a backward glance. She threw open the doors and rushed outside, seeming to gulp in air as if she'd been deprived of it for hours.

'Sorry,' she said. 'I just...'

'It's okay,' replied Fran gently. 'Camilla's death is a huge shock and, given everything else that's happened, it's not surprising it catches up with you every now and again.'

'I was fine this morning,' Sara replied. She moved over to a table and chairs laid out on an expanse of stone slabs, pulled out a chair and sat down heavily, leaving Fran staring at her. 'I'd got my head around Diane's news, although I still felt a little upset that in all this time she'd never felt able to confide in any of us, but generally I could understand where she was coming from. I was pleased. I thought it meant that none of my friends were murderers. But then the police arrived and...' She looked up, panic contorting her features. 'I hadn't been able to get hold of Camilla. I tried ringing her last night, but her mobile just went to answerphone. I didn't think anything of it, Fran, I just thought Camilla was busy. And instead, she was dead, alone in her house. I should have done something, I should have—'

'Sara, you weren't to know anything had happened. If it was a heart attack, it may have been very sudden; there was nothing you could have done. It isn't necessarily connected to Becky's death and you mustn't think—'

'No! Someone killed Camilla, just like Becky. Someone hated them enough to... What's going on, Fran?'

Fran moved swiftly to her side. 'It's going to be all right, Sara, don't worry. It's horrible and upsetting and... evil. But we're going to find the person who did this.' She sank to her haunches, reaching an arm around Sara's shoulders. 'Shall I get us a drink? What would you like? A coffee?'

'Could I just have a glass of water, please?' Sara gave a weak smile. 'Sorry, I...'

'There's no need to explain, Sara, really.' She straightened up. 'I'll be back in a minute.' Fran walked assuredly back through Sara's house, ignoring the dining table as she passed. She was trying her hardest to appear composed but, inside, her head was screaming questions. Was she really about to get a glass of water for a murderer? She took a deep breath, holding on to the wall for support. *Come on, Fran, you need to keep your wits about you.*

The kitchen was neat, just as it had been on every other occasion Fran had been to the house. A mug sat upturned on the draining board, no doubt the one Sara had used for her morning coffee and then... Sara had moved on to some house-work by the time the police arrived, clearly interrupting her. Fran paused for a moment and surveyed the room, her spatial memory kicking in, reminding her how it had looked on the night of the party when she was there working alone. Was there something she had missed? Some detail about that night which might help? She frowned, peering as if she was searching for something. There *was* something, some flicker of a memory, but the harder Fran looked for it, the flightier it became, like a will-o'-the-wisp, glimpsed but never seen.

Shaking her head, she took down two glasses from a cupboard and filled them from the cold-water dispenser on Sara's fridge before carrying them back outside.

'Here,' she said, handing one glass to Sara and taking a seat. 'Why don't you tell me what happened? And start from the beginning, when the police first arrived.'

'I didn't know they were coming,' began Sara. 'I think that's what threw me. If I'd had some warning, I would have rationalised their visit, put it into perspective, but...' She gave a tight smile. 'I think it might be a generational thing, but whenever I see a policeman I feel guilty, even when I haven't done anything. Does that make sense?'

'It does. I feel just the same.'

Sara took a sip of water. 'Thank you, that makes me feel better. Anyway, I don't think I heard them at first, I was hoovering the floor and so I think they must have been knocking for a while. That made me flustered too, thinking it looked bad that I'd kept them waiting, as if I was stalling or something. So when I opened the door and saw them there, I just froze, I guess. I'm not sure I really took in what they were saying.'

'Do your best,' replied Fran in an encouraging fashion. 'Just tell me what you can remember.'

'They didn't tell me about Camilla straight away. They wanted to know about the game and I—'

'You mean the party game?' Fran frowned. 'I didn't think they knew about that.'

'No, that's just it. Nick has told them. I suppose he had to, seeing as it was looking like his head would be on the block. He told them everything. How, in the game, Becky had played the victim, and that she'd admitted to finding it a little spooky. Then, when she actually fell ill and knew she was going to die, how freaked out she'd become, saying the game had been a bad omen.' Sara paused for a moment. 'They asked me why I thought Nick had neglected to mention any of that before.'

'What did you say?'

'Only that I thought he'd probably paid no heed to Becky's words. I mean, can you imagine the state she must have been in? I'm sure she said a lot of things that didn't make sense.'

'And did they buy that?'

Sara tipped her head on one side as if to ease an aching neck. 'They seemed to. But then they asked me if *I* had made the connection between the game and real life? I said I hadn't because it was way before Becky died. Besides, it was only a game, so how could there have been a connection?'

Fran was beginning to wonder that herself. 'Go on,' she said.

Sara hesitated, nervous panic beginning to show on her face again. 'They asked me about the game itself, and I had to tell them, Fran. What else could I do? So I said it had been for my birthday party, how we had picked the game and what had happened as we'd played it – that the characters were all being blackmailed by Becky's character, and that during the course of the evening she'd been killed, her character, that is. That was the point of the game, to work out who'd done it.' She held her glass to her lips with a shaky hand. 'That's when they asked me if Camilla had been blackmailed too.'

'And what did you say?'

'I answered like it was still the game they were talking about so, yes, I told them she had. That's when they asked me if I knew she was dead. Just like that, Fran, blunt as anything.'

Fran nodded.

'I didn't know what to say at first, and I was so shocked I

don't really remember what I did say. But I know I told them that I'd been trying to get hold of her. The one policeman made a note at that, and asked me what about, so I said she'd left me a message to give her a call when I was free. I explained I'd missed her call because I was working, but that her message wasn't unusual; she was probably just trying to fix up a get together.'

'So what did they say about how Camilla died?'

'Only that it appeared she'd died of a heart attack, so at the moment they're not treating it as suspicious. There'll be a post-mortem though, and depending on the results I might be asked to give a statement.'

Fran nodded. 'Did they tell you when she died?'

'Her husband called an ambulance when he got home from work, around eight thirty. They reckon she'd been dead about an hour or so, maybe longer.'

'Okay, well, it's most likely it was just natural causes, Sara, horrible though it is.'

Sara's eyes were wide and staring. 'Do you honestly believe that?'

Fran dropped her gaze to her lap. At that moment in time, she really didn't know what she believed. 'I think we have to, until we know otherwise. But I'll tell you one thing – if Camilla died at around seven thirty last night, then you have an alibi, Sara – you were with me at the time. A fact which also alibis Diane.'

'My God, you're right. Then who?'

Fran refused to speculate. 'Let's get back to what the police know about the game for a moment. When you explained why Becky's character had been killed, did they know the culprit was you, on the night, that is?'

Sara's look was fearful. 'Yes. It was like they'd asked me to explain everything about the game to check I was telling the truth. They already knew everything there was to know. Nick must have told them.'

Fran nodded. 'Okay, but that's not a problem. Did they say anything else?'

Sara thought for a minute. 'Not really... at least I don't think so. But that's almost worse because I couldn't tell what they were thinking. If they'd asked me a direct question, even suggested I'd actually killed Becky, I could have refuted it, but I never got the chance. They just nodded and made notes. It was all very unnerving.'

'So do they know that everyone at the party had a secret? In real life, I mean. Do they know that the game mirrored reality?'

Sara shook her head. 'No, they didn't ask me about that, so I didn't tell them. Whether they've already worked that out, I don't know, but they certainly didn't ask me about any secrets I might have.'

'Good, then we're still ahead of them. We still have some time.' She stared out across the garden. 'But to do what, I don't know.'

'The police are going to start looking though, aren't they?' said Sara. 'They're going to start questioning everyone.'

Fran could hear the anxiety in her voice.

'Yes, I think they probably are,' she replied gently. 'But it's going to take them a while to find out what we have,' she replied. 'And don't worry, the police are not going to accuse you of murder without any evidence, Sara. So, if they ask you anything else, just be truthful. We're so close, I know we are. We just have to figure out the last little bit of the puzzle. There must be something we've missed.' She had a sudden thought. 'Or someone else... Someone who's a part of this but that we've overlooked. It's either that or—'

'Someone isn't telling the truth.'

'Exactly!' Fran thought a minute. Camilla's death didn't necessarily reduce the number of suspects. She could have still killed Becky. She could have had a heart attack because of the stress she was under. She could have even taken her own life, out of guilt. Could she? Was that something you could make look like a heart attack? And there was also the possibility that she knew something and had been silenced...

Fran thought back to the phone message she had left for Sara. *I've made a mistake*, she'd said. But what kind of a mistake? Fran sighed. There was no use trying to answer those questions until they knew why Camilla had died and she tutted in frustration.

'Before I go, do you think you could let me have a list of Becky's other friends, just in case a name crops up somewhere or... I don't know. I thought we were narrowing things down and now it seems like we might have to open them back up again.

'Something isn't quite right about the blackmailing business,' she continued. 'It seemed obvious that Becky had created the characters to suit each person at the party, and had sent them out with a personal note, making sure the recipient understood that the character mirrored their own situation. And yet, as we now know, Becky didn't send you a note, neither was she blackmailing everyone. So what if it wasn't her who had set up the game? What if she was working with someone? Someone at the games company maybe?'

'But, I don't understand. Why would they do that?'

Fran shook her head wearily. 'I have no idea.'

Sara's brow creased in puzzlement. 'Wait a minute.' She leaned forward slightly so that she could pull her phone from her jeans' back pocket. 'This company... I'd forgotten the name, but here it is. The not very originally titled Red Herring Games.' She gave Fran a look full of regret. 'The other day, Adam was talking about this interview of his and, I'll admit, I wasn't really paying attention, not to all the details anyway. But I'm sure he said "red" something. Could it be the same compa-

ny?' Fran could almost see the cogs going around in Sara's head.
'But that's too much of a coincidence, surely?'

Her eyes found Fran's. 'You don't suppose he could be in
danger, do you?' she blurted. 'He hasn't really said much about
how he came across the details for this job, but what if they
contacted him directly? Intimating that they were head hunting
him or something. He's on loads of forums for gaming and
design...' Her hand went to her mouth. 'Is this all about me?' she
asked, clearly horrified. 'Is someone trying to get at me and now
using Adam to do it too?'

Fran stared at her. *Blimey, Sara has an even wilder imagination than I do. But even so... Could that have been what
happened?* She thought for a minute. No, that really was a
stretch too far. She gave Sara a reassuring smile, leaning across
the table to squeeze her arm.

'Sara, you're just seeing shadows, which is completely
understandable, but don't forget, it was Becky who died. If
someone was planning to get at you all along, what possible
reason could they have for killing Becky?'

Sara swallowed. 'Yes, you're right.' She picked up her glass
of water again. 'Sorry, I'm just letting my imagination get the
better of me.' She rolled her eyes. 'Even so, I still did the whole
"mum" thing and made Adam promise to call me once he'd
arrived safely.'

Fran smiled. 'So did I. That's definitely a mum thing, isn't
it? Fussing when there's no need and—' She stopped abruptly.

But Sara's head had already lifted to hers and now her eyes
were fixed on Fran's. 'Why would *you* ask Adam to give you a
call?'

Fran dropped her head. Ever since Becky had died, this
whole sorry business had been built on lies. Lies and secrets.
Fran had demanded honesty from everyone, except herself. She
took a deep breath.

'Sara, there's something you should know. About Adam.'

She gave a sheepish smile. 'And I know I should have told you about this long before now, but when I tell you, I hope you'll understand why I haven't.'

Sara pulled a face. 'I might have known he'd be in this mess somewhere. He's very good at getting up to things he shouldn't.' She sighed and rearranged her expression into something rather more patient. 'Go on. What's he done now?'

Fran ignored the question. 'Do you remember when I first came to see you?' she said instead. 'Concerned because I'd over-heard two friends talking at your party? Well, it wasn't actually me who overheard Lois and Diane, it was Adam.' She stretched out a hand to forestall Sara's comment. 'And before you say anything, just listen a moment. Then you'll not only understand why I didn't tell you, but also why Adam really is the most remarkable young man.'

At Sara's perplexed expression she hurried on. 'Adam was able to overhear Lois and Diane talking because they had no idea he was within earshot. Had they done, they probably wouldn't have said anything, in which case there would have been no one to warn of the possible consequences of Becky's death – consequences for you, that is. You see, Adam came to see me as soon as he found out that Becky had died. He realised immediately the importance of what he'd heard; a sentence which when taken out of context could have meant anything, but when viewed alongside the circumstances of Becky's death, said something very different indeed.

'He also very swiftly made the connection between the actual poisoning and that in the murder-mystery game, taking it to its logical conclusion and deducing, quite rightly, that it would only be a matter of time before the police came knocking on your door. As Becky's murderer on the night of your party, you would quite naturally rise to the top of the suspect list. He was frantic, Sara, he didn't know what to do. But all his instincts were telling him to do something, anything, in order to protect you. And he has – his quick thinking has given us a massive head start on the police, given us time to figure this thing out before they jump to any conclusions.'

Sara's expression had softened while Fran was speaking, but now anxiety flickered there too. 'And now they *have* come to see me.' Her eyes grew wide. 'And I have no alibi for the night before Becky was first taken ill.'

'Yes, but we're almost there, Sara, I can feel it. It's only a matter of time before we figure out who poisoned Becky.'

'So, Adam has been involved in this right from the beginning? He's helped you follow up the clues?'

'He has. He's the one who convinced me that Becky's death wasn't simply a tragic accident.'

Sara blinked rapidly, turning her head away a little. After a moment, she spoke again. 'But why would Adam go and see you in the first place? I didn't think you knew one another.'

Fran coloured. 'No, we didn't.' She paused, wondering how much she should say. Maybe now *was* the time to come clean. About everything. 'It's a little embarrassing, actually, but Adam and I met on the night of your party. In your understairs cupboard.' She raised a hand. 'And it's nothing untoward, I promise you. Simply that because I'm a coward and hate confrontation, I'd been trying to avoid Camilla. She'd been harassing me to give a talk to the school for the careers programme and so, during the party, when I saw her heading towards me, intent written all over her face, I panicked, dashed out of the room and the cupboard was the nearest place to hide. I had no idea that Adam was already in there and nearly died of shock when I realised he was. As first meetings go, it was certainly memorable.'

The edges of Sara's mouth were twitching. Despite the circumstances she was trying very hard not to laugh.

Fran smiled. 'I know, it's ridiculous, but there we are.'

'Sorry. I'm just picturing you and Adam meeting. My son does do some very odd things at times.'

'Maybe, but as you now know, he's not the only one. Not surprisingly, perhaps, we get on rather well.'

Sara was quiet for a moment, but when she finally looked at Fran, her expression was warm. 'I had no idea that Adam had done all that. I imagine it must have taken quite a lot for him to do it too, he finds being with people a little awkward at times.'

'It's okay, Sara. I understand why.' She smiled again. 'Adam's told me a lot about his past. How he's struggled. How he still struggles. But we wouldn't be where we are now if it wasn't for him.'

Sara looked up. 'He did that for me, didn't he?'

Fran nodded. She didn't need to say any more.

'I think...' A deep breath. 'I think that Adam and I need to have a chat, don't we? About quite a few things.' She traced a pattern on the table with her finger. 'I feel rather ashamed that he wasn't able to come to me with any of this.'

'Sara, you have nothing to reproach yourself for. It's often easier to talk to someone who isn't family. And, as you've quite rightly concluded, Adam's actions have spoken very loudly on this occasion. He wouldn't have come to me if he didn't care about what might happen to you. He cares very much indeed, it's just that somewhere along the line, the child who got into a whole heap of trouble at school has grown into an adult who hasn't quite cast off the repercussions of that time. But he's a very quick learner. I think you already know that.'

Fran lifted her glass of water and drank deeply. 'There is one other thing you should know, however.'

Sara raised her eyebrows.

'That time, in your kitchen, when we got talking about the secrets which everyone had and I asked you what yours was...'

'Oh God...' Sara closed her eyes. 'He overheard that too, didn't he? He heard everything I told you about his dad.'

Fran nodded. 'It wasn't intentional.' Perhaps she would keep the detail about the bug Adam had placed on her car keys to herself for a while. 'But yes, he did hear. Although... Let's just say he isn't quite as upset about it as you might think. In fact, it answered quite a few questions for him, about who he is, and the relationship he had with his father. If anything, it's made him far more accepting of both those things.' She thought for a moment and realised it was true; Adam *had* been far more sure of himself, more confident, since they'd spoken. 'You *do* need to talk to him, but you already know that. And, remember, having this out in the open is a good thing. Like you said, no more secrets.'

'No, no secrets,' repeated Sara. And then she smiled. 'Thank you,' she said. 'I'm glad you were there when Adam needed someone to talk to.'

'Hey, don't worry. He's proved himself to be pretty useful to me, on more than one occasion.'

Sara shook her head in amusement. 'So this job interview that Adam's gone to then? It isn't real, is it?'

Fran dragged her mind back to the reason why she was visiting Sara that morning. 'Oh no, it is, it's just that he's going to hopefully do a little digging while he's there too. It seemed too good an opportunity to miss. He applied before we knew about the letters that Becky sent, or that everyone's dirty secrets might not be quite as dirty as we thought. But now, like I said, Becky must have had help from someone at the games company, whether innocent or not. I'm not sure that Adam will get the chance to find anything out, but it's worth a shot.'

Sara laid her hand across her heart. 'And there's me thinking he might be in danger. I feel a bit stupid now.'

22

Adam hated motorways. But the alternative route was so mind-bogglingly complicated that it was out of the question.

He was also eternally grateful that Red Herring Games was not actually in Bradford itself, but in the hopefully more delightful setting of Kirklees Hall. Had Adam actually been looking for a new job, he would have taken that as a good omen. Kirklees Priory was synonymous with the Robin Hood legend and as a creator of stories he was well read on the subject.

A series of progressively bigger and bigger blue signs flashed past him, alerting him to the fact that he had reached his turn off on the M62, and he signalled left, wondering why he was so nervous.

The wonderful thing about being a freelance games designer was that he rarely had to go anywhere. He had a few established contacts who kept him pretty much supplied with work, and almost all of it came via email. Occasionally, he bid for jobs which had been posted on the various forums he followed, but Adam could count the number of interviews he'd physically attended on one hand. Or rather on two fingers. And he had a feeling his Saturday jobs weren't going to be of much use to him now.

Reaching the roundabout at the bottom of the slip lane, Adam signalled right, pulling up behind a lorry which was belching fumes. It was also blocking his view and he craned his neck to see around it; the left turn he needed was only a short distance along this road, and if he wasn't careful, he could— He wrenched the wheel sideways, flicking a glance in his rear-view mirror. Thankfully, nothing had been close behind him as he shot, without warning, into what was best described as a layby. It wasn't a proper turning at all. A high stone wall faced him, in the middle of which was a pair of large wrought-iron gates. He inched forwards, reaching for his phone.

His interview instructions had informed him that this first set of gates would open automatically, but once through he would need to drive along a winding road for some distance before reaching another set. These gave access to the estate and he would need a code to open them. He waited as the wrought-iron barrier in front of him slid smoothly back on a polished rail, and once the opening was wide enough to pass, Adam drove through.

The way ahead was dark. Bordered on both sides by thick woodland, little natural light shone through and the warm sunshine was suddenly gone. By now the heavy ironwork would have closed silently behind him. The world outside had vanished.

After a few moments, however, the trees noticeably thinned and, seconds later, he emerged into sunlit parkland, rolling, vibrant and studded with majestic trees. Adam gave a low whistle and, with a smile, pulled away up the meandering road ahead of him. He wasn't at all materially minded, but this was the kind of place he'd love to live in; it was gorgeous. A collection of warm stone buildings grew larger and larger as he neared, until, as expected, the road swept around and another gateway appeared. He slowed to a halt and wound down his window.

Once through, he turned into a car park on his left and, thick gravel churning under his tyres, he drew up and stopped. A bubble of nerves bloomed in his stomach and he killed the engine, staring out at the impressive set up ahead of him.

This wasn't all owned by Red Herring Games. In fact, they only occupied a small part of it, running their business from their home, which was nestled within part of the main building under the clock tower. It seemed staggering that someone had once owned the building in its entirety. Adam couldn't be certain, but he guessed that, just as the clock tower had been subdivided, so had the remaining parts of the building and perhaps six or seven different houses had been created. A long low stable block stood to one side of the car park while a short distance away a hexagonal building sat bordered by lawn and formal gardens.

Checking his watch, Adam realised that he still had well over an hour before his interview time. He could either sit in the car and wait or take his chances they'd let him into the building early, and he wasn't going to learn anything while sitting here, that much was certain. He collected his messenger bag from the passenger seat and climbed from the car, stretching his legs.

He'd only gone two paces when he suddenly heard Fran's voice in his head, and he slipped off his beanie, returning it to his car. He ruffled his hair, checking in the wing mirror that he looked presentable, and proceeded to crunch his way over the gravel towards a flight of stone steps which led into a courtyard.

He'd been told to look out for a corkscrew-shaped topi-arised bush on his left, and on finding it, to ring the doorbell of the red door beside it. It seemed straightforward enough. The only thing troubling him was the number of windows which faced the courtyard. Presumably they belonged to other houses, but Adam had been hoping for a little snoop around while he was here, and clearly that wasn't going to be easy.

The red door was opened by an incredibly attractive woman, who smiled at Adam so warmly that the bubble of butterflies residing in his stomach broke open, flooding his system with the fluttery devils. He could barely manage to introduce himself.

She smiled again at his stuttered opener, and that almost made it worse. 'Hi, Adam,' she said. 'Come in and let's see where we are. I'm Mel, by the way.'

He followed her into a wide open space which stretched the full height of the building. Unlike his hallway at home, which was cluttered with coats and shoes and stuff that had just found its way there over time, there was nothing here save for a round table in the centre of the room which held a bowl massed with flowers. As he gazed around, he realised that a small desk had also been added to the rear of the space, but he could tell by the positioning of it that it had been placed here solely for the interviews.

Mel crossed to the desk and took a seat, busying herself at the keyboard of a computer which had been perched on one end, wires trailing across the floor to a plug socket in one corner.

'Goodness,' she said. 'You *are* keen, aren't you? Your interview isn't for over an hour yet.'

Adam nodded and swallowed. 'I usually get lost,' he said, wondering if that explained anything. 'But I didn't, obviously...'

Mel glanced through a doorway to her right, his left, and frowned slightly. 'Right...' She looked back at him, now almost as ill at ease as he was. 'The thing is, I can't really let you in just yet, Adam. Mr and Mrs Harrison are conducting the interviews and they already have someone in with them at the moment. It's a bit of an unusual set-up here. This is their home, as you might have guessed, and there's just the one office, which is through there, where everyone is. Plus, they have another candidate to see before you.'

There was another doorway to Adam's right, but clearly this wasn't an option.

'Oh okay... so I can't really wait anywhere?'

She smiled at his grasp of the situation. 'Maybe the garden? It's quite a nice day today. Quite warm... Just walk around the side of the house, back the way you came. There's a bench or, if you carry on to the stable block, there's a table and chairs in there, we use it like a summer house.'

Adam nodded, already backing away. 'Yeah, sure. No problem. It's my fault, I—'

'No really, it's not a problem. Just, we don't have a reception area and... Is that okay?'

'Perfectly,' replied Adam, feeling completely stupid. 'I'll come back nearer the time.' He looked back towards the front door. 'So I just go...' He pointed to his right.

'Yes, that's it. Back towards the car park but instead of going straight, take the path around the end of the building. It will take you into the garden.'

Adam smiled, hitching his bag higher on his shoulder. 'Right, well... see you later then.'

He slunk towards the door and had almost reached it when Mel's voice came again.

'Listen, Adam. Can I get you a drink? You can take it with you while you wait.'

Adam's head lifted. The most audacious thought had just popped into his head. 'Would you mind?' He took a couple of paces back towards the desk. 'Only I left my water bottle on the table at home. Stupid. If you have tea, that would be great, thank you.'

'Not a problem.' Mel smiled. 'How do you take it?'

'Just milk. Thanks.'

Mel got to her feet and walked around the desk as Adam

stepped closer. His heart was beginning to beat uncomfortably fast. He was level with the door on his right now and, as he suspected, it opened onto an elegant living area. If he was right, the kitchen would lie somewhere at the other end of it. He smiled as Mel passed him.

'Thanks so much,' he called after her.

He watched her back retreating while doing a rapid calculation in his head. Exactly how long *did* it take to make a cup of tea?

With a furtive glance through the door to his left, he stepped quickly behind the desk and waggled the mouse. He had no idea how long it would be before Mel's screen saver came on, but he was taking no chances. Once the computer locked, he'd have no way of getting what he wanted. As it was…

Pulling his phone from his jacket pocket, he leaned over the computer, eyes flicking to the taskbar at the bottom of the screen. A few clicks were all it would take to give him the information he needed. His hand settled round the mouse. Click, and the Wi-Fi network appeared. Some bright spark had renamed it Whodunnit, and he smiled in appreciation of the wit. Another click on 'properties' brought up the IP address, and he flicked open the camera on his phone to snap a quick picture.

He straightened up, about to close down the window and then changed his mind. He might as well make this easy for himself. Still in properties, he clicked on the security tab, checked the box marked 'show characters' and groaned inwardly. So they had a network called Whodunnit, the password to which was *Jeeves*. He smiled again; the butler always did it.

By the time Mel reappeared with his cup of tea he was standing nonchalantly in the middle of the hallway peering at his phone, and had been for some time. Mel would assume he was checking his emails, or Facebook, or even messaging his mum to let her know he had arrived safely. The fact that he had just connected to the company Wi-Fi probably wouldn't even occur to her.

He accepted the mug gratefully. 'I'll bring this back, I promise.' Then he frowned, seeing the expression on her face. 'Is everything okay?'

She winced slightly. 'Touch of indigestion, I think. Not to worry.'

Adam nodded. 'So I go around to the right...?'

'Yes, that's it, you'll see the path.'

Adam carried his tea carefully to the door. 'Thanks, Mel, that's really kind of you.'

Once outside, he checked his watch. An hour would probably be plenty of time. Now all he had to do was find a spot where he could still pick up the Wi-Fi signal from the house.

The title 'stable block' didn't really do the building justice. It would certainly have housed horses at one point in its lifetime, but was now a summer house, and a rather luxurious one at that. It even had a clay oven built into one wall and Adam could just imagine the wondrous pizzas which would come out of it.

He sat down, looking around him. Bench seating ran around two sides of the structure, piled high with an assortment of brightly coloured cushions. Similarly coloured lanterns swung in an arc along the walls and there was even a circular seat hung from the ceiling. Whatever impressions of Red Herring Games he had already formed, the company certainly seemed to be turning in a healthy profit if their surroundings were anything to go by.

Half-heartedly, he lifted his phone, bringing the screen to life. He'd been glued to the tiny fan-shaped row of Wi-Fi signal bars for the last few minutes and wasn't expecting to see anything at all, let alone the solid rows that stared back at him. His gaze swung around the room, and he tutted with amusement when he saw the bank of power sockets tucked into one corner, one of which held a Wi-Fi extender. If you lived this kind of lifestyle, working from home, then of course your business would be accessible from any place you chose to work, hot summer's day or not. He grinned and pulled his laptop bag towards him.

He was about to open it up when he heard a cough, coming from somewhere close by. Yet the stable block sat at the rear of the garden. He didn't think there was anything behind it, save for another building he could see, which he presumed was part of another house, or an outbuilding of some kind. He got up and peered around the open front of the stable. The chances were that if anyone did spot him, they would simply think he was working on his laptop and never give a thought to what on. But it didn't hurt to be on the safe side.

Following the line of the building, he skirted the outside wall, realising as he did so that there was a flight of stone steps midway along its length, leading to a door set in the wall above. There must be a storage room of some sort up there. Probably the old tack room from when the house had a full complement of horses too. He climbed the steps, pondering how many other feet had passed this way before his. The door in front of him was solid oak, with black metal-studded furniture, and his hand was on the doorknob before he could stop himself. To his surprise, it turned easily.

He stepped over the threshold, peering into the darkness as he waited for his eyes to adjust to the gloom inside. He could only just make out the rectangular shape of the room in front of him. He was about to call out a tentative hello when something hard struck him between his shoulder blades, sending him sprawling. He hadn't seen the three stone steps in front of him, but he felt them now as his body curled reflexively into a ball and met each one on the way down. One, two and three....

Winded, he lay for a moment, feeling cold stone rough

against his cheek but rather pleased that he could actually feel something. When he was younger, as an awkward, too intelligent loner among boys who were much bigger and, importantly, more popular than him, Adam had become used to the goading and the teasing, accepting the blows which were dealt him by making his body as small as he could, tucking his head under his wing and rolling with it. It was quite possibly the reason why, as his tentative movements now would seem to suggest, none of his limbs were broken.

With a groan, he sat up and touched a tentative finger to his temple, dislodging a few bits of debris that were clinging to it as he did so. He couldn't see, but he didn't need to look at his finger to know that it was sticky with blood. His knees smarted too but, miraculously, apart from a general feeling of ouch, that hurts a lot, he didn't seem to be particularly injured. His heart was thumping from a heady combination of adrenaline and fear, and his head felt as if it were floating several inches from where it should be, but it could have been a lot worse.

He got to his feet. He dimly recollected the sound of a key being turned in the lock as he fell, but he would try the door anyway. Just to make absolutely sure that the whole thing hadn't been some bizarre accident and he had, in fact, been locked in there deliberately. He felt for the bottom step with his foot and slowly, and very carefully, lurched towards the door. One damned good rattle of the handle later and his fears had been confirmed. Adam wasn't about to go anywhere.

He let out another noise, which might have been a sigh, but turned instead into another groan and rapidly became a shout of anger. His laptop was still on the table downstairs. Or more likely it wasn't. And with it went any chance he had of finding out what was going on here. He thought about Mel, with her lovely eyes, and warm smile. Surely it wasn't her who had done this? But he hadn't had the chance to annoy anyone else yet, no one else knew he was here.

Adam thought briefly about hammering on the door and yelling for help, but decided against it. All that would achieve was a sore hand. The door was made of solid oak; he'd seen how thick it was when he opened it. So instead he sat down on the top step to think. It occurred to him that this was exactly how Fran must have felt when she was locked in Camilla's shed. That being the case, what would be really nice now was if she could rescue *him*.

With another sigh of frustration, he realised belatedly that his phone was still in his pocket. *Please God, let it still be intact.* But his optimism soon became despondency when he saw that there was no phone signal. Not only that, but the lovely solid bars of Wi-Fi signal he had seen before had now gone as well. Either whoever had done this to him had pulled the extender from the socket downstairs to curtail his communication, or, more likely, the solid and very thick walls of the building did not allow the signal to travel through.

He tried anyway. Call after call to Fran. But not a single one of them connected.

He was on his own.

23

Fran's kitchen seemed like an oasis of calm after Sara's house. It wasn't – it was a mess of discarded utensils, unwashed bowls and plates, and unwiped surfaces – but it was hers and, even among such chaos, she felt comforted by the familiarity of it all. In a world where everything felt upended and confused, here at least was a place where she could restore order. And some gentle pottering was exactly what she needed right now.

Fran's visit to Sara's had sent her head into a flat spin and, right now, she had no idea how to keep everything from crashing to the ground. Adam was on his way to Bradford and Fran was beginning to have real doubts about Sara. How could she possibly tell him that? Okay, so Sara had been with Fran at the time of Camilla's death, but as the circumstances of Becky's death had taught her, that meant nothing. Plus, there had been the phone call from Camilla, asking Sara to ring. Innocuous sounding, but what if it wasn't? What if it was a message to a killer, saying that Camilla had made a mistake? Was she trying to tell Sara that she knew something? And so Sara had had to silence her too? Fran had met Sara just after seven last night, but the time of Camilla's death hadn't yet been fixed, Sara could quite conceivably have had time to go over there first.

Plus, there was the fact that Sara was the only one who hadn't received a note from Becky about the character she was to play. It was Sara who had noticed the similarity between her life and that of her character's. But what if Sara had lied? Maybe she *had* received a note. In which case, was there something about her secret which she hadn't divulged? Something which would mean she had a great deal to lose if Becky were to blackmail her, enough even to give her a motive for murder?

Flicking on the kettle, Fran began to run water in the sink and collect the dirty dishes for washing. Ordinarily, she would have thrown things in the dishwasher, but washing up was good for letting the brain slip gears and freewheel. And Fran needed answers. There was something she wasn't seeing, there had to be. Perhaps something might pop into her head while she worked.

She turned to look around her kitchen, finding comfort in the familiar, in the routine. Kitchens were interesting places – they could tell you a lot about their owners, and Fran was always intrigued by this most revealing of spaces which gave such blatant clues to character. Most people followed a similar pattern when it came to storage of their mugs and glasses – for example, almost always close to the kettle, usually in the cupboard above or just to one side. It meant that whenever Fran started work in an unfamiliar setting she could instinctively work out where things should be. Only occasionally did she work for someone for whom those rules didn't seem to apply.

But it wasn't just the use of cupboards that was common. Everyone seemed to have a particular spot where they dropped their car keys for example, or their reading glasses; where the notebook and pen lived so it was always to hand; where the post was left until such time as it could be thrown away or filed. People were creatures of habit and, as she looked around her now, it was as if she were seeing her kitchen with a fresh eye, as if she were seeing it for the first time. Hardly surprising, she'd spent so little time in there of late, and yet... She narrowed her eyes. There was something bugging her, she knew there was, but she just couldn't get a hold of it properly. She rubbed at an itch over one eye and stared out the window, only turning at the last moment when she realised that the tap was still running. What *was* it...?

And then it came to her. She knew where she'd seen the driver of the car who had sped past her earlier that morning. It was the same woman who had been leaving Nick and Becky's house the first time Fran had visited him. She crossed to the pantry and took down her bag from the hook on the back of the door. Inside was the list of Becky's friends Sara had given her. But which one was this young woman? Fran's phone was in her hand before she'd even glanced at the names.

Sara picked up almost immediately.

'Fran? Is everything okay?'

'Hi, yes, I'm fine. But I've just had a sudden thought. You know how when we spoke this morning, I said that we seemed to have hit a brick wall? That we've spoken to everyone who might have been a victim of Becky's blackmail and are no further forward? Well, this morning, as I was leaving my house to see you, someone drove past who I recognised, but couldn't place. I've just remembered where I've seen her before: at Nick's house. And it made me think about that list of friends I asked you for. I wondered if she might be on it.'

'Okay... what did she look like?'

'Long blonde hair, tied up in a ponytail. She was driving a black Golf.'

'Sounds like Ronnie,' replied Sara. 'That would make sense. She was the one who couldn't come to my party.'

'Oh my God....'

'Sorry?'

Fran gripped her phone a little tighter. She was desperate for anything which might mean Sara was innocent. Could this be it?

'What if Ronnie was an intended victim of blackmail all along?' she asked. 'What if another character had been drawn up for her to play at your party? Another note sent out, hinting at the blackmail to come. And if it was… that means she has a secret too, one that we don't yet know about.' *Could that have been it? Could Ronnie have been the fifth party guest?*

'Even if she'd cancelled last minute,' continued Fran. 'It wouldn't necessarily have changed anything. She would still have known that her secret was about to be revealed. She might still have believed Becky was about to start blackmailing her.'

'But that can't have happened because everybody knew Ronnie wouldn't be at the party, right from the start. She had a visit planned to see her sister.' Sara sighed. 'In fact, Ronnie was the one who first offered to organise the party, but then, when she realised that might be difficult if she wasn't around, Becky offered to do it. We had a real job trying to find a date when everyone was free. Trust me to have a birthday when everyone was busy.'

Fran felt her heart sink. For just a second there'd been a tiny glimmer of hope.

'Was anyone else supposed to have been at the party?'

'No… I just wanted my closest friends. Otherwise… well, it's where you draw the line, isn't it? Before long, you end up with fifty people on the list.'

Fran smiled. There would never be even a remote possibility of Fran having fifty people on her invite list, but then she was more like Adam than his mum; a few very good friends and that was it.

Fran looked down at the list of names Sara had given her, reading them aloud: 'Louise Dawson, Maggie Holmes, Suzie Denton, Ronnie D-Jones, Stella Courtney, Helena Swift and

Lyn Chapman. So none of these others should have been at the party?'

'No, sorry,' replied Sara. 'They're more Becky's friends than mine. People she knew from school mostly.'

Fran peered at Sara's writing. 'Ronnie *D*-Jones? What does the "D" stand for?'

'It's her married name – Dankworth – but she's divorced, so she goes by Jones now.'

'Okay, Sara, thanks. I thought I might be on to something, but it doesn't look like it. Not to worry, I'll call you if I think of anything else.'

'I'm out visiting a client all afternoon, Fran. There's virtually no reception there, but leave a message, please, if *anything* occurs to you.'

'I will.' Fran hung up, chewing at the corner of her cheek, deep in thought. She'd heard that name somewhere before. *Dankworth...* quite an unusual name...

A ripple of fear suddenly prickled the back of her neck. She *had* seen that name before... and she was pretty sure she knew where. Fran quickly opened an internet tab on her phone and typed her query into the search bar. She waited for the page to load, drumming her fingers. 'Come on, come *on....*'

It took some time to find. Her name hadn't even made Red Herring Games' 'Meet the Team' page. But there, in a sub menu, under 'Help and Support', was the name she had remembered – Melanie Dankworth, Head of Support and Customer Care.

Fran quickly checked her watch, almost dropping her phone. *Why hadn't she been paying more attention?* Adam should have arrived at his interview by now. He should have called her, but hadn't. She dialled his number quickly, praying he picked up.

Nothing.

She tried again, and again, but each time the phone cut out, as if the call wasn't even getting through.

Without so much as a backward glance, Fran picked up her bag, and ran.

ADAM TRIED ONE MORE TIME. It was all he could think of to do. He had paced out every inch of his prison and there was nothing up there except for him. Whatever this storeroom had been used for in the past, it was now completely empty, offering nothing which might aid his escape. Without the light from his phone, the room was also completely black. There were no windows, and not even the slightest chink through stone to allow light in, and so for bouts of time, Adam simply sat, in darkness, cradling his head.

It had begun to ache quite some time ago. And the blood which he had felt on his first examination of it had trickled down the side of his face. Some of it had dried, and his skin felt taut and strangely thick. Some of it had trickled over his cheek to the top of his mouth, probably when he had had his head bent forward over his phone, and he had touched his tongue to it, just lightly, recoiling at the metallic taste.

But simply sitting there wasn't a long-term option either. He either needed to get out or find a way to contact someone. He had shouted for a while; his voice bouncing back at him off the thick walls until his head rang with the sound of it. Likewise, he had pounded on the door too, had incurred the expected bruises and abrasions, but he was still no further forward. No one could hear him. The thickness of stone and ancient oak had rendered him all but invisible.

So he was taking the only option left to him, and walking the room, pace by pace, methodically and systematically, trying to find a spot where the Wi-Fi had found a hole through which to leak.

It was the suddenness of it all which had taken him by surprise. And yet, as he thought about the sequence of events which had occurred since his arrival at Red Herring Games, he realised he was wrong. Because someone had known he was coming. Someone had seen him, and they had lain in wait for him at the summerhouse, enticed him up the stairs with a cough, only to spring their trap once he had opened the door and metaphorically touched the trigger wire. And that spoke of planning, or premeditation, so no, there was nothing sudden about it at all.

But, if that was the case, then just what exactly was going on? And who had done this to him? The only person he had seen so far was Mel, but... He examined his subconscious. She was very attractive, but was this really a reason to discount her guilt? In fact, he reasoned, it might make her an even more obvious choice. Had she used her appearance and friendly welcome like an actress applies greasepaint; to amplify what she wanted him to see?

He thought of his laptop, laying on the table downstairs with the programme on it which would allow him to hack Mel's computer. If he could connect to the same Wi-Fi network, it would only take a matter of minutes. He knew her computer's IP address, he knew the network password; just a couple of command prompts later and he would be able to search all her computer files. Because whether or not Mel was guilty, the question still remained – why had someone locked him up? He didn't know Mel, they'd never met before today, so what possible reason could she have for shoving him in there? And if it wasn't her, then who?

He was getting too close, that much was obvious. But close to what? He took a deep breath and rubbed his neck, trying to ease the furious ache that was gathering there. He could do with something to drink, too; fear had made his mouth dry. His cup of tea would still be downstairs, cold now, only half drunk, quite possibly with a skin of milk on the top but, if he could, he would drink every last drop.

Getting wearily to his feet, he steadied himself a moment, then put his back to the bottom righthand corner of the room and held up his phone. Nothing. He took a pace forward and then another, slower this time, giving time for any signal to register.

He was almost in the top right corner of the room, pressed up against the stone wall, but there! One tiny spot with a flicker of something. He brought up Fran's number, hit dial, holding his breath, holding as still as he could. The silence sounded tinny, as if he were no longer listening to silence in the room, but of some far-off place instead. There was a beep. Call failed. He swallowed and tried again.

Navigating back to his phone's home screen, he checked the signal again. It was still there, but so weak as to be almost non-existent. He shuffled slightly to his left, putting the teeniest distance between himself and the wall. Was that something? He blinked hard. His eyes were getting fuzzy from staring at the screen so intently.

He brought up his internet browser, and clicked to open a new tab, biting back his frustration. He was standing so still, so tense, he thought he might fall over, but he tried to breathe as evenly as he could, unclenching his jaw and hoping this might ease his head. Suddenly the browser's search bar opened. He typed quickly and hit go.

Please let it connect, please let it connect.

A box of text appeared, which Adam recognised from his previous perusal of Red Herring's website. The pictures would be the last things to load, but Adam didn't need them. Just the words. He scrolled the page, looking for anything which might give him a lead. There had to be a connection between the company and Becky's death. It was the means by which the stage had been set, the characters primed and, in turn, the deed executed.

The page footer had loaded now. *Privacy policy... Delivery... Join the Team...* None of these things were what he wanted. He needed to know why he had been thrown in here. He was only there for a job interview, so what was it about *him* which had given the game away? How did anyone know he had a connection to Becky, however indirect? He'd done some homework when he'd applied for the job. The 'Team' consisted of only three people: the managing director, his wife, also a director, and another man who was head of sales. But none of the names of these people meant anything to him. And who was Mel? And what position did she hold in the company? Because someone here had knowledge of the information sent out to his mum's party guests, even if they hadn't manipulated it. So who would be able to do that? And then he saw it: Help and Support.

He clicked on the link, screwing up his face as the whole screen went dark. He'd swamped the browser with redirects when the first page hadn't even loaded properly. It was incredibly tempting to keep clicking, to keep jabbing at the keypad, but he knew he mustn't. He must just wait, patiently, while the teeny bits of information tried to flow from one place to the other, rearranging and sorting themselves into the right configuration. *Come on... come on...*

A line of text appeared. Then a box, which was empty of the picture it should contain. White space stared back at him. His heart beat even faster.

And then he saw it. *Dankworth...*

And his brain made the connection almost instantly. Synapses fired, impulses stimulated his hippocampus where memories lived and, along with it, the amygdala, the portion of his brain responsible for fear and intense emotion. In a splinter of a second his brain had churned the name Dankworth and spat out another: *Ronnie*.

Adam lurched for the door, pounding his fists against it. Kicking it with all his might. Crying out for someone, *anyone*, to hear him. He rattled the door handle, cursing himself that he hadn't come prepared for anything except his interview. His lock-picking kit lay in a drawer beside his bed. He had nothing to help him, save for... *Wait*.

If he could get enough of a signal again, he could keep trying Fran. She was the only one who could help him now.

He limped back down the stairs. Moved to stand exactly where he'd been before, wiped away the wet from his cheek. This was all his fault. If he hadn't started all this he'd be in his bedroom right now, lost in some fantasy world he was creating. His mum wouldn't be... He couldn't finish the sentence, even in his head. Fran had been about to visit his mum when he had left for his interview. What if they had worked out what he had? Worked out any of it? His mum could be in terrible danger, they both could, and it was all his fault. Why hadn't he realised that the closer they got to the killer, the more danger they were all in? He had gone to Fran seeking to protect his mum in the first place, but now... He daren't think about the consequence of his actions.

He tried to calm himself, to breathe again, softly, gently. He checked the signal and dialled Fran's number. And prayed.

24

Fran had no idea where she was. She'd barely looked from side to side the whole of her journey, her focus solely on the road ahead, on the satnav screen telling her where to go. Nothing else was of any consequence. The only thing she was concerned about right now was the display counting down the miles, counting down the minutes until she might be able to help Adam.

She hadn't even thought about what she would do when she arrived at Red Herring Games, but she had to get there first. She glanced at the clock on the dash display. It was nearly a quarter to three. Adam's interview would be well in progress by now, or even over. Dear God, please don't let anything have happened to him. He had been there for over two hours already; one hundred and twenty minutes during which anything could have happened. She pressed her foot a little harder on the accelerator.

The sudden chiming of her phone might as well have been a gunshot echoing around the car. She jabbed at the button on the display which would connect the call.

'Adam...? Thank God! Where are you?'

There was burst of static so loud that Fran screwed up her face in response, struggling to make out anything coherent from the raucous crashing noise.

'*Adam!*'

'... Fran... stuck... it's...'

A beep ended the call and she wailed in frustration. '*Adam, come back, talk to me.*' She gritted her teeth, flashing one eye up to the road and one to her contacts list, stabbing wildly at Adam's name from those displayed.

Instinctively, she slowed, checking her rear-view mirror and pulling into the left-hand lane, dropping her speed to match the other vehicles. She was so close, less than ten minutes away.

She watched the screen – her name on one side, and Adam's on the other, and between them a series of dots. She willed them to connect.

Call failed.

Call failed.

Call failed.

She flicked on her indicator and pulled onto the slip lane. Adam was alive. And he had his phone with him. He had no signal, but... *Think, Fran, think, what did that mean?*

She peered at the satnav display. That couldn't be right. The place she was headed for was almost on the roundabout, but then, as she watched, the screen changed again, showing a larger scale. She was almost at the island now... indicating, slowing... traffic still coming from her right... there, a gap, pull out... round... round... signal left and... somewhere... somewhere... there, turn!

Fran lurched to a halt. In front of her was a set of large iron gates that she certainly hadn't been expecting. They were set between a high boundary wall that she could neither see over, nor hope to climb. Even if she did have the courage to do so in full view of the traffic. What did she do now?

Tutting at her stupidity, she snatched up her phone and

navigated back to the page for Red Herring Games. She found the phone number and dialled it, biting her lip as she did so.

Eventually, a woman's voice came on the line. 'Sorry to keep you. Red Herring Games, can I help?'

Fran forced herself to remain calm, to speak clearly without jabbering. She had no idea who she was talking to and she needed to be careful. 'Hi, I'm at your front gate and... how do I get in? I have a package for you.'

There was a noise which made it clear how many times they had been asked that question. 'No problem. The front gate is automatic, just drive through. Follow the road and when you come to the next set, you'll need the code 753.'

Fran grimaced at the unoriginality of the code: the diagonal numbers on a numeric keypad, she probably could have worked that out herself after a few attempts. 'Thanks. And where do I go when I get there? Are you easy to find?'

'Just head for the car park and then we're on the right. Red door with a sign outside. But if it's anything big, you'll have to carry it. I'm afraid we—'

'Great, thanks, no, it's only small, I'll manage.' Fran hung up before anyone could ask her any more questions.

For some reason Fran had imagined an industrial estate. Not an actual estate which, from the looks of things, had all the makings of Downton Abbey. She drove on through the gates, heart in her mouth.

A couple of minutes later, Fran pulled into the car park, clocking Adam's car and stopping beside it. She stared at it in dismay. On the one hand it meant that he was still here, but on the other, that was really bad news.

She had already decided to go for the direct approach; she would simply ask where Adam was. He had come for an interview, for a job which was advertised through proper channels, and for which he had applied in good faith. And no one would know who she was, after all. But, as she climbed from the car, stiff from her journey, her tongue felt thick and her legs like they might give way at any minute. She was also desperate for the loo.

She followed the directions she'd been given open-mouthed as she took in the array of buildings. All different angles and sizes, with bits of garden here and there, tubs of flowers and different-coloured doors delineating one property from another. It would be an amazing place to live, but Fran couldn't think about that now. She had spotted the red door and hurried across the courtyard.

Her knock seemed to take forever to be answered and when it was, Fran was met with a harried face that enquired none too gently: 'Yes?' A blank pause. 'Oh, the parcel...' A hand was thrust in her direction.

'Actually, I don't have a parcel,' replied Fran. 'I'm looking for someone. He had an interview with you today, and—'

She stopped at the expression on the woman's face.

'Sorry, could I come in? I've just driven rather a long way and...' She squirmed slightly. 'I really need the loo. Would you mind if...?'

There was a sigh of exasperation. 'We're a private residence, not a public toilet.' Her face was that of a woman who had already encountered far too many problems that day and Fran was simply another of them. Except that Fran hadn't had the best of days either and was quite prepared to be an even bigger problem.

'I'll wee in the garden then, shall I?' she asked, smiling sweetly. She had no time for this.

The woman stepped back from the doorway. 'I'll take you,' she said frostily.

Fran was admitted into a wide and airy hallway, whose elegance told her exactly the kind of people who ran Red Herring Games. A table held about two hundred pounds' worth of flowers in a bowl for starters.

'It's this way.'

Fran followed the woman through a doorway to her right and into a sumptuous living space, which was beautifully decorated. It was all she could do not to stand and stare. A kitchen followed and then, finally, the cloakroom. The woman pointed to the door without a word.

Fran was as quick as she could be and, on emerging, wasn't surprised to find the woman still waiting for her. She was, however, surprised by the expression on her face. She looked utterly distraught.

'Is everything all right?' Fran asked, taken aback by how anguished she looked. *Please God, let it have nothing to do with Adam.*

'Fine. We're just having rather a busy day of it, that's all. But you need to leave now,' she said.

Fran shook her head. 'I can't do that, I'm sorry. I'm looking for a friend of mine and it's really urgent that I find him. He was supposed to have an interview here at two o'clock.'

'Yes, well, he didn't turn up, so I'm afraid I have no idea where he is. Now, like I said...' The woman was already walking back towards the doorway, clearly expecting Fran to follow her.

'No, you don't understand. This is an emergency!'

'Yes, and one of our employees, and a good friend, incidentally, has just been taken ill and rushed to hospital, so if you don't mind...'

The hairs on the back of Fran's neck began to stand to attention. 'When was this?' she asked. 'What was wrong with her?'

The woman all but glared. 'I don't see how that's—'

'No, wait, listen... Please!' Fran was practically begging. She hurried after the woman. 'I think the two things might be connected – my friend disappearing and yours being taken to hospital. Please, just listen to what I have to say.'

They had reached the hallway, where a man was now

standing. He looked as harassed as the woman. 'What on earth is going on?' he asked.

Fran stood still, calming herself as best she could. 'I'm really sorry for barging in, but I don't have time to explain everything. It's vital I find my friend. I'm really scared something has happened to him. And, if I'm right, I think it might be connected to your friend becoming ill.'

'Melanie? I don't see how.'

Fran seized her opportunity. 'Melanie?' she said. 'Melanie Dankworth?'

The pair exchanged glances. 'Yes... but—'

'Has another woman been here today?' asked Fran, becoming more panic-stricken by the second. 'Her name is Ronnie. Veronica. Veronica Dankworth-Jones?'

'I don't see how—' began the woman, but the man put out an arm as if to hold her back. He took a step forward.

'I'm Clive Harrison and this is my wife, Marnie. We own Red Herring Games. I'm not quite sure what's going on here, but Ronnie is Melanie's sister-in-law... *was* her sister-in-law, technically they're not any more. But she comes here on odd occasions, yes. Why? What's the problem?'

Fran took a deep breath. 'I think Melanie might have been poisoned,' she said. 'You have to let the hospital know, straight away. If I'm right, she could die.'

Marnie's hands flew to her face. 'Poisoned? What with? Christ, Clive, I told you this was more than just stomach ache. Mel was in agony.' She stared at him in helpless indecision.

'Can you ring the hospital?' asked Fran. 'I can't be certain, but it could have been mushrooms. Death cap mushrooms!'

'I'll go,' cried Marnie, in a flurry of action. 'It's only five minutes away.' She ran into a room opposite and returned, clutching some car keys. 'I'll ring you,' she shouted from the front doorway, leaving it wide open.

Fran reeled from the sudden activity, buffeted by the swirling air which Marnie left behind. Clive was staring at her.

'I think you'd better explain,' he said. 'I don't know who you are, but—'

'Please, I haven't got time to explain. I need to find my friend. His name is Adam Smith, and he was supposed to be here for an interview today.'

'He didn't turn up,' Clive said. 'Or rather he did. Mel said he arrived far too early, so he went away to wait. Then he just didn't show up again. We had quite a few people to see and now we've had to cancel everything. I don't know what the hell is going on.'

'What time was Mel taken ill?' asked Fran, ignoring his concern. She didn't give a stuff about his interviews.

Clive looked at his watch. 'I don't know, just after two. Maybe a bit later. The ambulance has not long gone.'

Fran must have just missed it. 'Can you think of anywhere my friend might be? His car is still in the car park.'

'I've no idea. He could be anywhere. But he isn't here, if that's what you think. And if he's had anything to do with Mel, then—'

'He hasn't!' Fran was becoming more and more exasperated by the moment. 'He's trying to *save* someone's life. So am I for that matter! Where did Ronnie go? Has she definitely left?'

'Again, I have no idea. I would imagine so.' He was staring at the front door as if he hoped his wife might materialise again at any moment.

But Fran had had enough. She could see he was worried about Mel, frustrated about the lost interviews and the way his day had disintegrated around him, but she'd had enough, and her patience finally snapped.

'Do you have neighbours?' she asked. 'I bet you do... I bet there are loads of people out there who could be quite interested in seeing a small, dark-haired woman, wailing like a banshee out in the courtyard. Because I can, you know. I can make quite a bit of noise when I put my mind to it. And my tether has well and truly *reached its end*! So, are you going to stop being so unhelpful, and help me start looking for Adam, or do I have to start yelling?'

Clive stared at her as if suddenly seeing her for the first time. 'No... Yes. Yes, of course I'll help. There's no need...' He stopped and gave her a suddenly warm smile. 'I'm sorry.' He nodded. 'Mel mentioned she'd made him a cup of tea and pointed him in the direction of the garden. Come on, I'll show you.'

Clive was a big man, but he moved with surprising speed, and Fran hurried after him.

'The garden's this way, but I don't know if he'll be here. I didn't see him – you can't, you see, from the garden, our office windows only overlook the front courtyard.'

They emerged into a large, squarish space, which clever design and planting had subdivided into different areas.

'Adam!'

Fran's yell took them both by surprise. It was instinctive. She turned back to Clive.

'You don't know where Mel suggested he wait?' She didn't know why she was asking, really. An ambulance had been and gone, as had Adam's interview time. He wouldn't be simply sitting on a bench, calmly drinking tea.

Clive shook his head. 'I don't, I'm sorry. It wasn't that sort of a conversation. She mentioned it because we were waiting to start his interview, but then she felt... She began to feel really ill and... I suppose someone should have gone to look for him.'

'It's okay,' replied Fran kindly. 'You weren't to know.' She spun around, frantically scanning the garden, searching the grass, the bushes, anywhere Adam might have fallen, anywhere he might be... she couldn't finish the thought.

'Are there any outbuildings? A shed? Or storeroom maybe?' She thought about his phone call, the lack of signal.

Clive's face lit up. 'The stables,' he said. 'This way.'

He led them towards a stone building, which Fran had taken for another property. 'We have Wi-Fi in here, he might have been trying to work.'

Fran scanned the room, entirely open to the garden at the front. 'Adam!' She hurried to the table. 'Oh God, this is his bag, look.' She spun around. *Was that...?* She thought she heard something. 'Adam!' she yelled again, straining to hear. *There...* there *was* something. She looked at Clive.

'I know where he could be!' he shouted, disappearing back out into the garden. He raced up some steps at the side of the building and yanked at the handle of a door set into the wall.

Fran had heard Adam, she was certain. And if she'd heard him, then he was still alive.

'Damn!' Clive peered down at her. 'It's locked. And the key's gone. There's a spare in the house, I'll go and get it.'

Fran nodded. 'Please, be quick,' she urged. She waited until Clive had run past her again before running up the steps and flinging herself at the door.

'Adam! Can you hear me?'

There was a faint sound from within, and then another.

'Adam!'

'Fran...?' And then louder. 'Fran, is that you...?' She could hear him now, on the other side of the door.

'Yes, it's me. Are you okay? We're just getting the key... Oh God, hold on... Tell me you're okay.'

'I'm okay. Fran, it's Ronnie,' he yelled through the door, his voice harsh and raspy. 'She's the one who's done all this, and—' He broke off, coughing.

'Don't,' she said. 'Wait until we get you out.' She lay her head against the door and talked, a string of nothingness, but reassurance she hoped, while they waited out the eternity for Clive to arrive.

She made way for him as he approached, taking the steps two at a time. And then the door was open, and Adam was flinching at the light, falling into her arms as she pulled him through the door. Battered and bruised, hoarse and trembling, but alive.

'It's okay, it's okay,' she murmured, every maternal instinct within her firing. She pulled away to look at him, peering at the blood on the side of his face, her eyes filled with compassion. 'Can we get him back to the house, Clive, please?'

'I'm okay,' protested Adam. 'I just need a drink.' He looked up into her face. 'Fran, we need to go, we—'

But she shushed him.

'In a minute. Let's make sure you're okay first. What happened to you?' She helped him gingerly down the steps.

Adam shook his head, wincing. 'I don't know, really. I came out here to wait and heard a noise. Next thing, I'm pushed inside. I fell. There're steps.' He touched a hand to the side of his head. 'It must have been Ronnie. She's been here, Fran, I'm sure of it.' His eyes narrowed, searching her face. 'But you know that, don't you? You know it's her.'

Fran nodded. 'I saw the name, Dankworth. I'm guessing that's how you found out too.' She waited for his answering nod. 'I know it's Ronnie, but I still don't understand. I still don't know why she's done all this, I'm just very glad it's not your mum. God, Adam, I was really beginning to think it was her!' Her gaze glued itself to the blood on his head and she swallowed. 'Adam, Camilla's dead. We don't know how, it looks as if it was a heart attack, but...' She didn't finish. There was really no need.

They were at the bottom of the steps now, Clive waiting anxiously. 'We need to call the police,' he said. 'I don't know what's been going on here, but this kind of thing – what with Mel as well – it just shouldn't be happening.'

'I think Mel's been poisoned,' explained Fran to Adam gently. 'She's been taken to hospital. She's Ronnie's sister-in-law.'

Adam stared at her, horrified, nodding as he fitted the pieces of information together. 'My laptop's down here. I left it when I heard the noise and—' He stopped, staring at the table where his bag lay, but nothing else. 'Okay, so she's taken that as well. Damn.' He turned to Clive. 'Please, I need to see your computers. Mel's in particular. I was just about to check her files, and I'm almost certain that when we do, we'll find evidence of how this whole game was organised; how Ronnie manipulated the whole thing.'

Clive looked at Fran and then slowly back to Adam. Adam's words were brusque, but he now understood the importance of them. 'I don't think I want to know how you were going to check Mel's files, but come on, I'll show you.'

Once inside the house, Fran manoeuvred Adam into the office at Clive's suggestion and waited while he went to fetch Adam a glass of water.

'We've got to get back home,' Adam began, refusing to sit down despite his injuries. 'There's no telling what Ronnie might do. What if Mum discovers—'

'I know,' agreed Fran. 'But we need to understand what's been going on as well. Whatever Ronnie has done, we need proof. And don't worry about your mum. She was going to be with a client all afternoon. Wherever she is, she's out of harm's way.'

Adam nodded. 'Okay.' He accepted the glass of water from Clive gratefully and downed it in one continual swallow. 'Thank you.'

Clive crossed to another desk. 'My wife always keeps these in her desk drawer. They might help too.'

Adam smiled at the packet in Clive's hand. 'Tunnock's wafers,' he said. 'It's a shame I'm never going to be working for you if that's what treats are on offer.'

Clive smiled, but then his face sobered. 'What do I need to do?' he asked, sitting behind a desk.

'Right. I haven't got time to explain everything, but my mum ordered a game from you, a bespoke one. And I don't know all the details but, somewhere along the line, I think Mel was asked to send out some very specific instructions for it.' He glanced at Fran. 'A friend of my mum's was murdered, and this game lies at the root of it somehow. It wasn't Mel's fault. My guess is that Ronnie asked her to do it, saying it was just a bit of fun, or something like that. I don't suppose Mel ever realised the consequences of what she was doing, but Mel is our only witness to what has gone on, the only person who can testify to what Ronnie asked her to do.' He gave Clive an anguished look. 'I'm really sorry, but I think that's why Mel has been poisoned, to take her out of the equation.' He paused a moment. 'Do you have a memory stick or an external hard drive?'

Clive nodded. 'Yes, both.' His fingers tapped on the keyboard. 'What am I looking for?'

'Okay, so my mum's name is Sara Smith, and the game was played for her birthday party on the third of April. The game was ordered by her friend though, Becky Pearson...'

Adam waited until Clive had jotted down the names and dates on a piece of paper by his side.

'It would have been sent to an address in Shrewsbury. Please, just look for anything and everything you can which related to that order, electronic files or otherwise. Make a copy of it on whichever external drive you want, and then keep it somewhere safe. If anything happens to this computer, or the files on it, we need to make sure we have a copy. The police are going to want to see it.' He gave Clive a tight smile. 'And pray your friend's okay. She may be our only witness.'

Clive looked up from making another note. 'Okay, I've got all that. What are you going to do?'

'We have to get home, and quickly,' Adam replied. 'But call the police. Tell them what I've told you, and if you see Ronnie, don't try and be clever, just stay out of her way.' He clenched his jaw, wincing in pain. 'But if I'm right you won't see her, she's long gone.' He stared at Fran. 'And I think I know where...'

25

'Don't argue,' said Fran, 'You're in no fit state to drive.'

'Yes, but my car is faster than yours.'

They were crunching back across the car park, Adam still noticeably limping.

'Adam, you are not driving for two-and-a-half hours when you can barely walk. Besides...'

She stopped, pointing at Adam's car.

Adam groaned. '*All* four tyres, really? She had to slash all four... Do you know how much those things cost?'

Fran, who had walked around one side of the car, stooped to pick something up. 'You might be needing a new laptop too.' She dangled what was left of the computer, the lid hanging off, a huge crack across the screen. 'Okay. I was scared before, now I'm bloody furious. Get in the car.'

Adam gave her a wary look and hurried over. She waited until he was settled beside her with his seat belt on.

'So, what do we do now?' she asked. 'Apart from drive home at speed, find Ronnie and...' She made a twisting motion with her hands. ''Cause we still don't know what's been going on. It's as if there's a whole chunk of the puzzle missing, and I can't help feeling we've been looking in the wrong place.'

Adam nodded, a pained expression on his face. 'You wouldn't happen to have any paracetamol, would you?'

'You ought to get that looked at,' she said, frowning as she peered at his head. 'I think it's just a surface wound, but you might have concussion.'

'Later maybe. I'm okay, it's nothing, really. Actually, I'm not sure I haven't broken my toe, but—'

'*Adam.*'

'I kicked the door and it was a lot harder than I thought. That oak's been there a very long time, it's like iron.' He shook his head. 'Never mind.'

Fran lifted her bag from the passenger footwell. 'In there,' she said. 'Have a rummage. And there's water in that bottle in the door pocket. Help yourself.'

'Aren't women's handbags sacrosanct? I seem to remember my mum saying something of the sort.'

'Mine isn't,' replied Fran, pulling out of the car park. 'I have no secrets.' She bit her lip. It wasn't a lie, not really. She was going to tell Jack about all this... when it was over. She waited while the gate slowly swung open, muttering for it to hurry up under her breath. 'So, what's your thinking?' she asked, looking across at Adam, who was still swigging water, tipping his head back. Despite the situation, she smiled. She couldn't take tablets easily either.

'I'm still trying to puzzle it out. I'm hoping it will come to me.'

'Okay, but don't keep it to yourself. Two heads and all that.' She touched a finger to the satnav screen, checking that it was taking her in the direction of home. She was about to pull out onto the main road when the display lit up with an incoming call. She grimaced.

'Fran? Where are you, is everything okay?'

'Hi, Jack, yes, I'm fine. I'm just... driving at the moment, so I can't really talk.'

'Okay, as long as you're all right. When I came home and found water still in the sink and dishes everywhere, it looked like you'd abandoned it. I wondered if someone had been taken ill or something. Your dad's all right, is he?'

'She's fine... at least I think she is. Jack, I'm really sorry, but I've got to go.'

'No problem, I'll see you later, yeah? Oh, Fran? Before you go, this thing tonight, it's not posh, is it? Have I got to wear a tie?'

Shit... Fran could feel heat flooding her face. 'No, I don't think so, just wear a shirt, that'll be fine.'

'Great. Okay, love, see you later.'

''Kay... bye, love you.'

'Love you too.'

Fran ended the call and closed her eyes momentarily, swallowing.

'Is everything all right?' Adam was staring at her from the passenger seat.

'My daughter has her dance show this evening. At seven. What with everything else, I'd completely forgotten.'

'We could still make it,' he said.

Fran shook her head. 'It's fine. Come on, let's go.' She put both hands back on the steering wheel, angling her arm slightly so she could see her watch. Everything was far from fine.

Neither of them said a word until Fran had safely navigated back onto the motorway.

'Right, so let's put Ronnie aside for a minute and go over what we know,' Fran began. 'Starting with Becky's murder. Firstly, we needed to know the motive, and it soon became very obvious that Becky was blackmailing everyone who was a guest at the party.'

'Everyone except Mum,' put in Adam.

'Yes, everyone except Sara. But all the other guests had clearly been targeted. The game itself was all about a black-mailer, and Becky herself played the titular character. So when she wrote to all the guests saying she had devised a character for them, who just happened to have a secret which bore an uncanny similarity to their own, and then she included a note which hinted very strongly that she *knew* that secret, it didn't take much to put two and two together.'

'Except that the secrets weren't really worthy of blackmail at all,' said Adam.

'Yes, I'm coming to that,' replied Fran. 'Hang on.' She over-took a lorry and then pulled back into the slow lane. 'So, on the face of it we had our motive, and any of the guests could have been the killer. But investigations subsequently seemed to discount Camilla and then Lois because, while they did have a secret, it wasn't anything to be ashamed of, and certainly wouldn't be worth blackmailing anyone over.'

'But the blackmailer clearly didn't know that.'

Fran paused. 'How do you mean?'

'Well, if you hadn't gone to the trouble of finding out about those secrets, if you'd just *assumed*, like we did to start with, you'd jump to entirely the wrong conclusion.'

Fran flashed him a look. 'My God... that's true. So what does that tell us? That the blackmailer was sloppy? Or that they didn't really care what the secrets were, they just needed there to be *something*... Okay, let's think. After we discounted Lois and Camilla that left us with Diane who, again, without digging any deeper, seemed to have the biggest secret of them all *and* the most to lose. But even that has turned out to be innocuous. So, just like that, our motives have all gone up in a puff of smoke.'

She grimaced. 'And then we come to opportunity... Camilla had an alibi, as did Lois and Diane, although a bit of fishing uncovered this to be a lie. Even then though, given that Diane had no motive for murder, her dinner with Becky doesn't seem to have been anything other than two friends getting together. It would have been hard to slip mushrooms into a salad, and why even would Diane do that? It doesn't make sense.'

'Which is precisely the problem, isn't it?' replied Adam. 'None of this makes any sense. It did. It all seemed to make perfect sense, but now...'

Fran tutted. 'That's just it. It's as if we've run out of suspects, motives *and* opportunity. And now there's Ronnie. We know there's a connection. We know she's involved. For God's sake, she locked you in a storeroom, slashed your tyres and mangled your laptop. She's most definitely involved. But why? And how? I even thought she might be another potential victim of blackmail, even though she couldn't go to the party, but that's not it either. Everyone knew she wouldn't be there.'

'There is one other thing we no longer have.'

'Go on.'

'We no longer have Becky as a blackmailer. I don't think she was blackmailing anyone. The notes that she supposedly sent weren't handwritten, remember, they could have been sent by anyone. I think Ronnie was framing her.'

'Then why was she killed?'

'Why indeed?' Adam wiggled his fingers. 'See, that's the real thing that doesn't make any sense. I know that Ronnie got Mel to send out all the details for the game, but why would she do that? That only makes sense if Becky was a blackmailer. But now we think she isn't and...' He broke off, throwing both hands in the air.

'Oh, *now* I get it,' he said. 'The dead can't speak, can they? So we can't ask Becky if she was blackmailing anyone. And this whole thing hinges on that very fact. With no blackmailer, there's no need for motives or opportunity, because in fact that's not what this whole thing has been about at all...'

Fran could hear the incredulity in Adam's voice, the dawning realisation of something.

'What?' she asked, desperate to look at him.

'Oh God, I've been so slow. This whole thing... Jesus, I can't believe it.'

'What?' asked Fran frantically. '*What?*'

'It's all been a huge bluff. There never was any blackmail. Becky never did anything wrong, and neither did Mum nor any of her friends. It's all been a cover, a smokescreen, designed to hide the real motive and the real killer. Identifying Becky as a doer of evil deeds meant that when she was murdered we automatically looked for suspects, and when we did, Ronnie had set the perfect stage on which they could play, literally. It's just like one of my games, Fran, simulated reality, not the real thing at all, instead a game within a game.'

This time Fran did look at him, her mouth hanging open in astonishment. 'But that's... that's...'

'Very, *very* clever,' supplied Adam. 'Think about it. Becky was killed after she'd eaten some mushrooms. Mushrooms which, although deadly, are actually pretty common in the wild. There's a possibility then that her death might have been ruled as misadventure, a tragic accident, no more. But if not, what then? If foul play becomes suspected, then the finger of suspicion moves to point first at the loving husband. Once *that* possibility becomes exhausted then, like a gift, the most brilliant scenario is offered up. A whole group of suspects with multiple motives between them and a victim who wasn't the loving and loveable wife and friend everyone thought she was, but instead a callous blackmailer, driven by her need to have a child. And poor Becky, already dead, was never able to defend herself. Who wouldn't grasp at that heap of possibility? We fell for it hook, line and sinker, just like Ronnie intended.'

Fran could tell that Adam was on a roll now, all the little nuances of Ronnie's machinations falling into place.

'And it was risky too,' he continued. 'Don't forget that Ronnie had to plant the whole idea of the murder-mystery party in the first place. She even offered to organise it but then, given that she wouldn't be attending, suggested that someone take over that role. Ronnie took a calculated gamble that Becky would be the one to offer, but that gamble came good. Don't forget what Lois said about Becky, that she was the friend who tried to keep them all together. Becky was the most obvious person to offer but, even if she didn't, it wouldn't have made much difference in the long run. The fact that she did just made it all the sweeter for Ronnie.'

'Except that Ronnie didn't do quite enough research, did she?' offered Fran. 'If she had, she would have realised, like we have, that the secrets everyone has been hiding don't provide any motive for blackmail at all, let alone murder. So maybe she hasn't been quite as clever as she thinks she has.'

Fran thought for a moment. 'But all of that still doesn't tell us *why* Ronnie would want to kill Becky. They've been friends for years. So did Ronnie have a secret that Becky discovered after all?'

'It's possible,' replied Adam. 'But somehow I don't think so. It seems too close to the smokescreen that Ronnie set up. I don't think she would draw attention to herself in that way, it's too obvious.'

Fran flicked an anxious glance in her rear-view mirror as a car cut in front of her. 'So what else do we know about Ronnie? I've never met the woman.' But she *nearly* had. That morning when she first met Nick.

'Not much,' said Adam. 'I try to stay out of the way of my mum's friends. Not that Ronnie's ever been any worse than the others. Calls me her favourite barmpot, which is irritating but, up until now, I'd have said she was pretty harmless. Divorced, works as a sales rep, I think. Mum mentioned once that when her husband left, he also left her with a huge pile of debt, but she's always seemed cheerful enough when I've seen her.'

Fran tried to concentrate on what Adam was saying, but a sudden thought had cut across his words. 'Wait a minute,' she said. 'I've had this weird feeling for ages that I've missed something. And it was niggling me again today while I was standing in my kitchen. That was relevant somehow, but—' She broke off, eyes widening in alarm. 'Oh my God, I've just realised what it was. It wasn't anything about *my* kitchen which was bugging me. Or your mum's. It was Becky's.' She turned her head to Adam. 'Where was the liquidiser?'

Adam looked blank.

'Becky's liquidiser. I *knew* something wasn't right. It was in the cupboard, that's where, pushed right to the back, which makes no sense at all.'

'Doesn't it?' Adam smiled sheepishly.

'No! Don't you remember me telling you about the fridge in Becky's kitchen? The salad drawer was full of kale and carrots, and other leafy stuff, most of it turned to slime. That's what she used, you see, that was the clue!

'Becky was a runner. And she'd been for a run on the day that she was taken ill, Lois told me that. She also told me that when she and Becky met for a coffee, Lois had a piece of cake but Becky didn't have anything. She liked to watch what she ate, and she'd had one of her smoothies that morning, straight after her run. Nick told me the same thing too! God, how could I have been so slow?'

'You're going to have to slow down for *me*, Fran, I'm struggling here.'

'Think about it a moment. Becky and Nick were trying for a baby. Becky was doing everything she could to keep healthy – running as often as time allowed, making herself nutritious smoothies – so her liquidiser wouldn't be stuffed at the back of a cupboard, would it? It would be somewhere to hand, where it was easy to get at and use, every day...' A sudden spike of adrenaline shot through her.

'The mushrooms must have been slipped in the smoothie before it was blended... How easy would it be to pop one in among the mixture of other stuff in there? Once liquidised, you'd never be able to see it, or taste it. Becky had been out for a run on the morning of the day she was taken ill, had come home, showered, changed, all the usual routine, and then begun to make a smoothie to provide her fit and healthy body with a dose of everything that was good for her. Except that, at some point, while she was doing all those things, Ronnie, knowing her routine, paid her a visit. Nothing unusual about that. Ronnie was her best friend and would have probably popped in for a chat quite often, for a coffee, anything. And then, under some pretence or other, while Becky's back was turned, she popped a mushroom or two into the liquidiser. Becky whizzed it up, drank it down and, unwittingly, allowed Ronnie to murder her.'

'I don't believe it,' said Adam, shaking his head incredulously. 'No, I do believe it. I think that's absolutely what happened. And I bet Ronnie was there the whole time, watching Becky while she enjoyed her drink. How can anyone be so callous?' He swallowed, his voice hoarse and ragged with emotion. 'She must have really hated Becky to do something like that.'

Fran let out a shaky breath. 'But why? Dammit! That still doesn't tell us why.' She drummed her fingers against the steering wheel. 'This has got nothing to do with blackmail, and nothing to do with secrets either. It's something far less complicated than that. We've been led a right merry dance, when all the while the motive was probably the same as any other. Good old-fashioned hatred.' She put her hand to her mouth. 'I feel sick now. Worse, I have a horrible feeling that Ronnie hasn't finished yet. We have to catch up with her, Adam, and soon. If only we could figure out why Ronnie hated Becky so much.' She waggled her fingers. 'Give me some motives for murder.'

There was a momentary pause. 'Greed,' suggested Adam. 'Jealousy, a crime of passion, revenge... um...'

'No, that's good,' replied Fran. 'Now let's see – greed. Admittedly, I don't know Ronnie, but did Becky have vastly more money than Ronnie? I wouldn't have said so. And, as far as we know, there's no large inheritance or life insurance policy which would pay out to Ronnie on the event of Becky's death. I've always associated greed as a motive within families, not between friends.' She stared at the road ahead, thinking. 'No, I can't see greed as a motive. So, what's next? Jealousy... Now that seems a bit more like it. Something Becky had which Ronnie coveted. It would have to be something big – on the face of it, Becky didn't have anything which Ronnie would kill for. House, car, jewellery, none of that would make much sense.' She sucked in a breath. 'Oh!' Her round note of surprise sat in the air between her and Adam like a bubble waiting to be popped. 'What about a husband? Could *Nick* be the thing that Ronnie coveted?'

'Yes! It's the only thing that would make sense. But...'

Fran could almost see the procession of thoughts through Adam's brain.

'But for Ronnie to want Nick, does that imply that Nick might want Ronnie too, to some degree at least? Or else Ronnie is simply delusional which, given her behaviour, would make sense. I don't think there's ever been any suggestion that Nick and Ronnie were in a relationship, has there? And don't forget Becky and Nick were just about to start the process of applying to become foster carers, that's a very long-term commitment.'

Fran shook her head. 'True, and something about an affair doesn't feel right. No one has made even the slightest suggestion that Nick was involved with anyone else, and it's the kind of thing that friends pick up on. I'm sure someone would have said something, were that the case. Or Becky herself might have confided in someone if she thought Nick was having an affair. It's still entirely possibly though... Which brings us lastly to a crime of passion. That would make more sense. If Nick had rejected Ronnie. Perhaps she'd made a play for him and he rebutted her. The woman scorned...'

'Or, if they *were* having an affair, Nick could've told her he wanted to end things, that he loved his wife. Ronnie's divorced, she's been unlucky in love before.'

'Hmm... and then there's revenge, which could tie in with that.'

'A dish best served cold,' replied Adam, blowing out a puff of air.

Fran was about to reply when she realised Adam's words had snagged on her brain. 'What did you say?'

'A dish best served cold,' he repeated. 'It's what they say about revenge, so—'

'No, I know what it means, just...' She pressed a hand against her forehead, groaning with frustration. 'There's something there again, something one of us has said which...' She took a deep breath. 'Tell me again what you said about Ronnie. What you know about her.'

Adam sighed. 'Well, she's divorced, she's a sales rep, she—'

Fran held up her hand. 'Why would she call you a barmpot? You mentioned that before, right at the very start of all this.'

'I don't know, it's just a saying, isn't it? For someone stupid. I think Ronnie meant it ironically.'

'Yes, but the word "barmpot". Why not idiot? Or dimwit? Dummy?'

'It's just a word, isn't it? Where Ronnie comes from, it's the word they'd use.'

'*They'd?*'

'Someone from Yorkshire.'

'*It were proper chew-eh...*' Fran murmured. 'Becky and Ronnie come from the same area....' She turned to Adam, a triumphant look on her face.

He stared back. 'They do. I've never thought about it before, but they both have the same strong accent.'

'And your mum said they'd been friends a long time. What if they've been friends for a *really* long time? What if Becky did something to Ronnie years ago? Something that Ronnie had never forgotten. *Revenge is a dish best served cold.* That's it, Adam, that's got to be it!'

26

'Keep trying your mum,' said Fran, glancing at Adam as she increased the pressure on the accelerator pedal. 'Her client lives in a blackspot for phone reception, but she should be back on the road now. As soon as she picks up signal, she'll get our messages. We're only half an hour away, we need to speak to her as soon as we can.'

Fran glanced at her watch and then the dashboard. She had said only half an hour, but for Fran, time had run out. There was no way she could be in two places at once and she had a decision to make. Except there really wasn't a choice. She knew what she had to do. And what the consequences might be.

She had her phone dial Jack's number and waited with a sinking heart as the call connected.

'Fran? Where the bloody hell are you? I thought you would have been home by now. I've made a start on tea, but—'

'Jack, I'm sorry, I should have been. And thank you, but something came up and I was late leaving and well, now I'm stuck in traffic.'

'Where are you?'

'I'm still about half an hour away,' she replied, hoping he wouldn't notice she hadn't actually answered his question.

'Okay, well just get here when you can. We can still make it.'

She paused a moment, her heart pulling her in two directions at once. 'The thing is, Jack... I might not be able to come straight home. There's something I need to do first.'

'*What?* What can you possibly have to do?' His exasperation was clear. 'Whatever it is can wait, surely? You're on "you" time now, Fran, not work time. It's gone six o'clock and Martha will be leaving soon.'

'I know... And if I could do it differently, I would, but this is really important.'

'And your daughter's show isn't?'

'Jack, I didn't say that. I've never missed a show, an end-of-term concert, sports day, parents' evening... I've marked every occasion in our daughter's life and I wouldn't be thinking about missing Martha's show now if this wasn't something vital.'

A pause. 'Well, what is it then?'

'Oh, Jack... I can't... It's really complicated. I'm sorry.'

A pause. 'Has that lad you've got working with you got anything to do with it? Because you've been acting weird since he came on the scene. Taking phone calls at all hours, secretive ones, mind. Working late, disappearing at odd intervals. Your normal working pattern has gone right out the window these last couple of weeks.' A longer pause. 'Is there something going on between you?'

Fran took a deep breath. 'Yes, Jack, there is, but it's not what you think, so don't for one minute think we're having an affair. I'm your wife, Jack. We've been married for sixteen years and I want to be married to you for the next forty at least. I bloody love you, you daft idiot. *But...* Adam and I *have* been working on something, and I can't tell you about it now, you're just going to have to trust me. I've never had to ask you that before and I'm not doing anything wrong now, I swear, but I'm still not going to tell you what it is.'

Fran's heart pounded as she waited for her husband to say something, anything, to put her out of her misery.

'I love you too,' he said softly. 'You're not going to make Martha's show, are you?'

'No,' she whispered, the words sticking in her throat. 'I'm sorry, I don't think I am.'

'Then I'll just have to be enough for both of us, won't I? It's okay, Fran, don't worry. She'll be disappointed, but I'll think of something, and if I can't, then I'll just have to resort to bribery and corruption to make it up to her. Pizza Hut at the weekend, or something like that.'

'Thank you, Jack, really. And tell her I know she's going to be amazing. Tell her I love her.'

She could hear Jack's smile. 'I will. Oh, and Fran? Promise me you'll tell me what this is all about when you get home.'

'I will, I promise.' She hung up and a heavy silence filled the car. 'That was unfortunate,' she said when she couldn't bear it any longer. 'I'm sorry, Adam, you probably didn't need to hear that.'

'No, it's okay, I... What's the show you're going to miss? Is it what Martha and her friend were rehearsing for the other day?'

Fran nodded. 'The dance group she belongs to hosts a spring show every year. And now that she's a bit older, she has quite a nice part this time.'

Adam cleared his throat. 'I'm sorry you're going to miss it,' he replied. 'This couldn't have come at a worse time, could it?'

Fran gave her best smile. 'There'll be other shows, and it's not like I don't ever get to see Martha dance – she does it all the time at home.'

'Even so...'

'Even so,' Fran repeated. 'Crap, being an adult is hard sometimes. Being a mother can be next to impossible.'

Adam was quiet beside her.

'And don't you go thinking any of this is your fault,' she added. 'Because it isn't.'

'Unusually for me, I wasn't actually thinking that. I was thinking about Mum. About how hard things have been for her. Things that didn't have to be so hard until I made them that way.'

Fran thought for a moment, unsure how much she should tell him. 'You were a child, Adam, caught in a system that had no room for someone like you. That's the system's fault, not yours. And, you know, I think your mum understands that just fine. I haven't had a chance to say this yet, but when I went to see her this morning, the police had paid her a visit and it seems as if Nick has had to tell them about the game. They don't know everything we do, not by a long stretch, and I managed to reassure her that it was all going to be okay. And it is. But I had to tell her that we thought someone at the games company might have had something to do with the sending out of the blackmail notes, instead of Becky. It didn't take her long to realise that your interview at Red Herring Games wasn't simply coincidence. She was worried about you, Adam, and I had to tell her all of it, how we've been working together right from the start. I'm sorry, I didn't know what else to say.'

Adam let out a long, slow breath. 'I guess it was only a matter of time before she found out,' he said. 'The same as Jack. Things seem to be coming to a head, don't they?'

'It's time to finish this, Adam,' said Fran, sounding grimmer than she'd intended. 'And, once it is, then we'll have time to talk to those we need to.'

He nodded. 'Okay...'

Fran glanced at him. He was clearly still thinking about something. 'And...?'

'Does your husband really think we're having an affair?'

She smiled. 'No, but when you've been married a while it's

easy to spot when something isn't quite right.' She darted Adam another look. 'Don't worry about it, honestly. He's not going to come chasing after you with a big stick or anything. In a way, it's quite flattering.'

'Is it?' He blinked back at her. 'I had wondered whether people might think I'm your son. I mean, your husband wouldn't think that, obviously. Although he might, I suppose. I could be a long-lost son from before he knew you, but generally —' He stopped. 'That came out wrong, because I wouldn't have a problem being your son... and I'm not saying you look old enough to be my...' He paused. 'So maybe what I'm feeling is relief, and that, out of the two, I might prefer to be considered a catch.' He ran a hand over his face. 'I'm babbling. You should ignore everything I'm saying.'

Fran sounded her amusement. 'Actually, Adam, in a very roundabout way, that was extremely eloquent.'

She drew his attention to a road sign which was rapidly approaching. 'So what do we do now?' she asked. 'Where do we go? To your mum's or...'

'Hang on, I'll try her again. Mum?' Adam added seconds later as the call connected. 'Where are you?' He tapped his phone to put her on loudspeaker.

'I'm almost home. Why? Is everything okay?'

'Yes, I'm fine.' He pulled a face at Fran. 'And I'm on my way home too. But listen, Mum, something's happened and... There's no time to explain it all, but we know who killed Becky. It's Ronnie, Mum, you need to—'

'Ronnie? But how on earth can it be Ronnie? She wasn't even at the party. And I saw her only this morning.'

Fran exchanged a look with Adam. 'Sara? It's me, Fran. Hi, yes, I'm with Adam. But you didn't tell me you'd seen Ronnie, when was this?'

'A little before the police arrived, but I was in such a tizz after their visit, I probably just forgot. Anyway, why would I have mentioned it? I didn't think anything of it. Ronnie popped in to see how I was doing – she's just as worried about this whole thing as the rest of us.' There was a long pause. 'Are you really sure she—'

'Yes,' said Adam quickly. 'Absolutely sure. Listen, Mum, you didn't have anything to eat or drink, did you?'

'No, but—'

'You're sure?'

'Yes, Ronnie didn't stay long, she had to dash off, something about work.'

'Okay, but if you see her when you get home, call the police, okay? Don't let her in.'

'What?'

Fran spoke again. 'Sara, this is really important. How long have Becky and Ronnie known one another? I know you said a long time, but how long?'

'They went to school together, so twenty-odd years, I should think. They've always been the best of friends.'

'And what about Nick? When did Becky meet him?'

'Crikey. At uni, so... ten years or so, I don't know exactly. It was Ronnie who introduced them.'

'And did anything ever happen between them? A falling-out maybe?'

'Not that Becky's ever mentioned.'

Fran looked across at Adam, eyes wide. 'Okay, Sara, we're about ten minutes away, but do as Adam said. If you see Ronnie, just call the police. Actually, do that anyway. We'll see you soon.'

Fran pulled up behind a lorry at a set of traffic lights. 'It's what Ronnie is going to do now that worries me,' she said. 'She must know that we've figured things out, or at least are close to doing so. But somehow I don't think she's finished yet.'

'Unfinished business,' murmured Adam. 'When I first realised who Ronnie was, and what she'd done, it was my mum

I was scared for because of what she might know. But Ronnie has spoken to her this morning, so she already knows that Mum hasn't figured out anything. So she's hardly a loose end, is she?'

'No, I don't think she is. But Ronnie knows you're on to her now. Possibly me too.'

'She had a chance to get rid of me though, and she didn't. She just tried to slow me down. I don't think I'm her target either. But who's the one person who knows the history between Becky and Ronnie? Who knows everything that went on?'

'Shit.' Fran flicked her indicator left, pulling forward and, with a nervous glance in her rear-view mirror, angled the car into the next lane. A lane that would take her in a completely different direction to the one she had originally planned. 'Come on, come on,' she urged, inching forward as she willed the lights to change.

Adam wasted no time in picking up his phone again. 'Mum, it's me. Listen, there's been a change of plan... And I need you to do something.'

27

Five minutes later, Fran drove past Nick's house, craning her neck as she did so. 'Ronnie won't have parked outside, that's far too obvious. There!' she added, as they drove past a side turning, where Ronnie's black Golf was parked a little way down behind another car. Stopping, Fran reversed quickly and turned down the same street.

'What are you doing?' asked Adam.

Fran gave him a determined smile. 'You'll see.' She pulled into the kerb behind Ronnie's car, inching forward by degrees until bonnet and boot were almost touching. 'Now let's see her try to get away in a hurry.'

'You're good at this, aren't you?'

'I'm learning,' she replied grimly, climbing from the car.

'So how are we going to play this?' asked Adam as he walked alongside her.

'I'm going to waltz right up to the front door and ring the bell,' she replied. 'I'm banking on Nick being a little unnerved by Ronnie's visit and desperate for an interruption. Failing that, I'm going round the back. As soon as we're in there I'm just going to ask her what she thinks she's up to.'

'Okay... if you're sure.'

Fran turned to face him. 'Adam, you're black and blue, she's trashed your car and your laptop. I've just driven for five hours straight, I'm tired, hungry and I'm missing my daughter's show this evening. Quite frankly, I'm at the end of my tether, exceedingly grumpy and quite possibly hormonal too. I think Ronnie might be a good person on whom to relieve some of my stress.'

Adam held her look and gave the slightest of nods. 'Fair enough.'

Nick answered the door after a period of time which felt heart-stoppingly like forever. His face mirrored the surprise he undoubtedly felt and Fran reckoned he'd never had so many visitors all at once. Although his reaction could have been at the sight of Adam's head, which was still a little bloody and a variety of colours too.

'Hi!' said Fran brightly. 'Thanks, we'd love to come in.'

She strode past Nick and on down the hallway into the kitchen, where Ronnie was just getting up from the table. Nick was evidently halfway through his tea.

'Oh, don't leave on our account,' said Fran, as Nick and Adam came into the room. 'Actually, don't leave at all. I've got some things I'd like to ask you.'

Ronnie stared at her. 'And who the hell are you?'

'I think you know very well who I am,' she replied, staring right back.

It was the first time she'd had a proper good look at Ronnie, aka Veronica Dankworth-Jones, murderess. And she looked entirely ordinary. She looked like any other woman you might pass in the street and to whom you wouldn't give a second thought. She was wearing jeans, a striped top, and trainers, which were exactly the make fashion dictated they should be. She didn't look at all like someone who had forgotten what it was to be human. And the normality of her appearance made the hairs stand up on the back of Fran's neck. A monster had been walking among them, and none of them had been any the wiser.

'I'm a friend of Sara's,' she continued. 'The one who's been trying to keep her from being arrested. Nick too, of course. I've been trying to keep a lot of people from being arrested, as it happens. All except for you. I'd quite like to see you arrested. *Why* did you kill Becky?'

'What?' Ronnie's head snapped up as she looked first at Fran and then at Nick, incomprehension writ large across her face.

For one awful moment Fran thought they had everything wrong, but then Ronnie smiled and she turned her eyes back to Fran, who paled under their dead gaze.

'I *have* heard about you,' she said. 'Firstly, it was all about your wonderful cooking, as if that was something that no one else had ever managed to do. I'm quite a good cook myself, as it happens. And yet I didn't think anything of it when Sara talked about you in such glowing terms. That should have been the first thing to warn me about you, of course. An interloper in our midst... Not one of the "girls". Not one of the group of friends who thought they knew everything there was to know about one another. I should have known you might see things differently than the rest of them.'

Ronnie ran her fingers through her hair, an irritated gesture. She sighed as if to say: *Did Fran not realise how easy it would be for Ronnie to dismiss her, to render her impotent?*

Her message was clear. Ronnie believed she had power now.

'Of course, by now, it seems that everybody's secrets have come crawling out of the woodwork, thanks to you, oh glorious Fran, with your questions and your *understanding*. And it would appear that some of our friends haven't been as naughty as I first thought, but no matter. You think you understand, but let me tell you, you don't understand a thing.'

'I probably don't,' replied Fran, thinking quickly. She mustn't be the one to reveal Ronnie's crimes. That was a noose she had to string up herself. 'Why don't you enlighten me? Us. I'm sure we'd all like to hear how clever you've been.'

Ronnie snorted a humourless laugh. 'I'm glad you think so,' she said. 'Compared with some people, I'm a fricking genius. That's you, Nick, in case you were wondering. God, you're slow.'

Fran turned her attention away from Ronnie for the first time since entering the kitchen. Nick and Adam were still standing just inside the doorway. Adam, she knew, was standing there in case Ronnie decided to use her legs, but Nick... Nick looked as if he couldn't move even if he wanted to. His mouth was working, opening and closing, but no words came out, just a horrified rictus distorting his features as his brain tried to make sense of Ronnie's words.

'In what way am I slow?' he managed after a moment.

Ronnie was pacing the kitchen, circling, as if waiting for the right moment to strike. And then she stopped and gave Nick a curious smile.

'Because you never ever realised what was going on, did you? I blamed myself to start with; I should never have listened to Becky. She wanted to meet you, and I thought she was my friend, so what harm could there be in that? I thought she wanted to meet you because she was happy for me, happy that I'd found you. But no, she had to go and take you all for herself, didn't she? And you, you let her! You should have pushed her away. You should have listened to what I told you about her, but you were so stupid, you thought she was nice. You couldn't see that she was making a play for you, and you walked right into her trap.'

'It wasn't a trap, Ronnie, we fell in love. And your memory's playing tricks on you. You and I were over by then. For God's sake, you knew that. You were happy for us, said you thought Becky and I made a much better couple than we ever did.'

'Yes, well, I *lied*, Nick,' she sneered. 'Have you never come across that before? I lied. And I've been lying ever since. Only you're too thick to realise that. So you see, none of this is really my fault at all. It's yours.'

He stared at her, a muscle twitching in his neck.

'But you and Becky were friends! You have been, all this time. And you told me you were happy for us. You met Peter, you got married yourself, and I know you're not together now, but you were happy for years.'

'No. I only pretended I was because what else was I supposed to do while I waited for you to realise what Becky was really like? How wrong she was for you. But you never did, did you? Just like you were supposed to realise it was me you loved.

'When you couldn't have children I thought, finally! Finally, something that Becky was crap at. Something that would drive a wedge between the pair of you. But what do you do? You're so bloody perfect, you decide to foster. Well, how very public spirited of you. Just another thing that you decided to do *together*. When are you going to realise that she was no good for you, Nick?'

'I don't believe this. You were *jealous* of us?' he said incredulously. 'Jealous of all the heartache we've been through? Do you *know* how it feels when everyone else on the planet but you seems perfectly capable of churning out children? How that niggles away at you, how you feel more and more worthless as time goes by. But you know what, Ronnie, there's something you will never understand – when you make a commitment to something, you give it your all, and when you make a commitment to a *person*, it's a partnership. It's equal and trusting and loving, not—'

'God you're so *reasonable*.'

'We were adults, Ronnie. And that's what adults do. They

take a problem and they set about solving it, never once forgetting what's important. They don't behave like spoiled children,
throwing toys out of their pram when they don't get what they
want.'

'Really? Oh, but it's *such* good fun, Nick. I really enjoyed
throwing Becky out of the pram.'

Fran's legs felt as if they were about to give way as she
stared at the callous sneer on Ronnie's face, at the triumphant
gleam in her cold eyes. It felt as if all the air had been sucked
out the room, consumed by Ronnie's hatred.

It was Nick's gasp which shattered the stunned silence. His
face crumpled, but only for a second. Then, incredibly, as Fran
watched, his features rearranged themselves into a mask. Reso-
lute, and hard as iron. He pushed his glasses higher up his nose.

'Becky and I were heartbroken that we couldn't conceive a
child, and we *were* unhappy, but not with each other. We questioned everything, except how we felt for each other. We
grieved for everything we lost and everything we would never
have, except for *each other*. Are you getting the picture yet,
Ronnie? Can you even begin to understand how love works?
No, I didn't think so.

'You're pathetic,' he hissed. 'Because even now you still
believe there's a chance for us. Do you really think I could ever
feel anything worthwhile or positive about someone who's done
what you have? I *hate* you, Ronnie. Is that good enough for
you?'

Ronnie's eyes were wild, twin spots of colour burned into
her cheeks. 'Love and hate,' she spat. 'They're both sides of the
same coin, everyone knows that.'

'Not in my world, they're not. I loved Becky with everything that was pure and good and joyous and beautiful. What I
feel for you is dark and ugly, twisted and evil. Just like you.
What you sow, you reap.'

Ronnie paced the kitchen. All the way to the far side and

back again. Spun on the spot as if to do it all over again, but then she strode towards Nick at speed. She pushed her face close to his, only inches from him.

'You think you're so clever,' she hissed. 'But you're not, you're weak and always have been. Becky this, Becky that, like a puppet on a string. You couldn't stand up for yourself and say what you really thought then, just like you can't do it now. But that's okay, I've always known how you really felt about me. And that's all I need. I've won, Nick. And you, you've lost... everything.' She gave a high-pitched bark of laughter. 'Including me. You'll never have me either. In fact, you won't have anything, ever again.'

She walked backwards, her gait almost a dance, her face wreathed in a smug smile. She trailed a finger along the table where the remains of Nick's dinner lay. 'Well, I have enjoyed our little chat,' she said. 'But it's time for me to go now, if you don't mind. I'm a bit bored with all this, and there's really no reason for me to stay. Did you enjoy your meal? It looks as if you did, you've almost finished it. I had to force Camilla to eat hers, whereas you... so easy, almost child's play.'

Shock rippled through Fran as she stared at Ronnie. 'You killed Camilla!'

'I had to. The silly cow phoned me. Told me how you'd been talking to her about poisonous plants and that it brought to mind a conversation *we'd* had on just that subject. I could hardly let her tell everyone she'd given me the idea for the perfect murder weapon, now could I? And how ironic that Camilla should die the same way, although I chose something different for her, not mushrooms.' She looked pointedly at Nick's plate.

Fran gasped. She couldn't really mean that, could she? No, no, no... after everything, it couldn't end like this.

'What have you *done*?'

Ronnie's chin lifted. 'I had a few mushrooms left. It seemed such a shame to waste them. And casseroles always taste much better with them than without, don't you think? A richer flavour. Poor Becky, she never even realised what I'd done. *Amanita phalloides* to give them their proper name. They taste a bit like honey apparently, or so I'm *told...*'

Fran stared at Nick, horrified, her gaze drifting to the remains of his meal on the table. Maybe he didn't understand it yet, but Ronnie had killed him too.

They were too late. Everything they had striven to do, and now none of it mattered. Ronnie had won, she had beaten them all. She would pay for it, of course – her life would never be the same again – but that was of little recompense now. Fran's eyes filled with tears. It was over. It was all over.

She turned away, no longer able to look at Nick. They should do something. They should call an ambulance or... Her eyes sought out Adam's, expecting to see her own emotion mirrored on his face. But he was staring at Nick, mouth hanging open, but not in horror, in surprise.

Nick's eyes were locked on Ronnie's, no longer terrified, but instead burning, calm and unflinching.

'Maybe I'm a whole lot cleverer than you give me credit for, Ronnie. You see, I was going to eat your casserole for dinner, but then, when I sat down, I suddenly didn't fancy it any more. I'm not sure why. So I scraped half of it in the bin. Funnily enough, it was you ringing the doorbell which interrupted me, so I put my plate back down on the table, and went to let you in. I haven't eaten any of your casserole, or *evidence*, as I like to call it, so I don't think I'm going to be losing anything just yet, let alone my life. You, however, have just confessed to two murders and attempted murder. In front of witnesses—'

'One of whom happens to be bugged,' said Adam, stepping forward. 'So your confession is also on tape.' He raised his eyebrows at Ronnie. 'Yes, really. It's okay, Mum, you can come in now.'

Ronnie's gaze swung first one way and then the other, but she was outnumbered and Adam still stood between her and the door. Eyes hard, jaw clenched and standing at least a foot and a half taller than Ronnie. She'd never make it out of the room.

The front door opened behind Adam, heavy footsteps thudding down the hallway. Booted footsteps belonging to the uniformed police officer who strode into the kitchen, radio burbling. Sara brought up the rear, white-faced with shock.

'Veronica Dankworth-Jones, I'm arresting you on suspicion of the murders of Rebecca Pearson and Camilla Swinton. You do not have to say anything, but it may harm your defence if you do not mention, when questioned, something which you later rely on in court. Anything you do say may be given in evidence...'

28

THREE DAYS LATER

Fran stole a glance at Adam. He'd never been in her garden before, let alone sat at a table with her husband, a pile of sandwiches and a couple of bottles of beer in front of them. But he looked as if he was holding up okay. He had even taken off his beanie. And he was smiling, a genuine, broad, relaxed, and not at all embarrassed, smile.

She touched a finger to the corner of her eye and turned her attention back to the lawn where Martha and Louise were finishing their dance routine. As the accompanying music crashed to a crescendo, a loud whistle split the air as Adam stuck two fingers in his mouth. All three of them got to their feet, applauding wildly, as the girls took a bow, chests heaving from exertion, but pleased as punch.

One of their number had already seen the performance, of course, on the night that she and Adam had... She was still struggling to put words to what had happened on the night when she and Adam had caught a murderer, missing Martha's performance in the process. Jack had gone to watch her alone, but she'd been forgiven; they both had.

The girls tumbled towards them, spirits high, snatching up

chocolate biscuits and taking a glass of lemonade each. Martha flashed her a smile.

'Can we take these up to my room now?' she asked, smiling shyly at Adam, who was still grinning at them.

Fran nodded, holding her arms out for a hug. 'You can,' she said, pulling her daughter close. 'Because that was amazing.' She touched a hand to her face. 'I'm sorry I missed the show, though.'

Martha rolled her eyes. 'I know, Mum, you've said it enough times.' But she wasn't hurt, her eyes still twinkled. 'Besides, catching a killer is pretty cool.'

Fran caught Jack's eye and smiled, watching as the girls went giggling into the house.

'Well, that was worth waiting for,' she said, sitting back down again.

'Wasn't it?' He followed suit, fingers reaching for hers across the table. 'It seems we have quite a few talented people in the family, not just dancers.'

Fran blushed. 'I think most of it was down to Adam, he—'

'No, it wasn't,' protested Adam. 'It was you who worked out how Ronnie had killed Becky.'

'Yes, but only because you deduced that the murder-mystery game had nothing to do with the murder in the first place. Plus, thankfully, and I'm only going to say this once, because you still had that blessed bug on you, we managed to get the murderer on tape.' She tipped her head to one side. 'How's your mum feeling about that now?'

Adam smirked. 'She pretended to be angry, but mostly I think she was pleased no one else would be going to prison. And having me back relatively unscathed, of course.'

'She was really worried about you, you know.'

Adam nodded. 'She might have mentioned that, once or twice.'

Fran smiled, catching the look in Adam's eye. She'd heard

from Sara only yesterday how pleased she was that she and Adam had finally managed to have a long overdue chat, about all sorts of things. And, justifiably, she was very proud of her son.

Fran picked up her glass. 'What shall we drink to?' she asked.

'Normality,' quipped Jack. 'Please. I'd just like things to be normal, for a really, really long time.'

Fran wrinkled her nose. 'I'd agree, but we're still helping the police, don't forget. It's going to take a while before all this is finished for good. Before Ronnie is tried and goes to prison for the rest of her life.' She dropped her gaze. 'And poor Nick. Life for him is going to be very far from normal.'

Jack squeezed her fingers. 'You did everything you could. He almost lost his life too. Probably would have if some little voice hadn't told him to bin Ronnie's food. That voice would never have been there if it hadn't been for you asking questions in the first place. Not that I approve, of course.' He raised his eyebrows and then smiled. 'But there are a lot of people who owe you both a debt of gratitude. Have you heard how that other woman is doing?'

'Melanie?' said Adam. 'Oh, she's fine. She wasn't poisoned by death cap mushrooms, but had a rather more common allergic reaction to dairy products, albeit one severe enough to make her really ill for a few hours. Ronnie didn't want to kill her, just get her out of the way so that she couldn't tell us what she knew. She gave Melanie a cake, supposedly like others she'd baked for her in the past and completely dairy free. Only that one wasn't. Not at all.'

'And it was Mel who sent out the game and all the instructions with it?'

He nodded. 'It was, but just as we suspected, Mel had no reason to think there was anything sinister behind what she was doing. As far as she was concerned, it was just another party for a group of friends. Mel did everything Ronnie asked her to, believing her when she said that it was all simply a bit of fun.'

Jack frowned. 'But what I don't understand is where Ronnie got the mushrooms from in the first place. They don't grow around here, do they?' He looked at Adam.

'Don't you dare say Amazon,' Fran warned.

'No, it wasn't them,' replied Adam, 'but sadly, you can order a whole host of lethal things on the internet, if you know where to look. And Ronnie had had a very long time to work out the perfect murder. She even told people at the funeral she'd looked up the death cap mushroom. Which she had, of course, except no one ever suspected why.'

'It's just all so unbelievably sad,' said Fran. 'That hate could fester to such an extent that it caused a life to be taken. Poor Becky. Do you think she ever had any idea what Ronnie thought of her?'

'No, I don't suppose she did,' replied Adam. 'But Ronnie's behaviour wasn't normal, Fran, even I know that.'

She shivered. 'No, and she seemed so... ordinary. The best friend; who would ever suspect her?'

'Something must have tipped her over the edge,' remarked Jack. 'Otherwise, why now? Becky and Nick had been together for years, you said. It's an awful long time to wait for revenge.'

Fran toyed with the rim of her glass. 'You know, I've been thinking about that. I couldn't understand why Sara was the only one of the friends who hadn't received a "blackmail" note from Becky. Granted, it was Sara's birthday party, but even so, if Ronnie had wanted to frame Becky as a blackmailer, then Sara should really have received a note, in turn making her a suspect too. But it's obvious when you think about it. The reason she didn't was because Sara had already told her secret to Becky. She knew about Adam's dad.'

'Yes, but Becky never sent the blackmail notes, Ronnie did,' said Adam.

'Exactly. So Ronnie also had to know. She had to know that Becky could never blackmail Sara. It was a bit of a slip up on Ronnie's part, and it's taken me far too long to work that out.'

Adam frowned. 'I'm not sure what difference that makes, though.'

'You might be right,' Fran agreed. 'It might have made no difference at all, but I couldn't help thinking about how Becky might have come to tell Ronnie about Sara's secret. We won't ever know, of course, unless Ronnie chooses to tell anyone, but I think maybe one night, when the two women were having a girly night in, and perhaps had had too much to drink, she told Ronnie what Sara had told her. Becky trusted Ronnie, don't forget, she had no reason to suspect anything was amiss, and so, without really thinking of the possible consequences she shared a secret that wasn't hers to share. It doesn't take a huge leap of imagination to wonder whether that same evening, perhaps in a drunken confession, Becky admitted to stealing Nick from Ronnie. She didn't know how much Ronnie hated her for it; she thought her friend had long got over that particular episode in their lives. Everything pointed to the fact that it had. But instead, without even realising it, Becky unwittingly signed her own death warrant.'

Jack stared into his bottle of beer. 'Oh my God...'

'Makes sense, doesn't it?'

'It makes perfect sense,' agreed Adam. 'This whole affair has been about secrets, right from the start. And maybe that's what gave Ronnie the idea for blackmail. She must have been chuffed to bits when she found out about Diane.'

'And then Lois too... even Camilla, who had no idea it was her who had given Ronnie the idea for the murder weapon all along until I spoke to her and jogged her memory. It was knowledge for which she paid the ultimate price. Ronnie must have found the means by which to kill Camilla the perfect irony.'

'So she *was* poisoned then?' asked Jack.

Fran nodded. 'Hemlock. There was a huge bunch of it in a vase on Camilla's table. It looks quite pretty, a little like horse parsley, but there's no way Camilla would have mistaken it; neither would she have eaten any of it. No, she was forced to, by Ronnie. Camilla had to die, she was a loose end Ronnie simply couldn't afford.'

'Except that Ronnie didn't do her homework quite as well as she thought she had,' said Jack, taking a long swig of beer. 'Not like the two of you. If this was *Scooby-Doo*, it would be the part where the villain says *if it weren't for them pesky kids.*' He smiled, but then his face fell. 'Except that this is real life and people have actually died, and you aren't children. I'm incredibly proud of you, but you have to promise me you'll never do anything like this again.'

'Oh, come on,' said Fran, picking up her glass. 'When is anything like this ever going to happen round here again?' She took a sip of her wine. 'Right, that's enough talk about horrible things. The sun is shining and it's a beautiful day. Come on, let's have that toast.'

'To normality,' said Jack immediately. 'To everything being back the way it was.'

Fran raised her glass. 'To normality then,' she said, grinning at Adam.

'I'm serious though,' added Jack, slurping a little beer from the top of his bottle. 'You have to promise me that you won't ever get involved in murder again, and if you do happen across one, you'll leave it to the police next time.'

'Honestly, Jack, nothing like—'

'Promise,' he repeated. 'You too, Adam. I'm sure your mum would like to hear you say it too.'

A slight movement underneath the table caught Fran's eye.

She smiled up at Jack, pretending she hadn't seen Adam's crossed fingers.

'Of course we promise, don't we, Adam?' she said, eyes twinkling as she crossed hers too.

'Oh, absolutely,' he said. 'Promise.'

A LETTER FROM EMMA

Hello, and thank you so much for choosing to read *Death by Candlelight*. I hope you enjoy reading my stories as much as I enjoy writing them. So, if you'd like to stay updated on what's coming next, please do sign up to my newsletter here and you'll be the first to know!

www.bookouture.com/emma-davies

I grew up reading murder mysteries – at one time, before bookshelf space became rather limited, I had all seventy-odd Agatha Christie books, and I still re-read them today. Regular readers of mine, however, will know that this is a bit of a departure for me, and rather different from the contemporary romance novels I've written in the past. So, in many ways, these books are very special for me and came about simply because of my love of this genre and a long-held desire to write a murder mystery of my own. I also love the setting of these mysteries – particularly the grand houses, which I had great fun with in *The Mystery of Montague House*, and the parties too. So the inspiration for the setting for this novel, the first in a brand new series, came very easily, because who doesn't love the idea of a murder-mystery party?

I'm also incredibly grateful to my wonderful publishers, Bookouture, who leaped at my suggestion to write some cosy crime books for them and decided that four books in a new series would be a great place to start! And this book in particular would never have happened without the support and skill of my wonderful editor, Therese Keating. Huge thanks to her and also the incredible team of people at Bookouture, who take my stories and transform them with the utmost skill and care, delivering them into your hands. And finally, to you, lovely readers, the biggest thanks of them all for continuing to read my books, and without whom none of this would be possible. You really do make everything worthwhile.

Having folks take the time to get in touch really does make my day, and if you'd like to contact me then I'd love to hear from you. The easiest way to do this is by finding me on Twitter and Facebook, or you could also pop by my website, where you can read about my love of Pringles among other things.

I hope to see you again very soon and, in the meantime, if you've enjoyed reading *Death by Candlelight*, I would really appreciate a few minutes of your time to leave a review or post on social media. Every single review makes a massive difference and is very much appreciated!

Until next time,

Love, Emma xx

www.emmadaviesauthor.com

facebook.com/emmadaviesauthor
twitter.com/EmDaviesAuthor
instagram.com/authoremmadavies